HOLLY

Also by Albert French

BILLY

HOLLY

ALBERT FRENCH

VIKING

VIKING
Published by the Penguin Group
Penguin Books USA Inc., 375 Hudson Street,
New York, New York 10014, U.S.A.
Penguin Books Ltd, 27 Wrights Lane, London W8 5TZ, England
Penguin Books Australia Ltd, Ringwood, Victoria, Australia
Penguin Books Canada Ltd, 10 Alcorn Avenue,
Toronto, Ontario, Canada M4V 3B2
Penguin Books (N.Z.) Ltd, 182–190 Wairau Road, Auckland 10, New Zealand

Penguin Books Ltd, Registered Offices:
Harmondsworth, Middlesex, England

First published in 1995 by Viking Penguin,
a division of Penguin Books USA Inc.

1   3   5   7   9   10   8   6   4   2

PUBLISHER'S NOTE
This is a work of fiction. Names, characters, places, and incidents
either are the product of the author's imagination or are used
fictitiously, and any resemblance to actual persons, living or dead, events,
or locales is entirely coincidental.

LIBRARY OF CONGRESS CATALOGING IN PUBLICATION DATA
French, Albert.
Holly / Albert French.
p.   cm.
ISBN 0-670-85746-7
I. Title
PS3556.R3948H6   1995
813'.54—dc20   94-41250

This book is printed on acid-free paper.

Printed in the United States of America
Set in Garamond No. 3
Designed by Katy Riegel

To

Agnieszka

nevertheless

And now thou sayest to me: Go, and tell thy master: Elias is here.

—3 Kings 18:11 (Douay Version)

*Thanks to all
the helping hands
along the road.*

HOLLY

SUPPLY, NORTH CAROLINA

SUMMER NINETEEN FORTY-FOUR

There was a sign out on the blacktop highway that said WELCOME TO
SUPPLY. Some folks that would see the sign from the highway might
slow down, read it, try and peek over and take a quick look at the
cluster of buildings, houses and them little roads goin here and
there. Might see the courthouse stickin up real tall and wonder what
it was, see out behind the buildings and all, see that brown and
green till it got to that blue sky. Then the blues would just seem to
go forever, most folks would keep on goin, too.

The train tracks right along the highway, had to cross them to get
down into town. Had to watch out for them fast-movin trains because they weren't slowin down for no stoppin at Supply after just
gettin started good from that stop they'd made in Wilmington.
Some folks said that the only thing good about Supply was that it
wasn't far from Wilmington. Said, You can go on up there, see some
things. Some folks been known to go on and walk up there—might
take some time, half that day—but they go on and do it.

Supply folks, especially them old men, would sit out on them benches in front of the courthouse. Some of them had their own sittin seats. Folks might see a empty seat on a bench and ask, Where's Pete today? Sheriff LeRoy was like Supply, didn't bother nobody and didn't like to be bothered. Folks didn't bother him at all, gave him a Good mornin, Sheriff, and let him go his way. Supply didn't have a newspaper, didn't need one, Chester Higgens the mailman sorta gave folks the news when he gave them their mail. He even took that mail out on the other side of the Velvet Creek and give it to the coloreds. That's where Supply's coloreds lived, folks just called out past the creek the Back Land.

Time had its own way in Supply, it would sorta sit with them old men down by the courthouse and just watch things go by, didn't seem to change things much at all except once in a while it would have to get up and make it rain or be ready when some poor soul's days were up. But when the war came, time had to change its ways. Folks started pullin on it, wantin to know what it was doin, wanted it to bring things faster, then wanted it to slow things down.

Supply's lumber yard got real busy, even had to take on some coloreds to help get that wood to the government. Folks said, The government need our help, gots to get that wood cut for em, gots to stop them Japs over there. Folks didn't mind helpin either, once they start seein that good dollar comin their way. Some of them Supply men got some good jobs up in Wilmington, workin on them docks. Most of Supply's young boys went on and signed up to fight them Japs just as soon as they heard Pearl Harbor was bombed. Chester Higgens went around and told folks, "Them Japs attacked us first, sneak-attacked us, too."

Freckle-face Chucky Flyn was the first boy from Supply to get killed, the body didn't come home, just the telegram sayin his ship went down. It wasn't until the third boy, Chester Dobson, got killed, that Eugene Purvis, Supply's courthouse clerk, started puttin their names up on the courthouse wall and always made sure there was some fresh flowers under them.

Early mornings still sounded the same, chickens get to makin noisy, them yard dogs get to barkin, but folks would be movin a little faster. Them folks that had the electric line would hurry and get up, get that radio turned on to hear what was happenin, give them somethin to talk about all day. Them folks that lived out past the electric line figured they'd find out sooner or later.

Folks hadn't started talkin about Holly Hill. Everybody knew Holly, knew she was Gus Hill's daughter and her mama was Ginger. Folks that knew Ginger when she was a young quick walker and a good looker said, That child the spittin image of her mama. Holly had that Hill blond hair and them sky-blue eyes. She had her daddy's height, but could take her mama's quick steps. Holly's nineteen.

Gus Hill lived right outside of town, no more than a half mile down that old broken patched road. His house was the last house before the creek. Gus Hill been workin down the lumber yard since folks could remember. Ginger stayed home and hoped the war would end soon and wished it never started.

Sundays still had their slow ways.

Ginger is up, but Holly won't be up for a while, hates to get up early on Sunday, don't see no point in it. Holly's little brother Jason is gettin up now, he will be seven come spring, but Ginger is thinkin of Robert. She thinks of him as Bobby, her first child. He is twenty-one and the last she heard he was on Saipan. Every morning Ginger sits in a distant silence, maybe further than Saipan could ever be. She knows the island in the Pacific has not fallen yet and the fightin is ragin through her mind. The day he came home so excited sayin, "I'm a marine, Mama," won't go away and he ain't been back. The coffee Ginger is sippin on has long turned cold. She gets up from the kitchen table and goes to the sink, then stands and stares out the window before she hears Jason comin down the steps. She knows he will come in the kitchen and she must think of him, now.

"Mama, can Ah have this?" Jason asks over his shoulder as he looks and pokes inside the icebox.

"What, honey?" Ginger asks over her shoulder.

"This, Mama. Can Ah have this?"

"What, Jason? Can't ya wait? Just get some bread and jelly till your daddy and Holly get up."

"Mama, can Ah fix somethin else?"

"Ah told ya now, get some jelly and close that icebox door."

It wasn't too long before Holly heard her name slashin through her faraway thoughts. Them ones she was smilin about, wantin to think about. She had wokened and was just lyin with her face buried in the pillow. Her mother called again, but Holly was good at not listenin to things she didn't want to hear. It was that brat of a brother she knew her mother would send up to get her and just the thought of it was botherin her already. With her face still buried in the pillow she mumbles, "That little, if he come up here botherin me, he better not . . ."

"Um up, Mama," Holly yelled, then put her face back in the pillow.

The morning sunlight was comin through the window, but Holly didn't want to see the light, she kept her eyes closed. She could see Billy Felter, see him in his sailor suit, see him comin home with his cute little smile she can make him put on his face. But in her darker thoughts where she sneaks away to, she can feel things she's never touched. Garet Foster is kissin her, she feels his arms around her. She wants him, even closer, but she pushes him away.

"Holly, Holly, Mama says ya git up."

"Git out of here. Git out of here, ya better."

"Mama says ya git up, Holly."

"Ya better git out of here if ya know what's good for ya."

"Mama says . . ."

"Ya better git out of here, now. And close that door ya hear me?" Holly shouted and put her face back in the pillow.

"Um tellin Mama ya went back to sleep."

"Git out of here right now." Holly jerked the covers off her, jumped to her feet, gathered her nightgown and pulled it down over her legs. Then her mouth got to runnin the same time her hand got to flickin her hair out of her eyes. Holly could fuss and got to mutterin, "Can't sleep past the chickens. Same thing every time Ah turn around. That little brat, wait till Ah git him. Can't wait ta git out of here. Do this, do that, do that, do this, do that . . ."

Mirrors in Holly's life could make her smile. She had washed her face, let the water glisten on her skin. She combed her hair, shook it out and combed it again. Billy Felter always liked her hair, especially when she would wear it down over her shoulders. She would wear it that way today, even though he would not see it, she would do that for him. She would put on the blue dress, the one with the ruffled sleeves, she'd put it on and save Mama from yellin at her to get dressed for church. But she knew her mother would yell anyway about the low neckline.

"Mornin, Daddy," Holly spoke softly over her shoulder as she left the bathroom and heard Gus Hill's footsteps in the hall. Back in her room, Holly had to find that red barrette, that's the one she wanted. Quickly, she got to openin them dresser drawers and pushin bobby pins and brushes aside. Her hair swayed with her sudden moves.

"Holly, Holly, come on if ya want ta eat before we go," Ginger had yelled for her again.

"Um comin, Mama."

Holly found the red barrette, stuck it in her hair as she watched herself in the dresser mirror. But the moment was filled with Garet Foster, she heard herself mutter his name, then she posed and let her movements settle in the mirror.

"Ah hate this damn thing. This dress is ugly," Holly hissed through clenched teeth, then spun around and tried to keep her eyes on the mirror, but she still hated the dress no matter which way she turned. She sighed, then stood quietly.

The silent moment brought Billy Felter's face. His ring was on her finger. "Ah love ya, too, and um goin ta wait for ya, Billy," she had said, then cried when he left.

"Jason, turn that off and git in here to the table. Ya hear me?" Ginger yells into the living room above the scratchy voices comin from the radio. She does not want to hear of the war news.

Heads are bowed at the breakfast table. Gus Hill has taken his seat at the head of the table. It is quiet until he utters his thanks to his God for thy food that has been prepared for him. The stillness lingers, then he slowly raises his head. Jason eats quickly, Holly picks at her food, Ginger sighs. She has quietly uttered her own prayer, it was for Gus Hill.

The gentle chippin sounds of forks nippin at the food on the plates fall beneath the stillness in the kitchen. Ginger's eyes twitch when they look, then stare at the empty supper seat. Quickly she turns to Holly.

"Why don't ya wear that white dress? It looks so nice on ya." Ginger's askin.

Holly sighs, then picks at her food.

"Ah thought ya were goin ta wear it today?"

"That old thing, Ah hate that dress."

It is silent again at the table, Ginger lets the silence swell before she says, "Don't ya think that's ah little too much for church?"

"No, Mama. Besides it's hot. Be sittin in there wit all them folks, it's too hot for all that dress anyway . . ."

Holly is still poutin, Gus Hill begins to stir in his seat. Ginger looks up from her plate, looks at her husband and lets her eyes settle on him until she sees his fist clench, then she looks away.

Ginger says, "We ought ta be gittin ready."

Holly picks at her food.

Jason is still eatin.

Ginger says, "Hurry up, Jason. Then ya go and git washed up and comb your hair, too."

Jason is up, he hurries to the steps, then scampers up them. He wants to be first to go out and get into the car. Ginger sighs and glances at Holly, then speaks softly, "Holly as soon as ya done pickin at what ya ain't eatin, git this table cleaned up. Um goin to start gittin ready. Hurry up so we ain't the last ones there."

Gus Hill is silent until Ginger looks at him, then lowers her eyes and says, "Gus, it's about time ta be goin. Ya still goin or ya stayin home?"

Slowly, Gus Hill nods his head yes.

Ginger is up from the table, she is hummin as she takes her plate to the sink. Every time the days near Sunday, she pleads with Gus Hill, tells him in the late of night, or sun's first light. "Bobby needs our prayers. Come with us ta church, ya never know it might help some."

He says, "Ah pray, but don't need that singin and shoutin. Don't need it."

But he has said he will go today and Ginger is still hummin as she looks in the mirror in her bedroom. Her face is thinnin, the lines on her forehead have deepened. Her hum softens, Gus Hill's footsteps are near.

"What time she come in last night?" he asks.

Ginger is silent.

"When ya goin ta talk ta her?"

Ginger sighs and begins to comb her hair.

Gus Hill's voice rises, but his words come slow and drip from his mouth. "If ya ain't goin ta talk to her, Ah will. Last thing Ah need is for her ta be runnin out there. Ah ain't standin for it."

Ginger had not turned to him, but watched him go away in the mirror.

Alone, Gus Hill stood amid the harsh rays of the electric light hangin from the bathroom ceiling. The light could not brighten the dark shadows around his eyes. He tried to straighten his shoulders as he began to shave but the mirror made them sag again.

Town wasn't that far, no more than a half mile. The church sat on the other side of town, which wasn't much further, a good half hour walk at the most, but Gus Hill would not walk the road. The small stones and pebbles of the old broken patched road bounce beneath the car, a trail of dust follows. The morning air is still cool and feels good on Holly's face, her chin is up and she watches the blurs of greens and browns and sometimes blues whisk by the car window. Far fields lie beyond the roadside trees and bushes. Beyond the silence of the trees hot within the stillness of the far fields, the Velvet

Creek can be seen. It has cut away from the Back Lands and curves southeast to the distant seas.

The car was slowin, now turnin and the road was bumpier. All the morning sounds, the bouncin of Gus Hill's Ford, the distant sounds of birds and the yappin of some yard dog seemed to take rhythm with the floatin sound of a piano playin. Slowly, Holly turned and looked toward the church and the sound of the music. She always loved the sounds of the piano, its gentle swells of melody would seep into her soul.

The church was always there, sittin at the end of its own road. From a distance, the cross atop its steeple stood stark against any day's long sky, its white walls gleamed in the sunlight. Some folks just thought about it on Sunday, some folks carried it in their minds all week, others tried to push it far from any thought.

The car stopped, its engine's last putter gave way to the soft piano music comin from the church. Holly sighed and looked out of the car window and stared at the folks gatherin beneath the shadows of the cross.

Ginger looked at the church, smiled, then glanced back at Gus Hill.

Gus Hill sat silently and stared at the steerin wheel.

Holly was lookin out the window and tryin to see Elsie in the crowd of folks.

Ginger spoke softly. "Looks like its goin ta be a nice service, look at all the folks here. Jason, don't have me havin ta git after ya now. Ya hear me?"

Jason was stirrin, then blurted out, "Mama, can Ah go over June Boy's house after church is over? Huh, can Ah? Ah be back fore it's suppertime. Can Ah go home wit June Boy?"

"Hush," Ginger only whispers.

The music is good to Ginger's ears, the old piano eases her thoughts, cools the fires on Saipan. The car doors open, Gus Hill climbs out and takes his steps slowly. Jason jumps out and does not get two steps before Ginger has him by the hand. Holly stands in the sunlight, throws her head back to get the hair out of her eyes, then pulls and yanks at her dress. She is irritated, the dress is wrinkled already. Holly hisses and mutters to herself as she tries to yank the wrinkles away. Ginger has moved ahead, still has Jason's hand, but turns back to her daughter as she hears the sharp hisses.

"Holly," Ginger speaks quickly and beckons with her eyes. The look on her face tells Holly to come quietly and stop that fussin around. But Ginger's eyes soften as she sees her husband comin. She is reminded that she is pleased he is with her, even though he is trailin.

In the shade of the cross, good mornins are only nods. Supply folks come to their worship in silence. Mothers hush their children, fresh-shaven-faced men humble themselves in the stillness. Gus Hill keeps his eyes down, his head is already bowed. Folks must slow at the church door, ease and soften their steps as they squeeze through. Inside the church it seems dark, darker than it really is. Eyes squint as they seek a new vision in the shade, look for empty seats, look away from other searchin eyes. But Holly is peekin around, lettin her eyes sneak quick peeks at other faces. She sees Elsie Fagen, Elsie is peekin, too. Holly smiles, but very quickly. They are women now, no longer the playful girls of summers ago, but they are still the friends of that time when baby dolls were held tightly in secret places, whispers carried promises of dreams to come. Elsie wiggles her nose, Holly almost laughs, but the piano still plays.

Folks have taken their seats, the stirs and rufflin sounds dwindle, the piano is playin softer. Some folks are beginnin to sway with the music, but they are gentle sways. The music stops, then silence beckons all eyes forward to the hunchbacked old man in the Sunday black preachin suit. He is the Reverend Odem Powell, folks say he came to Supply about the same time the Velvet Creek started flowin through. Seemed to most folks that he was always old and bent, born that way. Might have been born with that walkin stick he had all the time. Folks could see him comin and go on doin what they were doin, knew it would take him a little time to get anyplace they were. He talked slow, until Sunday morning would come, then sometimes his words could come real fast, almost get away from him. He'd get to talkin about things he ain't thought about yet.

Jason begins to squirm in his seat, he wants to close his eyes, but he knows the old preacher will still be there when he opens them up again. So he squirms and lets his eyes flash about. He sees the window, can see the outside light, then watches it beam into the church and disappear into the shadows in the corner.

"It is a quite precious Sunday mornin, isn't it?" The Reverend is speakin slowly while he looks down into his preachin book.

Holly wants to cross her legs, sit back and let her eyes wander. She is not comfortable and twists some in her seat, but she will not cross her legs. She knows she is in church and should not be thinkin of things in the dark of her mind. She sighs, lets her breath blow slowly through her lips.

"Who in times past suffered all nations to walk in their own ways . . ."

Ginger watches the old man speak, but her vision is in the purity she seeks. That world beyond her mind where peace and children play.

"God will show His mercy . . ."

It is stuffy in the church. The woman Gus Hill is sittin next to is fat with bulgin hips that plow into his side. He scoots closer to his wife, but the fat woman only seems to expand, pushin him even further and the words keep comin.

"It will say in Psalm Six, Oh Lord reduce me not in anger, neither chasten me in thy displeasure . . ."

Gus Hill looks away, lets his eyes wander from the preachin man. But he can still see him in his mind carryin that Bible he totes around all the time. He can see him sneakin out to the Back Lands, sneakin up that twisted path that just goes one place. Been seein him carryin that Bible and that walkin stick and sneakin up there to see that big yellow colored woman, Flossie Mae Hicks.

The morning shadows in the church begin to lift as the sun nears the noon hour. The piano begins to play and muted voices utter final prayers. Some eyes are still closed as thoughts are almost willed across distant seas of war. Ginger still prays and calls beyond her grasp, beyond her silence, calls Bobby's name. Then begs with silent words, "Please bring him home, Lord, please bring him home again."

Sunlight and faces blend, hands are extended in greetins. Names are called and good mornins float gleefully amidst the gatherin. Holly moves swiftly through the crowd and out of the fading shadows of the church to where she knows Elsie is waitin. There is a distant tree; Elsie waits there.

As Holly nears, Elsie asks, "Why ya wear that for?"

"Shit, it was this or that white long-sleeve thing Ah hate."

"Ya git yelled at?" Elsie asks quickly.

"No, ain't nobody said nothin. Your mama say anythin?"

"No. My daddy was asleep, reckon he drunk, too. Mama was up, but she wasn't studyin about me. Ah think her and Daddy must have been fightin again. Ya know how he gits when he gits ta drinkin."

"Ya got any cigarettes?" Holly asks.

"Ah got some in my purse. But we light up here, your mama and mine be screamin crazy."

Holly gets that poutin look on her face, then starts lookin at things she ain't thinkin about.

"What is wrong wit ya this mornin?" Elsie asks.

"Ah tell ya later, Ah don't want ta talk about it now."

"Why not? What's wrong wit ya, huh?"

"Ah just don't want ta talk about it."

"Is it Billy? Did ya hear from him?"

"No, it ain't him. Ah ain't heard from him, anyway."

"Ya said ya got a letter last week."

"Damn it, Elsie. Ah just don't feel like talkin about it."

"Are ya comin down later, like ya said?"

"Yeah."

"What time, huh?"

"Ah don't know yet."

"Well, ya still goin tonight, ain't ya?"

"Yeah."

"Ah wish ya git out that pissy mood."

"Who's in a pissy mood?"

"Ya. Who else is standin here be all pissy actin?"

"Gimme a couple cigarettes, Ah ain't got none."

"Here, take what's there, Ah got some at home."

"Ah be down after suppertime. Ya know how Mama is about Sunday supper and all. Ah see ya after that . . ." Holly lets her words trail behind her as she spun around and headed for the car.

Gus Hill had said his quick good mornins, then had nudged Ginger's arm and got to whisperin to her. "Let's go on now. I said I'd come, but I ain't said I'd stand around here all day, now."

Ginger had felt Gus Hill's tuggin and had whispered back to him, "Just goin ta say hello to Mrs. Bruce, see how she's doin. See if she heard from her boy Charles. Ya know he's in the Pacific, too."

The car was hot, the sun had baked down on its roof and glared through its windows. The ride back home had its ways. Jason was stirrin in the car seat and whinin about not bein able to go over June Boy's house. Holly just sat quietly lookin out the window at things she wasn't lookin at. She could hear her mother talkin, but she kept lookin out the window.

Ginger was sighin and sayin things at the same time. "Mrs. Bruce is just a-worried. She was sayin, she ain't heard from Charles either. She says, the last time she heard anything was almost three weeks now. She said, last thing she heard he was shippin out from his base. Said he couldn't say where they were goin or nothin like that. He ask about everybody, seem like he's all right. But she says she still can't sleep at night . . ." Ginger let a moment go by before turnin and askin Holly, "Did ya write Billy?"

Holly's eyes stayed fixed on the distant blues and greens.

"Holly, did ya write Billy?" Ginger asks again.

"What, Mama?" Holly answers but keeps watchin things out the window.

"Did ya write Billy?"

"No, Mama."

"Didn't ya git a letter from him on Tuesday?"

"Yes, Mama."

"Well how come ya ain't written him yet?"

"It just came Tuesday, Mama."

"He writes ya all the time, honey. Why don't ya write him back a little more?"

Holly stares past anything she can see, takes a deep breath and keeps the air held tightly down in her chest.

"Why don't ya write him today, honey? Maybe ya can write your brother, too. Ya ain't written him in a while, he always ask about ya."

Holly turns sharply, quickly the air rushes out of her mouth with words rushin out, too. "Um goin ta write. Ah can't write everyday. Ah ain't married ta him. Ah mean, why ah have ta write him everyday for. Ah just wish." Holly stops talkin, grabs her breath and jerks her head back toward the window. The hot breeze blows in her face, the loose strands of her hair flicker across her eyes.

"Mama, can Ah stop at June Boy's?" Jason wants to know. Ginger hushes him quickly, lowers her head and seeks the peace she left at the church.

The blue dress came off quickly and was tossed across the bed, then the red barette came out of Holly's hair and was pitched onto the dresser. The bedroom still had its morning shadows lingerin. The mirror showed Holly her face, let her watch her eyes starin back into her own. Slowly, she let her hands move to her hair and pick at the other bobby pins holdin it up, holdin it in its Sunday place. She watches her hair fall and hang loosely over her shoulders, then she looks back into her eyes. She stills herself and just stares in the mirror as moments from a time ago come again.

It is years ago, almost a secret time. A long time for moments to live, still smile and laugh, but they do. Ninth grade, songs and senior boys. Whispers to Elsie, Billy's cute, ya think he knows Ah like him? Thick curly hair and a cute smile, big brown eyes, tall and sorta bowlegged. Quick-tempered and schoolyard fights and Elsie whispers, He likes ya, Holly. Ya like him? Holly jerks away from the mirror, a deep sigh fills the room.

Suppertime came, then slowly moved on. Ginger was in the kitchen washin the supper plates and starin out the window. She turned from the sink when she heard Holly comin down the steps.

The hemmed-up peach-colored summer dress swayed with Holly's walk. Fresh makeup and lipstick gave her face the glow she wanted it to have. A scent of perfume slowly followed every step she took.

"Where ya goin?" Ginger asked.

"Up Elsie's, Mama." Holly threw her words over her shoulder and kept walking.

"What time ya comin home?"

"Ah don't know, Mama."

"Ya know it's Sunday, ya know that and ya were out late last night . . ." Ginger's words chased Holly onto the porch. Holly quickened her steps.

"Holly," Ginger yelled.

"What, Mama?" Holly shouted back, slowed and let her heels scrape across the porch.

"Um sick and tired of ya comin in here all hours of the night. Ya hear me?"

Slowly, Holly turns her head and looks at her mother, then speaks quickly. "Mama, Ah told Elsie Ah was comin up, maybe go for a walk or somethin. That's all Um doin."

Ginger was still standin in the shade of the porch, Holly knew she was there, but didn't look back as she hurried up the path. She slowed when she reached the old broken patched road, then quickly looked the way she didn't want to. She could see down the road, see where it began to curve, see the shade lurkin beneath the trees. She turned and started up the road, leavin a sigh behind. The way to Elsie's was never a span of time, only a space between it.

"Girl, what took ya so long?" Elsie yelled from her porch steps as

Holly came into her yard. Holly just twisted her face, didn't say anything and sat beside Elsie.

"What took ya so long? Why ya still all pissy for?"

"Who's in the house? Anybody home?" Holly asked with a whisper.

"No, Mama still over Aunt Judy's, ain't no tellin where Daddy is. Ah ain't seen him all day, Ah think him and Mama still fightin or ain't talkin."

Holly sighs and leans back against the porch post.

"What's wrong wit ya today, why ya so puffed up?" Elsie asks.

"Ain't nothin wrong wit me."

"Is so."

Holly jerks away from the porch post and gets to fidgetin with her purse. She has the cigarette in her fingers, but is still diggin in the purse for matches.

"What Garet say? Did he say anythin about Lucy Belmar?" Elsie asks.

Holly has lit the cigarette, tasted its smoke, now holds the smoke and the taste of it in her mouth.

"What he say, huh?" Elsie asks again.

Holly blows the smoke out her mouth and is silent as she watches it curl through the air.

"Well, what he say, huh?"

"He said they're just friends," Holly answers and stares into the smoke.

"Friends my ass."

"That's what he said."

"What ya say when he said that?"

"Nothin."

"He's doing it ta her."

"No he ain't."

"Yes he is, everybody knowin that."

Holly is silent, the cigarette burns and the smoke floats away. Her thoughts go with it.

"Ya crazy," Elsie says.

"Ah told him Ah was engaged ta be married and all. Ah told him that," Holly blurts out of her silence.

"He knew that anyway."

"He says he really likes me. He says he always been likin me."

Elsie makes a face, then quickly says, "He's full of shit, Holly. Ya know that. Everybody knowin he's doin it ta that fat-ass, Lucy Belmar. Everybody knowin that. What about Billy?"

Holly shouts, "Ah don't know."

"Ya still love him, ya know that."

Holly is silent.

"Ya write him back yet?"

Holly shakes her head, flings her hands in the air, the cigarette goes flyin. Now she is yellin, "How come everybody keep askin? Did Ah do this, did Ah do that? Ah mean he, what if he . . . ? Ah write him back, Ah ain't got ta write every day, just be sittin and writin all the time. How come Ah can't do what Ah want ta witout everybody gittin in my business? Um sick and tired of it. Ah want ta go someplace where folks ain't never heard of this place. And Ah ain't comin back either if Ah gits there. Um sick and tired of this old place."

Elsie asks, "Ya want ta go in ta town? Go in Ben's, see who's in there?"

"Yeah, let's do that."

2

Elsie Fagen had her ways, but they were never too different from
Holly's. She was a little shorter, but had a quicker step, sorta
bounced when she walked. Her hair was a little darker than Holly's,
but just as long and flowin, her eyes could be just as blue. Folks not
from Supply would just know they were sisters, havin them same
looks and ways. Supply folks was used to seein them together, if
they'd see one without the other they'd seem to keep on lookin to see
if they saw right. Holly and Elsie could have their different ways of
thinkin about the same thing, get real mad at each other, fuss about
stuff for days. Then they could have the same way about somethin,
get to sayin the same thing the other one just got done sayin.

Nothin special ever happened in Supply on Sunday, folks just like
to come out and walk and talk that day. Even some coloreds came to
town, come in from the Back Land in them mule wagons. Everybody
sorta wantin to be around somebody else, especially since the war
came, folks had plenty to say and needed somebody to say it to. Pale
painted buildings stood backdrop to folks movin about in their col-
orful Sunday dress. Children bounced and skipped in their play,

women talked and waved as old men sat in the shade. Young folks would go on over to Ben's, see who else was there listenin and dancin to that jukebox music he had in that back room he added on.

Holly and Elsie were halfway to the center of town before they hushed and started lookin around to see who was walkin the streets, see who was lookin at them, too. Then down by the courthouse, they scooted around the corner and went into the shade of them back-streets. Ben's wasn't too far from there.

"Ya think he's in there?" Holly slows her steps and asks Elsie.

"Ya want ta see him or not?" Elsie asks back.

"Suppose she's in there. Ya think she's in there?" Holly stops and twists her face up. She can hear the music comin from Ben's, a slow thumpin melody seeps into the street.

Elsie blurts out, "If she's there, and she's wit him, just act like ya ain't seen em."

Holly makes some kind of gruntin sound, jerks her head so the hair gets out of her eyes, then says, "Um sick and tired of her fat face. She can kiss my ass, Um goin in there."

Elsie smiles.

Ben's place had its Sunday crowd of soda and hamburger seekers. But some of them Supply young men and them out-of-town sailor boys always had somethin tucked away, a little liquor or a bottle of moonshine they got someplace. Sheriff LeRoy sorta let them boys be, long as they behaved themselves and didn't start no trouble. Sheriff LeRoy didn't like no trouble. Some of them out-of-town sailors couldn't help but point and stare at Holly and Elsie as soon as they see them comin through the door.

Holly held her head high, made sure her chin was straight. She knew them sailor boys were lookin at her, wanted them to, but she wasn't lookin for them.

Elsie nudges Holly's arm and whispers, "Ya see em?"

Holly gives a quick "No," shake of her head. Ben's counter is full and the booths along the wall are bulgin with folks tryin to squeeze into them. Holly eases her way past the folks standin around the counter, keeps her eyes lookin ahead and moves to the sound of the music. Ben's back room just had one overhead lightbulb hangin down that seemed only to light the center of the room, made a big wide circle of light in the middle of the floor. Along the walls were tables that were always in the shadows. The music was floodin the room with its rhythm. The song was slow, some deep voice beggin for his woman to come on back home. Holly kept lookin around and tryin to look like she wasn't. The only thing she could see was shadows full of faces and backs of heads.

"Shit, ain't no place to sit," Holly is whisperin over her shoulder.

"Ya see em?" Elsie whispers.

"No," Holly hisses.

Elsie feels a hard tappin on her shoulder.

"No thank ya," Holly hears Elsie sayin, she turns around and sees some buck-toothed red-faced sailor and she can hear him pleadin with Elsie, "Oh come on now. Me and my buddy over there seen you coming in . . ."

Elsie and Holly turn away from the sailor and let his pleas seep into the melody of the jukebox song. Holly hasn't given the sailor a second thought, it is his sailor suit that stays in her mind, makes her turn a little quicker, take a few more steps into the sound of the music.

Quickly, Elsie whispers, "Holly, don't look now, she's over in the corner by the jukebox. She over there wit Francine Hamond."

Holly's lookin at Elsie, got her back turned to where the jukebox is and whisperin real fast, "Ya see him, he over there wit her?"

"Ah can't see. He might be, that Calvin is over there."

"Shit," Holly mutters.

"Hi, my name is Jack. This is my buddy, Melvin. We were wondering if you two pretty ladies would like to come and sit with us?" The buck-toothed sailor had caught up with Holly and Elsie and was tryin to introduce himself again. He was speakin quickly but kept the same big smile on his face. Holly looked past him and glanced at the other sailor standin behind the buck-toothed one. The other looked like a little boy all dressed up in a costume. Holly saw his eyes stare at her, then suddenly drop and look down at the floor when she kept her eyes on him.

"This is our first time here. Our ship is docked up at Wilmington. Maybe you two pretty girls would like to have a soda?" the buck-toothed sailor was asking with that big smile on his face.

Elsie flinched when she heard Holly sayin, "That would be so nice of ya, we'd love ta have a soda."

"Would you like to come over and sit with us, too?"

Holly smiled at the sailor and followed him over to a table. Elsie took the seat next to Holly and was across from where the buck-toothed sailor sat. The little shy sailor sat across from Holly with his head bowed and starin down at the table when he wasn't takin quick peeks up at her.

Some other song was playin, Holly let her head turn with the melody and look across the room, but she could still hear the other sailor talkin faster than the music was playin. Elsie was sayin somethin back to him, but she wasn't sayin too many words before he'd start sayin somethin again. Holly kept lookin away.

"What's your name?" the fast-talkin sailor slows his words and asks Holly, but she don't say nothin back; acts like she don't hear him and makes him ask her again.

"What's your name, sweetheart?" the sailor asks and keeps lookin at Holly while she keeps lookin away. He sees her close her eyes, open them up again, but not look at him, only say, "It's Holly."

The sailor turns away from Holly and takes his smile to Elsie, then asks, "Do you have a boyfriend?"

Elsie shakes her head yes, then looks away.

The sailor turns back to Holly and asks, "What about you, do you have a guy?"

"Um engaged ta be married," Holly is sayin as she starts to dig around in her purse for a cigarette.

"Oh, you have a boyfriend, too? Getting married, huh? When's the big day?"

Holly keeps diggin for a cigarette, finds one. A flash of fire comes quickly as the tip of the cigarette touches her lips. The shy sailor has flicked his lighter and is holdin it out for Holly. She keeps her eyes on the flame, when she sees it shakin she sees the boy's hands are shakin, too. The tip of the cigarette turns red in the flame, the taste of smoke comes to Holly's tongue. She looks up and over to the shy sailor, stares through the smoke, then smiles.

"So when's the big day, huh?" the other sailor is askin again.

Holly has decided to relax, sit back in her chair and cross her legs. She looks at the buck-toothed sailor still grinnin at her with all those teeth stickin out his mouth, then looks away but is sayin, "We gittin married when he comes home. He's a sailor, too. He's on the *Bunker Hill,* he's in the Pacific."

The sailor turns to Elsie and starts askin her about her boyfriend, but Holly looks at the shy sailor, sees him lookin down until she asks, "What's your name?"

The boy's eyes pop up and he answers quickly, "Melvin Ames, but everybody just calls me Mel."

Holly is smilin a little and askin, "How old are ya?"

"Seventeen."

"Ya just seventeen?"

"I'll be eighteen next month."

The songs kept coming from the jukebox. From time to time, Holly would glance around the room, see what she could see, then settle back against her chair. The shy sailor was talkin now, telling Holly about himself and some small town outside of Toledo, Ohio. His eyes were bright, even in the shadows of the room. Holly watches his eyes dance and glow when she smiles at him.

Elsie was gettin tired of the buck-toothed sailor and all them teeth and words comin out his mouth. She started pickin at them and throwin them back at him.

"Ain't none of your business. Why ya keep askin about boyfriends and all, huh? Ah ain't tellin ya nothin," Elsie sayin.

"I was just asking, that's all, sweetheart. Just trying to be nice to you. Why don't we get on out of here and go someplace where it's quiet? What do you say?"

Elsie rolls her eyes.

"Oh come on, just want a chance to talk to you, get a chance to know you."

"Ah told ya, Ah have a boyfriend. Can't ya hear me?"

"Why don't you give a guy a chance?"

Elsie is twistin her face up and lookin away.

"I'm just trying to be friendly."

Elsie tugs on Holly's arm and is whisperin, "Come on, Holly, let's go."

"What's with you?" the sailor blurts out.

"Listen, Ah told ya Ah have a boyfriend. And Ah ain't wantin ta git to know ya or go someplace else wit ya. Can't ya hear me?" Elsie sayin and lettin her words hiss.

The grin leaves the buck-toothed sailor's face, now his teeth protrude through the sneer.

"Come on, Holly, let's go," Elsie sayin again.

The shy sailor is lookin at Holly, watchin her eyes and askin, "Do you have to go too, Holly?"

Holly smiles and shakes her head yes.

Elsie is up out of her seat, and lookin any place that buck-toothed sailor ain't.

"Why don't you set back down, come on, sweetheart?" The sailor talkin real fast with that smile back on his face.

"Why don't ya go and git lost somewhere?" Elsie is mutterin, then hisses, "Ya asshole."

Elsie took a few quick steps away and Holly gave the shy sailor a last smile and followed. She glanced through the shadows and over shoulders to the far end of the room where the jukebox sat. She caught a glimpse of Lucy Belmar sittin near the jukebox, she could see her smilin.

"Um goin over there," Holly whisperin to Elsie.

"Huh?"

"Um goin over there. Come on, Um goin ta play a song." Holly quickened her steps through the crowd, then edged her way up to the jukebox, leaned over and began readin the little black letters on the white selection keys. She threw her hair back and let it fall over her shoulders, let her face be seen, let her looks taunt Lucy Belmar, let Lucy Belmar know she was there. A gentle tap touched her back, she turned.

"Holly, I was hoping you would let me write to you. I really liked meeting you and maybe I could have your address and write to you, please?" The shy sailor had followed and stood starin up into her eyes. Holly looked, then lowered her eyes a little as a moment came from a time ago. Billy Felter was in the moment, he didn't have a name or face, but Holly knew the feelin and knew it was him. The sailor stood starin at her, the music played, but the music would not go away.

"You're the prettiest girl I've ever met. I'd just like to write to you, that's all. Would that be okay?" the sailor is sayin.

"Ah don't know," Holly answers with a sigh.

The sailor is silent.

"Well, Ah mean, Ah told ya Um engaged and all," Holly is sayin.

"Can't we just be friends?"

Holly is silent, she turns from the boy and stares back down at the black little letters inside the jukebox. A song is endin and the little arm is carefully pickin up the record. She watches it move, so slowly.

The shy sailor waits quietly.

The swayin melody of another song came and Holly threw her head back, let her hair flow with the music, then she asked over her shoulder, "Do ya really want to write me?"

"Yes, I just want to be friends."

"Ah ain't too good at writin letters."

"That's okay, if I could just write you."

Holly turns and looks at the boy, then turns back and stares into the jukebox. She is smilin a little before she is sayin over her shoulder, "Ah don't know, maybe it would be all right."

"Then it's okay?"

Holly keeps starin into the jukebox and swayin with the music. Elsie is leanin over and whisperin in Holly's ear, "Ah see him. He's here, he just come in."

"Hey Garet, Garet." Holly hears Garet Foster's name bein called and knows it's that Lucy Belmar callin for him. She keeps her eyes in the jukebox and is holdin her breath and bitin her lip.

"Can I have your address, Holly?" the sailor is asking.

The record spinnin, somebody is singin, the beat of the music is poundin.

"Shit," Holly mutters to herself as she lets her breath out, then takes another deep breath. She tries to hear over the music, keeps listenin for Garet Foster to call her name, but she can only hear Lucy Belmar laughin. Now the shy sailor is leanin closer and sayin, "Holly, I have a pencil and some paper, can I write down your address?"

Holly spins around, looks at the sailor, then glances beyond him to where she sees Garet Foster standin by that Lucy Belmar. She looks back at the sailor and is sayin real fast, "Ya want ta come wit me?"

The boy's eyes light up.

Elsie whispers, "Holly Hill, what in the Sam Hill ya doin?"

"Nothin," Holly whispers back, then lets her words flow gracefully to the sailor, "Um goin for a walk, would ya like too come wit me?"

Sunday's sun was coolin and glowed red in the far sky. Supply's streets were thinnin out, most folks had gone home and was gettin ready to listen to that radio, see what they might have missed.

When Holly wanted to walk, she could walk. Throw that head back, that chin sky-high, stretch that stride an extra step and don't show no care about how far her hips got to swayin. Elsie could barely keep up with her sometimes.

Elsie is whisperin somethin, Holly blurts out, "He can kiss my ass."

"Where ya going?" Elsie askin.

"Ah don't know," Holly sayin as quick as she walkin.

"What about him?" Elsie is whisperin and pointin back to the sailor.

"Let him come," Holly says and keeps on walkin.

The walk became silent, the sailor came up to Holly's side and tried to talk to her. His questions were long, Holly's answers were short. The end of the street came quick and the old broken road began. A little ways up the road Holly slowed and turned up a path, Elsie and the sailor followed. At the end of the path, the old Supply schoolhouse stood. The coolin sun had left it in the deep shade of the evening. Holly walked through the schoolyard and up to the steps of the school, then slowly climbed the steps until she reached the top one. She turned and sat, crossed her legs and leaned against the school door. Elsie climbed up beside her and took a seat, too. The sailor stood, looked around the schoolyard, then sat on a lower step. Holly and Elsie got their cigarettes out, the sailor lit both.

"Is there something wrong, Holly?" the sailor looks up and asks.

Holly is sittin back and puffin on her cigarette, then blowin the smoke into the evening shade.

"Something wrong, Holly?"

"What ya say your name is?" Holly is askin through the smoke.

"Melvin Ames, but you can just call me Mel, that's what my friends call me."

"Where ya from again?"

"I'm from Ohio, Perrysburg. It's not too far from Toledo."

"What ya all do up there in Ohio?" Holly is askin and smilin a little.

"I work with my daddy on our farm. We have four hundred and thirty-seven acres, it's a real nice farm. Good fishing, too, the river cuts right through our land."

Holly is smilin and the sailor's eyes brighten as he asks, "Do you like to go fishin?"

Holly is puffin on her cigarette, then gets to smilin a lot and lookin at Elsie before she says, "Elsie likes ta go fishin, she loves ta do that."

"Kiss my butt, Holly Hill. Kiss my butt," Elsie blurts out.

The sailor looks down, and then away.

Holly is gigglin, can't stop until she grabs her breath and straightens up her face and starts sayin, "Elsie Fagen, Ah declare. Shame on ya, talkin like that in front of menfolk. What in the world done got into ya?"

Elsie looks at Holly and makes a face and Holly gets to gigglin again. The sailor looks up and is just starin up at Holly, then he looks over to Elsie and asks, "Have you known Holly for a long time?"

Elsie is lookin at Holly, then she turns and looks down at the sailor and says, "Ah ain't known her that long. Her mama comin up ta me and ask me ta act like Um her friend, cause she ain't havin any. Her mama real nice, she give me a dollar evey time Ah take this crazy thing out wit me."

Elsie flinched when Holly poked her in the side. In a while nothing was left of the sun, the far sky had even lost its glow. The schoolyard had darkened and except for the occasional glimmer from cigarettes burnin, shiftin gray smoke, laughter, quick words, it lay still in the dark.

Holly had let her shoes fall off and was wigglin her toes in the night. Both her and Elsie were still amusin themselves with the shy sailor's questions and answers.

"What would ya do if ya had a girlfriend? How would ya treat her? Ya be just like the rest of them no good men, wouldn't ya?" Holly is askin and laughin.

"Oh no, Holly, I'd be real nice. I'd be real good to my girlfriend, I'd never go out with another girl or anything like that. I believe in, well, when you love somebody, you have to be faithful."

"Shit, ya'd be just like the rest," Elsie blurts out.

"No I wouldn't," the sailor insists.

"How come ya want ta send me letters and all, huh?" Holly is askin.

"I think you're real nice, I think you're pretty, too. I just want to be friends and have someone real nice to write."

Holly giggles when Elsie butts in sayin, "How come ya ain't wantin ta write me, Melvin, huh? Ya think Ah ain't nice and pretty, too? Don't ya like me, Melvin, huh?"

"Oh, I'll write you too, Elsie. I think you're real nice."

Quickly, Holly says, "Ah thought ya said ya wouldn't go cheatin on a girl. Ya sayin, ya likin me and all, sayin that first and wantin ta write me letters. Now ya wantin to write another girl same time ya wantin to write me, and she's funny-lookin, too."

Elsie sticks her tongue out at Holly and Holly wiggles her toes at the sailor. The boy starts lookin away until Holly gets to nudgin him with her foot and sayin, "Well, Melvin, which one of us ya really likin, huh?"

The time in the schoolyard seemed to slow, dwindle into a few last moments of soft laughter and quiet words. The sailor left with a smile on his face. Holly and Elsie had given Melvin their addresses and walked out to the road with him. Holly and Elsie's walk back home had spurts of quietness, then laughter and talk would fill the night air. Elsie would always walk a little further down the road to the halfway point between her house and Holly's. Then the old broken patched-up road could have its way in the night.

Ghosts of times gone by were always by the roadside. Cricket calls and night-bug cries filled the dark skies. But Holly can be alone on the road, distant from the songs of the night, separate and not a part of the dark. She can think of things and the night leaves her alone. She wonders if the sailor will really write, she smiles and leaves the thought behind in the dark. The jukebox songs come again, she can hear them and see the record spinnin around, hear Lucy Belmar callin Garet Foster's name. She sighs and turns from the thought, looks out to where the moon hangs in the dark. Near her yard, she slows before turnin off the road and stares to where she can see the old road still curvin in the dark.

"Is that ya, honey?" Ginger calls as Holly enters the house.

"Yes, Mama." Holly answers slowly through the soft music coming from the radio in the living room. She goes into the kitchen where she knows her mother will be sittin.

Ginger speaks with a smile. "You're home early."

"Oh, Mama, Ah said Ah wasn't goin anyplace. Me and Elsie just went down Ben's. We didn't even stay long, we spent most of the time just down at the schoolyard sittin on the steps talkin," Holly answers and sits at the kitchen table with her mother.

Ginger sits quietly sippin on her coffee and starin at the table-cloth. It has become her way, sometimes to early morning hours. She will not sit in the living room where the radio plays its music and speaks of battles. She cannot listen, but she can never stray far from the sound.

Ginger's words come as faint as the fleetin music from the other room. Her eyes are still starin at the tablecloth, and Holly is lookin down, too. "Ah wrote your brother," Ginger is sayin. "Ah told him your daddy went to church this mornin, Ah told him, Ah saw Mrs. Bruce and let him know Charles is over there, too. Maybe they'll see each other, they just might, ya know."

"Oh, Mama, it's so big over there, a whole wide ocean and all . . . ," Holly is sayin before she cuts her thoughts and words short.

"Do ya think he's all right?" Ginger is askin.

Holly is silent and stares at the tablecloth, too. Then she jerks her head up and is sayin, "Mama, Bobby is all right. Ain't nothin goin too happen to him. He just can't be writin all the time, that's all. Ya know Bobby, he probably be forgittin ta write if he gits the time anyway."

Ginger is silent.

Holly sighs and begins to get up as she is sayin, "Mama, Um goin on up and git this dress off me."

Ginger is still starin at the table, but as Holly leaves the kitchen, she calls out, "Honey, now don't ya forgit ta write a letter to Billy."

Quickly, Holly gets that dress off and lets it fall to the floor and lie wherever it has fallen. A puffy sigh fills the room as she snatches the blue shabby nightgown from the bottom of the bed. She hurries and puts it on, then quickly turns the light off and scoots up on the bed. She grabs for her pillow, then cuddles with it as she lies still in the dark. She keeps her eyes open as her deep breaths fill the silence in the room.

"Shit," Holly whispers and pushes the pillow away.

The light comes on, Holly is up and starin at the dresser drawer. It is yanked open, then slowly Holly reaches in. She plucks a pencil from the bottom, then very slowly pulls out the pretty-colored light blue writin tablet.

Cool breezes that had come have gone away. The night's hot, everything is hot, but Holly lets the sweat roll down her face and just stares at the pretty writin paper.

Dear Billy,
    I'm sorry I have not sent you a letter sooner. I been

The pretty paper is torn from the tablet and ripped into little pieces.

Dear Billy,
    I am sorry I have not sent you a letter. I have been very busy doing things

Holly snatches the paper from the tablet and crumbles it up and squeezes it in her hands. The cracklin sound fills the room and won't go away. Holly leans forward on the dresser stool and pushes brushes and lipstick casings away from where the tablet lies, then stares down at the new empty page. Billy Felter's eyes come ten thousand miles. Elsie comes, too, whisperin, "Ya like him Holly, just say it, just say it. He likes ya, everybody in the world knowin that."

Holly closes her eyes, then tries to close them more and squeezes them shut. Nothin comes in her dark and nothin will go away and when she opens her eyes the paper is still there, but it ain't pretty no more.

Dear Billy,

    I am writing to say I love you very much and I always will, but maybe I am not the right girl for you. I have been thinking about you and me a lot and

Holly stops writin and slowly lifts the pencil from the paper, then reads over the few lines she has written. She sits quietly, then gently lays the pencil down. She looks down at the ring on her finger, the ring she has never taken off.

The pretty-colored light blue piece of paper is quietly pulled from its tablet and quietly torn to pieces.

3

Supply's days came as they always had, dark grays of the night would linger for a while, then the sun would show its face. Some days took folks' smiles away, brought that kind of news that made them just shake their heads. Eugene Purvis put another name up on the court-house wall. Fat Tommy Benic was killed in Sicily, his daddy said he got a letter after the telegram, said the letter was from Tommy's captain. Tommy's daddy showed everybody the letter, said Tommy had a real nice captain that would say things like that. Say how Tommy was so brave and his best soldier, said it was nice of him to say that. Tommy's mother, Ellen, has not come out of the house since and that was a couple weeks ago.

One of them colored boys from out in the Back Land got killed, too. Folks said it was one of Dusty Moore's boys, that colored that hauls them vegetables into town on Saturdays. Said it was one of his boys, but didn't know which one. Sheriff LeRoy had to beat the hell out of one of them Moore boys a ways back for stealin out the lumber yard, folks were wonderin if that was the one that got killed.

Every time another Supply boy got killed, Ginger seemed to become thinner with worry. Gus Hill started sippin some of that moonshine that Harry Miller has over behind his place. When Gus Hill was home, which wasn't too often, he'd get to hollerin and cussin about everything. He hit Jason real hard for just turnin the radio dial. Yelled at Ginger all the time for anything. Got to tellin her, You gettin on my nerves too much, here.

Gus Hill sorta kept his distance from Holly, she was the only one he'd turn away from, listen to what she was sayin to him. She could put her hands on her hips just like her Mama used to do and let him have it. Daddy, ya drunk. Ya go on right this minute and git up there and git in the bed. Go on, Daddy, go on up there and lay down.

Holly had a way with her father. They never talked much anymore, but when she was younger it was his lap she'd crawl up on and go to sleep. And if she really wanted somethin, she'd wait all day for her daddy to come home. Then she'd jump up on his lap, or pull and jerk at his arm until he bent over close enough for her to whisper in his ear. Gus Hill would smile then, tell Ginger, She's as connivin as her mother and she ain't knee-high yet.

Ginger had not heard from Bobby. Saipan had fallen, but she had not received the letter she had prayed for. Each day she'd wait for Chester Higgens to bring the mail. Chester would see her waitin, knew she'd be waitin, too, and would shake his head no as soon as he'd see her. Then he'd say, Maybe tomorrow, ya know how the mail be these days Mrs. Hill. Ya probably git a whole dozen letters anyday, now.

Holly had not heard from Billy, his last letter said he was shippin out, said he didn't know where. She had written him, had to, to shut her mama up. Holly had sighed when she finished the letter, but didn't smile when she signed it with love.

Holly and Elsie had spent their evenings and some late nights down Ben's. Garet Foster was followin Holly around like somethin that was stuck to her already. Lucy Belmar had just about rolled her eyes out of her head.

It was August now, the first week was endin. It was a hot Friday afternoon, folks had talked about the heat all day. Said they wouldn't mind havin a little rain. Ginger was sittin out on the porch. The sun had passed overhead and was on its way toward the Back Land. There was a little shade on the far side of the porch, but Ginger sat in the passin sunlight just starin up at them trees on the other side of the old road. Jason was still over June Boy's, had been over there all day, like every day, or June Boy would come over and be chasin around with Jason. Drive Ginger crazy sometimes with all that noise and in and out the kitchen all day. Gus Hill was still down the lumberyard, wouldn't be gettin off till past dark, then no tellin when he would be gettin home. Holly was down Elsie's, had been down there half the day.

Ginger really wasn't watchin the folks that might be passin by on the road. This far back on the road, wouldn't be too many folks passin anyway except them coloreds comin and goin to the Back Land. If they were them town coloreds, them ones that worked for folks in town and Ginger knew them, been seein them for years, she give them a wave and a good mornin. How ya all doin today? But if they were them field coloreds, them ones that do that pickin for folks out in them fields, them ones that sorta stay out in the Back Land and keep to themselves and keep them ways they got, Ginger would sorta let them pass without payin them any mind.

Time was sorta leavin Ginger alone, wasn't tellin her to get up and go fix this or that, it just let her sit for a while. The sun bein so hot had a way of keepin folks in their own fever, keepin them distant from things that weren't far away, sorta not carin about anything beyond their own burnin souls. Chester Higgens wasn't there, he wasn't comin up the road totin that old beaten brown mail pouch he been carryin since when. He had come earlier that mornin when he was supposed to, said the things he was supposed to then. He wasn't up on the road now, comin again, wasn't him, wasn't nothin.

Ginger's eyes saw the squiggly figure in the glarin heat, but her mind wasn't lookin at what her eyes were seein. Chester Higgens turned from the old road and started down the path.

Suddenly he is there.

Ginger is jumpin to her feet and gatherin her skirt. Her eyes are wide, starin at Chester Higgens. She wants to see his eyes, see what they might be sayin, but he got his head too low.

"What is it, Chester? What is it?" Ginger is askin, her voice quiverin.

Chester Higgens sighs and keeps on comin.

Ginger is gaspin, tryin to make breaths say, "Is it Bobby? Is it Bobby?" Her hands have come up and cover her mouth, then just tremble as she watches Chester Higgens near.

"Mrs. Hill, this here come in late. Ah thought Ah best be bringin it on out to ya, knowin ya be wantin to know anything. It bein from the War Department, Ah thought Ah better bring it on out."

Chester Higgens is sighin, lookin at Ginger, then lowerin his eyes when he sees her. The bright telegram envelope in his hand is still there. Ginger will not reach for it. Tears start seepin from her eyes.

"Oh God. Oh God. Please Dear God, no . . . ," Ginger is screamin, her hands are shakin and twistin in front of her face before she reaches out and touches the envelope. It is in her hands now, but she is not openin it, not lookin at it, it is just there shakin in her hands.

Chester Higgens is silent and still.

The envelope falls from Ginger's hands. She becomes rigid, stiff, silent and just starin down at the ground where the envelope has fallen.

A moment will not move away for another one to come until Ginger screams, "Oh God, not my baby. Please no, please no, no not my baby. No, no . . ."

Slowly, Chester Higgens is bendin over and pickin up the envelope and sayin, "Mrs. Hill, Mrs. Hill, maybe Ah ain't the one to say, but if ya want Ah open this here up for ya. Ya never can tell, ya know it could be somethin we ain't thinkin."

Ginger's face is only tears.

Chester Higgens is lookin at her, waitin for her to speak. He sighs and slowly and neatly opens the envelope. He reads silently, then looks up at Ginger and says, "Mrs. Hill, ya might be wantin to read this. Your boy ain't dead, he hurt. It say here he in a hospital."

Holly and Elsie had been sittin on the porch the good part of the day talkin about anything and everything that done come to their mind. It bein Friday, talk done turned to goin down Ben's, maybe up to Wilmington to one of them USO dances.

"Ya make up your mind on what ya goin ta wear? Ya ain't still thinkin about that blue thing are ya?" Elsie is askin Holly.

"Ah don't know yet. How come ya askin, ya ain't even knowin what ya wearin. Ya just sayin things about my blue dress cause ya want ta wear it, Elsie Fagen," Holly answers and gets to gigglin at the same time.

"Ah ain't wantin ta wear that old blue thing of yours, be lookin funny-lookin in it and all. What ever Um goin ta wear, Ah ain't wearin no stockins wit it, too damn hot for them things," Elsie sayin.

"Ah might wear . . ." Holly let her words drift and looked out toward the old road, she stared, then turned back to Elsie sayin, "Ah might just wear . . ." Holly's words drift again, she jerks her head toward the road and stares. "Ya hear that, that's Jason yellin," Holly is sayin and still starin over to the road. Elsie is lookin, too, and sayin, "Where he at, what's he doin that carryin on for?"

"Holly . . . Holly . . . Holly . . . ," Jason is yellin with every poundin beat of his heart. Each runnin step he takes, he tries to go faster.

Slowly Holly gets up and walks to the edge of the porch, then stares off down the road. Her eyes widen when she sees her little brother runnin blindly up the road with his hands flingin in the air.

"Holly . . . Holly . . . Holly . . ." Jason's screams fill the air.

"Somethin wrong," Holly is mutterin to Elsie as she runs down the steps and starts runnin up the path.

"Jason what's wrong? What's wrong wit ya?" Holly is shoutin.

"Holly . . . Holly . . . ," Jason is yellin as he sees his sister.

"Jason, Jason, answer me. Answer me, what's wrong?" Holly is runnin and shoutin.

"Holly . . . Holly . . . come home. Mama wants ya, come home Holly. Mama says come home right now. Mama wants ya, them Japs shot Bobby. They shot Bobby."

"Huh . . . Huh . . . ?" Holly is shouting.

Jason stops and yells, *"Come home, Holly, come home. Them Japs shot Bobby, they shot Bobby. Mama say, come home."*

Holly is gaspin, "Oh my God," then grabbin Jason's hand and runnin back down the road. Tears stream from her eyes, the greens and browns of the roadside become mushy blurs. But she sees Bobby's face, him tryin not to cry when he fell out that tree and broke his arm. Him, comin back and kissin her good-bye after he already had.

Elsie is followin, tryin to catch up and shoutin to Holly, *"What's wrong, Holly, what is it?"*

"They shot Bobby, they shot my brother," Holly twisted around in her run and yelled back to Elsie, then turned, stumbled and kept runnin. Elsie stopped, stood and shook in the road, then started runnin again.

Sweat and tears dripped from Holly's face as she ran from the road and started down the path. She could see her mother sittin on the porch step, a light-colored envelope glarin in the last rays of the sun. Chester Higgens had left, said he would go find Gus Hill, tell him what he be needin to know. Jason had finally gotten hungry and come on home from over June Boy's. Ginger was still sittin on the porch steps cryin when he got there. She told him, "Go git ya sister, ya brother been shot. Tell her ta come home, now. Go on, now."

"Mama . . . Mama . . . ," Holly's shouting as she nears. Ginger is still sitting quietly, holdin the telegram in her hands.

"What's it say, Mama? What's it say about Bobby? Is he, Mama, is he? What's it say, Mama?" Holly's voice is quiverin as she slows and comes to her mother's side.

Ginger starts shakin, then mutterin, "Ah can't tell what it's all meanin. A bullet or somethin went in his head, they say they gittin him to a hospital and they sayin they'll let's us know how he comin. They say it happened two weeks ago, it got the date on it and all. Ah just knew somethin was wrong, just knew it. Ah guess all's we can do is just wait, just wait and pray."

Holly sighs, then is quickly askin, "What hospital, where is he?"

"It don't say," Ginger answers and starts shakin her head back and forth.

"Let me see, Mama, let me see?" Holly is askin and reachin for the telegram. She quickly unfolds the paper, her eyes are twitchin as she begins to read. Silently her lips are shapin the words as she reads,

I REGRET TO INFORM YOU THAT YOUR SON, PRIVATE ROBERT P. HILL, SN. 1226443 USMC, SUFFERED A GUNSHOT WOUND TO THE HEAD ON OR ABOUT 22 JULY 1944 WHILE ENGAGING IN OFFENSIVE ACTIONS AGAINST THE ENEMY ON THE ISLAND OF SAIPAN IN THE MARIANAS. HE IS BEING TRANSFERRED TO A FMF NAVAL HOSPITAL. YOU WILL BE NOTIFIED UPON HIS ARRIVAL.

Holly is wipin the tears out of her eyes and pullin the hair back away from her face and sayin, "What's a FMF hospital? When they gittin him there? He ought ta be there now. How come they ain't sayin where he at and can he talk and is he all right and all?"

Elsie is nearin slowly, she is holdin both of her hands up and over her mouth makin her face just a mask with bulgin eyes. Holly hears her whisperin, "What happen, is he, is Bobby, is he?"

Holly keeps her eyes on the telegram and lookin back and forth over its words, but is sayin over her shoulder to Elsie, "He's, he's still alive. They gittin him ta some hospital, they ain't sayin where he's at or nothin."

Elsie sighs and keeps takin deep breaths as she waits for Holly to say something more, but it becomes silent. Jason has sat next to his mother, he has been quiet and just starin down at the ground. He is lookin up and askin his mother, "Is Bobby goin to die, is he, Mama?"

Ginger turns and looks at him, tries to still her quivers and sucks in her breath as she says, "He's goin ta just be fine, honey. He's goin ta be in a hospital where he can git better."

Quickly, Elsie is wipin the sweat and tears from her eyes. She looks at Ginger, glances at Holly and sees Jason, sighs and says, "Come on, Mrs. Hill. Ya too, Holly. Let's git on inside. Maybe Ah can fix somethin for ya all, ain't no sense in sittin out here."

Elsie nudges at Holly's arm, but Holly shrugs away and blurts out, "It says here it happened on the twenty-second of July. How come they just findin out and tellin us? How long it goin ta be takin them ta git him ta this here hospital? Ain't nobody goin ta know Bobby at the hospital. They better be nice ta him and all."

Elsie had gotten Ginger and them into the house and into the kitchen. She had fixed some coffee, given Jason some milk and cookies he had asked for. Then Elsie sat and eased herself into the silence that had already fallen over the kitchen table. Ginger did not look at the coffee before her, she just kept starin down at the telegram she held in her hands. In its way, the telegram was hope and Ginger held onto it tightly. She could see Bobby and all the faces of his life. The tears comin from his eyes when he was a baby and sick for days with that fever. She can feel him now, tuggin at her dress and wantin to be picked up, held and carried. She trembles but keeps hold of the paper in her hands when she sees his last face, him with that uniform on and turnin around one more time to wave good-bye to her.

Holly has lit another cigarette, she inhales deep and long. She sits quietly and watches the smoke float. The cigarette burns out and Holly lights another one real quick, then slowly she lowers her head and stares at the table. She feels the tears comin to her eyes again and quickly reaches up to wipe them when she thinks Bobby might be dead already. She wipes them away, but they just come again.

The glass of milk is still half full and Jason is only lookin at it. The cookies don't have any taste, Jason lets them lie on the table. He stares at the cookies but in his mind can only see the Japs shootin Bobby and blood comin out of Bobby's head.

Elsie sits quietly, if she speaks, she only asks Ginger if she wants her coffee warmed. She wants to say more, sometimes she looks at Holly and wants to whisper a secret, but she is as silent as the secret has been. So she lowers her head and stares down at the table too. She sees the night again, watches it as she stares down at the table or watches the smoke floatin about the kitchen. She was goin home that night, she had left Holly's house and was hurryin because it was goin to rain. The quick rushin winds seemed to hiss of the coming of the rain. She had slowed when she seen him comin down the dark road, knew it was Bobby when she seen his bouncin way of walkin, couldn't have been anybody or anything else. She knows she was sixteen then, because he was eighteen and comin from seein that Pam Epps. The rain came and they were still talkin, had huddled under them low-hangin branches just off the road. She had giggled when he touched her, but did not shy from his kiss. She had kissed him back, had always wanted to kiss him. Then it was the rain, the dark, the wind and a secret in the night.

It is dark now, even in the far sky past the Back Land, there is no light hangin in the sky. Holly has walked Elsie up the path and half-way up the road. They stood and talked, then held each other tightly before parting. Holly hurried back down the road, but when she reached the path she slowed, then stopped and stared down the dark road. A silence seemed to call, the old fat-bellied oak tree seemed to wait. Holly sighed and turned from the dark road and its silent call and hurried down the path.

Ginger was still sittin at the kitchen table. She had taken Jason into her arms and was holdin him, his eyes were closed. Holly slowed her steps as she entered the kitchen, then quietly sat at the table again. She was thinkin something, wanted to whisper her thoughts to Ginger, but let the thought of Chester Higgens, and what he might bring in the morning, drift. Holly was starin at the floor and slowly looked up when she felt her mother movin. Ginger had only turned her head and looked toward the window, then sighed and lowered her head again.

"Ya daddy should have been home by now," Ginger is muttering quietly.

Holly is silent and looks back down at the floor.

Ginger gently nudges Jason, eases him out of his sleep, then gets him up and takes him to bed. She stays with him a while until he settles in his bed. She tells him Bobby is goin to get better, maybe be home soon, too. But he still wants to know if Bobby is goin to die.

When Ginger comes back into the kitchen, Holly is smoking another cigarette and has made another pot of coffee. Ginger walks to the window, leans toward it and looks out into the night.

"Ah know ya daddy knows, Chester said he'd go on over the yard and tell him. Chester's mighty good about things like this. Ya daddy be knowin now," Ginger is sayin out into the night.

Holly is twistin in her chair a little, but still lookin down at the floor. Ginger turns from the window and sits back down at the table, but keeps lookin toward the window.

"Why ain't he home, why?" Ginger is mutterin.

Holly keeps twistin in her chair a little, then stills herself and just stares at the floor. And the floor becomes an ocean she can see, little specks become islands and boats. The space between is the emptiness of the sea she sees. It is a quiet sea, a still sea, but it is not peaceful. Holly looks for Billy Felter's ship among the specks on the floor, she does not know which one it is, sighs and closes her eyes.

Ginger is sippin on her coffee and sometimes glancin at the window and the dark beyond it. Her head is lowered now and she is sighin, almost whisperin, "Maybe we hear somethin more tomorrow. Maybe the hospital let us know somethin. Maybe it ain't that bad, ya know as bad as it sounds. Them boys wear them helmets, ya know. That might've helped some. Ah figure they got him in the hospital by now, we ought ta be hearin somethin again."

Holly is silent.

"Ya daddy," Ginger says, then quickly takes the words from her breath and hushes.

Holly looks up toward the window, then looks at her mother. A moment is restless and will not go on and pass with the others. Ginger's hands are holdin one another tightly, fingers twisted around fingers.

"Daddy might have had ta stay workin, Mama. Maybe he couldn't come away, them bein so busy and all, he might have had ta stay some," Holly is sayin.

Ginger sighs, takes a quick glance toward the window, then lowers her head. In a moment, Holly takes a deep breath, then sorta whispers, "Mama it's too hot ta be just sittin, Um goin out on the porch some."

Holly walks to the edge of the porch, leans against the porch post and curls her arms around it, then gently lets her head rest on it. She slowly searches the dark skies, sees the yellow stars, then looks down at the dark ground and stares at the worn footpath. Crickets and night bugs seem to silence their songs, yard dogs lie still, but Ginger's muffled cries seep out of the house and spill into the night. Holly leans closer to the porch post and squeezes it a little tighter.

When the hours passed, they did so silently and without changin the night, makin it lighter, shorter, longer. Tears that had come, still came. Deep sighs filled silent moments. Hope kept comin and goin and when it went away, stayed too long, silent prayers brought it back.

Holly sat with her mother again. She had stood on the porch, searched the night for things she couldn't see. The kitchen had cooled some in the later hour, the coffee was cold, but Ginger would still take a sip. She had looked at Holly, smiled a little and said, "Honey, go on and git some sleep, Ah wait for ya daddy." Holly had just shaken her head no.

Distant yard dogs barked and barked. Ginger's eyes widened, she turned her head to the window, listened, then turned back and stared at the table. Holly stood and walked to the window, put her head to the glass and peeped out into the dark, then quickly turned and went out onto the porch. The dogs still barked, but everything in the night was dark until the lights flickered in the distance. Holly took a deep breath and let it come out slowly, then went back into the kitchen.

"He's comin, Mama," Holly is sayin as she sits back down.

Ginger is silent.

The bangin noise of a car comin down the road becomes louder and louder, then its lights jab through the kitchen window. Rocks and stones bounce up and hit the bottom of the car as it turns from the road and comes down the path. The lights die out, their glare vanishes from the window. It is silent for a while, then the squeakin sound of the car door bein opened seems to last forever until the crashin sound of it bein slammed shakes the night. The sound of footsteps comes, slow slidin footsteps that seem to scrape across the ground, then slowly pound up the porch steps.

Ginger cringes, but keeps starin at the table.

Holly starts bitin her lip and lookin at her mama.

Footsteps stumble into the house, hallway, then near the kitchen door. Gus Hill comes into the kitchen, his shirt is open and stained with sweat. The sour smell of alcohol comin from his mouth fills the air in the kitchen. Holly is lookin at him and keeps starin at his face. He staggers by her, then bumps into the back of Ginger's chair until he gets to the icebox. He pulls the door open and tries to steady himself by holdin on to it. The icebox door swings on its hinges, Gus Hill sways and swings with it. Holly keeps her eyes on her father, but Ginger won't look at him, just keeps her head down and stares at the table.

"Daddy," Holly hisses.

Gus Hill ain't answerin, keeps tryin to bend over and reach inside the icebox.

"*Daddy,*" Holly shouts.

Gus Hill doesn't turn to her, just makes some gruntin sound. Holly is pushin her chair back from the table, her eyes widen, her hand quickly brushes the hair from her face. Ginger jolts at Holly's sudden moves, but keeps her head down.

"*Daddy,*" Holly is shoutin, "*did Mr. Higgens come find ya? Did he come find ya and tell ya, did he? Bobby been shot, shot bad in the head, do ya know that? Do ya, huh? Did Mr. Higgens come and tell ya? He told ya, didn't he? He came and told ya, Ah know he did. How come ya ain't come home? An now ya all drunk, look at ya. Bobby might even be dead, and ya out there gittin all drunked up and all.*"

There is a piece of roast on a plate in the icebox, Gus Hill is reachin for it, but it keeps slidin away from him. He touches it, it moves, he grabs again, it ain't where it was. A bottle of milk gets in the way, it is pushed aside, Gus Hill is mutterin, his words stick together into thick grunts. The bottle of milk is in the way again and will not move. He grabs it and tosses it out of the icebox, it splatters and splashes over the kitchen floor.

"*Daddy, Daddy,*" Holly is screamin, "*what in the Sam Hill are ya doin? What's wrong wit ya, huh? Look what ya doin.*"

Ginger is tremblin and has put her face in her hands where it is dark and she cannot see, she doesn't want to see, hear anything. But her heart is poundin, beatin against the inner walls of her chest. Her head is rattlin, makin her face shake in her hands. She jerks her hands from her face, smashes them down on the table and screams, "*Gus, goddamn ya. My God, just look at ya. Look at ya, look at ya, look at ya. God only knows where Bobby is or if he's still alive. Where were ya this time that ya couldn't even come home when your own son might be dyin, God only knows where.*"

Gus Hill has the piece of roast in his hand and is tryin to stand. The icebox door swings wildly as he sways back and forth on his feet. The piece of meat is pushed into his mouth, his fingers poke at the little pieces that hang from his lips.

Holly runs out of the kitchen and onto the porch where she grabs onto the porch post. The dark hides her twisted face, crickets and night bugs hear, "Ah hate him, Ah hate him. Damn it, Ah hate this whole damn world."

The icebox door slams, Gus Hill's yells come out into the night, *"What do you want me to do? Ah didn't start the goddamn war, Ah can't stop the goddamn thing either. He's a man, not your little baby. Worry, worry, worry, that's all you do is worry. You'd do better if you keep that girl in sometimes. You don't think Ah know what time she gets her ass in here? You'd need to worry some about that, you hear?"*

Ginger's shouts come out into the night, *"At least she's here, she's here, Gus, and not layin somewhere with a bullet in her head. And she's here where she can see ya, see her daddy so drunk he can't even show no care for her brother."*

The porch is shakin, the sudden thumpin sounds inside the house burst out into the night. Holly hears the sharp crack of a smack, then her mother's screams pierce the yard dog's ears. Holly spins from the porch post and runs back into the house, through the dark hallway and into the kitchen.

"Goddamn ya," Holly is yellin and jumpin up in her father's face, *"Stop it, Daddy, stop it. Look what ya did ta Mama. What's wrong wit ya? Stop it."*

Everything in Gus Hill's skull is spinnin and twistin. Everything that did not move, walls, floors, chairs, coffee cups, wiggle and shake inside his mind. Screams and cries stab at the center of his mind.

"Stop it, Daddy, stop it . . . ," Holly is yellin.

Gus Hill's eyes flash around the kitchen, then suddenly stop and settle on Holly's. He stares into her eyes, then slowly looks beyond her to where Ginger sits holding her face. He looks back at Holly, breathes heavily and turns away. His steps are slow, his feet seem to drag behind his will. Except for the sound of Gus Hill's footsteps goin into the hallway, then beginnin to climb the steps, the house has stilled. Ginger doesn't cry, just holds her battered face and stares at the table. Holly stands by the kitchen door and looks at her mother sittin at the table. She sighs and just keeps lookin at her mother.

4

Supply hadn't had much rain all summer, seemed like it hadn't rained at all in July and now it was dead center in the middle of August. Some folks just seemed to be sittin around waitin on the rain or anything else to cool things off some. Then when the sky started gettin all dark in the middle of the day, folks that were just sittin and them folks that had to be up and tryin to make a dollar got to lookin up and wonderin if it was really goin to rain. Supply's old men, them ones that spent most of their time just sittin, shrugged their shoulders and got to sayin, Just a little shower comin up.

When it rained, anything dirt quickly turned into mud. Town folks looked up for a split second, then covered their heads with anything they could get their hands on and ran inside wherever they could get. Coloreds out in them back pickin fields got to hollerin and runnin all at the same time.

Rain was blowin up on Elsie's porch, but Elsie was still standin there just a laughin at Holly runnin down her yard path.

"Ya crazy girl. Everybody knowin the rain was comin," Elsie is shoutin.

Holly's shoutin something back, but Elsie can't hear what she is sayin. Holly's words are fallin in the mud with the rain, only her gestures can be seen and they seem to be vanishin in the downpour, too.

"Hurry up girl fore ya drown out there," Elsie's shoutin out through the rain.

Holly stops in the middle of the path, her dress is a cloth of water that clings and sticks up on her legs. The rain has soaked her hair, it hangs in slick strands over her face. Her hands go up in her hair and slide to the top of her head. She gets a look in her eyes that ain't seein no rain and slowly starts wigglin her hips.

Elsie's laughin and shoutin, "Girl, what's wrong wit ya, ya drunk?"

Sudden winds blow strong gray streaks of water across the mud-soaked path. Yard weeds bend to the ground, thunder breaks in the distant sky, lightning flashes fire, but Holly is shakin her hands to the sky and wigglin her hips from side to side. She got a smile on her face and is shoutin something, but Elsie can't hear her in the windblown rain.

"Ya damn fool," Elsie yells.

Holly dances.

Elsie runs from the porch and down the steps holdin her hands over her head until the water soaks her hair anyway, then she throws her hands to the sky and sways with the wind and rain. Laughter and yells whirl with the wind. The old black face of the sky seems to get mad about Holly shakin her ass up at it and spits some more thunder and fire. Holly and Elsie just keep laughin, then keep laughin while they run on up onto the porch.

"Ya crazy, Holly Hill. Ya plum out of ya mind, girl," Elsie is shoutin when she reaches the porch.

Holly is shoutin back and laughin so much she can hardly shout, "Ya could have stayed on the porch, Elsie Fagen. Ya ain't had ta come out there. Ah got caught in it, ya come out and jumped in it. Who's crazy, Elsie Fagen, just who bein crazy, huh?"

Elsie's shoutin back, "Ya damn fool, ya the crazy one."

Holly's yellin, "It was fun."

Elsie's smilin, laughin and sayin, "Ya want ta do it again?"

"Ah told ya, ya were the one that's crazy. See, ah told ya. See, Ah ain't the one crazy-actin, now," Holly's sayin.

Elsie's mother, Becky Fagen, comes to the door and looks out onto the porch and just starts shakin her head and sayin, "What in the hell are ya two doin? Ah swear the older ya two git, the younger ya all act. Look at ya, both ya all together ain't got the sense one of ya should have. Come in this house and git them wet clothes off ya."

Elsie giggles and says, "It was Holly's idea."

Holly is gettin one of her serious looks on her face, but can't keep a smile away as she is sayin, "Oh no, Mrs. Fagen, ya daughter was already out there dancin and just carryin on when Ah come runnin down the path tryin ta git out of all that rain. She grabbed my arm and kept me out there wit her."

Becky Fagen gets to just shakin her head again and sayin, "Git on in here, the both of ya. And git them wet clothes off before ya be gittin so much pneumonia in ya, ain't goin ta be nothin lefta ya."

Holly and Elsie go on into the house and up to Elsie's room, where everything is still funny as dancin in the rain. Holly stands in front of Elsie's mirror lookin and laughin at her thin summer dress soakin and saggin from her, then she sees her face all covered with long wet strands of hair. Elsie pops into the picture in the mirror and together they laugh and make faces.

"Shit, this ain't never goin ta dry," Holly is hissin as she begins wringin out her hair.

Elsie has already taken off her dress and slips and laughs when she tugs at her bra as it sags from her breasts. Holly pulls her dress over her head, along with her bra, stands laughin in front of the mirror askin Elsie, "Ya want ta git butt naked and go out there again? Huh, ya want to?"

Elsie just laughs at Holly and starts dryin herself off, then she asks Holly, "What ya want to put on? Ah still have that print dress ya hate, ya want it?"

Holly looks at Elsie and makes a face. "Ah don't hate that thing as much as ya like it. Ah know Ah should have never let ya borrow it. Ah knew ya be tryin ta tell me Ah didn't like it anymore."

"Ya tellin big stories, Holly Hill. Ah don't like that dress, it lookin like some old hand-me-down hussy dress or somethin," Elsie blurts out, then says, "Ah give ya my maroon skirt and that pink top ya like."

"Hell no, that thing's tight on ya, it be too big on me."

"Look who's talkin, Miss Skinny Hips herself," Elsie is sayin and laughin, then throwin the towel over to Holly.

Holly throws the towel back in Elsie's face, giggles and yells, "Ah can't help if my ass ain't as big as yours, Elsie Fagen."

The rain still poured down through the hours, the moments crept by slowly. Holly's and Elsie's giggles had settled into whispers. Holly had put on a pair of Elsie's dungarees and one of her big shirts she got from her daddy and was sittin on the edge of the bed. Elsie had just put on her housecoat and was sittin in the chair next to the dresser. Holly sighed, put her head down and stared at the floor. Elsie had her head down, too, then looked up askin, "How ya goin ta do that, huh?"

"Ah don't know yet."

"If ya do, what ya think is goin ta happen?"

"Ah don't know, maybe nothin."

"Why don't ya wait some, ya know see how ya be feelin then?"

"Ah can't, Ah mean, shit, Ah just can't. Besides . . ." Holly let her words die with her breath.

"Besides what?" Elsie is askin and lookin at Holly.

Holly's words start pourin like the rain. "He ain't comin home no time soon. Ain't no tellin how long this damn war be lastin and all. Ah think Ah ought ta tell him. Ah mean, it ain't just Garet. It's just, well, Ah don't feel, Ah don't feel things anymore. Since Bobby got hurt, Ah written Billy a bunch of times, try and say some things, sweet things and all. But Ah just don't feel Ah want ta be married all my life ta him. Ah mean, Ah want ta git married and all. But, Ah just don't want ta be wearin his ring. Ah mean, Ah just don't want ta be wearin his ring and be feelin like Ah do. Ah think Mama have a fit if Ah do it. Ah know she go havin a fit, her thinkin old-fashion like. She gits pissed every time Ah don't send a letter ta Billy when she sends one ta Bobby. She still sendin letters ta Bobby now. That Red Cross lady said it be a while before he could read and send a letter back, but Mama just keep sendin one every day anyway. Besides, they say he bein shipped back to Pearl Harbor. Lord knows how long that be takin, it's just like writin ta Billy. Ah mean, him bein on a ship and all. Ah git letters from Billy he done sent over a month ago, sometimes. Even if Ah write him and tell him, ain't no tellin how long it be fore he really know."

Elsie just sat in her chair and listened, even to the silence when it came. Holly had lifted her head, brushed the wet hair out of her eyes and looked out the window at the rain and sighed. She stared out the window for a moment, then spoke over her shoulder sayin, "Ah bet the creek done flowed over, bet them coloreds out in them Back Lands gittin washed out."

Elsie looked over at the rain comin down, then asked Holly, "When ya goin ta do it?"

Elsie had some cigarettes lyin on her dresser, Holly got up from the bed and went and got one, lit it up and sat back down on the bed. She took a few drags on the cigarette, slowly blew the smoke out and sat silently.

Elsie was silent, too.

Holly started talkin again, tellin Elsie, "Ah took the ring off this mornin, just left it upstairs, didn't put it on all day. Just before Ah was comin up here, Mama start askin me if Ah lost it or somethin. Ah didn't feel like startin somethin, her bein worryin about Bobby and all and ya know how Daddy been bein. Ah just told her Ah forgot to put it on. Ah went on and got it, keep her quiet and all. When Ah write ta him, Ah think Ah just keep wearin the ring for a while, keep Mama happy. Besides, it come in handy sometimes wit some of them assholes we be meetin, they always wantin ta know if ya married or somethin. Them ugly ones, Ah just keep showin the ring ta."

Elsie got up out of her chair, went over to the window and looked out for a while, then turned and sat on the window ledge. For a moment, she sat quietly, sometimes lookin back over her shoulder at the rain, then lookin at Holly sittin in the gray light that the storm was castin through the window. Then she put her head down, but starts to whisperin and pickin at words she wants Holly to hear. "Ah always liked Billy." Elsie is talkin real soft. "He's always been nice, ya know. Ah think he can be a little crazy-actin, but he got nice ways about him. Ah tell ya, he a hell of a lot more than that damn Garet ever be. Ah think that Garet Foster ain't nothin but a big asshole. If ya ask me, Ah thinks ya ought ta wait some."

Holly blurts out, "Ah can't wait, Elsie. Ah mean, it's feelin like bein on some invisible chain. Can't do nothin without feelin ya tryin ta sneak away from somethin that don't own ya anyway. And just because ya want ta go some place, do somethin that ya allowed to anyway. That's important, real important. It's important ta do things that's important ta ya."

Elsie shakes her head back and forth like her mama does, looks at Holly and starts sayin, "Ain't nothin so important about some damn Garet Foster. What's so important about that asshole, huh?"

Holly's yellin, "Ah ain't meanin that, Elsie."

Elsie's sayin, "Garet ain't but wantin one thing. And as long as Lucy's around and he can git it the only thing he wantin is somethin new. That's all, the same thing but just new. That's all ya be, some new piece of ass. And ya know he'd be runnin around tellin and braggin how he screwed Billy's girl. Them two ain't never got along, and if Billy was here, he'd kick that Garet Foster's butt."

"That ain't what Ah was meanin, Elsie. That ain't what Ah was meanin, and Garet ain't like that, either." Holly is shoutin, now.

Elsie shouts back, "Shit, Holly, he is too. He's a asshole."

"No he ain't."

"Then how come every time he's around ya and that Lucy Belmar around, he actin like ya some cousin or faraway-livin friend, how come?"

"He just that way, he say he just ain't wantin ta hurt her feelins and all."

"Lucy Belmar ain't got no feelins. She'd screw anything, might even let some nigger on her if no one was watchin."

Holly jerked her head toward the window and looked out at the rain, but only saw its grays.

Elsie hissed loudly, "He's an asshole, Holly."

Holly didn't turn from the window and didn't answer.

Elsie's yellin, "Do ya just want ta do it, is that it, huh?"

"It might be," Holly turns and shouts back. "It might be. Ya can't say anything ta me. What about that redheaded army guy? That one bein from Texas, what about him? What about him, huh? Ya knew he wasn't comin back, he even told ya his group was shippin out. He told ya, don't say he ain't."

Elsie jumps to her feet shoutin, "So what, huh?"

"Ya knowin. So what, ya know what ya did."

"At least he wasn't an asshole and fuckin some Lucy Belmar, then runnin around like he ain't knowin her or like she some goddamned good friend or somethin. She's a fuckin whore and he's a fuckin asshole. And ya a fool if ya ain't seein that, Holly Hill. That boy from Texas, Ah really liked him and he liked me."

"He ain't never sent ya a letter, did he, huh? If he liked ya so much, how come he ain't sent ya a letter, how come?"

Elsie sighed and lowered her head, then told Holly, "Ah don't care what ya do, go on and send Billy any kind of letter ya want, go ahead."

The sound of raindrops poured into the silence that came into the room until Holly sighed and said, "Guess who Ah got a letter from today? Ah forgot ta tell ya, guess who?"

"Who?" Elsie asks quietly.

"Go on guess," Holly says and smiles a little. "Melvin," Holly blurts out.

"Who in the hell is a Melvin?"

"Melvin, ya remember Melvin. Member that boy we took down ta the school yard, that one from Ohio someplace, that big-eyed boy," Holly's sayin and smilin.

Elsie smiles back and says, "He said he was goin ta send me a letter too. He's another asshole."

Holly's laughin and sayin, "Ya think everybody is an asshole."

Elsie smiles and says, "Ya can be one, too, Holly Hill."

"Hey Elsie."

"What?" Elsie answers, looks at Holly and starts laughin when she sees Holly makin the ugliest face she could make.

The rain had settled into a heavy drizzle, the far skies were tryin to lighten. Elsie glanced out the window, smiled and said, "Um goin ta throw somethin on, let's go on back out ta the porch. It's gittin stuffy in here with all my cigarettes ya done smoked."

Late afternoon came and brought a little sunlight. Holly was on the old road, still had Elsie's jeans and big shirt on and was tryin to get around them puddles the rain had left on the road. All that rain and thunder seemed to set back everybody's time, had folks doin things now they usually did an hour or so before. Them pickin-field coloreds were on the road and still had them soaked clothes on just a hangin all from them. They never did walk fast, comin or goin, them big puddles in the road didn't seem to make no mind to them, they just curled on around them.

Holly was in a hurry, didn't have the time them coloreds had. She was walkin fast, zigzaggin around the puddles and them coloreds, too. Some of them that seen her comin or knew she was comin without even lookin back, sorta edged over some and got out of her way. Holly was just a hurryin until she looked up and saw Tessie up in front of her. Holly knew it was her, could tell her from anybody forever.

"Tessie, Tessie," Holly got to yellin and smilin at the same time.

A dark gold-colored face turned to Holly's call and glowed with a bright smile. "Hey Holly girl, hey."

"Tessie, Tessie, Tessie," Holly shouted and waved her hands as she ran to catch up.

Tessie lived right on the other side of the creek, was one of them children belongin to Big Calvin, everybody knew Big Calvin. Anytime anybody had somethin to move that they couldn't get a mule to budge, they'd call Big Calvin. Sheriff LeRoy, as big as he was, didn't even come up to Big Calvin's shoulders. Holly used to play with Tessie down by the creek, splashin in the water all day and makin more mudcakes than any Supply bakin mamas.

"Holly girl, Holly girl," Tessie yelled and waved as she waited for Holly to catch up to her. She had grown tall, full since the days down by the creek, but still had that baby-doll face and her big bubbly smile.

As Holly neared, she got to jumpin up and down in the mud, yellin. "Where on earth ya been? Tessie, where ya been, huh?"

Tessie got to jumpin up and down in the mud as much as Holly. Different colored smiles gleamed in the gray of the passin storm. "Looky, looky at Holly. Look at Holly girl," Tessie yelled and kept smilin, then got to sayin, "What ya been doin, huh? What ya doin in that big old man shirt lookin like ya comin from the wood yard or someplace. What ya been doin, huh?"

"Ah just been around, ain't been doin nothin," Holly is answerin, then askin, "Where on earth ya been hidin?"

"Girl, Ah went on up ta Baltimore. Ah was up there wit my Aunt Rachel."

"What ya doin way up there?"

"Had me a good-payin job . . ."

"Tessie, Tessie, Tessie," Holly is shoutin as she looks down at her. Tessie's smile glows brighter than the comin sun.

"Tessie, ya goin ta have a baby," Holly says and her face is aglow, too.

Tessie is still smilin.

"How come ya ain't come and told me ya havin a baby, huh?"

"Ah didn't know myself, didn't know till Ah knew somin wasn't the ways it was supposed ta be. Ah had some of that fever that come around, just thinkin Ah was sick for a while. Didn't think nothin of it till Ah look down one day."

Holly is whisperin, "Did ya git, did ya git married already?"

Tessie's smile goes where the storm has gone, her eyes drop to the muddy dirt she is standin in. Holly looks down, too.

They got to walkin and Tessie got to talkin. "His name was Tyler Allen, he was livin across the street from my Aunt Rachel. We's talks about gittin maried, then he goes on and goes up to Pittsburgh when the war started. Says he can git in them mills they's got up there, says they hirin colored and all. He say he be sendin for me, Ah ain't heard from him. Ah come on back here when Ah know about the baby. Aunt Rachel send Mama a letter about it, ya know, not wantin me there wit a baby. Mama say come on back down here."

Tessie was smilin again, askin Holly, "Ya still got that curly-head boy ya had, ya all gits married?"

Holly sighs, looks far down the road and says to things she can't see, "He's in the Pacific, he's in the navy and all. We got engaged ta be married fore he went. But, Ah mean, Ah don't know. Ah been thinkin, ya know, thinkin about things and all." Holly let her words drift a little, then got to sayin, "My brother Bobby done got shot over there. He in the hospital in Pearl Harbor, now. He got shot real bad in the head, can't talk or nothin. Mama's worried sick."

Holly was walkin with her head down, sayin some things and listenin to what Tessie was sayin. But it wasn't the puddles along the way she was lookin at and sometimes it wasn't Tessie's words she heard. Tessie was the same age as Holly, and she was havin a baby. Somewhere there was a baby and it would be a girl, too, bright eyes, that might be blue. And then the puddles were there, Holly stepped around them.

"Where ya comin from, ya ain't out there workin in them hot fields and all, wit the baby comin? Ya ain't doin that are ya?" Holly is askin.

"Got ta, Holly girl, gots ta make some money."

"How long ya think it's goin ta be fore the baby come?"

"Ah ain't knowin that. Mama say, the way Um carryin it be 'bout in November."

Holly reached her yard path and stood and kept talkin for a while, then she stood and watched Tessie go on down the road. "Ya stop by, ya need anything, ya hear?" Holly yelled as Tessie vanished in the darkness of the curve of the road, where the shadows always live.

Jason was sittin on the porch steps and started callin to his sister as she neared, "Did ya see the rain, Holly? Did ya see it? Me and June Boy went down by the creek, ya should see it down there, it got real big. Ya know down by that big rock, ya can't even see that no more, the water is all over that real big rock. Ya should see it, ya want ta go back down there wit me, Ah show ya?"

Holly makes her straight face come on, the one she uses when she wants to be serious, but is gigglin inside. "No, Jason, Ah don't want ta go and see no big rock," she is sayin and almost gets it said before she smiles and sits next to her brother.

"Ya should come see it, Holly."

"Ah told ya, Jason, Ah ain't goin down there lookin at no rock."

"It looks just like a big river down there."

"No, Jason, and ya and June Boy keeps your butts away from down there. Ya just stay away from that high water and all. Ya know how it can wash up all them snakes, ya know that. Ya go down there and git bit by one of them big water snakes, Mama goin have a fit."

"Where did ya git that boy shirt at?"

"Ah got it from Elsie. Where's Mama?"

"Where Elsie git a boy shirt from?"

"Never ya mind. Where's Mama at?"

Jason was sittin still for a moment, then bounced up and started dartin across the yard. Holly hollered after him, "Jason, don't ya go down there and git bit by no snake, ya hear me. Um tellin Mama."

Ginger was over by the sink lookin down and fixin somethin in a bowl. She just started talkin when she heard Holly come in the kitchen. "Did ya eat down Elsie's? Me and Jason just ate. Wasn't that rain somethin? Ah hope things cool off for a while. Ah fixed the rest of that stew, there's some corn bread in there, too."

Holly went over to the icebox and busied herself with gettin somethin to eat. She had not thought about bein hungry until her mother started talkin about eatin. Ginger turned from the sink, smiled a little and got to sayin, "Ah thought that rain got ya, the way it come down here right after ya left out of here. Lord just look at ya, Ah told ya, ya ought ta be waitin."

Holly was still gettin her plate fixed, but blurted out, "Ah saw Tessie, Mama. She's back, been up in Baltimore and she goin ta have a baby, too."

Ginger shook her head, sighed and said, "Tessie's havin a child?"

"Yeah, Mama, Ah saw her on the road. She say, she didn't even know it for a while, she thought she was just sick or somethin. She say, this boy named Tyler or somethin, up in that Baltimore is her baby's daddy. But he went on up to Pittsburgh, get a job and told her he'd send for her. She say, he left fore she knew about the baby and all. Then her mama sent her a letter and told her ta come on home. She say her aunt, somebody, ain't wantin her up there havin no baby."

Holly ate and talked some more with Ginger, then went on up to her room and closed the door. The room was filled with shade and cool air that lingered from the passin storm. What light was comin through the window was weak and fell into dark gray. Slowly, Holly got out of her dungarees but left the big shirt on. When she lay across the bed, she grabbed her pillow and brought it close to her, then hugged it. Silent moments went by and Holly had closed her eyes to them, but she could see Tessie's face. It was smilin again. Tessie was lookin down at her stomach, then lookin back up with that smile on her face again. Holly sighed and kept her eyes closed, but she smiled a little when she thought of the day when her child would be within her. She thought of Billy and slowly her smile went away.

5

September came, but the heat of the August nights stayed. Friday night and the nickel jukebox at Ben's was blarin. Sweat, smiles and dancin songs gave base to the night. Holly's red lipstick gleamed in the light.

Elsie is whisperin, "Stay here, don't go wit him."

Holly whispers back, "Um comin right back, Ah ain't goin noplace far."

Garet Foster has said, "Let's get out of here and go someplace where we can talk. Ah got somethin Ah want ta show ya too, come on, Holly, please?"

Outside the grays of buildings hunch in the dark. Sailors go by, smiles and laughter flash and fade. The dancin music comin from the nickel jukebox becomes a distant thud in the night. Garet Foster reaches for Holly's hand, she shies away from his touch. He gently places his hand on Holly's elbow and guides her across the street. Even in the night, the parked blue car seems to have a glow of its own. As Holly nears the car, she slows, then stops.

"Do ya like it?" Garet is askin.

"Is it yours?" Holly asks.

"Yep, all mine and paid for. Been savin up for it," Garet is sayin with a big grin on his face that Holly doesn't see as she smiles at the car.

"Ah didn't know ya were gittin a car, Garet, it's real nice."

"Would ya like ta go for a ride in it? Maybe just out ta the highway and back? It really goes good, it got a real good engine in it, purrs just like a kitten. Oh, it got a radio in it too. It's a good car, 'thirty-nine Hudson," Garet has said in one breath, then looks at Holly and tries to see her eyes.

"Ah don't know, Garet."

"We won't go far, just out the highway and back."

"Ah don't know, Garet. Ah told Elsie Ah wasn't goin noplace."

"Ah promise, we won't go far, just out ta the highway and turn around there. It will just take a minute, Holly. Ah been really wantin ya to see it and go for a ride in it with me," Garet is sayin, then reaches and opens the car door.

A faint rhythm of dancin music comes across the dark street and seeps into the moment. Holly is sayin, "All right, but we can't go far."

Garet grins, Holly slides into the front seat of the car and sits lookin at the shiny dashboard. Quickly, Garet closes Holly's door and rushes around the car, then gets in his side. He leans back in his seat, looks at Holly.

"This is real nice," Holly is sayin as she keeps lookin at all the shiny knobs and buttons glimmerin in the dark.

Quickly, Garet puts the key into the ignition. The car shakes, then settles under the hum of the engine.

The highway wasn't far, right down Main Street, a quick turn and over the railroad tracks. Holly had leaned back in her seat and glanced out into the night, the little wind comin in the car's window was gently blowin on her face.

The car slowed as it neared the highway, then stilled in the emptiness of the crossroads. Holly heard Garet speakin softly. "Can Ah take it out on the highway for ya? It really goes out there. We won't go far."

Holly whispered back, "Not too far, Garet."

"Which way, north or south?" Garet asked and smiled at Holly.

"Ah don't know. Let's go south, but not too far, Garet."

Garet put the car in its gear and sped out onto the highway. Holly leaned back and rode the jolts of its shiftin gears, fast dark winds blew past the window.

Garet reached over and flicked the radio on, then sat back in his seat. In a moment, the night was full of music. Garet started talkin and Holly listened to his words and the melody of the song the radio was playin. When she spoke, she only whispered above the sound of the music. She was tellin Garet, "Ah still love Billy, Ah know that Ah always be lovin him. Ah mean carin for him and all."

Garet was quiet for a while and Holly spoke again. "Billy is real nice ta me. Him bein my first boyfriend and all, Ah really care about his feelins a lot, but . . ." Holly sighed and let her thoughts and words go with the wind passin by the window.

Garet started talkin again sayin, "Ah like ya a lot, Holly. Ah always been wantin ta come right up and tell ya, but Ah knew ya were Billy's girl. Ya think, maybe we could just go out, ya know since Ah got the car now, maybe go up to Wilmington to a picture show or somethin?"

"Ah don't know, Garet."

"Ah like ya a lot, Holly, Ah can't change the way Ah feel. Ah just like ta get ta know ya more. Maybe ya could get ta know me some, too."

"What about Lucy, you're always wit her? Ah mean ya told me ya all were just friends. But she likes ya, anybody can tell that."

"Look, Holly," Garet was saying quickly, "Ah like ya a lot. Lucy is nice, but Ah want ta be with ya. Ah know ya love Billy, but Ah don't know how much."

Holly sighed, turned and looked out into the night. The ride became quiet, but slowed as the car turned off the highway and eased down a dark dirt road. Holly kept lookin out the window watchin the car lights light up the trees and bushes along the road, then watched the trees and bushes vanish in the dark as the car passed. Somewhere in the dark, frogs croaked, crickets squeaked. The car slowed and then stopped. Garet turned the engine off, then flicked the lights out. The radio went silent. Holly sat starin into the darkness, then slowly turned and softly asked, "What we stoppin here for, Garet?"

Garet turned in his seat and leaned back against the car door. He sat lookin at Holly, watched her lower her head and stare down into the darker dark in the car, then reached over and put his hand on her shoulder.

"Ah think we better go, Garet," Holly was sayin, her head still lowered.

"Ah just want ta talk ta ya for a while."

Holly sat quietly.

Garet slid over some and touched the back of Holly's neck. A sigh came from him and he whispered, "Ah know about Billy, but Ah know how Ah feel about ya, too. Ah had been wantin ta say some things, even when he was here, Ah can't wait for him ta get back. Ah like ya a lot, Holly, Ah think about ya all the time."

Holly raised her eyes a little, but only to where the little shiny knobs were tryin to glow in the night. The warm feelin of Garet's fingers on her neck and the coolness of the night air touched her. She raised her eyes up from the dark and looked at Garet.

"Ah think we ought ta be goin, Garet."

Garet slid closer and Holly turned and looked out into the night. "Holly." Garet called her name. Frogs croaked, crickets sang in the night, Garet called Holly's name again."

"Ah ain't said it yet, but Ah love ya, Holly."

"Ah think we should go, Garet," Holly utters as she slowly turns to Garet. His eyes are there starin into hers. The warmth of his breath nears just before his lips touch hers. They cover the sigh comin from her mouth. Holly closes her eyes, then her mind. The feelin of the kiss becomes everything, silences the cricket songs. Garet pulls her closer to him, then Holly presses even closer. Slowly Garet takes his lips from hers, then begins to kiss her neck. She throws her head back, sucks in the night air. She feels the buttons on her blouse bein opened, the sudden cool air of the night on her breasts, then the warmth of Garet's breath nearin them. The night can't get dark enough so Holly tries to close her eyes even more tightly.

Softly, Holly had tiptoed up onto her porch and eased the door open. Then she quietly walked through the dark hallway and very slowly and softly up the steps and into her room. When she closed the door, she eased it shut but did not turn on the light. Quietly she took her skirt and blouse off and let them fall to the floor, then sat on the side of the bed. The late hour was haunted with silence and the lingerin thoughts from the hours that had passed. Holly sat for a while, then slowly eased the ring from her finger, held it in her hand and tried to see it in the dark.

When she reached the dresser, Holly stopped and just stared down at it as if she were in a daze and did not know why she was standin there. A moment passed slowly, then very quietly Holly opened the dresser drawer. She put the ring into the drawer, slid it way back in one of the corners. She stood silently for a moment with her head down and starin at the open drawer, then she slowly closed it. She waited for the sound of the drawer closin to go away. It did, then she turned from the dresser.

Holly pulled the cover over her bare shoulder and brought her pillow up into her arms, but sleep would not come. Songbirds began to sing, the dark hours were fadin as morning neared. Holly pushed the pillow away, jerked the cover from her shoulder and sat up on the side of the bed. Then she lowered her face into her hands and held it there for a while. Slowly she got up and went and sat on the stool in front of the dresser. She got out the pretty blue writin paper and the pencil. The early light comin through the window fell softly across the paper as Holly wrote her first words.

> Dear Billy,
>
> I hope that where you are nothing bad is happening there and you are alright. I worry about you and never want anything bad to happen to you.
>
> You know I love you very much. I have loved you since the very first day I saw you. I will always love you and will always want to be your friend. I am sending you this letter because I have something important I have to say to you. You are very nice and I love you, but I don't think I am the right girl for you . . .

Holly wrote slowly, sometimes stoppin and puttin her hand to her face and just starin down at the paper, then she'd write again. Each word had to mean something, say things forever. When the letter was finished, Holly folded it carefully and put it in its envelope. Then she left the letter lyin on the corner of the dresser.

The midmorning sunlight beamed through the room and across the bed where Holly still lay sleepin. Ginger had taken a peek in at her, had opened the door earlier, then closed it quietly and went downstairs. It wasn't until noon had neared, that the sunlight was able to nudge Holly's eyes open. When she woke, she got up quickly, washed, got dressed. She moved quickly, everything she did she hurried. She made her bed, picked up her clothes from the floor, put things away she hadn't touched in weeks, but kept her eyes from the letter lyin on the corner of the dresser.

Ginger was by the sink, washin and cuttin up vegetables when Holly came into the kitchen. She did not turn to Holly and remained silent when Holly was sayin, "Mornin, Mama."

Holly made a cup of coffee and left it on the kitchen table while she ran back upstairs to get her cigarettes. She went into her room, grabbed her purse, searched for her cigarettes and saw the letter. She stared at it, thought of the time of day it was and wondered if Chester Higgens had come yet. She let the letter lie, but the thought of the ring went back downstairs with her.

Ginger did not turn from the sink as Holly got her cup of coffee from the table, and did not utter a word when Holly said, "Um goin out on the porch, Mama."

The sun felt good, Holly took a deep breath and wiggled her shoulders, then sat on the porch steps. She started sippin on the coffee, then lit a cigarette and looked out into the day. Everything seemed so far away from where she sat until she saw Chester Higgens comin down the road. She kept her eyes on him, watchin him turn down the yard path without lookin or watchin his step.

"Mornin, Mr. Higgens," Holly called.

"Good mornin, Holly. How ya today?" Chester Higgens was sayin, but still had his head down sortin his mail.

The door opened and Ginger's footsteps came out onto the porch. Holly did not turn around. Chester Higgens looked up and said, "Good mornin to ya, Mrs. Hill. How are ya today? Got a few letters here for ya all today."

Chester Higgens extended his hand with the letters in them to Holly. She took them, thanked him and wished him a good day as he started back up the path. Then she got to sortin through the four or five letters and spoke over her shoulder sayin, "Mama, ya got two from the Red Cross lady."

Ginger took the letters Holly handed her, sighed and quietly went back into the house. Holly kept the other three letters, she knew two of them were from Billy, could tell his handwritin anywhere. The other she held up, looked at, then smiled when she remembered Melvin. She remembered he had written before and she hadn't written him back. She amused herself with the thought of sendin him a sweet letter. She put the two letters from Billy down on the steps beside her and carefully opened up the one from Melvin and began readin it. Holly smiled a little as she read. When she finished, she folded the letter up and put it back in its envelope and looked down at the unopened letters from Billy. Quickly, Holly jerked her head back up and stared out across the road. She sat for a while, sipped on her coffee, smoked and blew the smoke as far as she could. Then she placed Melvin's letter on top of Billy's and took them up to her room.

Ginger was sittin at the kitchen table with letters from the Red Cross woman lyin open in front of her. When Holly came into the kitchen, Ginger kept her head down and kept lookin at the letters.

Holly asked, "What the Red Cross lady say about Bobby? She say when he can write a letter by himself, did she say that?"

Ginger didn't look up, just said, "She doesn't say. She says, he seems ta be doin a little better."

"She say if they were goin ta send him home? Ah mean, back ta America."

"She didn't say."

Holly has stood by the kitchen door lookin at her mother and waitin for her mother to look up at her. Slowly, she walks over to the table and sits. Ginger is quiet and Holly softly asks, "Mama, what else does it say? Does the other one say anything?"

Ginger shakes her head, no, then gets up from the table and goes over to the sink.

"What's wrong, Mama?" Holly blurts out.

Ginger keeps slicin the vegetables and mixin them with one another in the pot she has.

"Mama, is there somethin wrong, is there?"

Ginger keeps slicin, keeps silent.

"Mama, what is wrong wit ya? Is there somethin wrong wit Bobby, huh?"

Ginger keeps slicin, but Holly can hear her whisper, "What time did ya come home? What time did ya finally decide ta come home?"

Holly stills herself, lets the twistin, joltin, wigglin in her stomach settle, then says, "Huh?"

Ginger wipes her hands on her apron and goes to the pantry.

Holly looks down at the table, stares until she hears her mother askin, "Where were ya? Ah want ta know."

Holly's face is twistin up, she's bitin down on her lip. Quickly, she jolts from the table and hisses, "Ah wasn't noplace, Mama, just out, that's all."

Ginger's whispers blow into shouts. *"Don't ya walk out of here when Um talking ta ya. What time did ya come in here last night?"*

Holly stops, spins around, sayin, "Ah don't know, Mama."

"Where were ya, Ah want ta know. Ya hear me?"

Holly stands still, silent, and glares at her mother, then lowers her eyes and stares at the floor.

"Where were ya? Ya hear me talkin ta ya?"

"Ah was just out, Mama. Ah didn't know what time it was gittin."

"Don't ya stand there and tell me ya didn't know what time it was. Ya hear me, Holly? Don't ya tell me that."

Ginger's eyes are in Holly's face. Holly keeps lookin down at the floor.

"Ya look at me when Um talkin ta ya."

Quickly, Holly moves toward the kitchen door.

"Come back here. Ya hear me? Come back here."

Holly stops and stares out into the shadows of the hallway.

"Turn around when Um talkin ta ya, turn around here."

Holly spins, shadows go away, hair flings across her face, her mama is a blur that is standin there and lookin at her. She yells, *"Ah just was out, Mama. Ah was just out and went for a ride wit somebody, that's all, Mama."*

Ginger screams, *"Who were ya wit ta that time in the night?"*

Holly blows the breath out of her and stares down at the floor.

"Ah want to know, who were ya wit? Ya hear me, who were ya wit?"

Holly jerks her head up and shouts, *"Ah was wit Garet Foster. Ah was wit him, we went for a ride in his new car, that's all."*

Ginger shouts, *"Garet Foster, what were ya doin wit him? What were ya doin wit that boy, Holly?"*

Holly's eyes turn red, she throws her chin up and yells, *"We just went for a ride, Mama. Um not married, Ah can do what Ah want."*

"*What about Billy?*"

Holly looks away, looks at the window, the light comin through it, the green somewhere far off.

"*What about Billy?*" Ginger screams again.

Holly turns from the window and looks down at the floor and asks, "What about him?"

"*You're supposed ta be engaged ta him and not runnin around here like some nickel slut. It was almost daylight when ya come in here.*"

Holly keeps lookin down at the floor and says, "Um not engaged no more."

"*What?*"

Holly throws her eyes up into her mother's face, yellin, "*Ya heard me, Ah said Ah ain't engaged. Ah ain't engaged no more ta be gettin married.*"

"*Ya what?*"

Tears come streamin from Holly's eyes, words she wants to say get caught in gasps for air, but she's holdin up her hand and pointin to her bare finger and sayin, "See, see, see, see, Mama? Can't ya see, Mama, Ah ain't wantin ta be engaged. Ah know it was important, Ah know it was important, Mama, but Ah ain't want that. See, Mama, Ah, Ah . . ."

Holly turns from her mother, runs through the hallway. Ginger yells, "*Holly, Holly, come back here.*"

"No, Mama, leave me alone," Holly cries over her shoulder as she runs out onto the porch and wraps her arms around the post.

Ginger comes to the door yellin, "*Come back in here.*"

"No," Holly cries, runs down the porch steps and starts runnin up the path.

"*Come back here, come back in here, Holly. Come back here.*"

"No, Mama."

Greens, browns, grays, all the colors of the world are just misty blurs in tears. Holly stops at the end of the path, looks down the road to where the creek would be flowin and the fat-bellied oak is sure to be standin. She jerks her head away and starts runnin up the road. Each step comes quick, but won't never go away, seems to leave her where she don't want to be. The old broken patched road teases and taunts, gets longer than it's ever been. Holly won't stop runnin, colored drivers pull them mule wagons aside, let her pass on by.

"Elsie, Elsie."

Elsie comes to the door, peeks out and sees Holly runnin down the path with her arms swingin every which way and all red-faced and cryin. She runs out on the porch and yells, "Holly, what's wrong? What's wrong wit ya?"

Holly stops midway on the path, turns around, places both hands behind her head and just stands there lookin away.

Elsie runs up to her, shoutin, "What's wrong? What happened, Holly?"

Holly keeps her back to Elsie and starts kickin at the ground. Elsie runs up behind her and keeps yellin, "What's wrong, Holly? What's wrong wit ya, huh?"

Elsie grabs Holly and turns her around. Holly's face is a bright mask of tears and sweat. Elsie screams, "What's wrong?"

Holly starts shakin her head and sayin, "Nothin, nothin."

"What happened, Holly? Somethin happened ta Bobby?"

"No, it ain't him."

"Then what's wrong, what's wrong?"

Holly glances toward the house and asks, "Anybody home?"

Elsie answers quickly, "No." Then asks, "Why ya cryin?"

"Me and Mama had a big fight. She sayin Um a slut. She askin all where Ah been last night. Sayin Um engaged and all. Ah ain't no more, Elsie. Ah told Mama, she started yellin more. Everything all damned messed up now," Holly says and starts kickin at the dirt again.

Elsie shakes her head, then takes Holly by the hand and into the house. Upstairs in Elsie's room, Holly sits on the bed and wipes at the tears in her eyes. Elsie doesn't say anything for a while, she just sits over by her dresser until she asks, "Ya want a cigarette?"

"No. Yeah," Holly answers, then takes a cigarette and gets it lit real quick. Her sighs come out of her mouth with the smoke as she lowers her head.

Elsie whispers, "Ain't ya goin ta wear Billy's ring no more?"

Holly keeps her head down and just shakes it no.

"What happened last night? How come ya ain't come back? Ah waited on ya till it got real late. Were ya wit that creep the whole time?"

"Nothin happened. He ain't no creep," Holly hisses through clenched teeth.

Elsie sits quietly again, reaches over and takes the cigarette from Holly's hand and takes a few puffs. Holly keeps her head down and without raisin it, says, "Ah got in real late. Ah didn't know what time it was or nothin, but Ah know it was late. Mama must have been watchin, or hearin me. This mornin, she actin funny, wasn't sayin nothin. Then when the mail come, she start wantin ta know that, wantin ta know this and all. She askin all at the same time, who were ya wit, what time ya come home. She keep on askin that, then she git to hollerin the same thing. Then she start sayin how Um engaged and what about Billy and what about this and what about that. She kept goin, Ah told her Ah just went out for a ride in Garet's new car, she start hollerin about that. Sayin, what Ah was doin was real cheap like. And when Ah told her Ah wasn't gittin married ta Billy and Ah wasn't engaged anymore, she really started yellin and just keeps goin on. Ah swear, Ah couldn't stand it no more."

Elsie sits quietly, but gets to lookin down, too. Holly sighs, puts the cigarette out and lights another one, watches the smoke for a while. Tears come to her eyes again, but she ain't even tryin to wipe them away. She just starts talkin, sayin, "Ah wrote Billy last night, Elsie. Ah did it when Ah come home. Ah told him that Ah still loved him and all. Ah told him Ah had somethin important ta tell him. Ah really love him, Elsie, but Ah told him, maybe Ah ain't the right girl for him. Ah didn't want to, Elsie, but it was important ta tell him so he know. Ah told him Ah ain't ready ta be married, but Ah still love him and all. Ah put the ring in the drawer, Ah give it ta him when he gits back, maybe Ah feel different then. Ah ain't mailed the letter yet. Ah was goin ta give it ta Mr. Higgens today.

Ah give it to him tomorrow, no tomorrow be Sunday, Ah give it ta him come Monday."

In a while, Elsie looks up at Holly, then lowers her head. Holly sits quietly, blows smoke, then watches it, "Did ya do it wit Garet?" Elsie looks up and whispers.

Holly jerks her head up, her eyes widen, but she don't say anything, she just stares at Elsie.

Elsie keeps lookin at Holly and waitin on her to answer. Holly takes a deep breath, looks away, then quickly looks back at Elsie and says, "We ain't did nothin, we ain't went all the way or nothin. Ah mean, we did some things, but we didn't do it. Ah mean, we didn't do it like it was supposed to be done. He kissed me a lot, he got me down on the seat and kissed me a lot. Ah really wanted ta do it, he can kiss real good, but Ah was sayin Ah didn't want ta. And Ah didn't want ta, but Ah did, but Ah didn't say that. He wanted ta, real bad, but Ah kept sayin Ah didn't want ta. Ya know what Ah mean? It was like somethin ya really want, but it still ain't seem right and special like. And me still havin Billy's ring on and all. And, ya know, not knowin Garet real good like, it just didn't seem real right and all."

Holly stayed and talked with Elsie until the sun went on and left them still talkin. The walk back down the road was longer than the run up. The early night had already darkened the road. Holly walked slowly, sometimes she'd stop, stand still for a while and stare down at the ground.

6

Supply folks used to wait for them hot summer days and nights to go away. When October came, the cool nights came, that time for sittin and bugs not doin all that bitin came. But that time for just sittin back and not thinkin about anything didn't come. Them radios stayed on, them soft melodies most folks listened to, they'd try real hard to keep in their mind when that war news would come on.

Eugene Purvis had put another name up on that courthouse wall, Herman Witek. Everybody in town knew Herman, tried to remember things about him. He was the son of Ryan Witek, Supply's undertaker. Ryan Witek had been buryin Supply folks for years and was real good about it, folks thought it wasn't fair that he'd have to bury his own boy. Herman's body was the first one to come back to Supply, them other boys were buried wherever they fell, or at sea. The train made a special stop down by the highway. Eveybody in town seemed to be there waitin in the midday sun for the train to come. Then they watched it stop, shiver on them tracks while them train men got the big train door slid open. Then they watched as that cart got rolled up to that big train door and Herman's coffin

with that American flag on it was pushed on out on that cart. Menfolk watchin that had hats on to keep that sun out their eyes,
reached up and took them hats off, rested them on their chest. Then
they watched Herman's daddy haulin that cart away.

After Herman's body was put in the ground up behind the
church, folks say that what happened next, just wasn't right. Reverend Powell said, "Maybe it was God's will. God has His ways
sometimes."

The day after Herman's funeral, Dewey Evans, that old colored
man that been workin for Ryan Witek for years, found Ryan hangin
dead in his coffin shop. Dewey Evans said, "Ah come in there in the
mornin, just like Ah do every mornin. Ah went in the back of the
shop and Ah sees Mr. Ryan hangin up back there. He was just
hangin there, Ah knows he was dead, Lord Ah knows he was dead.
He was just a hangin there, Ah come on out of there. Ah ain't
knowin what Ah was supposed to do. Ah knows he just wasn't actin
right, Ah knows it, knows it since he opened that boy's box. Ah told
him, Ah say, Mr. Ryan, ya sure ya want ta do this here? Ah told him,
ya sure? That boy's box bein sealed and all, wasn't supposed ta be
opened by nobodies. But he say, he had ta make sure, had ta know
for hisself, just had ta know. Ah was there when he got it opened, Ah
was there and had ta come on out of there. There wasn't nothin in
that boy's box but pieces of him. Just pieces in one of them bags
theys put them in. When he opened up that bag, Ah tell ya, Ah had
to come on out of there."

Everything in Supply seemed to change a little after Herman got
killed and his daddy hung hisself. His mama ain't been right, since.
Folks still whisperin about it, then wonderin, who's goin to be doin
the buryin now.

Ben's was quiet for a while, some of them sailors got into it with
some of them Supply boys. Before Sheriff LeRoy could get in there,
they had that jukebox all over the floor, some of them tables and
chairs were in big chunks of what they were. Sheriff LeRoy had to
use his stick on them, said he had ta whip them like he had ta do
niggers. Said they just wouldn't come out of there.

Holly and Elsie started going up Wilmington on Saturday nights, went up there to them USO dances they had. Gettin a ride up wasn't too hard for them, gettin a ride back was easy.

Ginger didn't know what to do with Holly, seemed the more she'd yell at her the later Holly would stay out. Sometimes Elsie couldn't keep up with Holly, she got to askin Holly, "Girl, what done got inta ya?" Holly was wantin to stay out, do things all the time. Billy Felter's ring was still in the drawer and she didn't talk about it bein there either. She had sent Billy the letter and didn't talk about doin it at all. Told Elsie, "That's done wit and Ah don't want ta talk about it no more."

Garet Foster got to be and was wantin to be Holly's shadow. But sometimes Holly could step, spin on her heels so fast, Garet would end up bein just a dark spot on the ground she'd done stepped past.

If there was any color left in the skies over the Back Land, it was only a faint red glow of where the sun had been. Holly was on the road, her quick steps slicin through the last fadin colors of the day. Elsie was waitin on the road, Holly could see her up ahead and quickened her stride. As she neared Elsie, she was smilin. Elsie asked, "Ya still goin ta try and do it?"

"Ah said Ah was," Holly says and keeps smilin.

"Suppose he sees ya?"

Holly is quiet for a moment, then blurts out, "So he sees me, that ain't goin ta mean Um goin ta be seein him."

The road became dark as Holly and Elsie neared town, then the lights from them town buildings and some of them cars passin lit their way. Ben's was packed, even the front room was filled up. Holly whispered to Elsie, "Go in the back and see if he's back there, Ah stay here. If ya see him and he git ta sayin somethin, just tell him Ah be here later or somethin. Say, Ah said Ah was goin ta meet ya here, just say that and come back out. Then we'll go back outside and wait, maybe see Raymond or somebody that will ride us."

Holly squeezes her way over to the corner and stands. She feels a gentle tap on her shoulder. When she turns, dark eyes that look into hers get bigger, then brighten. A sailor that looks like what she would want him to, lookin like Billy a little bit, lookin like a face she been lookin for. One she could touch and wants, too. Quickly Holly looked up into the face, looked beyond to the dark hair hangin from underneath the white cap, then looked back at the face.

"I saw you come in, my name is Mark. What's yours?"

Holly looks off into the crowd, but whispers, "Holly."

"Are you from around here?"

Holly keeps lookin off, but nods yes.

"Are you waiting on someone?"

Holly looks back, looks up at the sailor and says, "My girlfriend, she's in the back. What time is it, ya have a watch?"

A quick flick of the wrist and the sailor is sayin, "Yeah, it's nineteen thirty-five."

Holly is smilin and sayin, "It's what? Ah don't know what that dumb time ya all use means."

A little laugh comes from the sailor.

"Well, what time is it for real?"

"I'm sorry, it's seven thirty-five. I'm so used to thinking military time. I'm sorry, we've been at sea so long, I'm still thinking military stuff."

Holly finds herself talkin before she knows it. "What kind of ship ya on, is it one of them real big ones?"

The sailor is talkin and Elsie comes behind Holly whisperin, "He's back there, he ain't seen me, but he's back there talkin ta Jimmy Lucas and them."

Holly steps from the sailor, whispers quickly, "Shit."

Elsie whispers, "Who's that?"

"He just come up and started talkin, he's cute."

"He have a car?"

"Ah ain't ask him, Ah hope so. Let's go outside, see if he comes. Let's go now fore Garet come out here."

Holly steps back to the sailor sayin, "It was nice meetin ya, but we leavin now."

"Where you going, you're not going home already, are you?"

"No. We just leavin, we don't like this place."

"Well, where you going?"

"We don't know yet," Holly is sayin and smilin at the sailor as she scoots around him. Elsie is followin and givin the sailor a quick look and smile.

Outside, the night is still and seems empty without Ben's crowd jammin into it. Holly and Elsie take a few quick steps away from the door, then slow.

Elsie whisperin, "Where we goin now, huh?"

Holly stops, flashes her eyes back over her shoulder, then looks back at Elsie sayin, "Ah don't know, we can just stand here for a while. We can act like we waitin on somebody or somethin. Ya see dumb old Raymond back there? Ah know we can git him ta ride us."

Elsie is lookin over Holly's shoulder, then looks back quickly whisperin real fast, "Here he comes."

Holly whispers, "Who, Raymond?"

"No, that sailor."

A faint "Hey," then the sudden sound of footsteps comin fills the emptiness of the street. Holly keeps her back turned from the sailor's call. When he nears, she slowly turns.

The sailor is asking, "I hope I'm not butting in on you?"

"Ya ain't buttin in," Holly says.

The sailor is askin if Holly has made up her mind about where she's goin. His questions are comin quick. Holly smiles and is askin while he is still talkin, "What did ya say ya name was?"

"It's Mark, Mark Pitman."

"Where are ya from?"

"I'm off the *Baden,* she's docked—"

"Not what boat, where ya come from?"

"Oh. I'm from Pennsylvania, right outside of Philly, West Chester."

"Ya sound like ya from somewhere way up there."

Elsie gets a quick look from the sailor, she is smilin back. He's askin, "Do you two live in town?"

Holly is sneakin peeps beyond the sailor's smile, glances at Ben's

door, looks back at the sailor, then peeps at Ben's door again. Elsie
looks at Holly when she hears her sayin, "Well, it's been nice talkin
ta ya again, but we have ta be goin."

"Where you going?"

"We were goin up ta Wilmington, but Ah think we done missed
our ride. We were goin ta the USO, but Ah guess we just goin on
home now. It's been nice meetin ya," Holly sayin, gives the sailor a
smile, then she's turnin real quick and walkin away. Elsie is still
standin where she was and is just a-lookin at Holly, but she ain't
sayin nothin and gets to turnin and walkin, too.

"Hey wait," the sailor is callin.

Elsie stops, Holly slows and they both look back.

"Wait here," the sailor is sayin quickly, "you can ride up with us,
we're leaving anyway. Wait here, let me go and get my buddy, he's
inside. We'll drive you up with us. Okay? Just wait right here, I'll
be right back."

"Oh, no," Holly is sayin, "we can't be lettin ya all do that."

"Just wait right here, let me go get my buddy. I'll be right back,
just wait a minute."

Holly smiles as the sailor darts back toward Ben's. Elsie is sorta
whisperin and sayin, "Holly Hill, what ya gittin us into, now? Ah
hope his buddy ain't no jerk or nothin."

"Oh, hush, it's just a ride. Any old way, he's cute. Ah hope he hurries up."

Elsie blurts out a quick whisper, "Oh, look at him."

Holly whispers back, "He'll do, he's cute, too."

Elsie is standin and watchin the other sailor comin, he's as tall as
the one that was talkin to Holly. She is tryin to catch his eye so she
can give him a quick smile. She likes the quick way he has about
him that she can even see in the dimly lit street.

The sailors get closer. One is whisperin to his buddy, "See, I told
you." Then sayin to Holly, "This is my buddy, his name is Jerry."

Holly gives Jerry a little smile and says, "Hi, Jerry, this is my
friend Elsie. Ya all don't have ta be givin us no ride . . ."

Jerry got a big grin on his face, he's lookin at Holly, then looks over to Elsie. Holly is still talkin and he starts, too, sayin, "Come on, dolls, we'll take you anyplace you want to go. Come on, let's get out of here."

Elsie quickly says, "We want ta go ta the USO club, ya all goin ta take us up there?"

"Come on, let's go," Jerry says, turns and starts walkin across the street. Holly gives Elsie a quick look and smile, then she glances back over her shoulder and peeps at Ben's door.

Elsie's eyes widened some as she neared Jerry's car and knew it was his. She took a quick look at Holly, tried to catch her eye, but Holly was starin at the car too. Jerry and Mark got the car doors open, Elsie smiled as she gathered her skirt and eased into the front seat. Holly looked up at Mark as he held the door. She didn't smile, just kept her eyes on his for the moment that was passing, then slowly slid onto the backseat.

Elsie was sittin quietly as Jerry got in the car and started it up, then she just went on and asked what she wanted to know. "What kind of car is this? It sure is pretty."

"You like it?" Jerry asks, grins a little and says, "It's a Cadillac, doll."

Holly had leaned back in her seat, got her legs crossed and the hair brushed away from her eyes. Mark got in and slid over some in the seat, Holly looked away and out the window. Ben's door and the dimly lit street, seemed to glide away as Jerry started the car and slowly drove off.

The car seemed to slide through the street, it turned at the corner and rolled slowly by the courthouse and out of the lights of the town. The car crept across the tracks, then lunged into the night. Wheels screechin left their shrill sound dyin in the dark.

Out on the highway, the night was fast and everywhere, except for where the car lights beamed, its black air came blowin through the car windows. Elsie leaned against the back of her seat, then looked over the seat to Holly. Elsie got to smilin, Holly got to smilin, too, then they both got to gigglin. Elsie turns to Jerry and yells through the air blowin around in the car, "How fast ya drivin us?"

Jerry got that grin on his face, laughed a little and said, " 'Bout eighty. It will go faster, you want to see?"

"No. Ya crazy," Elsie yells, then gets to laughin and rushin gettin the windows rolled up.

Holly had turned her face from the wind and Mark was there smilin at her. For just a moment she lowered her eyes and stared at the darkness hoverin over the floor of the car. Mark was saying somethin, Holly heard him talkin, but only reached in her purse for a cigarette. Mark hurried and lit it for her, then slowly watched the flame from the lighter brighten up her face. Holly was colors in the dark, she had worn her bright red blouse, but Mark could only see the blue of her eyes. When the flame died and only the cigarette glowed, Mark whispered, "I think you're so pretty." Holly sighed, let breath float with the smoke she could not see. She lowered her eyes, then quickly looked up and at Mark, askin, "Where ya say ya were from?"

"Pennsylvania, West Chester."

"Oh."

"Do you have a boyfriend?"

Holly is slow to answer and when she does, it is only a quick shake of her head in the dark no. She cannot see the smile on Mark's face, but she hears him sayin, "You don't have a guy?"

Holly looks out the window, then looks down at the cigarette she is holding. She stares at its red glow. Her words come, distant and apart from one another. "Ah was . . . Ah was engaged once . . . but . . . that's . . . we ain't engaged no more."

"Who were you engaged to? Does he live back there?"

"How come ya want ta know all that for?" Holly asks, then turns and looks for her answer. The sailor lowers his eyes, then looks back up and is sayin, "I just wanted to know, just asking."

Holly is silent.

"You're a very pretty girl."

"How come ya keep sayin that for?"

"I just think you are."

Holly turned and looked out the window. The car has slowed some, but the ride is still fast. Elsie has curled up in her seat with her back toward the door and is answerin Jerry's questions. "No, we ain't never been ta noplace like that, we just go up ta Wilmington, go shoppin when we can, movies and all. East side of what?"

"How old are you?"

"How old Ah look," Elsie asks back with a smile.

"Twenty-one, twenty-two." Jerry ain't askin, just sayin, then askin, "You never been over on the east side?"

"Ah done told ya, Ah ain't been on the east side."

"You ever hear of Fannie's."

"No, Ah ain't never hear of no Fannie's. Where's that?"

"It's a joint over on the east side."

Far off in the night, twinkles of light begin to glimmer. The car is nearin the outskirts of Wilmington. Jerry slows it down from its highway speed, leans back in his seat and lets the car cruise the road. Elsie is askin, "Where ya from, huh?"

"Up north."

"Well, Ah knew that. Where at up there?"

"Chicago, you ever hear of it? You're a good-lookin doll, what are you doing staying in that hick town back there?"

"Supply ain't no hick town."

Jerry laughs, but it's a quick laugh that leaves a grin on his face as he gives a glance over the seat and asks, "Hey Mark, what you say we stop off and get some refreshments?" He catches Holly's eye, grins a little more, then looks back to Elsie and says, "How about it, would you two like to get some refreshments?"

Elsie turns in her seat, glances back at Holly.

"What kind of refreshments ya havin in mind?" Holly blurts out.

"What would you like?"

Holly smiles at Elsie, then gets to sayin, "Where ya want ta take us?"

"Anyplace you two little dolls want to go. There's a lot of fun places, you just have to know where to go."

Holly looks at Elsie real quick, then looks back at Jerry and wants to know, "How come ya know so much about Wilmington? Ya been here before or somethin? Ain't ya just gittin here, too?"

"I'm stationed here," Jerry says, lets a little moment slide by like he wants it to, then says, "I've been here since April, I'm a SP. Me and Mark went through boot camp together. We were on the same ship for a while, but I got off that tub and got transferred to SP duty here."

"What's a SP, what's that?" Holly ask.

"Shore Patrol, I'm in the military police."

"Ya in a what?"

"I'm a MP, doll. Military police."

"What ya do, ya arrest folks? Who ya go around arrestin and all?" Holly blurts out and sits up in her seat.

Jerry laughs, looks at Holly, then back at the road, sayin, "We just make sure guys stay out of trouble, keep guys in line, make sure they have their liberty cards and leave papers. We keep them out of the off-limits areas mostly."

"What ya meanin, 'off-limits' and stuff?" Holly wants to know.

"Doll." Jerry gets his big grin on sayin, "There is a lot in this town you ain't seen. You got more queers running around here than Chicago, especially over on the east side."

"Ah ain't never been over there. Ah ain't seen no queers. What do queers do?"

The car filled up with Jerry's and Mark's laughin.

Elsie blurts out, "What ya all laughin at?" Then Holly says, "Ya all can," but cuts her words and smiles at Elsie. Elsie smiles back and Holly gets to sayin, "Whats kinds of places ya all meanin? How come ya keep talkin about the east side for?"

"You two want to go over there and ride through?" Jerry asks and gives Mark a little quick look and grin.

Holly glances at Elsie and Elsie glances at Holly, then they both get to gigglin. Holly sits back in her seat and asks Jerry, "Ain't no-body goin ta come out and grab us, are they? Ah don't want no boogie man come chasin after us."

"Not as long as you're with me, doll. They know who I am," Jerry sayin quickly, then says, "Let's make a stop over at Fannie's first."

The car was cruisin in the light of the main street of downtown Wilmington. Jerry made a quick turn, then made a few more before he turned the car up some back alley. Back-alley dogs got to barkin, some dark-colored face was lit up by the car lights and stared in as the car passed. Holly stared back at the dark face in the night. Jerry slowed the car, then stopped it and got out sayin, "You all stay here, I'll be right back."

Holly stills herself, looks at Elsie, then whispers to Mark, "What is this place? What we doin back up in here for?"

"Jerry's just goin to get us something to drink."

"Get us somethin ta drink, like what?"

"You'll see."

"Ah see what?" Holly says real quick, turns and looks out the window. She can see Jerry goin up some bare path that looks like it's windin through weeds and a whole bunch of old junk lyin around. Then she can see somethin that looks like some old outhouse, but it got a window in it and got some lights in there, too.

Mark's sayin, "He's just going to get us some wine, then we'll go get something to eat before we go over to Fannie's."

Jerry comes back down the path and gets in the car with a couple of brown paper bags stuck under his arms. He starts up the car, jerks it in gear and does a quick turn around, then speeds back down the alley. Elsie asks, "Where ya takin us now, huh?"

"I'll tell you what," Jerry sayin, "let's run over to Mack's, get something to eat there, it's closer than Fannie's. You girls hungry?"

Elsie looks back at Holly, then looks at Jerry and says, "We wantin ta go to the USO. Ain't ya all goin ta take us there, huh?"

"You dolls stick with us," Jerry sayin, and gets a real big grin on his face. Then gives Elsie a little wink and says, "Stick with Jerry, doll, I'll show you a time you haven't seen in the movies, yet."

Elsie looks into Jerry's eyes, but he turns quickly, she looks back at Holly, then sits back in her seat and settles with the movements of the car. She has seen the smile on Holly's face and it has tickled her own. She lights a cigarette and looks back at Jerry as he keeps his eyes on the road. Holly has leaned way back in her seat, got comfortable again.

Mack's place was like Ben's, except it was smaller and didn't seem to have a back room. Everybody in there seemed to know Jerry and got to givin him some good greetings. He got a booth and ordered anything that anybody wanted, then asked the waitress to bring some extra glasses. She smiled and said she would.

Holly and Elsie sat lookin at all the strange faces they seen comin and goin. Some drunk was goin noplace, was sittin at the counter talkin to everybody and nobody was talkin to him. Holly could hear the man talkin and giggled when he got to talkin about how his wife put him out. He was tellin folks, "She come puttin me out, tellin me don't never come back in there. Then she come sendin for me, got the nerve ta come sendin for me. She can't git the goddamned toilet ta flush and she want me ta come fix it."

A couple of girls sittin in the next booth gave Holly and Elsie a hard stare, but called and waved to Jerry. In a while the waitress brought a big plate of fried chicken and home fries. Jerry started eatin and sayin through some of that chicken hangin out of his mouth, "Come on, eat up, dolls. Mack got the best chicken in town."

Holly and Elsie started pickin at the chicken, then started eatin it when they got a good taste of it and the urge to fill themselves up. "Here, take this." Jerry got to whisperin a little and pourin somethin out one of them paper bags into them extra glasses the waitress had brought.

Elsie looked and Holly asked, "What's this?"

"Just try it, it's good. Go ahead, you'll like it."

Holly picked her glass up and sniffed at it, then looked at Elsie and took a sip. Elsie took a sip from her glass, then looked at Holly and smiled. Holly took another sip and enjoyed the warm tinglin feelin she was gettin as the wine trickled down to her stomach. "Ah like this," Holly said, smiled, giggled and took another sip.

Jerry and Mark ate and drank quickly, but sat and talked while Holly and Elsie finished their food. Jerry kept pourin and fillin up them extra glasses as soon as they got a little empty. After a while he was askin, "You two dolls ready to go?"

Holly took another sip of wine, glanced at Mark, then sorta whispered to Jerry, "Let's go someplace where we can dance, let's go there, Ah feel like dancin."

"Let's go." Jerry said.

Outside of Mack's, everything seemed to Holly to move and sway in the night. She was gigglin. Gray sidewalks looked all misty and seemed to float away from her steps. When she got into the car, she gave Mark a quick smile. He leaned near her to kiss her. She turned quickly and looked out the window, giggled a little as she felt him kissin her neck. Jerry started up the car, jerked it into gear and they cruised out into the night.

Elsie had twisted in her seat, had her legs curled up toward Jerry, knew her skirt had rode on up but didn't care. She's askin Jerry, "Where ya gittin all this money, buyin stuff and havin this big car, too?"

Jerry laughed, said, "I got a few things going on on the side, doll."

"What kind of things ya got on the side? Side of what?"

Jerry grinned and said, "Don't worry about it, just keep lookin good, doll."

Holly had peeked out the window, then stared at everything she saw, then got to sayin real fast, "Where we at now? Lord, look at all them niggers. Look at them over there, they all over the place. We ain't goin ta no place here, are we?"

Jerry twisted in his seat a little, smiled back at Holly and said, "This is the east side, doll. That's Lu Lu's, just some nigger joint."

"Look at that one," Holly shouted, pointed and laughed sayin, "He got more red on than Ah do, everything on him is red."

Sounds of drums were comin from somewhere and Holly could

hear a horn blowin, then some piano music, too. Jerry slowed the car and eased it up to the curb. Holly kept lookin out her window and asked without turnin around, "Where we at now?"

"This is Fannie's. You said you wanted to dance," Jerry answered.

"Ah ain't said Ah wanted ta go in there," Holly is sayin and lookin out the window at all them folks standin in front of some shabby-lookin place with its windows all painted some dark color.

Elsie gets to laughin and whisperin to Holly, "Ya see that? Look at that big redheaded hussy. It's a wonders she ain't breakin them heels she got on wit all that hip she carryin on them."

The horns stopped blowin, the piano sound was just an echo, but the drums kept beatin. Holly starts wigglin in her seat and askin, "They really dancin in there?"

The sidewalk swayed under Holly's feet with every step she took. Gettin into Fannie's was first squeezin through all them folks standin around the door. Red-faced guys hangin onto high-heeled quick-talkin women jammed the doorway. Smells of perfume and drinkin breath floated with the cigarette smoke. Some made-up woman waved and shouted, "Hey Jerry." He gave her a quick look and shouted something back as he took Elsie by the arm and started weavin through the crowd. Holly cuddled against Mark and let him take her hand.

Inside, Fannie's floor seems to bounce. Jerry looks back and yells over the sounds of shouts, laughter and music, "Follow me."

"Where we goin?" Holly shouts to Mark.

"Downstairs," Mark shouts back.

"What's down there?"

"You'll see."

The walls of the stairway were thick with folks. Holly's eyes widened as she saw the entanglement of legs and arms twistin and grindin against the wall. She kept her eyes on the sailor who had some girl pressed against the wall. His hands were holdin her butt real tight and her arms and legs where all twisted up in his.

The stairway walls were painted bright red and were still that color in spots that hadn't been written on, scratched on or all busted up with plaster fallin off. At the bottom of the steps, Holly's knee wedged against somethin that felt like it was movin. She looked down and saw some half passed-out sailor slumped down on the steps. His face was all red and he was slobberin as he stuck his tongue out and wiggled it up at her. Holly gave him a sneering look, made sure he saw it before she stepped around him.

Drums, horns and a piano seemed to be everywhere. Women were shakin their heads, twistin their hips and wigglin their butts to the beat of the drum. Some fat sailor got his pants off and was dancin in his white baggy undershorts. Holly giggled, watched and tried to see him after he vanished into the crowd. She kept Mark's hand and followed him through the sweaty faces and shakin butts.

The room had seemed small in its bright center, but got to expandin in the darkened shadows beyond the dance floor. Jerry saw an empty table against the back wall and led the way. Before Holly sat down, she stood starin back at the crowd dancin. The band was still playin, but it was the drums that seemed to make all the music. Holly tried to see the drummer, but she could hardly see the band. As she sat, she glanced at Elsie and saw her scootin up close to Jerry after he done put his arm around her. Elsie was smilin, her eyes seemed to belong to the music.

Mark had leaned over and was whisperin in Holly's ear, his lips were ticklin and makin her smile. When he was done whisperin in her ear, she turned and whispered in his. "Ya really think Um pretty? How come ya think Ah am?"

Jerry was grinnin and shoutin across the table, "Well, what do you think, you like it here?"

Holly looks at Elsie, sees the smile still on her face. Mark is whisperin in her ear again, his lips tickle again and now his breath whirls over her neck. The drums have not stopped.

"Let's dance, Ah want ta dance," Holly blurts out, grabs at Mark's hand.

"I can't dance," Mark says, leans closer to Holly and kisses her neck.

"Come on, Ah want ta dance. Come on, Ah teach ya. Come on,

Ah want ta dance. Ya comin, Elsie, let's all dance," Holly is sayin, askin, pullin on Mark's hand and swayin in her seat.

"I can't dance."

"Come on, Ah want ta dance. Come on, Elsie, ya come too."

Holly was up, pullin Mark by the hand. Elsie was whisperin somethin to Jerry, smilin and tuggin on his arm.

"Come on, ya all, come on," Holly yells back, pulls Mark's hand, then gets to stretchin her steps and slidin them into the rhythm in the light. Elsie's comin too, draggin Jerry and quick-steppin behind Holly and Mark. Jerry ain't lookin where he's goin, he's lookin down and can't get his eyes away from watchin Elsie's butt shakin.

Holly stops when she gets to the middle of the dance floor. She spins around, stills herself, looks at Mark and gets to smilin. Now her head gets to shakin, her hips get to rollin back and forth with the rhythm of the drums. Mark tries to move with her motions. Elsie's next to her, dancin too. Then it's just Holly dancin with the drumbeat. Others have stopped their dancin and are watchin her. Holly's not smilin, but she's keepin her lips parted as a leerin expression comes to her face and stays. The beat of the drum has slowed, Holly's slowly rollin her hips to the poundin rhythm. Her hands are up in her hair and her eyes are closed. The fat sailor in his undershorts dances up to Holly and gives a howlin yell.

Holly keeps on dancin.

Mark's smilin at the sight.

Elsie is callin out, "Go, Holly Hill, go."

Holly danced until her smile came back and she got to gigglin. Mark got her back to the table and Jerry was pourin wine into cups again. In a while he was shoutin, "Where you two dolls want to go next?"

Outside of Fannie's the night still seemed to be dancin. When Holly wasn't staggerin, she was still tryin to sway with the music comin from Fannie's. Jerry got the car doors open and Mark got Holly and Elsie into the car. The sounds of the car startin up and its tires squealin off into the night were left in front of Fannie's with the fadin music. Jerry was drivin and tryin to get another bottle of wine open. When he did, he handed it to Elsie. She took it with a smile, then asked, "Ya want me ta drink it like this, right out of the bottle?"

"It tastes the same, doll."

Elsie turned the bottle up to her mouth and gulped a couple mouthfuls, then gave the bottle to Holly, sayin, "Here, Holly Hill, don't ya drink all of it."

Holly sipped on the wine, Mark leaned closer, tickled her neck with a kiss. Holly giggled, said, "Ah want ta go dance again. Let's go dance up that nigger place, let's go do that."

"Ya crazy, Holly Hill," Elsie laughed and shouted back over her seat.

"Where we at now? Where we goin now, huh?" Holly wanted to know as Mark pulled her closer to him and kissed the corner of her mouth.

"We're just goin for a ride, doll," Jerry says and rubs Elsie's knee.

"Where we riding at? Ah want ta dance some more. Where we at?" Holly shouts, sits up in her seat and looks out the window.

Jerry gives a quick little laugh, then says, "Down by the docks, we're on Waterfront Street. This is where all the queers hang around."

Holly stares out at the dark streets, dark spaces between loomin buildings that stand silent in the night. "Where's a queer at? Ah don't see no queers out there. Ain't no queers out there."

Mark pulls Holly back from the window and back under his arm. Jerry grins and says, "Whatcha want to see a queer for?"

"Ah ain't never seen no queer. Ah want ta see what one looks like," Holly says, looks at Elsie and catches her eye, then says real quick, "Elsie wants ta see one too."

Elsie gives Holly a quick funny face and tells her, "Kiss my butt, Holly Hill.

Jerry laughs and asks, "You never seen a faggot?"

Holly says back, "Ya mean some funny kind of actin man?"

Jerry grins, laughs and says, "Yeah, if that's what you want to call them, doll. They're out there."

Holly leans up in her seat again and looks out the window, then looks back to Jerry and tells him, "Ah still don't see one. Where they at? Ain't nothin out there bein funny."

Jerry made a sharp turn with the car and drove it down an alley-way between two big dark buildings. All Holly could see were red brick walls until the car made another turn, slowed and drove up into some lot behind the buildings. The car stopped, Jerry turned the engine off, but left the lights on. Holly stared out the window, everything she saw, big old trucks, piles of crates, seemed to lurk and make big ugly faces in the night. Real, real quick, Holly wants to know, "What we doin comin in here? What's back here, huh?"

Jerry laughs, but it's a quiet laugh, then he says, "You wanted to see a queer, didn't you?"

"Yeah, but Ah ain't wantin ta see one back in here. Ya crazy or somethin? Ah don't see nothin back here anyway, cept some old trucks and stuff."

Jerry flicks the car lights on and off.

Holly askin, "What ya do that for?"

Jerry whispers, "Just wait a minute."

Elsie yells, "Wait for what?"

Jerry whispers, "You'll see, just watch."

Elsie gets to duckin down in her seat and yellin, "Ah ain't lookin at no funny queers. Ya all done went crazy."

Jerry whispers, "Here comes one now."

Holly's eyes widen, search the dark.

Elsie shouts, "Damn ya all."

Holly sayin, "Where? Ah don't see nothin."

Jerry's whisperin real fast, "He's over there by that doorway. See over there? He'll come over in a minute. He's watching us now. If he sees a lot of people in the car, he won't come up. Duck down some."

Holly whisperin now, sayin, "Duck down, how Um goin ta see if Ah duck down?"

"Is he comin?" Elsie whispers, then hisses, "Ah ain't lookin, damn ya Holly Hill."

"Here he comes, duck down," Jerry whispers.

"Shit," Holly says and gets to scootin down in her seat, but still peekin out the window.

Elsie's gigglin, scootin, hissin, "Holly Hill, better not be no damn queer comin over here. Damn ya, what's wrong wit ya, girl? Is he comin? Ah ain't lookin."

Holly can see some skinny figure easin its way through the dark, then stoppin and lookin over at the car. Holly keeps lookin and her eyes get real big when she hears the skinny figure whisperin with some funny kind of voice, "Hi, are you looking for some fun?"

Jerry laughs, then whispers out into the dark, "Yeah, we'd like to have a little fun. Come on over."

Elsie's whisperin, "What he sayin?"

Holly whispers back, "Shut up, Elsie, he'll hear ya."

The funny kind of voice in the dark whispers, "Do you want a real nice time? I can give you one."

Holly mutters, "What kind of nice time he talkin about?"

Mark leans over to Holly, gives her a little laugh and whispers, "You wanted to see, so just watch."

"Come on over," Jerry is callin again.

"Do you have friends with you? You're not going to beat me up are you?"

"No, sweetheart," Jerry whisperin, "just come on over, we just want to have a little fun."

"Is he comin?" Elsie wants to know.

Holly whispers real quick, "He just standin out there. He looks like a nigger, is he?"

"Come on over, sweetheart," Jerry is callin.

Holly askin, "What ya goin ta do if he come over here?"

Mark whispers, "We'll have some fun."

"Fun my . . ." Holly lets her words seep into a quick silence, but she's keepin her eyes on the skinny figure.

"If I come over there, you're not going to try and hit me, are you? Do you have someone in your backseat? I think I see someone back there. How many friends do you have with you?"

"Ohoo, look at him," Holly blurts out, "he actin just like some girl. Look, Elsie."

Elsie's gigglin, gettin to peepin too and sayin, "Damn ya, Holly Hill, Ah ain't want ta see nobody girl-actin."

"Come on over, sweetheart, and I'll let you blow me."

"Ya goin ta let him do what?" Holly shouts a whisper and looks at Jerry. Elsie is up and peepin, Mark's laughin.

"Do you have girls with you? Are there girls in the car, too?"

"Come on, sweetheart, you can give us all a nice blow job."

Holly shouts, "He ain't doin no blowin on me."

Mark laughs.

Elsie shouts, "Shit, damn ya, Holly Hill."

"Com'ere, sweetheart, get your fuckin faggot ass over here," Jerry yells, reaches and gets an empty wine bottle, pushes the car door open. The empty bottle flies and slices through the dark.

Holly screams, "What ya do that for?" as she watches the girl-like man throw his hands over his face and duck from the bottle flingin through the air.

Jerry shouts, "Com'ere, you asshole faggot."

Mark sits laughin.

The bottle splatters. Holly hears light footsteps scatter in the dark.

"Come back here you fuckin queer asshole fuckin faggot," Jerry yells, then turns back to the car and slides in his seat sayin, "I hate those fuckin bastards."

Elsie sits up in her seat, her eyes have widened, she looks back at Holly. Holly is still starin out into the night, then she looks at Jerry and yells over Mark's laughter, "What ya do that for, huh? What ya do that ta him for?"

Jerry gives Holly a quick look without his grin, sayin, "I hate those fuckin bastards."

"Where we goin now?" Holly asks, then giggles as Mark's lips play with the breath carryin her words.

Where dark buildings, houses, and things in the night had

loomed along the streets, black trees stood. Distant grasses and bushes were gray under the faint starlight. Jerry slowed the car, then eased it off the road and gently edged it beneath the low-hangin branches of the trees. Distant sounds of the dark—night bug hums, bat wings flutterin, some hoot oil hootin—seeped into the car when Jerry turned its engine off.

Elsie searched Jerry's face for his eyes, she wanted to see them before she closed her own. But his face was too close, the scent of his breath, the tip of his tongue nippin at her lips, quickly came through the dark. She closed her eyes and opened her mouth.

Whispers stirred with breezes of cool night air. Mark's soft words lingered past the moments in which they had come. Holly didn't whisper back, closed her eyes, and smiled in the dark.

A slow rhythm of deep sighs filled the car. Jerry pulled Elsie over to him and had her in his arms. Mark gently leaned Holly back until she rested against the car door, then she pulled him closer. Breezes blew, Holly sucked in the cool night air, then let it hiss back out. She knew her blouse was open and didn't care, went on and put her fingers in Marks' hair as he nestled his face in her breast.

Jerry stops sighin and starts groaning. Elsie's squirming, her whispers spill out into the dark, "No, Ah ain't doin that."

Jerry whispers back, "Come on, sweetheart."

"No, Ah ain't doin that. Ya hear?"

"Come on, sweetheart."

"No, Jerry, Ah ain't doin that ta ya."

"Aw, come on."

"No, stop it, Ah said Ah ain't doin that ta ya."

"Yes you are, sweetheart, now come on."

"Ah told ya, Ah ain't."

"Why not, huh?"

"Ah just ain't, Ah told ya Ah ain't doin that ta ya."

"Okay."

Elsie jumps, shouts, "No, Jerry. Stop it, ya hear me?"

"You little hick bitch."

"Ah ain't no hick bitch. Ah told ya Ah ain't doin that ta ya."

Holly's eyes open.

Jerry shouts, "You little fuckin hick bitch, take it."

"What ya think Ah am? Ah ain't doin that."

"Here, take it, bitch."

Holly jerks, pushes Mark away, then stills herself.

Mark whispers, "What wrong, huh?"

"Nothin," Holly says.

Jerry shoutin, "You little fuckin hick bitch. I hate you fuckin dumbass hillbillies."

"Ah ain't no hillbilly and Ah ain't no bitch and keep ya hands off me, ya hear me, ya hear me? Ah said, keep ya hands off me, ya hear me?"

"Take it, bitch."

"No, goddamn ya."

Holly pushes Mark further away, whispers, "Ah think we better go."

Mark whispers back, "Go where?"

"Ah think . . . Ah think maybe it's time for ya all ta be takin us back."

Mark comes closer, puts his lips back over Holly's and tries to cover her words. She pushes him away, then keeps her hand on his face. He moves it, she puts it back, sayin, "Ah think we aught ta stop, it's late. Ah think ya all best be takin us home now, ya hear me?"

"Why?"

"Because."

The car shakes.

Elsie shouts, "Stop it. Ya hear me, stop it, Ah ain't doin that. Ya hear me, ya hear me, ya hear me? Stop, Ah said . . ."

Elsie's words become smothered in muffled groans. Holly pushes Mark away, gathers and pulls her skirt down from where it has risen and gets to buttonin her blouse. "Ah want ta go now, ya hear me? Um ready ta go."

"Go where?" Mark asks with a little laugh.

"Look," Holly shouts, "Ah told ya Ah want ta go home. How many times Ah got ta be tellin ya that, huh? What ya think this is or somethin? Can't ya all hear? We want ta go home."

Elsie's head is bein pulled and pushed down, Jerry shoutin, "Damn you, you little fuckin bitch, take it, take it. You ain't gettin away with this hick shit with me. You know what to do. Now do it, do it."

"Leave her be," Holly screams at Jerry.

"You shut the fuck up," Jerry shouts back.

"Don't ya be telling me ta shut the fuck up. Ya leave her be, ya hear me?"

Mark reaches for Holly's arm, sayin, "He's just havin fun, that's all we want is to have a little fun before the night's over. We thought you two wanted to have some fun, too. We're nice guys, Jerry just gets like that some when he has a little too much. He's a nice guy, look how nice we've been treating you. Look at all the fun we had, look how nice we've been treating you. Come on, why don't you two stop acting like this? We're nice guys."

"Look, just take us home," Holly says.

"Aw come on . . ."

"Ya all take us home, now. Ya hear me?"

Elsie has pushed Jerry away from her and sits up in her seat, buttonin her blouse and straightenin her skirt. Jerry has slid back over behind the wheel of the car and is muttering under his breath, "Fuckin hick bitch."

Mark reaches and touches Holly's shoulder, but she shrugs away. Jerry starts the car, throws it into reverse, then roars it backward until it's back on the dark road. Only the dark winds rushin by the windows give sound to the night.

7

It was November eighteenth, it was a Saturday and it had finally come. Its early morning moments were still silent. Ginger sits at the kitchen table sippin on her coffee, she has been waitin on this day to come. The train that is bringin Bobby Hill home is on its way, but Ginger is still waitin. To Ginger, waitin has its ways. Sometimes she cannot remember what she is waitin for. She can get to doin dishes, yellin at Jason for somethin, wonderin where Holly is, hopin Gus Hill ain't someplace drunk. But the waitin is always there, she turns to it when the dishes are done and dryin, Holly done come home, Jason done ate what was on his plate, Gus Hill come in actin right. Sometimes the waitin can be gentle with Ginger, not always naggin at her and keepin on her mind what she's waitin for. Sometimes waitin can be like a friend, wait for the right moment to tell her what she's waitin for. The waitin could hold the horrors of her soul away from her, keep her from thinkin about how hurt Bobby was, keep her from wonderin how deep that bullet went into his head, keep her from screamin all day long.

The steam keeps risin from the coffee cup sittin on the table and vanishin in the cool morning air. Ginger keeps starin through it, sometimes she places her face into her hands and utters a prayer of thanks for the comin day. Then sometimes she sighs when she wonders why Gus Hill isn't up yet.

Holly heard her mother callin to her, at first it was just a sound scratchin at her sleep, then she heard, "Holly, Holly, come, honey, get up." She kept her eyes closed, tried to stay in the night, then a gentle feelin touched her. Holly's eyes opened quickly, she could see the mist of morning light, she shook. Bobby was comin home today. Her eyes widened. She brushed her hair from them and sat up on the side of the bed. She had not smiled yet, but there was a softness to her face.

Ginger had pulled at Gus Hill's arm, whispered to him, "Gus . . . Gus . . . It's time now, Ah got some coffee on." He opened his eyes slowly, took a deep breath and blew it back out of his mouth. The house was still quiet and he lay in its stillness for a while, then eased himself up and sat on the side of the bed. He could still taste the liquor on his breath, it had lost its sweetness from the night before. He shivered from the morning chill.

Jason bounced up like a jack-in-the-box. As soon as he heard his mother callin his name, his eyes popped open and he was up shoutin, "Is it time ta git Bobby, is it?"

The kitchen filled with early light and the smell of bacon, Ginger moved around the table and pantry as quickly as she could without spillin anything off the plates. Holly sat sippin on her coffee, Jason kept on askin questions until Ginger put his food in front of him, then he busied himself eatin and askin questions too. "Is Bobby bringin me a big Jap sword, is he? Ah bet he is, huh, Mama?"

"Hush, Jason and go on and eat," Ginger says softly, then quickly gets to sayin to Holly, "Honey, ain't ya goin ta eat anything? Ya better eat somethin, suppose the train is late, we may not be back here till noon or so. Ya better eat somethin."

Holly pouts a little, smiles, then tells Ginger, "Oh, Mama, that train going ta be right on time. It ain't goin ta be late or somethin just cause Bobby is goin ta be on the thing."

Gus Hill ate in his silence.

Ginger sat and nibbled on a few pieces of bacon, had a little toast but kept glancin out the window. Sometimes a smile would come to her face, then she would turn from the window and hurry her breakfast.

Holly had put her bright red dress on and had borrowed Elsie's blue sweater to go with her purse and shoes. She had put her hair back in a ponytail, the way she wore it before Bobby left. She had put it up, took it back down, then put it back that way after she made up her mind that Bobby would like it. She'd show him that she was still his little sister, even though she was all grown up now.

"What's wrong, Mama?" Holly askin as she sees Ginger stop in the middle of the floor with her hands full of dishes. Ginger stands silently for a moment, all the distant sounds of the morning seem to still with her.

"Mama," Holly calls again.

"Huh?" Ginger seems to jolt and answer at the same time.

"What's wrong, ya forgittin somethin?"

"Oh, no," Ginger says with a sigh, then goes on over to the sink and lets her words trail behind her, "Ah was just thinkin."

"Thinkin about what, Mama?" Holly askin and gettin up to start helpin.

"Oh, nothin, let's hurry up. Ah want everything ta just be right when we git him home. Ya know the first thing be on his mind is ta be fillin himself up, nothin could change that."

Chester Higgens had brought the letter, the one that Ginger had been prayin for. Bobby had still not written with his own hand, but the Red Cross lady would write down things he wanted to say. Then the Red Cross lady would stick a little extra letter in the envelope. She'd tell Ginger things she knew she'd want to know, have to know. She told Ginger, "Try not to worry, Mrs. Hill, Bobby is coming along fine. He's going to need some time. He is always so nice to me, you have a fine boy here. I know he is thinking of you and your family. I think he'll be able to come home soon."

Then in a few days Ginger got another letter, it was from the War

Department. It said, Bobby was comin home. It said his train would reach Wilmington Saturday, November eighteenth, at 0830 hours. Another letter came from the Red Cross lady. Holly had been up Elsie's. When she came home, Ginger was sittin at the kitchen table with tears in her eyes. Holly had asked what was wrong but Ginger only smiled and said everything would be all right in time.

Holly took the letter from her mother's hands and silently read it to herself. "Dear Mrs. Hill," the Red Cross lady had written, "By now you have probably been notified of Bobby's medical discharge." The letter went on to say, "You may have to give him a little time, he's been through a lot. I've become very fond of him and wish all of you well and God's love." The letter ended with a name and an unseen face.

The highway was sunlit already but it was a gentle sun, a November sun. Soft light that swept across the early hours of the day. Far greens of trees seemed to touch the sky while lowlands of browns and brighter greens were dappled with the red, blue and yellow head scarves on the coloreds in the fields. Sometimes the sunlight would carry their song to the highway, flutterin notes would follow alongside the car but only for a while. Gus Hill drove through the sunlight and the morning songs, he did not hear the music. He stared through the soft glow, kept his eyes on the gray of the highway. Ginger sat next to him but on the far side of the seat. Holly and Jason sat in the back, Jason watched the big trucks pass and gave them a "Wow" as they sped by. Holly sat lookin out the window to the far colors.

Jason had jumped up on his knees and was lookin out of the back window and twistin around with questions of all things comin and goin. Then he blurted out, "Mama, do Bobby still have them bullets in his head, or do they come out after ya shot?"

Ginger turned in her seat, a frown covered her face and stayed over it as she whispered, "Jason, don't ya ever talk that way about ya brother again. Ya hear me? Don't ya ever talk that way, or think that way about ya brother. Now ya turn around and sit and shut your mouth."

Jason slid back in his seat, Holly turned from the window and looked at her mother, then looked into her eyes. It was a quick look that Ginger didn't notice. Then Holly turned back to the window and the far colors. She could not see Saipan, it had always just been a sound to her, now it was an ugly sound. It had hurt her brother and she could not hurt it back. She sighed as she kept starin out the window.

Gus Hill drove silently and kept the speed of the car steady until he reached the outskirts of Wilmington. The early morning traffic was thickenin, big trucks headed for the docks were lowerin their gears. Street sidewalks were fillin with folks carryin lunch bags and pails. Gus Hill let his eyes wander, but made his turns carefully. When he reached the train station, he eased the car into a parkin space and turned the engine off. Then he sat quietly for a while in the midst of Jason's quick and noisy movements and Ginger's hushin him. He still sat quietly after Ginger, Holly and Jason stood beside the car, waitin on him to get out too. Jason yelled, "Come on, Daddy, the train might be comin." Holly and Ginger just stood and looked at Gus Hill until he opened the car door and got out. He stood and looked around at the old train station, its pale yellow brick walls stood as silently as Gus Hill's stare.

Sleepy-eyed sailors and soldiers passed by carryin their big brown bags as Ginger, Holly, Jason and Gus Hill entered the station through the big gray-toned doorway. Low-hangin ceilin lights hung from big high ceilins, big round gloomy circles of light lay still on dark wooden floors. Long deep brown benches sat along cold dark-colored walls. Some sailors and soldiers lay sleepin on the benches, jackets pulled over them for cover, big brown bags were pillows. Jason ran ahead, but was stoppin and yellin back, "Which way? Which way ta where the trains are at? Come on, one might be comin."

Ginger looked around nervously and muttered to Holly, "Git him."

Holly hissed out to Jason, "Jason, git back here. Mama says ya git back here now, ya hear?"

It had been years since Holly had been in the train station. It had been in a different time when trains were choochoos and Bobby ran all over the place, even ran back up there in the colored section, Gus Hill had to get him out of there. But Ginger wouldn't let her hand go, wouldn't let her go chasin after Bobby. It would have been on a Saturday that time, too. A bright sunny summer Saturday. She would have pulled on Ginger's apron, looked up and started askin, "Mama, when we goin, huh? When we goin ta see the choochoo station, huh? Daddy goin ta take us for a ride on it, is he, huh?"

Holly took Jason by the hand, leaned over and whispered, "Ya just behave yourself, ya hear?" Then Jason's eyes got real big but he kept lookin around as Holly gave him a quick kiss on the cheek. Ginger looked over her shoulder at the big-faced clock on the distant wall. In ten minutes it would be eight o'clock, then the time would slow to long final moments of waitin. She sighed, turned away from the clock and slowed her pace before she went through the heavy wooden doors and out onto the outer platform.

The platform had a silence, muddled passin voices, footsteps, all seemed to quickly seep into an uncanny stillness. The sun seemed brighter but cast long shadows down the walkway of the platform. Gus Hill wore his Sunday suit, had even put on his red tie. When Ginger had told him, "Gus . . . Gus . . . he's comin home, they're lettin him come home. Thank God," he had just come into the house, the hour was late into the night but Ginger had waited for him. She wanted to see his face, see it light up with smiles, see years leave it, but he turned to the wall and just stood starin at it. She could only see his back quiverin.

"Let's sit here," Ginger whispered and stepped toward the bench along the wall. Jason ran to the bench and marveled at bein there first. Ginger and Holly sat but Gus Hill stood. Jason leaned out from the bench and looked up and down the tracks, then asked, "Which way is it comin, Holly?"

"Ah don't know, Ah reckon it will come that way," Holly answered and pointed up the tracks.

"Will it be comin fast, real fast? How is it goin ta stop? Can it stop right there?"

"It will stop right there and let everybody off. Ya see when it comes," Holly answered and let her eyes wander up the tracks. Jason kept askin questions but Holly kept silent for a moment. She turned from the tracks and looked down into the shade of the shadows at her feet. The shadows were still but her thoughts were restless, it seemed like Bobby had just left. She could see him in his room again, see herself standin there and watchin him put his tie on, then puttin on that Marine Corps jacket. She had teased him, said things that were not important, told him, "Ya better not come back here wit some ugly wife wit a bunch of comic-book-lookin kids. They gonna have girls over there? Ya better write me letters, Ah write ya too." When he left the house, she had hugged him before he started up the path, then he turned around and came back and gave her another hug. She waved and kept on wavin until he was gone and she couldn't see him anymore, then she ran upstairs and cried.

Ginger sat quietly but Gus Hill began to pace back and forth. Each time he'd go to pacin, he'd go a little further up the platform, stand and just look up the tracks. The platform began fillin, others came and sat and stood. Sailors and soldiers came carryin and draggin their bags, worried-lookin women walked at their sides. A stocky man in a dark blue suit and a little blue brim on the front of his cap strutted back and forth. He'd pause, but just a little bit, pull his gold-colored watch out his vest pocket, flick it open, close it and strut away. Two or three young colored boys browsed about with shoeshine boxes. From time to time, they'd shout out a rhyme of, "Shoeshine time, gimme a dime for a shine." Sometimes only their chants would mark the passin of the time.

Jason could not sit still, he'd sneak up, stand and skirt out toward the tracks until Holly called him back. Gus Hill had slowed his pacin but stood beyond the bench starin up the tracks. He turned and took a step, stopped and turned back around, then stood starin up the tracks.

A flutter of mist floated in the far sky, then disappeared. Gus Hill kept starin up the tracks. In moments the flutter of mist was there in the sky again, then it became little white puffs of smoke. Gus Hill stared, made sure the smoke would not go away again, then he turned and walked back toward the bench.

The stocky man in the blue suit took his watch out of his pocket, looked at it, leaned out over the rails and looked down the tracks, then put his watch back and walked away. A soldier called to him. The stocky man stopped, turned to the soldier and shook his head yes. The soldier started gatherin his bags.

"Ya see it, Daddy, is it comin?" Jason jumped up and asked. Ginger looked up into Gus Hill's eyes for the answer to Jason's question, she watched him nod yes, then she lowered her head and quietly thanked her God.

Holly had lifted her head and looked toward the tracks, then leaned from her seat to see if she could see the train comin. It was not there, she listened and tried to hear the big coughin sounds but beyond Jason's yells the only sound she could hear was, "Shoeshine time, gimme a dime for a shine."

Ginger's head was still lowered, the shadowy pavement before her became blurry. She looked down at her hands and they were blurry, too. Quickly, she reached in her purse, fidgeted around in it until she got the handkerchief. Jason could see a puff of distant smoke and a little black ball lookin like a marble rollin beneath it. "Holly . . . Holly . . . Here it comes, see it, see it?" he yelled to his sister.

The stocky man in the blue suit strutted away into a door, then a big voice soundin like a radio voice flooded the platform. "SOUTH-BOUND . . . CHARLESTON . . . ATLANTA . . . ALL POINTS SOUTH . . . COMIN IN . . . CLEAR THE TRACKS . . . ALL SOUTHBOUND PASSENGERS PREPARE TO BOARD . . ." Everybody on the platform seemed to move at the same time, quick movements that suddenly slowed into just stirs. Then everybody started lookin up the tracks.

Holly stood, then eased herself up on her toes. She could see the distant white smoke and the little black engine face beneath it.

Then the faint sound of the comin train seeped into the chatter on the platform. Holly heard the distant sound and turned to her mother, sayin, "It's comin, Mama, looks like its goin ta be here in a minute."

Ginger wiped her eyes, sniffled and put her chin up. The sound of the train whistle blew into the station. Folks standin on the platform began stirrin, quick whispers and long sighs filled the air. A small skinny colored man with a tattered blue suit on and a red band around his cap pushed and weaved a large pale brown cart through the crowd. A soldier passin by with his heavy bag over his shoulder slowed and stared at Holly until he caught her eye. He smiled, then moved on. Holly watched him walk away, let his bag fall from his shoulder and peek back at her through the crowd. She smiled, then dipped her chin and looked away.

Ginger came to her feet and stepped away from the bench and stood silently. Soon the monstrous sound of the comin train engulfed her stillness. Bulgin, bellowin steamy white puffs of smoke blew from the big dark engine as it came into the station. A low chillin squeakin sound from big iron wheels scrapin across cold steel rails lingered beneath the roar of the engine.

Holly could see Jason's mouth movin, see his hands pointin, see him bouncin up and down, but she could not hear any of his sounds. She turned to her mother but could not catch her eye. The hard concrete beneath her feet began to tremble, then everything shook and quivered. Holly's nose twitched from the steamy cloud of smoke shiftin about the platform. She turned her face away, turned it to the wall as the big dark engine went surgin by.

The engine rolled on past the platform, its ridin cars slowed to a stop, then stilled. Ginger's eyes searched through the smoke, stared into every window of every ridin car that went by. And when they stopped, she kept lookin through the smoky glass. The ground beneath her feet settled, but the poundin of her heart was shakin her apart.

Folks started movin swiftly, bags were gathered and flung over shoulders, tear-stained faces hid in the crevices of hugs. Ginger kept her eyes on the windows of the ridin cars. Holly came to her side, put her hand on her mother's arm and looked through the mist with her. Some faces in the windows just stared out and turned away, others seemed to press against the glass and become a part of the glare. "Do ya see him?" Ginger whispers to Holly.

Holly looks back and forth at the windows, then softly tells Ginger, "No, Mama, Ah can't see yet. He might be on one of them cars back there at the end."

Ginger turns quickly and looks at her husband. Gus Hill's eyes are searchin the windows. They move quickly, lookin back and forth, but there is a calmness about his face.

Ginger sighs, asks, "Do ya see him, Gus?"

Gus Hill shakes his head.

Blue-suited colored men, and some with white jackets on, begin openin the car doors. They lower steps from their ridin cars to the platform, then climb down and stand silently by the steps. Ginger watches the doors, sees a few young-faced sailors come out quickly, jump down the steps and whisk through the crowd. Other travelers follow, some pausin on the steps, lookin around and then wavin and smilin. Jason is askin, "Mama, where's Bobby? Did he come, where's he at?"

Holly steps out and away from her mother and looks up and down the platform. She tries to see all the faces in the crowd, then steps back but keeps lookin around. "Mama, Ah don't see him, yet," Holly whispers.

"Gus, ya think we should walk up some? He might be on one of them cars in the back," Ginger is sayin and keeps lookin at Gus Hill until she sees him nod his head and she knows he will follow. "Holly, get Jason," Ginger whispers, then sighs.

The crowd is thinner at the far end of the platform, Ginger walks slowly, lookin ahead, then quickly turnin and lookin back. Holly keeps Jason's hand and walks beside her mother. Gus Hill follows but does not look back.

Nervously, Ginger asks Holly, "Do ya see him?"

Holly whispers back, "No, Mama."

Jason is yellin, "Where's Bobby? Did he come, did he come?"

Ginger whispers, "Hush, Jason, hush."

Jason jerks away from Holly's hand shoutin, "Bobby, Bobby, there he is."

Quickly, Holly yells, "Come back here . . . ," then lets her words drift forever. She can see Bobby standin near the end of the platform. Her steps slow. Holly grabs her mother's hand and can feel it tremblin, hear her gaspin sound utterin, "Thank God."

Jason runs through the space of the far platform, his yells— "Bobby . . . Bobby . . . Bobby . . ."—fill the emptiness. Colored men standin by their ridin-car steps watch Jason run. He cannot run any faster but he is tryin and does not stop until he reaches Bobby's waist and throws his arms around it.

Ginger and Holly hasten their steps.

The big radio-soundin voice sends its message, "SOUTH-BOUND . . . CHARLESTON . . . ATLANTA . . . ALL POINTS SOUTH . . ."

Softer calls of "Shoeshine time . . . Gimme a dime for a shine" ring through the air.

Ginger can see Bobby's face, she got to run now. Holly lets go of her mother's hand and hurries her steps, then runs, too. She can see her brother's face, see it in the silence around it.

"CHARLESTON . . . ATLANTA . . . ALL POINTS SOUTH . . . BOARDIN . . ."

"Bobby, Bobby, did ya bring me somethin, huh? Did ya, did ya?" Jason is yellin.

Ginger's hands are nearin her son, she can touch him soon. Maybe another step, another moment, another heartbeat. She touches him, then throws her arms around him and pulls him closer to her whispers of "Thank God, thank God you're home."

Holly can hug him too, lean her head into his chest and close her eyes. Now she knows, she is cryin, been cryin. Tears drop from her eyes onto her cheeks.

Ginger is kissin Bobby, gentle kisses on his cheek. Then she is lookin into his face, starin into his eyes. Softly she hugs him again and silently whispers to her soul, "My God."

Bobby Hill does not lean to touch, stands straight and rigid. His lips are quiverin and the tears roll from Ginger's eyes when she hears him utter, "Mama."

Holly looks up into her brother's eyes, steadies herself against his chest, then lets her words rush with her feelins, "Ya all right, Bobby? Ya all right?" Slowly she lowers her head and presses her face back into his chest.

Ginger turns to the hand on her shoulder, she knows its touch and turns to it. Then she steps back from Bobby, Holly moves with her mother's motions, Jason silences in the presence of his father. Gus Hill speaks, his words come slow but steady, "Bobby, you're home now, son . . . you're home. . . . Come on, let's take you where you belong."

8

Thanksgiving day came to Supply, then December days followed. Some were bright and sunny, almost like them hot summer days, but the nights were cold. Folks made sure they had enough kindlin. Dark red fires with jittery streaks of yellow flames burned quietly in the chill of nights. It would be a while before the sun came and melted the frost, warmed things up, then Chester Higgens would come and bring the mail. When he'd get to the Hills', he would always ask Ginger how Bobby was doin. She would smile and say, "He's just comin along fine."

Billy Felter kept writin to Holly, she kept takin his letters and puttin them in that dresser drawer, didn't open any of them. Then she put the ring on top of them. Sometimes she just opened up the drawer real fast and shoved them in there, wouldn't even move the ring out the way. She'd get to mutterin, "Shit, how come he still sendin me letters?" Melvin kept writin Holly too, she read his letters and sent him a few letters back. He was in the Pacific, said he was on one of them big battleships, said he was on one of them big gun turrets and they shot down four Jap planes in an hour. He wanted Holly to send him a picture of her, Holly told him she would but hadn't sent one yet.

Chester Higgens had come and gone, the coloreds were on the road headin back to the Back Lands. Holly hurried along the road until she got to Elsie's path, then she hurried down the path and scooted up onto Elsie's porch. "Elsie . . . Elsie . . . Where ya at, huh?" Holly yelled before she went into the house.

"Um up here," Elsie yells down the steps.

Holly goes up the steps, Elsie's sittin in the chair by the dresser. Holly sits and bounces on the bed sayin, "Shit, Ah thought ya were comin down. Ah waited on ya, how come ya didn't come?"

"Ah was comin," Elsie says.

"What ya doin?" Holly asks.

"Nothin."

"Ah see that. What ya doin just sittin up here for?"

"Just sittin, that's all."

"Oh," Holly mutters. Elsie sits quietly and begins combin her hair. In a moment, Holly is sayin, "Mama thought ya were comin down."

Elsie jerks at the comb in her hair and blurts out, "Ah told ya Ah was."

"What ya bein pissy for?"

"Ah told ya Ah was comin down."

"Well Mama was just askin. She was just askin where ya been and all. She sayin ya ain't been down for a while. She thinkin ya might have a cold or somethin. Ah told her wasn't nothin wrong wit ya but she keep on askin. Ya know how she can git her worryin. Ah thought ya were comin down."

Elsie sits quietly.

"Ya still want ta go tonight? Ya think it's goin ta be too cold?" Holly askin.

"Yeah," Elsie mutters.

"Yeah what? Yeah it's too cold or yeah ya still wantin ta go?"

"Yeah, Um still goin. What's wrong wit ya?" Elsie pouts.

"Nothin's wrong wit me. What's wrong wit ya?" Holly gets to yellin.

Elsie turns to the mirror and is combin her hair real fast.

Holly sighs, looks down and sits quietly.

"How's Bobby?" Elsie asks and slows the combin of her hair.

Holly keeps starin down and says, "He's all right."

"What's he doin?"

"When Ah left he was doin just what he always do, just sittin in his room and all."

"Ya want ta try and git up tonight, or ya want ta just stay at Ben's?" Elsie asks, then turns from the mirror and looks at Holly.

"Ah don't know, what ya want ta do?" Holly is sayin but keepin her head down.

Elsie mutters, "Ah don't know, what ya want ta do?"

Holly scoots up on the bed and leans back against the headrest, smiles a little, then asks Elsie, "Maybe we can go ta Fannie's?"

"Where?"

Holly giggles and says, "Ya know, Fannie's. We can go there and dance, too. Maybe see Mark and Jerry, maybe see them again."

Elsie makes a quick ugly face, sticks her tongue out at Holly and says, "Ya crazy, Holly Hill."

Holly's walk back home was quick, the late afternoon sun had gone way past the Back Land. Shadows and shades blended into the grays of the evening. The old road was bare, all the coloreds had vanished into the Back Land. When Holly got to her yard path, slowed and looked down the old broken patched road, it seemed to vanish too.

Ginger was sittin in the kitchen when Holly went into the house. Holly went into the kitchen sayin, "Elsie says ta tell ya hi. She says for ya ta stop frettin about her. She says if it be the last thing she do on earth she be comin down here tomorrow. Then she asks, what ya cookin tomorrow."

Ginger smiled, Holly took a quick look in the icebox and kept on lookin at things she wasn't seein when Ginger asked, "What ya two have planned for tonight?"

Holly kept her head in the icebox but got to sayin over her shoulder, "Nothin, Mama, we just goin out for a while." Then she quickly closed the icebox door and got to talkin about somethin else and anything before she went up to her room. When she passed Bobby's room, she slowed her steps, walked quietly by his closed door. It had become a ritual to do so.

Holly leaned closer to her dresser mirror to catch its light from the lamp, all the light from the day had gone. When her makeup was on and her hair was finally combed, she lowered her eyes. Friday night had come and Elsie was waitin, but for a moment Holly listened for any sounds comin from her brother's room.

Garet Foster was at Ben's when Holly and Elsie came in. Holly gave him a quick look and "Hi," then followed Elsie to a booth. Ben's crowd was small. Only the sound of the jukebox playin filled up the emptiness. Holly and Elsie had settled on just stayin at Ben's and not tryin to get a ride up to Wilmington. But Elsie gets to lookin around and rollin her eyes at Holly the same time Holly is lookin around and rollin her eyes at Elsie. Holly is makin faces and sayin, "Shit, Ah ain't stayin in here." Quickly, Elsie's whisperin, "Here he comes."

Holly looks up and Garet is there, then sayin, "Holly, Ah have to talk ta ya, come on outside, Ah want ta talk ta ya by yourself."

Holly looks down, looks at the table and says, "Talk about what, Garet? Why we have ta go outside and all?"

"Ya know."

"Know what, Garet?"

"Let's just go outside, Ah can tell ya there."

Holly takes a deep breath and a quick glance at Elsie, then says, "Garet, Ah come out in a few minutes. Ah got somethin Ah have ta tell Elsie first. Ah be out in a minute but Ah ain't goin ta stay a long time or nothin."

"Ah be right out front, Ah wait for ya there," Garet says, then turns and walks away.

"Shit," Holly gasps.

"Don't go runnin off wit him, Holly. Ah ain't feelin like sittin here by myself ta midnight hour," Elsie's sayin and shakin her head.

"Ah ain't wantin ta go out there wit him," Holly is mutterin and makin faces down at the table. Then she gets to shruggin her shoulders and brushin the hair out of her eyes.

"What's he want?" Elsie's askin and turnin up her nose.

"Ah don't know what he wantin. Ah done told him Ah ain't his girl like he thinks Ah am or somethin. He's cute and all and Ah told him we could be friends, that was a long time ago, too. He be wantin me ta say things, tell him things just cause he wants ta hear things. Hear me sayin Um his girl and all."

Elsie sighs, then blurts out, "Well, if ya goin ta talk ta him, go ahead. Ya mise well go and git it done wit. Why don't ya just go on and tell him ya ain't wantin ta see him no more, tell him that. That be the only way of gittin rid of him. Ah told ya he was an asshole anyway. He sayin all them things ta ya and probably still doin it ta fat-ass Lucy, go on tell him."

"Oh, he ain't still seein her. He said he don't even like her no more."

"Shit, Holly, he ain't got ta like her ta do it ta her. But he sure got ta see her. Ya believe everything that asshole tell ya. Ya crazy, Holly Hill."

Holly gets to poutin and starin down at the table. "Holly," Elsie's sayin real quick, "Go on out there, git it done wit. Ya be sittin in here all night just thinkin about it. He ain't nothin but an asshole anyway, ya know that. The whole time ya were wit Billy, ya ain't thought about no Garet Foster. Only thing ya be sayin was how he come ta school wit so much grease in his hair he look like somebody fried bacon on his head or somethin."

Holly's smilin and sayin, "Ah ain't never said that."

"Ya did so, Holly Hill," Elsie says gigglin, then says, "Why don't ya just let him go on and stand out there all night? See how long it take him ta figure out ya ain't thinkin about his butt."

"Ah can't do that."

"Well, when ya git out there, just remember he still doin it ta Lucy, Ah don't care what he say. And don't ya forgit Ah ain't sittin in here all night either."

Garet Foster stands leanin against his car, his arms are folded across his chest. "What took ya so long?" he's askin Holly as she comes up to him.

"Ah was talkin ta Elsie."

Garet jerks his head and makes it turn real quick, then stares out into the night. Holly says, "Ah wasn't that long."

Garet keeps his head turned.

Holly asks, "Well, what ya wantin ta talk about, huh?"

Garet gets to breathin real hard and keeps starin at a piece of dark somewhere. Holly just stands there and looks at him for a moment, then says, "Well, if ya don't want ta talk, Um goin back in. Ah ain't goin ta be standin out here in the cold just lookin at ya all night."

Garet sighs, jerks his head and looks back at Holly, then reaches in his pocket and gets a cigarette out. He lights it, then says, "Ah just want a chance ta talk ta ya."

"Well Um here, go on."

Garet opens up his car door and says, "Come on, let's sit in the car, it's warmer than standin out here."

"We can talk right here, if ya just wantin ta talk, Garet."

"Come on, Holly."

"No, Ah said."

"Come on, Holly, Ah just want ta talk."

"No, Garet, we can talk right here."

"Come on, Holly. Ah just want ta talk ta ya. Just a talk that's all. Ah just don't want to stand out here, not like this."

"No."

"Please?" Garet askin softly and starin at Holly's eyes.

Holly feels the chill on her back and the light wind come across her face. She looks at Garet and throws her head back, her hair still flows in the light wind, she steps toward the car. Garet hurries, closes the door after Holly gets in, scoots around the car and gets in the driver's seat. Holly is sittin quietly when Garet gets in askin, "What's wrong wit ya, Holly? Why ya treatin me like this for, huh?"

"Ain't nothin wrong wit me, Garet. Is this what ya bring me out here ta talk about?"

"No, Ah just want ta talk ta ya."

"About what, then?"

"Why ya stayin away from me? Every time Ah come around, ya act like ya don't know me, like ya too good or somethin. Since ya and what's-a-name been runnin up Wilmington. Ya actin like some little Wilmington . . ." Garet cut his words.

"Ah told ya, that ain't none of ya business where Ah go. We ain't engaged or nothin. Ah ain't engaged ta nobody," Holly shouts.

"But," Garet yellin, "ya still actin . . . runnin along wit the first damn sailor come along. Ya and that Elsie bitch. Everybody knows that, ya ain't foolin nobody."

"Ain't nobody's business, ya hear me? And it ain't ya business either," Holly yells, turns away and reaches for the door.

"Wait a minute."

Holly pauses but does not look back.

"Wait, what about us, huh? What about us, Holly?" Garet is askin, his voice is low and pleadin.

Holly keeps lookin out the window, she is silent for a moment, then says, "Garet, Ah like ya but Ah told ya Ah don't want nothin steady."

"Ah thought we had a feelin for each other. Ya can't say we didn't want ta be with each other, ya can't say that, Holly."

Holly turns and looks at Garet and says softly, almost whisperin, "But that was before, Garet."

"Before what?"

"Before a lot of things."

Quickly, Garet lunges forward and puts the key in the ignition. The car starts up and jerks into gear. Holly is shoutin, "What are ya doin, Ah told ya Ah wasn't goin noplace."

The car skids out its parkin spot and speeds down the street. Holly's eyes turn red in the dark. She yells, "What are ya doin, Garet? Let me out, damn ya. Let me out right now, ya hear me, Garet?"

Garet shouts back, "We ain't goin noplace, just away from in front of here, that's all."

Slowly, Holly leans back in her seat and stares out the window. The car races against moments and Holly's deep sighs, then stills as it comes to a stop behind the schoolhouse. Holly sits quietly, Garet reaches for her shoulder, she jerks away from his touch. "This ain't talkin," she mutters.

"What do ya want me ta do?" Garet askin.

"Do about what?"

"About us."

"Garet, there's nothin ta do."

"Are ya datin one of em sailors, is that it, huh?"

"No."

"Well ya sure runnin around wit em. What's wrong wit Supply boys? Ain't we good enough for ya?"

"Let's go, Garet, Ah told Elsie Ah be right back. She's sittin there waitin on me."

"We ain't goin till we talk, Holly."

"Take me back, Garet."

"Ah said, we ain't goin till we talk."

"Shit, Ah knew Ah shouldn't have come up here wit ya. Ah want to go, now, ya hear, Garet?"

"Why ya in such a big hurry, huh, huh? Ya can't wait ta git up ta Wilmington, that's it, ain't it? Ya want ta go up there with them fuckin sailors and run around like the rest of them Wilmington whores. Git the fuck out of my car, ya little tease bitch. Git the hell out of here."

Holly's eyes widen, she looks at Garet, then stares and hisses, "Why ya sayin stuff like that for, ya asshole."

Garet shouts, "Ah say what Ah want."

Holly shouts back, "Ah don't want anything ta do wit ya, ya just an asshole, Garet, that's all ya are and ever will be. Ya lucky ya got that pig-faced Lucy Belmar, cause ya such an asshole ya ain't goin ta git nobody else, especially me. From now on, Garet Foster, ya just stay away from me, ya hear me?"

Garet lunges forward to start the car but Holly pushes the door open and slams it before he has the key turned. He leans over and rolls down the window and yells out, "Holly, come on, Ah take ya back. Um sorry, come on."

Holly steps quickly, she does not look back. Everything is dark gray in the night, except for where car lights shine on dark school-yard walls, fences, trampled bare paths. Garet drives the car slowly, leaning across the empty seat and calling out the window, "Holly, come on, Ah take ya back to Ben's. Come on, Holly, Um sorry."

Holly spins around and shouts at the trailing car, "Ya can go ta hell, ya hear me? Ya can go ta hell, Garet Foster."

On the hard road in front of the schoolhouse the clickin sounds of Holly's heels echo in the dark. Garet drives alongside of Holly, leans to the window again and pleads with her to get in the car. But the monotonous rhythm of Holly's heels only hastens.

Garet calls, "Come on, Holly, git back in. Um sorry, ya hear? Ah really care about ya, that's all. Um sorry, ya hear? Ah didn't mean it, ya hear?"

The car followed, Holly's steps quickened, her head twisted and jerked from Garet's calls. The car and calls followed until she was just about in front of Ben's, then Garet shouted somethin that Holly couldn't understand. She saw the car whiz by and could see it stop and slide, then jerk back and forth. Holly rushed into Ben's before Garet could get out of the car. Ben's Friday night folks were filin in, she weaved through the crowd and found Elsie sittin at the booth with a couple of sailors. One of them smiled and asked Elsie, "Who's this?" as Holly neared.

"Shit," Holly mutters under her voice.

"Here, sit here." The sailor smiles and slides over on his seat.

"Ah don't want ta sit down." Holly pouts.

"What happened?" Elsie asks.

"Ah tell ya later. Come on, let's git out of here," Holly's sayin and takin quick glances over her shoulder.

The sailor sayin, "Hey stay a while, have a seat."

"No thank ya," Holly says quickly, gives the sailor a small smile.

"What's wrong with your friend?" the sailor is askin Elsie.

"Nothin but we have ta go," Elsie is sayin and scootin out of her seat. Ben's jukebox is blarin, Friday nighters are crowdin the dance floor. Elsie follows Holly as she zigzags through the crowd.

"What the hell happened, Holly?" Elsie is whisperin ahead.

Holly spins around sayin, "That asshole was carryin on wit me, ya should have heard what he was sayin." Then she spins back around and keeps weavin through the crowd.

Elsie turns to a jerk of her arm, Garet has grabbed at her arm and is askin, "Where's Holly? Ah know she come back in here, Ah saw her come in."

Elsie bolts away and quickens her steps to catch up with Holly. Now Garet can see Holly and pushes through the crowd toward her. He starts callin, "Holly . . . Holly . . . Holly, wait a minute."

Holly mutters over her shoulder, "Leave me alone, ya hear me?"

Ben's door is yanked open and Holly rushes out into the night. Elsie has caught up with her, Garet is runnin and callin ahead, "Holly . . . Holly . . . Ah want ta talk ta ya."

Holly shouts back over her shoulder, "Leave me alone, Garet."

Garet pushes past Elsie and is still tryin to talk with Holly. Elsie yells, "Look Garet, why don't ya just leave her be, huh? Just go on back and leave her be."

Garet shouts, "Shut up, Elsie."

Elsie shouts back, "Don't tell me ta shut up."

"Ah tell ya ta shut up anytime Ah want, bitch."

"Don't call me a bitch, ya asshole."

Garet calls, "Holly, just stop and hear me out. Hear me out, huh?"

"No," Holly shouts and keeps goin.

Garet grabs onto Holly's arm.

Holly jerks away, shouts, "Let me go, now. Ya hear me, let me be."

Garet is yellin, "Damn ya, stop Ah said."

"No."

Garet grabs and holds Holly's arm.

"Git off me, Garet."

"Damn ya, wait a minute."

"No, Ah said. Now git off me right now, ya hear me?"

Quickly Garet lets go, stands still and shouts as Holly walks on, "All right, go ahead. Ya ain't good enough for me anyhow." Then he stands starin before he shouts, "Ya goddamn bitch."

Holly stops, spins around and yells, "Hey Garet, ya can kiss my ass. Ya hear me? Kiss my ass."

Holly spins back around, throws her head up and keeps walkin down the street. Elsie gets to smilin and whisperin, "Holly Hill, Um proud of ya. If ya hadn't, Ah was."

Holly and Elsie keep walkin, Holly is tellin Elsie, "Ya should have seen his face when Ah got out his damn car. He start sayin how sorry he was and all, kept on drivin beside me sayin he sorry. Ah started ta tell him then what he could do."

The sound of words hissin through the air follows Holly and Elsie to the end of the street. They stop and stand lookin at each other until Elsie gets to laughin and askin, "Well, Holly Hill, what in the hell we goin ta do now? It is damn cold standin out here. That one sailor that was talkin ta me was real cute before ya come bustin in there."

Holly gives Elsie a quick stare, then twists her face up and says, "Ah can't go back in there. What's wrong wit ya? Ya think Um crazy? Ya crazy if ya think Um goin back in there tonight with him bein in there."

Elsie went back in Ben's first, then Holly followed but stayed out in Ben's front room while Elsie went into the back. Holly stood in the corner and kept lookin around until Elsie came back smilin and whisperin, "Raymond said he'll do it, he said, he'll be glad ta do it. Be nice ta him and don't be kiddin at him."

Raymond Vire was never called Ray or anything except Raymond. Most girls in town and everybody else over the age of twelve was at least a couple inches taller than him. Raymond's daddy was Norman Vire, he did folks dry cleanin for them. Raymond worked for his daddy and knew everybody in town. Holly smiled when she looked behind Elsie and saw Raymond comin through the crowd with that peculiar grin he always kept on his face. Raymond followed them out the door, then ran ahead to get his car doors open. Holly whispered to Elsie, "Ya sit up front wit him."

Holly slid in the backseat and lit up a cigarette while Elsie and Raymond got in the front. In moments filled with quick sounds of the engine startin up, Ben's jukebox music fadin and Raymond clearin his throat, the car drove into the night. Holly spoke softly, sayin, "Thanks for ridin us up, Raymond."

"Ah like ta drive, Ah like ta drive ta Wilmington, too. Anytime ya want a ride, just ask. Ah like to drive," Raymond answered slowly but kept his eyes on the road. Elsie spun around in her seat and gave Holly a quick smile, then asked for a cigarette.

Holly leaned back in her seat to enjoy the ride, the road became dark and soothin. She smiled to herself when she thought of Garet beggin, then got a sneer on her face when she thought of him callin her names.

Raymond was talkin Elsie to death but doin it real slow, tellin her all about his daily activities at his daddy's dry-cleanin shop. Elsie butted in, sayin, "Raymond, if Ah start bringin my clothes down there, how much would it be costin me? Ah mean, Ah wouldn't be bringin a lot."

Raymond told Elsie, "Oh, Ah be glad ta do them for ya. Ah wouldn't charge ya anything, Elsie."

Holly smiled and asked, "Raymond, can Ah bring mine too?"

"Oh, sure, Holly, ya can bring yours too. Ah can do yours the same time Ah do Elsie's."

Holly giggled and said, "Elsie, would ya please come down tomorrow and pick up my things so you can take them up ta Raymond?"

Elsie says real quick, "Ya know what, Holly Hill?"

The road became talk that could only go so far before it became laughter. As the car entered Wilmington, Raymond asked, "Where do ya want ta go? Do ya still want me ta take ya over ta the USO? That's over by the train station, isn't it?"

Elsie spins around in her seat and asks Holly, "Ya want ta go ta that place, just ride by?"

Holly asks, "What place?"

Elsie gets ta smilin and sayin, "Ya know, that Fannie's place. Ya want ta just ride by?"

"Yeah," Holly sayin, then leans up in her seat and gets to lookin around. "If we can find it. It was over on some east side." Holly still talkin and lookin out the window, then she blurts out, "Ya think we can find that other place, too?"

"What other place? That place where we ate?" Elsie askin.

"No, not that place," Holly's sayin, "that place where they got that, ya know what."

Elsie blurts out, "Ya want ta?"

"Ah feel like it," Holly sayin, then quickly askin, "Ah wonder how much it cost? Ya think we can find it? It was back in that old dark alley, remember?"

"Ah don't have no money," Elsie says, then says quickly, "Ah ain't goin in that place ta git nothin. Ain't no tellin what was in there."

Raymond says, "Ah got some money. What do ya all want?"

Holly blurts out, "He can go in and git it for us."

Elsie askin, "Ya think we can find it?"

"Let's go see," Holly says and edges further up on her seat and gets to lookin one way and pointin the other. Raymond drives the best he can with "Turn here. . . . No . . . no . . . turn here. . . . That way. . . . It's right down there.. . . . Maybe it's over there . . . . no . . . not that way. . . . Ah bet it was back there. . . . Holly, ya done got us lost again. . . . Ain't not Elsie. . . . Ooh turn here, Raymond. . . . Damn ya, Holly Hill, it ain't nowhere near here. . . . Is so, member it was real dark wit that little window and all . . . member it was behind that place. . . . Ah told ya, see . . . see . . . That ain't it. . . . Yes it is, member . . . see the window . . ."

Raymond sits and stares out the car window, then asks, "What's in there? It looks all dark, does somebody live there?"

Elsie's sayin, "That ain't it, Holly."

Holly's sayin, "Is so, Elsie." Then she gets to whisperin to Raymond, "Just go in and tell them ya want a bottle of wine, say that. Then say, ya a friend of Jerry's, say that ta them."

Raymond's grin gets more peculiar but he's sayin, "Oh, Ah can go in for ya."

Holly and Elsie peek out the window of the car and giggle as they watch Raymond disappear into the dark creepy yard of the back-alley shack. Elsie's whisperin, "Ah hope this is the one." Then she's gigglin and sayin, "Suppose it ain't and somebody shotgun him. How we goin ta git out of here? Damn ya, Holly Hill."

When Holly and Elsie weren't gigglin, they sat peerin out the window until they saw Raymond comin back through the yard. They knew it was him soon as they saw somethin moving that was just a little bit too tall to be a cat or somethin. Holly whispered, "Here he comes, see."

Elsie whispered back, "Does he have it?"

"Oooh, yeah, he got it. See he got a bag, see," Holly whispered and giggled.

Raymond got back in the car and his face had some big bulging eyes to go with its peculiar grin. He's tellin Holly and Elsie, "There was some big black nigger woman in there, she sure was mean-lookin. But she say, Ah can come back and git some more anytime Ah want ta."

Elsie's askin real fast, "Where we goin now? Where we goin ta drink it at?"

"Ah don't know," Holly's sayin and still peekin out the window, then she says, "Let's just git out of here."

Raymond started the car and carefully turned it around in the alley, then drove slowly back to the street. Holly and Elsie kept talkin and gigglin until Holly saw a dark spot on a quiet street and blurted out, "Let's do it here, want ta? Raymond, park here, pull over there."

The scent of the wine tickles and teases Elsie's nose as she opens the bottle, then looks over to Holly and says, "Ya do it first." Holly takes the bottle, takes a quick sniff of it, then a quick taste. She gets a funny look on her face, then closes her eyes and tips the bottle up to her lips. The taste of the wine gushes around her tongue, its chill is warmed by her mouth. Then the wine gets hot down in her stomach, makes her squirm. When her eyes open, Elsie is smilin and starin at her, Raymond is lookin too. Holly gets to gigglin and takes another drink from the bottle before she hands it to Elsie, sayin, "Here Elsie, ya drink some too."

Elsie takes the bottle, takes a couple of gulps, then takes one real big one before she passes the bottle back to Holly. Raymond sits watchin, then clears his throat and is askin, "Can Ah have some?"

"Sure ya can," Holly's sayin. "Ya were sweet enough ta git it for us, Raymond, ya can have some." She takes a few quick drinks, then gives the bottle to Raymond. Elsie gets to lookin at Raymond and laughin too. "Well go on, Raymond, take some," she's sayin.

Raymond is still lookin at the bottle. Then he turns it up and takes a quick drink. Elsie laughs when she sees his eyes pop open real wide. "Take some more, Raymond, go on," Elsie's tellin him and givin Holly quick looks and smiles.

Raymond turns the bottle up and keeps it up to his mouth, then takes it down real fast and wipes his mouth with his hands. He's quiet, starin at the bottle, now he's gigglin and takin another drink.

Holly's askin, "Ya like it, Raymond?"

Raymond tells Holly, "It's good, gives ya a funny feelin inside."

"Ya ain't never had any before?" Elsie asks.

"Yeah, Ah did but it wasn't this here kind." Raymond tells Holly and Elsie, then takes another sip.

The bottle was passed around, each sip from it brought more laughter into the night. Elsie had leaned her back against the side of the front door so she could comfortably talk to Holly and listen to what Raymond might be tryin to say. Holly sat leanin back in her seat with her shoes off and her feet up on the back of the front seat. In between giggles and quick words spillin out into the dark from the car, it could be quiet. Holly had lit a cigarette, she blew the smoke away and was starin into the red glow before she got to sayin, "Let's drive all the way to Hollywood, let's do that. Let's go out there and be in the movies. Ah can be the beautiful rich girl, and have lots of money and all. Elsie, ya can be my friend but ya can't be as rich as me. Raymond, ya can be the chauffeur, be the one that drive us around. No, ya can be Elsie's husband. Ah won't have a husband but Ah have lots of good-lookin movie-star men wantin me ta marry them."

Raymond says, "Ah like to drive ta California."

"Shut up, Raymond," Elsie sayin quickly, then she gets to sayin, "Um the one that would be in a movie and be a star. Holly Hill, your butt's too big to be in some movie."

Holly makes a face at Elsie and says, "It ain't as big as yours, Elsie Fagen."

Elsie twists her face up a little and says, "It's too big ta be in some movie, less it's a Tarzan kind and ya playin somethin that's real big and got a real long nose. Holly Hill, your butt been bigger than mine, since when."

"No it ain't and never will be, Elsie Fagen," Holly is sayin, then looks at Raymond and softly asks him, "Raymond, ain't Elsie's butt bigger than mine, ain't it?"

Raymond stutters, "Ah . . . Ah don't know . . . Ah . . . Ah . . ."

Elsie shouts at Raymond, "What do ya mean ya don't know, huh? Ya think my butt is bigger than hers, huh, Raymond?"

Raymond puts his head down, then gets to mutterin, "Ah . . . Ah . . . Ah can't tell . . . Ah ain't sure . . . Ah mean, Ah can't tell . . ."

Holly blurts out, "He knows, he just doesn't want ta hurt your feelins, Elsie Jane Fagen. That's why he ain't sayin. Huh, Raymond?"

Elsie smiles and teases Raymond, "Raymond, ya know Holly Hill's butt is bigger than mine and is too big ta be in some movie, don't ya? Now ya just go on and tell her, go on now, Raymond, tell her."

Raymond sits with his head still down and stutterin, "Ah don't know . . . Ah can't tell . . . Ah mean . . . Ah mean . . ."

Holly shouts, "Ya mean what, Raymond?" Then gets to gigglin.

Raymond sits quietly mutterin, "Ah . . ." a few times but keeps his head lowered. Elsie takes the bottle of wine and takes a good swig, then stretches her foot across the seat and nudges Raymond's leg. He still keeps his head down but she's sayin, "Raymond, are ya goin ta tell Holly Rachelle Hill that her butt is bigger than mine or not?"

Raymond lifts his head a little and is mutterin, "Ah don't know, Ah can't tell. Ah ain't never see her, Ah mean . . . Ah mean . . . Well, Ah don't know."

Elsie shouts back to Holly, "Show him your butt, Holly Hill. Go ahead, Ah dare ya. Show it ta him, so he can see how big it is. Ya goin ta do it, huh? Ah dare ya, Holly Rachelle Hill."

Holly smiles, laughs, then tells Elsie, "Okay, but if Ah do, ya better too."

Elsie shouts at Holly, "Go ahead, show it ta him. Ya goin ta do it? Ah dare ya, Miss Holly Rachelle Hill, Ah dare ya."

Holly gets a smooth smile on her face, giggles a bit, then twists around in her seat and gets up on her knees. Elsie gets to laughin and tellin Holly how crazy she is but Holly sticks her butt out toward Raymond, hikes her skirt up and looks back over her shoulder. Raymond ain't lookin and Holly gets to sayin, "Raymond, look, ain't mine smaller than hers, ain't it? Look, Raymond, how ya goin ta see it if ya keep lookin that way? Turn around so ya can tell her."

Elsie shouts, "Ya crazy girl, ya ain't got a bit of sense."

Holly shouts, "Raymond, look."

Raymond keeps his head down until Elsie pokes him with her foot and says, "Ya mise well look, Raymond, she goin ta stay there till ya do."

Slowly, Raymond turns around and looks at Holly up on the backseat with her skirt pulled up over her butt and her pink panties givin color to the dark. Holly's smilin and lookin back over her shoulder sayin, "See, Raymond, it ain't big, is it? Say it, Raymond, tell her it ain't big. Go ahead, Raymond, tell her."

Raymond looks, then looks away real quick but he's whisperin real slow, "It ain't big. . . . Ah mean it don't look big . . ."

"See, see," Holly says and gets a big smile on her face as she pulls her skirt down and twists back around in her seat. Then she looks at Elsie, makes a face and says, "Now, Elsie Jane Fagen, ya show him yours. Go ahead, show him."

Elsie kept gigglin and laughin until she started losin her breath. Holly shouts again, "Go ahead . . . Go ahead . . . Elsie . . . Jane . . . Fagen . . . Ya dared me and Ah did it. . . . Now Ah dare ya . . . Ya so smart talkin, now let's really see . . . Let's see, Elsie, let's see who got the fat butt."

Elsie gets enough breath to shout, "Ya crazy, Holly Hill."

Holly reaches for the bottle of wine, takes a quick swig, then says, "Let's go find that Fannie's place. Ah feel like dancin."

9

It was Sunday night, December tenth, when it happened. Supply folks will remember it as just the Big Storm, winds and rains comin from afar. Folks said, it wasn't the time of year for it, ain't never had anything like this come this time, must have come from way out in the ocean ta have all that water and wind. Some of them old colored folks out in the Back Land got to thinkin, God's ahh-mighty mad at somebody.

Holly would remember it as that Sunday night, the one right after her, Elsie and Raymond got drunk up in Wilmington, then went to that Fannie's place and danced all over the floor.

That Sunday morning, everybody had went to church, except Bobby. Gus Hill had been goin every Sunday since Bobby came home, had cut down on his drinkin, too. Ginger went to pray and Jason went because he had to. Holly went because she thought it would help get her mother off her back for comin in so late. She made Elsie promise she would be there too.

After Holly got back from church, took them church clothes off, had dinner, the rest of Sunday went its same old ways, she was runnin back and forth to Elsie's, lookin at the funny papers, sittin around thinkin about things, then sittin around tryin not to think about things.

Come evening, the skies over Supply got real dark and the winds came blowin. It stayed that way for hours, folks with that electric line started turnin off them lights and radios. Holly went on upstairs, thought there wasn't much sense in sittin downstairs with all the lights off. She tiptoed by Bobby's room and went into her own.

Outside, the wind kept blowin. Trees bent over, broken branches were flung through the air, yard dogs whimpered and whined. Holly stood by the window, looked out and then pulled the blinds down. But the howls of the winds still came.

She went on and got in the bed and pulled the covers over her head. Sleep was slow to come and when it did, it was restless.

Around midnight the winds brought the rains, quick swift drops at first, then the sky out past the Back Land lit up like day and crashed back into darkness with a thunderous roar. Everything shook, the sky became a flashy torch and the rain poured into the night. Holly woke with the thunder and held on to her pillow.

The night became wicked and everything wicked came.

Long curling screams burst out of the dark.

Holly cringed from the piercin sting of the sudden cries. Her eyes sprang open, then she lay quiverin as the screams clawed at her mind.

Somewhere in the dark, Bobby Hill stood screamin.

The wind had blown days away, the thunder brought back nights of ago, lightning flashed dead faces left on Saipan. Dead men's faces covered with bloody mud called out his name. *"Bobby . . . Bobby . . . Hey Hill . . . Hill . . ."* Bobby called to their cries, *"Um comin . . . Um comin . . . Stay down . . . Ah git ya . . . Hold on, Um comin . . ."* Bobby heard the cries, ran through the dark of his room, ran through the dark of the hall, ran down the steps and into the night.

Holly kept hearin the screams, then her mother callin, "Bobby . . . Bobby . . . Bobby . . . Gus . . . Gus, git up." Ginger ran from her room, Holly heard her mother's footsteps stumbling through the dark, then she could hear them runnin down the steps. Holly calls, "Mama . . . Mama . . . What's wrong?"

Winds kept blowin.

Rains beat down anything limp, made it droop dreary in the dark. Bobby ran wild in the night, called names that would never answer but he kept callin, *"Sarge . . . Um comin . . . Where are ya? . . . Sarge . . . Where are ya . . ."*

Holly could still hear her mother screamin and callin, "Bobby . . . Bobby . . . My God . . . Bobby . . ." She gathers her nightgown and runs into the dark hallway yellin, "Mama . . . Mama . . . What's wrong? . . . Where's Bobby? . . . What's wrong wit him? . . ."

Everything was shakin in the dark, Holly trembled as she ran down the steps toward the sounds of her mother's screams and calls into the night. Ginger had gone out onto the porch. Cold water swept across her face, winds twisted her hair and flung it with its scorn. Holly leaned into the wind, then pushed and fought through it until she reached her mother on the porch. "Mama . . . Mama . . . What's wrong? . . . Where's Bobby?" she shouts through the wind and the whippin rain. Ginger just shakes and keeps callin out into the storm, "Bobby . . . Bobby . . . Where are ya? . . . Come back . . ."

Holly is shoutin again as she gets closer to her mother and yells, "What's wrong, Mama? What wrong wit Bobby? Why he out there?"

Ginger turns her face from the wind, shouts, "He just ran out there screamin," then turns back to the wind and calls for Bobby again. Holly wipes the water from her eyes and looks out into the streakin rain. Ginger shouts to her, "Ah can't see him, do ya see him? . . . My God . . . Where is he? . . . He just started screamin."

Holly calls, "Bobby . . . Bobby . . ." Then she hears the screams in the wind calling, *"Sarge . . . Stay down. . . . Stay down. . . . Um comin . . ."*

"Mama . . . Mama . . . Ah hear him, Ah hear him. . . . He's over there somewhere, Ah hear him."

Ginger lunges from the porch and into the full face of the rain. She is screamin for Bobby and tryin to run in the mud. "Mama . . .

Mama . . ." Holly shouts and jumps into the streakin rain shout-in, "Mama . . . Mama . . . git back here. . . . Git back here, Mama. . . . Ah git him, go back."

Holly pushes and pulls her mother back up the porch steps, then turns back into the wind yellin, "Bobby . . . Bobby . . . Where ya at? . . . Bobby . . ."

The wind blows and rips at her hair. Hard cold raindrops beat at her face. Her blue nightgown is soaked and saggin from her, but she keeps yellin, "Bobby . . . Bobby . . . Where ya at, Bobby? . . . Where ya at, Bobby?"

Lightning is flashin and lightin up the night. When it does, Holly wipes the water from her eyes and searches the quick bright light, then shakes and closes her eyes when the thunder shakes the ground. The mud makes her slip, almost fall with every step she takes. Sometimes the wind brings Bobby's screams for Sarge, then just his cries. Holly keeps lookin, then screams, "Bobby . . . Bob-by . . . ," she sees him standin in the night lookin like a frightened scarecrow. When she gets to him, she can see him shakin, see him lettin the rain splash on his face, but he keeps starin someplace. Holly yells, "Bobby . . . Bobby . . . What's wrong wit ya, huh?" The winds carry her yells away. Bobby will not turn to her. She grabs for his arm, gets it and tries to whisper through the wind, "Bobby, whats wrong? Ya can't be out here. Come on, Bobby, come on." Holly pulls on his arm but Bobby still won't turn to her. She slips and slides in the mud until she can get in front of him and make him look at her. She can see his face, his eyes wide open and starin beyond her. She is pleadin with him now, tellin him, "Come on, Bobby, come back in the house. Come on, Bobby, ain't nobody out there. Mama's worried sick about ya. Ya all wet, come on now. Mama's waitin on ya, she's on the porch waitin. She wants ya ta come in the house."

A light swung in the darkness, the rains and winds let it through. Gus Hill came with his lantern and brought Holly and her brother back into the house. Ginger rushed to dry Bobby off and between her quick movements she kept glancin at Holly, askin, "Ya all right, honey?"

Holly sits at the kitchen table with a blanket over her shoulders and stares down at the floor. "Um all right, Mama, Um all right," she answers but keeps lookin down.

Gus Hill took Bobby back up to his room, told Ginger and Holly to stay in the kitchen, he'd be back down. Ginger fixed some coffee and gave Holly some, then sat at the table. The face of the night still frowned, battered Ginger's world with its winds and rains. She sighs and shakes, then asks Holly again if she is all right. Holly nods her head yes but keeps starin at the floor.

For a moment, a silence becomes stronger than the storm. Ginger stills in it and Holly keeps her head down but starts cryin and askin her Mama, "What's wrong wit Bobby, huh? What's wrong wit him, Mama? Why he go out there hollerin like that for? What's wrong wit him, Mama?"

Ginger sits silently.

Holly tries to wipe the tears from her eyes, sits up but looks down at the table and starts tellin her Mama, "He ought not be actin like that. He ain't actin nothin like he was. He out there lookin for somebody he called Sarge. When Ah told him wasn't nobody out there, he just look out there anyway. He was cryin, Mama."

Ginger sighs, a look comes to her eyes that shows the darkness of the storm. She doesn't say anything, she just sits silently and stares.

Holly's snifflin a little and sayin, "Mama, Ah hear him hollerin in his sleep sometimes. Ah ain't said nothin, Ah figure ya hear it too and Ah ain't wantin ta be worryin ya wit it. Mama, somethin wrong, he ain't actin like Bobby. Ah mean . . . Ah mean, that's why Elsie ain't come down that much anymore. She say it bother her ta be seein Bobby that way and all. Her rememberin how he was before. He ain't laughed at nothin, don't ask ya nothin either. And if ya ask him somethin it take him so long ta say somethin back, then he just say yes or no or just shake his head or somethin. He ain't even say that much ta Jason. Ah ain't told ya but Jason come cryin ta me, wantin ta know if Bobby still like him and all. Ah ain't say that ta ya either. Mama, is Bobby goin ta git better?"

Ginger is silent but the look in her eyes tells Holly all she doesn't want to know. Holly looks away, then puts her head back down. Gus Hill has come back down the steps and into the kitchen. He pours himself a cup of coffee, then turns to Holly sayin, "Why don't ya go on up and get back in the bed. Your brother will be all right, I got him to take one of them pills they sent with him. I figure that ought to calm him down, get him sleepin some."

Holly looks up at her father, stares at him, then asks, "Daddy, he goin ta be all right? He's goin ta git better, ain't he?"

Gus Hill takes a deep breath, holds it, then lets it out slowly.

Holly keeps her eyes on her father. When he doesn't speak, she says, "Daddy, Ah think . . . Ah mean . . . Ah think Bobby's . . . he's real sick and all."

Gus Hill's head jolts, he looks at Holly and says, "He'll be fine, just fine. He needs some more time, that's all. He got some things that need some more time."

"Gus," Ginger says and looks up at him. She waits until he turns to her, then she waits until she can gather her feelings into words. Slowly she's askin, "Ya think . . . Well maybe Doc Anderson could come out and see Bobby? . . . He might know somethin we could do for him."

"No," Gus Hill shouts, "I don't want this damn town thinkin somethin wrong out here. Bobby will just be fine, let him come his own way."

Ginger sighed and put her head back down, Gus Hill turned and left the kitchen. The roars of the storm's wind and rain fell silent beneath the sounds of his footsteps. Moments passed before Ginger raised her head and said, "Honey, why don't ya go on up now? Go on up now and git some sleep."

Holly sighed and got to her feet and started to the door, then turned and came back and kissed her mother on the cheek. When she turned to leave, Ginger called to her. Holly slowed and heard her mother sayin, "Honey, why don't ya think about writin Billy, he just keeps writin ya. It don't take that long ta write him somethin. Maybe sit down tomorrow and . . . Well, why don't ya think about it some? Ain't no tellin what these boys are goin through."

The darkness in the hallway seemed to be darker than the night. But it was soothing dark, a dark that Holly could hide in, that hid her from the storms and even the night but not from the feelings that were trailin her up the steps.

At the top of the steps, Holly holds her breath as she nears her brother's door, it is closed. She listens for any sound comin from his room, but she only hears the sounds of her breathing. She puts her hand on her brother's door, then slides it down until she can feel the doorknob at her fingertips. She turns it and gently pushes the door open until it squeaks, then she stops and peeks through the crack of the open door. It is quiet and all she can see is the dark in his room. She pushes the door further and eases her head into the opening until she can see Bobby lyin on the bed.

She whispers, "Bobby, ya wake?"

The room was as quiet as its darkness.

"Bobby . . . ya still wake?" she whispers again, then gently steps into the room and tiptoes up to the bed. She stills herself when she can see her brother's eyes starin up into the dark.

"Bobby, ya all right now?"

Slowly, Bobby turns his head and looks up at his sister, then just stares. Holly smiles a little, then whispers, "Ya all right now?"

Bobby shakes his head yes, then slowly turns and looks away.

"Ya sure, huh?" Holly whispers and eases herself down on the side of her brother's bed, then she whispers, "Bobby, what's wrong, huh? Why ya go out there for, huh?"

Bobby is silent.

The room has a chill from the rain and wind but Holly can still see the sweat glistenin on her brother's forehead. Slowly, she raises her hand and reaches for Bobby but her hand stops. She sighs and whispers, "Bobby, who's Sarge? Why ya callin him?"

Quickly, Holly jerks her hand back from Bobby's sudden shakes, then whispers while he still trembles, "What's wrong, Bobby?

What's wrong, does your head hurt? Does it hurt, is it hurtin again, huh?"

Slowly, Bobby stirs, then lies quietly again. Holly bites down on her lip, takes a deep breath, then with a very soft whisper asks, "Does it still hurt, is that what's wrong, Bobby? Isn't it better yet?"

Bobby is silent in all of his ways. Holly sighs, eases herself up from the bed, then stands and keeps her eyes on her brother. "Um goin now, ya goin ta be all right?" she whispers. Slowly, Bobby shakes his head yes.

There was warmth beneath the covers, Holly held her pillow and lay in the dark with her eyes open. The night swayed like a porch swing, thoughts swung back and forth in the dark. The rain came splashin into her mind and she could see herself runnin after her brother, she could see the wind blowin everything sideways. She could see Bobby standin like some pickin-field scarecrow, just starin with real eyes instead of them button ones. Sarge has a face now, it is a face with just eyes but it was callin her brother and now it is callin her, too. Holly takes a deep breath and turns in her bed, brings the pillow closer and tries to push her thoughts further away. She jerks, squeezes the pillow and turns again, the thoughts turn with her.

Morning came without a sun, thick dull gray light brought a dark day. Holly slept late. When she woke, it was a slow wakening. Everything seemed quiet and distant, damp air soaked the room. For a while she lay with the pillow in her arms and stared at the shadows in the corner of the room.

"Honey . . . Honey . . . ," Holly heard her mother callin, then Elsie yellin up the steps, "Girl, git up, ya goin ta sleep all day?"

In a moment, Elsie pushed the door open sayin, "Ya woke? Look at ya, ya look like the mess itself. How come ya ain't up? Everybody up and lookin at the floodin."

Holly brushed the hair away from her eyes and asked Elsie, "What time is it?"

"It's almost noon, girl. What ya still doin all up in the bed?"

"Ah tell ya later," Holly whispers and rolls her eyes towards the hallway, then looks back at Elsie and whispers again, "Ah tell ya later."

Elsie whispers, "Your daddy do somethin?"

Holly shakes her head no, then whispers again, "Ah tell ya later."

Elsie blurts out, "Ya hear what happened?"

"What?" Holly asks.

Elsie gets to tellin. "Ya know down where the creek makes the turn? . . . Ya know that place where all them big rocks stickin up at? . . . All them shacks back up in there got washed out. They say they ain't found some of them coloreds back up in there yet. Everybody talkin about it. Say its been one of the worst floods they done seen back in there. They still down there lookin and all for coloreds. Said they found one of em, it was an old woman. Said she was caught up on a fence and all wit her nightgown still on but she had died already when they found her. Ya want to go down there and see what happened? Everybody goin down."

Holly rolls her eyes up and down, sighs and says, "Elsie Fagen, what's wrong wit ya? Ah ain't goin down there lookin at dead folks. Ya must be crazy or somethin. All them snakes be washed up and crawlin around like worms. Ah ain't goin down there ta see dead folks and snakes."

Elsie kept talkin about the flood, Holly sat up on the side of the bed and brushed at the hair that got back in her eyes.

Elsie kept talkin.

Holly saw her blue nightgown lyin on the floor, it was still wet and covered with mud. She sighed and looked away.

10

Eugene Purvis, Supply's courthouse clerk, hung the big green Christmas wreath over the courthouse door. Folks across the street watched him, see if he would get it hangin straight. Some folks thought it looked a little strange havin the Christmas wreath on top the door, then right next to the door was that wall with all them boys' names on it that wasn't never comin home for Christmas. Folks didn't know whether to look at the wreath and be happy, or look at them names and them flowers beneath them and be sad. Just knew they couldn't be both at the same time. Them folks with boys in the war said it didn't seem like Christmas at all, didn't want to see that wreath or them flowers.

It was the Saturday before Christmas, December twenty-third, nineteen forty-four. Holly had promised Jason she would take him to Wilmington to see all the Christmas decorations if he promised not to act like a fool, then made Elsie come along to keep her company.

The trip to Wilmington in the daylight hours could be made by bus and only took about a half hour or so. Downtown Wilmington had its big Christmas tree up and brightly decorated. Right in front of the Christmas tree, folks had put up a platform where a church choir was singin carols. Shoppers with children, boys in uniform and quiet-faced old men stood and listened. Jason had stood still for two songs but was now pullin on Holly's arm to come. "Let's go, Holly. Ya said Ah could see the train sets in that big store, ya said," Jason pleads and pulls.

Holly and Elsie had stood listenin to the songs. Elsie had asked, "Ya make up ya mind on what ya gittin?"

Holly tells Elsie "No," real quick, then gets to hushin Jason. The choir had just finished a song when the director of the choir turned and spoke into the audience, sayin "We goin ta sing this next one here for all ya all boys that will be away from your loved ones."

Holly had always liked to hear "Silent Night," it was her favorite of all the Christmas songs. When the choir began singing it, she began to hum along with them. Jason pulled at her some but she kept hummin. A soft smile and a gentle glow had come to her face. Christmas was always a magic time for Holly. She felt special at Christmas. It was her birthday, too. Ginger used to tell her, "We just found ya in the stockin, didn't even know ya were there till ya started yellin. Sorta figured we keep ya since ya come on Christmas mornin, call ya Holly."

The choir was still singin "Silent Night," Holly hummed along. Jason kept pullin on her arm and whisperin, "Can't we go? Come on, Holly, ya said."

"Just a minute," Holly whispered from her hum.

The choir finished its last notes but the melody seemed to flutter in the breeze of the afternoon. Holly is still smilin when she asks Elsie, "Ya think Ah should have sent him somethin? Maybe just a card, huh?"

Elsie asks quietly, "Billy?"

Holly is silent for a moment, just takes Jason by the hand and starts to walk off before she turns to Elsie askin, "Ya think he done sent somethin? What if he sends me somethin, should Ah keep it, or try and send it back and all?"

Elsie is silent, she sighs and looks down at the pavement.

Holly starts talkin real fast. "He might have sent somethin, ya think he did? Ya know how long it be takin stuff ta git here, ya think he sent a birthday card or somethin? If he do, ya think Ah should send him somethin back, huh?"

Elsie butts in sayin, "Ya ain't opened up the letters ya got now."

Holly is silent for a few steps, then asks Elsie, "Ya goin ta git your Mama's gift at Miller's, or ya want to go over ta Dalton's?"

Elsie says, "Let's see what's in Miller's." Then she gets to laughin and askin, "Ya want ta see if they still got that fat Santy man? That one we git up on, member?"

Holly smiles and asks Jason, "Ya want ta go see Santa?"

"Ain't no Santa Claus, Ah know that, Holly," Jason says quickly, then turns to Elsie sayin, "Tell her, Elsie, tell her there ain't no Santa Claus."

Elsie is gigglin and sayin, "There's a Santa, your sister done come up here just ta sit on his lap."

Holly gives Elsie a quick look, then twists her face up and gets to tellin her, "At least if Ah sit on his lap, Ah wouldn't break the old man's knees, Elsie Fagen."

Elsie laughs and tells Jason, "Your sister come up here ta ask Santa if he take her on over ta Fannie's, that's where she wants ta go for Christmas."

Jason asks, "Huh, what's Fannie's?"

"Jason, don't be payin Elsie no mind," Holly is sayin.

Jason forgot about Fannie's and ran into the store ahead of Holly and Elsie. The store was crowded with shoppers. Holly kept her eye on Jason as he roamed the aisles lookin for all the things he wanted Christmas morning.

"Jason, don't ya be touchin that and breakin it, ya hear," Holly shouts ahead to where Jason is roamin, then turns to Elsie sayin, "Maybe Ah should have sent him a Christmas card. Ah mean, Ah wouldn't had ta say anything, just sign it. It ain't like Ah hate him or somethin. Or he been mean ta me and all."

"Go on and do it, if it be makin ya feel . . . ya know, better and all," Elsie says, then tells Holly, "By the time he be gittin it, it might be Easter or somethin."

"It wouldn't take that long."

"Well it ain't gettin there by Christmas."

"Shit," Holly mutters.

Elsie says, "Ya ain't even knowin where he's at, he might be all over that ocean someplace."

Holly is quiet for a moment, looks for Jason, then mutters to Elsie, "Ya want ta go see if they got that same Santa Claus? If he there, Ah ain't sittin on his lap."

Elsie laughs, but just a little bit, then says to Holly, "Why don't ya open his letters, see where he at? He might be at some base over there or somethin. It might not be takin a whole bunch of time ta git there. Ya know, he might be somewhere where his ship be gittin fixed or somethin. He might be on land somewhere."

Holly takes a deep breath and stares out into the crowd.

Elsie says, "Ya mise well open the letters, ya know he still loves ya and all. Him still writin all the time say he still loves ya. Ya ain't got ta open up the letters ta know that, Holly Hill."

"Ah still don't know yet," Holly says, then sighs.

"Know what?"

"Ya know, Ah just don't know."

"Ya ain't got ta be no genius or somethin ta know ya want ta send him a Christmas card or somethin. Ya actin like ya got ta git married in the mail. Ain't nothin wrong wit ya sendin him some kind of Christmas card."

"Ah don't know," Holly answers and sighs again.

"Damn, Holly Hill, it could be nineteen hundred zillion and ya still be walkin around sayin . . . 'Ah don't know . . . Ah don't know . . . Ah don't know . . .' Ya be too old ta know if ya did know."

"It ain't that," Holly says quickly, "Ah mean . . . Ah mean if Ah send somethin, suppose he start thinkin we . . . ya know, we still gittin married and all."

"Well, why don't ya git married ta Raymond? Make some midget babies. One thing for sure about Raymond, he likes ya ass," Elsie says with a giggle, then gets to laughin when she sees Holly's face.

Jason has found Santa Claus and is standin behind the roped-off area callin for Holly and Elsie to come over. "Is he real?" he spins around and asks Holly as she nears.

Holly smiles and tells Jason, "Yes, that's him. Ya want ta go and tell him what ya want?"

"He ain't real," Jason says quickly, then turns around and watches the other kids gettin up on Santa's lap.

Elsie leans over to Holly and whispers in her ear, "That's the same one, look at him. See, that's the same one, ain't it?"

Holly whispers back, "No it ain't, this one's skinny and all."

"That's the same one, look at him. Besides, how would ya know what was skinny or not?"

"Hey Elsie . . . ," Holly says, then lets her words drift.

Jason turns around sayin, "He ain't real, Holly. Is he?"

"Go on up, Jason," Holly says, then gives a little nudge.

"He ain't real."

"Yes he is, now go on up and tell him what ya want."

Jason goes on and gets in line behind the other kids but keeps lookin back at Holly and Elsie. Holly waves him on and whispers through the crowd, "Go on now, go on."

Holly's smilin as she's watchin Jason and whisperin to Elsie, "Ah was scared ta death of that old man when Mama brought me down here. Ah member Ah raised a fit."

Elsie smiles and says, "Ah member my mama sayin, if Ah ain't take my thumb out my mouth Ah wasn't seein Santa and Christmas, too."

When it was Jason's turn, he got on up on Santa's lap but kept lookin back at Holly and Elsie. Santa asked Jason a couple of questions and Jason got to talkin back and askin Santa a few questions, then he went on and talked Santa's ear off. Holly finally got Jason off Santa's lap and out of the store. The street was bright in the midday sun, the shoppin crowd had thickened with folks almost bumpin into one another. Them folks that did bump into somebody just smiled and said, "Sorry, Merry Christmas ta ya."

Holly and Elsie dragged Jason in and out of stores until Elsie got her mama somethin and Holly got some things she was lookin for, too. The last thing Holly bought was a Christmas card for Billy. She told Elsie, "He might git it after Christmas but at least Ah sent it before . . . and he can't say Ah didn't send him one."

The bus ride back to Supply carried the echoes of the Christmas songs. Holly kept hummin "Jingle Bells" and askin Elsie if she should have bought the card. When the bus pulled up in front of Supply's courthouse, the afternoon hours were fadin. Holly, Elsie and Jason got off the bus and headed back out the old road with their packages. Jason was still talkin about Santa Claus and how he just knew he was bringin him everything he asked for. A little ways out of town, Holly's hummin got to be singin and she starts makin dancin steps to "Jingle bells, Jingle bells, jingle all the way . . . Oooh what fun it is ta ride in a one-horse open sleigh . . ." It wasn't too long before Elsie got to singin, too, and swayin her hips to the melody.

"Let's do this one . . . let's do this one . . . ," Holly blurts out, then starts singin at the top of her voice, "On the first day of Christmas, my true love brought ta me . . ."

Elsie shouts with laughter, "Ya ain't got no true love, Holly Hill," then gets to singin, too.

"Ya comin later?" Holly's askin as they reach Elsie's yard path.

Elsie wants to know, "Your mama start on her cookies yet?"

"Ah don't know," Holly is sayin and smilin, "she said she was but she says she goin ta hide them from ya this year. She said she was goin ta do that since ya ate em all last year."

"Oh hush, Holly Hill, we all know who ate em all. Tell your mama, Ah be up just ta see her," Elsie says, then starts wavin as Holly and Jason go on down the road. Jason runs on ahead, Holly calls, "What ya in such a big hurry for?" then she starts her "Jingle Bells" singin.

When Holly reached her yard path, she looked further down the road, let the fat-bellied oak and the glistenin waters of the creek come into her mind. The singin of the "Bells" silenced into a quiet thought that brought a smile to Holly.

Jason had run on ahead and up into the house. Holly took her time and let her hum become quiet words of, "All is calm, all is bright . . ." As soon as she got in the house she could hear Jason tellin her mother about Santa and all the things he knew he was gettin. Holly smiled and started singin "Jingle Bells" again when she went into the kitchen, then she kept singin and tryin to say at the same time, "Mama, Elsie say ta tell ya she comin down ta help ya wit the cookies, like she did last year."

Ginger sits at the kitchen table with her head down, and her face is reddened. Jason is still goin on about the Santa he saw but Ginger's smile is faint. Holly is askin, "What's wrong, Mama, ya feelin all right?"

Ginger is silent for a moment, then looks at Jason, tries to brighten her smile and says, "Honey, why don't ya go on over June Boy's, tell him 'bout Santa. Tell him Ah got some cookies for him. Here, ya can take them ones over in the pantry. Ya take them ta June Boy."

"What's wrong, Mama?" Holly's askin again.

Slowly Ginger gets up from the table and goes to the pantry and wraps the cookies for Jason to take to June Boy's.

"Mama," Holly is askin with the breath of her sigh, "ya all right, ya feelin all right, huh, Mama?"

Ginger nods her head that she's all right but keeps her back to Holly. A moment passes and Holly stands and just stares at her mama, then she gets to puttin her packages on the table and talkin about all the folks up in Wilmington and how nice the choir was singin. Jason stuck around for a while and kept tellin Ginger about that Santa he'd seen, now he's scootin out the kitchen and on his way to June Boy's. Holly's still tellin about Wilmington and how Jason got to talkin Santa's ear off. Ginger turns to her, Holly is sayin, "Ya should have seen him, Mama. First he ain't wantin ta git up on his lap, then he ain't wantin ta git off." Now she is askin, "Mama, ya feelin all right?"

Ginger looks at Holly, then lowers her head and sits back down at the table.

"Mama, what's wrong?"

Ginger sits quietly with her head down.

Quickly, Holly is askin, "Somethin wrong wit Bobby, huh? Is he sick again?"

Ginger shakes her head no.

"What's wrong then, Mama? What's wrong?"

"Holly . . . honey . . ."

Holly's eyes are gettin big.

Ginger sighs, looks up and says, "Mr. Felter was by."

"Oh, what he want?"

"He waited for a while . . . but . . ."

"What he say, Mama?"

"He came ta tell ya . . ."

"Tell me what, Mama? Did Billy tell him ta tell me somethin, huh?"

"No, honey."

"What's wrong, Mama? What he want then?"

"The part of the ship that Billy was on was hit by a bomb."

"Is he hurt, Mama? Is Billy hurt, Mama? Huh, Mama, is he hurt?"

"Billy's dead."

"No, Mama . . . No, Mama . . . Jason saw Santa Claus . . . He saw Santa Claus . . . It was a skinny Santa Claus . . . wasn't that one they used ta have . . . Me and Elsie . . . Ah got Billy a Christmas card . . . Ya want ta see it, Mama? . . . Um goin ta send him a Christmas card . . . Cause Ah know he's sendin me one . . . And Elsie . . . Um goin ta send it ta him, Mama . . . Um goin ta send it ta him, Mama . . ."

"Holly."

"No, Mama . . . No, Mama . . . Um goin ta write ta him . . . Ya

said Ah should send him a letter . . . Ah got him a Christmas
card . . . No, Mama . . ."

"Oh dear God Jesus," Ginger is sayin and gettin to her feet.

"No, Mama . . . No, Mama . . ."

"Com'ere, baby," Ginger sayin and takes Holly into her arms.

"No, Mama . . . No, Mama . . . No . . ."

"Mama got ya, baby. . . . Let it come. . . . Mama got ya."

Holly quivers until she starts shakin. She keeps tryin to talk, say
somethin about the Christmas card. Her words can't come out as she
begins to gasp. Tears are fillin up her eyes, she screams and tries to
jerk away from her mother. Ginger's holdin on to her, pullin Holly
closer to her and pattin her back. She's whisperin to Holly, tellin her
she must trust God . . . God took Billy home . . . Billy knew she still
loved him. Holly's askin with the breath of her cries, "Will God let
him know . . . Mama, will God let him know Ah got him a Christmas card?"

"Oh yes He will . . . Yes He will, honey."

Ginger got Holly up to her room and laid her across her bed and
wanted to stay with her but Holly said, "Ah want ta be by myself,
Mama." Billy would not go away, his face filled the darkness when
Holly closed her eyes, then he was everywhere in the room if she
opened them. She held her pillow but it had no warmth and was
soaked with tears.

When Elsie came, Holly was still cryin, Ginger told Elsie of Billy's death and had to take her in her arms, too. Then quietly, Elsie
went up the steps to Holly's room, took a deep breath and gently
opened the door. Holly lay across the bed with the pillow in her
arms and just staring into the silence. Elsie's soft footsteps tiptoed
into Holly's mind and she turned to the sound. Elsie didn't say anything, she just sat on the bed bedside Holly and looked at her, then
they were both in one another's arms cryin. Holly kept utterin, "Ah
was goin ta send him a Christmas card."

Evening came and Holly was still in her room. Elsie had left, said
she'd be back tomorrow and would stay all day. Ginger had come to
the room and sat with Holly when Elsie went home. She had

brought Holly some coffee and soup, asked her if she wanted a cigarette too. Holly shook her head no. Ginger sat quietly on the edge
of the bed, then she trembled when Holly softly asked, "Mama, did
Billy's daddy say when they were goin ta bring Billy home . . . ta be
buried . . . huh?"

Ginger sat silently but her hands quivered around the coffee cup
she held. "Honey . . . honey . . . ," Ginger is sayin slowly. She takes
a deep breath and then says, "Honey . . . they buried Billy at sea."

Holly lay quietly for a moment, then asked, "Ya mean they just
put him in the water by hisself?"

Ginger was silent, she twisted her fingers around the coffee cup,
then she spoke slowly sayin, "It's not like that. . . . They have a min-
ister and all. . . . and all of Billy's friends would be there. . . . They'd
do it real nice, honey."

Ginger stayed for a while and then got Holly undressed and beneath the covers. When she left, she told Holly she'd come back and
sit with her if Holly couldn't sleep. Time had no moments, it had
stilled for Holly and just became a part of the silence and emptiness
she stared into. When the door opened, Holly shook and turned to
it. The room was dark but she knew it was her brother comin to her.
Bobby didn't say anything at all, he stopped and stood in the dark,
just lookin. Then, slowly, walked over to Holly and touched her
cheek.

Gus Hill had heard about Billy down at the lumberyard, when he
got home he asked Ginger, "How she take it?" He waited until
morning when she was awake and found her just lyin on the bed. He
said all the things he could say, told her time would make things
better, you got ta keep goin you know, try not ta think about it too
much.

Jason knew the Japs killed Billy, knew it made his sister cry. He
did just like his mother told him to, he went and gave Holly a hug.
Then he told her, "Ah git em, Holly, soon Ah git big enough and
can go. Ah git those Japs that killed Billy."

Christmas came and the cookies had no taste. Elsie came down
and spent the day and when she found the right time she said,

"Happy birthday, Holly, ain't ya goin ta smile just a little bit? Ya been waitin ta be twenty since Lord knows when."

Holly says, "Ah don't feel like it's birthday or anythin. Ah just keep thinkin about it, Elsie."

Elsie puts her head down a little bit and says, "Mama keep askin about ya, ask how ya doin and all. She say, ya git a chance and feel like it, ya come on up. She say she got somethin for ya."

Holly was silent.

Elsie says, "Come on, let's get some cookies? See what your mama's cookin, ya can't be stayin up here in this room forever. It bein your birthday, too. Come on, let's go downstairs, then maybe go up my house. Ya want ta do that, see what my mama got for ya?"

"Ah don't want ta, Elsie."

Chester Higgens had told the courthouse clerk, Eugene Purvis, about Billy Felter's death. Eugene Purvis just shook his head, said it wasn't right, bein Christmas and all. Then said, "Ah reckon Ah better git his name up. Make sure them boys have some fresh flowers come Christmas."

11

A couple of days after Christmas, Chester Higgens brought Holly some letters. He knew they were from the Felter boy and made sure he gave them to Ginger. He said, "Mrs. Hill, Ah think ya ought ta have these ones here, knowin how things be and all." Ginger waited for the right time and gave them to Holly, sayin, "Honey, why don't ya open them? Billy would have wanted ya ta. Looks like this one's a Christmas card."

Holly had taken the letters up to her room and sat for hours just holdin them in her hands, then put them in the drawer under Billy's ring and the other letters he had sent. Then, slowly, she opened and read the card he had sent. Read it over and over, could hear him sayin the little things he wrote at the end. "I'll always love you. . . . You're my Christmas every day. . . . Happy Birthday, too. . . . Love, Billy."

Holly cried again, some of the tears fell on the card. When she put the card away, she put it on top of the unopened letters, then gently placed the card she had got for Billy on top of the one he had sent her. Slowly, she put the ring on top of the cards and closed the drawer.

The winter of nineteen forty-five came to Supply and seemed to stay longer than it was supposed to do. Some folks just sat around and looked at it, tried to nudge it along but it wouldn't hurry. Skies always seemed that dark gray and the nights weren't good for nothin but stayin warm and listenin to the radio. The war news kept comin, a few more names were under Billy Felter's.

Spring came slow and shyly, seemed like it didn't want to come at all but it did. Them colored people got back in the fields, started gettin that dirt turned over. The lumberyard was still goin seven days a week, tryin to keep up with all that lumber the government was needin. Folks were gettin tired of hurryin all the time but still tried to give a day a smile.

Spring comin and them bright sunny days didn't light up Holly's eyes. Winter had not taken Billy away when it left, Holly wouldn't let him go. She kept his unopened letters, ring and the Christmas cards in the back of the drawer. Sometimes, she'd get them out and just hold them. Elsie stopped comin down as much, Holly would go up to Elsie's every once in a while but wouldn't stay long. She hadn't been to Wilmington since that Saturday before Christmas, had not thought about goin to Ben's.

Ginger had tried to talk to Holly, tried to say, "Honey, ya got ta let it pass. Let it go away." Holly would only turn away, go back upstairs and leave Ginger standin in her silence. Ginger thought with spring comin, Holly would get to bein herself again, get to doin things she used to do, ought to be doin. She was sittin on the porch, gettin some of the mild spring sun, when Holly came out the house and walked to the edge of the porch, then leaned against the post. Ginger let her stand for a while and look wherever she was lookin, let her be in the moments of the time. Then, softly, Ginger asked, "Ya goin up Elsie's? Looks like a real nice day, why don't ya walk up, see Elsie?"

Holly just kept leanin against the post, didn't say anything. The warm spring breeze gently blew her hair, made it flutter softly across her face.

Ginger is sayin with a little laugh, "Ya tell Elsie, Ah got a bone ta pick wit her. Tell her, she better git down here and see me. Ya tell her Ah said that, ya hear?"

Quietly, Holly eased herself from the porch post, then walked down the steps and started up the yard path. She stepped lightly, kept her eyes down until she reached the end of the path. Ginger sat smilin as she watched Holly go up the path, the smile lingered, then vanished but Ginger kept watchin. Holly had started up the road to-ward Elsie's, then stopped, stood still before she turned around and started back down the road toward the Back Land.

"Where ya goin, honey?" Ginger shouted from the porch.

Holly shrugged her shoulders and kept goin.

The grass along the roadside was still faint from winter's stay, a little fresh green was startin to show. Some yellow flowers had al-ready bloomed along where the old road began to curve. The trees grew tall at the road's bend, shadows always lurked within the curve. It had been like a tunnel between two worlds, a dark slow turn into another land. It had been, trailin Bobby and him sayin, "Go home, Holly . . . Ah said go home, ya can't come." It had been, sneakin to go play with Tessie, a dark gold face in a mystery land. "Ya stay up out that Back Land," Ginger had said.

Holly's walk was slow through the shady bend in the old road. Sometimes coloreds would come around the bend but today the road was empty and silent of songbirds' singin, field folks' hums. But the silence and emptiness was gentle. At the end of the bend the road slopes down, the top of the fat-bellied oak can be seen. Holly sighs when she sees it, a quiet sigh that is left in the silence of the road.

Ginger sat on the porch for a while, kept lookin up to the road and out toward the way it goes to the Back Land, then she got up and went into the house to get supper ready. From time to time, she'd put a pot down, wipe her hands on her apron and look out the window. She'd look for a while, then go to the door and stand a bit, look out to the road before she'd get back to fixin supper. When Jason came in, she asked, "Did ya see your sister? Were ya and June Boy down at that creek? Did ya see your sister down there?"

Jason looked up and said real fast, "No, Mama, Ah was over June Boy's. We just be out back his house." Then he was askin, "Why Holly go down ta the creek for, Mama?"

Ginger let Jason's question pass with, "Go git ya brother, tell him supper be ready in a bit."

"Mama, what's Holly doin down the creek, huh? When she go down, huh?"

"Just go on and git Bobby, go on now."

Jason scooted away.

Ginger busied herself fixin supper, then set the table. She summoned her prayers and asked that the table be blessed. Jason squirmed in his seat, Bobby sat quietly, Holly's chair was empty. Jason asked, "What's Holly doin, she still down at the creek, Mama?"

"She'll be home soon. Go on and eat now, ya hear?" Ginger said, then let her eyes wander to the window.

Jason was hungry, went on and got to eatin real quick. Bobby ate slowly, he would put his food in his mouth, chew it slowly, then sit still for moments before he'd take another fork or spoonful. He flinched when he heard the sudden footsteps comin up on the porch. Ginger kept her eyes on the hallway until she saw Holly comin through, then she quickly lowered them.

"Hi, Mama. What ya fix, it smells good, did ya save some for me?" Holly is askin as she comes into the kitchen and goes over to the sink to wash her hands. Then she's sayin over her shoulder, "Ah was down ta the creek, it sure is pretty down there. Ya should see all the pretty flowers comin up already, it looks like a little picture-book garden."

Ginger looks at Holly and waits for her to turn around, she wants to see her eyes. Holly turns from the sink and Ginger says, "Ah was just wonderin where ya went off ta, Ah was gettin kind of worried."

Holly sits down at her seat, askin, "Worried about what, Mama? Ah just decided ta go for a walk, what ya worried about?"

Ginger says softly, "Oh, nothin, Ah was just worried some."

"Ain't nothin ta worry about, Mama. Ah been goin down there since Ah was big enough ta chase Bobby," Holly's sayin and givin Bobby a little twisted funny face, then she smiles at him.

"Ya better go on and eat somethin, put some meat back on them bones," Ginger is sayin and lettin a little smile linger on her face.

After supper, Holly helped Ginger with the dishes, then went up to her room. In a while she came back down and yelled into the kitchen, "Mama, Um goin up Elsie's." Ginger waited a moment, then went to the window and watched Holly go up the path. She was still starin when she heard Jason callin for somethin, then she turned from the window. Holly had vanished behind the roadside trees and bushes but not from her mind.

Elsie's mother saw Holly comin down the path and went to the door sayin, "Well, looks like the spring bounced in ya."

Holly came on in the house smilin, told Elsie's mama, "Ah went down the creek, ya should see all them pretty flowers a-comin up, it looks so pretty down there." Then still smilin she's askin, "Where's that daughter of yours at, her butt in bed or somethin?"

Elsie's mother pointed to the steps, laughed a little and said, "She ain't eatin, she's sleepin. Go wake her up."

"Hey Elsie . . . Elsie Fagen . . . Git your butt down here," Holly yelled up the steps, then ran up and went into Elsie's room askin, "What ya doin, huh? Why ya up here for?"

Elsie was lyin across the bed, she looks up, her hair keeps hangin down over her face.

Holly's askin again, "What ya doin up here for, huh?"

"What ya doin here, Ah mean . . . ," Elsie says, brushes the hair from her eyes and sits up on the bed. She keeps lookin at Holly, then says real fast like she's tryin to catch up on them words she ain't finished, "Ah mean . . . Ah was goin ta come down when Ah got up."

Holly says, "Ah come up here ta see what ya doin. Ya ain't been down in a while, some Frankenstein man could have come got me and carried me off somewhere. Ya wouldn't even had known."

"Ain't no Frankenstein man want ya," Elsie says smilin.

"Take me fore ya," Holly says quickly, then laughs some and sits on the side of the bed.

Elsie asks, "What ya been doin?"

"Nothin."

"How's Bobby?"

"He's fine. Why don't ya come down and see him?"

Elsie curls around and sits up on the side of the bed with Holly, then looks away before she asks, "What ya so bubbly for? Sounds like . . . Ah mean . . . Ya sound . . ." Elsie's words fade into just sounds of her breath.

Holly's still smilin and gets to askin, "Why everybody think Um actin like somethin? What's wrong wit ya all . . ."

Quickly, Elsie says, "Guess who Ah saw?"

"Saw where?" Holly asks.

"Saw down Ben's."

"When ya go down Ben's? Ya ain't told me ya were goin."

"Ah been goin down sometimes. Ah ain't thinkin ya wanted ta go."

"Ah would have went wit ya."

"Well Ah . . ."

"Who ya see? Not that old Garet Foster?"

"No, not him. He was bein down there but Ah wasn't meanin him."

"Who, not silly Raymond?"

"Ah ain't meanin no Raymond."

"Who?"

"Mark, ya member, Jerry's friend. That one ya were wit."

"Oh, him."

"His ship was in again, he wasn't wit Jerry. He says ta tell ya hi."

Holly's smile goes away, then comes back again and she is askin, "Ya want ta go down Ben's tonight?"

"Yeah, Ah go," Elsie says quickly, then asks, "Ya sure ya want ta go?"

Holly's smile draws up, she says, "Yeah Um sure. How come ya askin me if Um sure, huh? How come ya askin me that for?"

"Ah just askin," Elsie says, and is quiet for a moment before sayin, "Ya ain't been out since . . . well . . . ya know, since it happened and all."

Holly lowers her head but quickly throws it back up, brushes the hair out of her eyes and says, "Ah was just tired of goin out. Got tired of them old same places all the time and all."

Elsie says, "Ah been meetin Tammy, we been goin down together. Sometimes we git a ride up ta Wilmington, or we git Raymond ta take us."

Holly's eyes get big and she says, "Tammy . . . Tammy Kelso?"

Elsie says, "Yeah, she's nice."

"She thinks she's cute and all."

"She's real nice, she just started comin out. Said her daddy wouldn't let her but he took off, went back ta Richmond. Said he just left fore Christmas, her mama ain't heard from him since. She say, she glad he gone. She say her mama glad, too."

Holly put her head down when Elsie mentioned Christmas. Elsie kept talkin about Tammy Kelso until Holly asked, "Is Lucy still chasin Garet?"

Elsie says, "Lucy got some sailor hangin around. He must be like that Jerry, stationed up in Wilmington or someplace. He's always around and got a nice car and all."

Holly asks, "What's Garet been doin?"

"Don't git mad, ya know what an asshole he is. He's been takin Tammy up ta Wilmington sometimes, took her ta some picture shows and all."

"What Ah git mad for, he can go do that."

Talk went on. Elsie was sayin somethin about some sailor she met when Holly got up, smilin and sayin, "Um goin now, Ah be back up soon as Ah get dressed and all."

Holly took her time goin back home. When she got home she went right upstairs and busied herself gettin dressed. Ginger poked her head into Holly's room askin, "Ya goin out?"

Holly turns, smiles and says, "Me and Elsie, we might go down Ben's."

"Oh," Ginger says.

"Yeah, Mama, we just goin down Ben's, that's all," Holly says and gets to lookin in the mirror.

Ginger smiles and says, "Ya have a nice time, honey."

Ben's didn't look any different, it was Friday night and Ben's Friday night crowd was already dancin to the jukebox music. Tammy Kelso was sittin with Garet Foster when Holly and Elsie came in. Tammy waved and called to Elsie, "Hey Elsie, come on over."

Elsie turned and whispered to Holly, "Garet's over there, ya want ta go over?"

Holly whispered back, "Yeah, why not?"

Tammy Kelso seemed tall even though she was sittin, she had a way of holdin herself up and showin her good looks. Her dark brown hair, almost black in Ben's dim light, hung loosely and swayed with her movements. In school, she had been a year behind Holly and Elsie and had kept to herself a lot but seemed to be comfortable in the company of her good looks. She saw Holly comin and looked at Garet, then looked up at Holly and said, "Hi, Holly, didn't know ya were comin."

Holly smiles at Tammy, says a quick "Hi," and tries not to look at Garet. Elsie is sayin some things to Tammy, and Garet is lookin up at Holly. He's watchin for her eyes to see his before he speaks. Holly starts lookin at little things lyin on the table. She stares at the little red circle on the pack of cigarettes, then stares at the dark wood of the table. Quickly she looks at Garet, says, "Hi, Garet, haven't seen ya in a while," then she looks back down at the table.

Garet sighs, then whispers to Holly, "Um sorry about Billy."

Holly nods her head a little, Tammy scoots over so Elsie and Holly can sit at the table. Love songs spin around Ben's back room, Garet keeps glancin at Holly until he asks her if she wants to dance. Holly says, "No, Ah don't like ta dance here."

Garet looks down at the table for a moment, then looks up askin, "Where ya been?"

Slowly, Holly's sayin, "Nowhere, Garet, just at home."

Quickly, Garet says, "Ah thought ya were sick or somethin."

Holly tightens up her face, looks at Garet and says, "No, Ah wasn't sick."

"Ah just thought so, ya ain't been down. Ah thought ya, Ah mean, got sick. Ah was just askin, that's all," Garet says, sighs and looks away.

Holly's face becomes soft again, she lowers it away from Garet and tries to listen to the music. The melody has a beat to it, a slow thumpin sound, Holly can feel the thud in her stomach. For a moment, Ben's seems empty, Holly has to look up to see if folks are still dancin, if Elsie's still there, too.

Elsie was sayin somethin to Holly, then said it again when Holly kept starin at her and not sayin a word. "Ya want ta ride up?" Elsie's askin again.

"Huh?" Holly says.

Elsie just looks at Holly, then gets to sayin, "Ya want to go? We goin on up ta Wilmington, Garet's takin us."

"Oh," Holly says, then gets a smile on her face and tells Elsie, "No, Ah just want ta stay here. Ya all can go."

Elsie whispers, "Oh, come on."

Holly says, "Ah don't feel like it."

Garet looks at Holly, then says, "Come on, Ah thought ya like ta go up Wilmington. Come on with us."

Elsie whispers, "Come on, we can have some fun. Ya ain't wantin ta stay here?"

Holly looks down at the table, then looks up smilin and sayin, "Ah just don't feel like it tonight. Ya all go on, go ahead, Elsie, ya can go."

Garet starts nudgin on Tammy's arm and whisperin to her, then she asks Elsie if she's still goin to Wilmington. Elsie sighs, gives Holly a quick look, then tells Tammy, "No, Ah might go up tomorrow. Um goin ta go on and stay here."

After Garet and Tammy have left, Elsie sits quietly for a while. Holly doesn't say anything either, she sits watchin some of the folks dance. In a while, Elsie asks, "How come ya didn't want ta go, huh?"

Holly whispers somethin that Elsie doesn't hear. Elsie's sayin, "Huh?" Holly turns and looks at Elsie sayin, "Ah said it ain't important. Goin up there ain't important no more."

There was a song playin on the jukebox but there was a silence in Holly's eyes. And when she started smilin again, the silence was still there. Elsie had seen it, but now she was feelin it. She took a deep breath, reached into her purse and wiggled her hand around until she found her cigarettes. "Here, ya want one?" she asked Holly as she got one out of the pack for herself. Holly said, "No."

The same song was still playin when two sailors came over and asked if they could sit down. Elsie looked up, smiled and said, "Well if ya want to." Holly looked up and gave a little smile to the one standin closest to the table, then looked back down. The two sailors sat down, one said his name was Paul. The other kept lookin at Holly, then said his name was Roland. He asked Holly her name. She looked up, smiled and told him, then looked off into the crowd.

The two sailors sat and talked, Elsie answered their questions and wanted to know where they were from. Paul was a stocky redhead guy who still had freckles. He said he was from Maryland. He laughed a lot, tried to say funny things. Elsie laughed and kept on answerin his questions, then she asked the other sailor where he was from. He hadn't said much, or asked much. He had a quiet look in his eyes that made them look darker than the brown they were. His hair was dark, too, he wasn't much taller than the other sailor but wasn't stocky-lookin, more lean. He was tellin Elsie, "I'm from Johnstown, Pennsylvania, it's not too far from Pittsburgh. I'll be here a while, got stationed up Lejeune."

Holly still had not said much, she had sat quietly amidst the music and talk. Roland kept glancin at her but had stopped askin her questions. He had just got back from the Pacific, waitin had become a way with him. Glancin at Holly and waitin for her to say somethin was a different waitin.

Paul was still talkin to Elsie and she was still smilin. He stopped talkin for a second, looked at her, then asked, "Do you want to dance?"

Elsie lowered her voice a little, almost to a whisper, and said, "Okay."

Paul took Elsie to the dance floor and Roland waited for a while before he looked at Holly, waited until she lifted her eyes, then asked, "What about you, do you want to dance?"

Holly looked off to the dance floor, looked into the dimly lit circle of light where Elsie had her head on Paul's shoulder and swayed with the slow melody of the music. "Ah don't like ta dance here," she says.

Roland says, "I don't like to dance at all. I just asked because I thought you might want to. I can't dance anyway. Why are you so quiet?"

Holly turns, looks at Roland and perks her nose up sayin, "Um not quiet, ya just don't know me. Ah talk a lot."

"You have pretty eyes when you're not trying to hide them," Roland is sayin, then watchin for Holly to smile.

Holly pouted. "Um not tryin ta hide my eyes."

"Why are you so quiet?" Roland asked again.

Holly smiled a little and told Roland, "Ah told ya, Um not quiet. And Ah ain't tryin to hide my eyes either. Why ya keep on tryin ta see them for anyway?"

"They're pretty."

"Huh?"

"I said, you're pretty, your eyes and everything about you is pretty. I mean that, I'm just not saying things. I know a lot of guys say the same thing to you and mean it, too. But you're very pretty and it makes me feel good to look at you. I guess I'm a little selfish in my thoughts, I don't mean to be. It's just, well it's a world gone wild, it's good to look at something pretty. What's your last name?"

Holly sat quietly for a moment, then said, "It's Hill, Holly Hill."

Roland didn't say anything more. Holly looked off to the sound of the music and watched Elsie dancin with Paul. When the music ended, she turned and looked down at the table. Elsie and Paul came back, talk filled the silence between Holly and her thoughts.

When Ben's neared its closin time, the music seemed to play

slower. Holly hadn't said much but had listened to Paul and his storytellin. Roland had talked a little but mostly just listened to Paul. Holly heard Elsie sayin, "Well it's been nice meetin ya all. We have ta be goin now."

"Would you mind if we walked you home?" Paul asked Elsie, then glanced at Holly a little. Elsie said, "Well . . . ," then got to lookin at Holly. She was sittin quietly, then seemed to shake a little when Elsie said, "They goin ta walk us home."

The old road seemed silent and peaceful under the full-faced spring moon. Paul and Elsie walked up the road a bit, hand in hand. A little ways back, Holly and Roland followed. Holly walked slowly with her arms folded in front of her, every few steps or so she'd look off into the darkness along the side of the road. Roland had started talkin, tellin Holly about Johnstown and what it was like. He asked Holly if she had ever been to Pennsylvania, she said, "No." Roland was sayin somethin, stopped talkin about what he was sayin and asked, "How old are you?"

Holly took a few steps, then says, "Um twenty."

"You're just twenty?"

"Yeah."

"When's your birthday?"

"It's in December."

"Oh, what day?"

Holly sighs, takes a few steps, then says, "It come on Christmas Day."

"Christmas?"

"Yeah."

"You're a Christmas baby?"

"Ah was, Ah ain't now. How old are ya?"

"Twenty-five."

"Oh."

"Do you have a boyfriend?"

Holly walked quietly, put her head down and listened to the soft sounds of her footsteps. Roland asked again, "Well, do you?"

A faint no lingered with the sounds of the footsteps.

"You must have some guy that's crazy about you, somewhere?"

Holly sighed and just kept walkin.

"You're not married, are you?"

"No," Holly's sayin, sighs, takes a few steps and says, "He was . . . he . . . Ah was engaged but . . . He was in the Pacific . . . He died just fore Christmas."

Roland is quiet now, his walk slows, he utters, "I'm sorry. Was he a marine?"

"No . . . He was in the navy, he was on the *Bunker Hill* when it got hit wit a bomb or somethin. . . . He . . ." Holly's words slow, then just become a breath.

The old road has come to Elsie's house, Elsie and Paul kiss in the light of the full-faced moon. When Holly and Roland near, they stop. Holly says to Roland, "Well, Um goin on home now. It was nice meetin ya." Then she turns to Elsie sayin, "Ya comin down tomorrow?"

Elsie says, "Yeah."

Roland calls, "Holly, where do you live? Can I walk you home?"

"Ah just live down the road some," Holly says, gives Roland a smile, then turns and starts down the road.

Roland hurries and catches up with Holly, he sighs and asks, "What's wrong?"

Holly keeps walkin, says, "Nothin's wrong."

"Can I walk you home?"

"Ah just live down there some."

"Well, I'll walk you down. Do you walk down here alone all the time?"

"Yeah, ain't nothin down here 'cept my house and the Back Land."

"What's in the Back Land?" Roland smiled some and asked.

"Nothin. Coloreds live out there but they don't be botherin nobody. Only see em in the daytime, they live on the other side of the creek down there."

"It's a little dark, I mean for you to be walking home alone like this. Aren't you scared?" Roland's sayin and lettin a little laugh follow his words.

Holly smiles a little and says, "Of what, the boogie man or somethin?"

"I'd really like to see you again."

A couple of steps go into the night, then Holly's words follow. "Ah don't know, ya nice and all but Ah don't know. It might not be the right thing ta do and all."

Roland sighs, looks down into the darkness of the old road, then he walks and talks but keeps lookin down. "What isn't right?" he sayin. "What wouldn't be right, huh? What's right with anything anyway? I didn't tell you, Holly, and it might not make a difference on how you feel, but it makes a difference on how I think about things. I was with the marines in the Pacific. I'm a corpsman, that's like a medic. I've seen it all, had so much death in my hands to last forever. I was at Tarawa, then a few other godforsaken hell holes, then came Iwo. I don't care anymore, I mean I don't care about a lot of things I used to care about. The only thing I want out of life, now, is to just settle down someplace, find someone and just settle down. I want to live, it may sound silly but I want to plant flowers, I want to watch them grow. I don't ever want to see anything die, ever again. It's not like I've known you all my life, I just want to get to know you. You're pretty but it's not just your face, it's a feeling I get when I look at you. That's why I want to see you again."

Roland became quiet, then whispered, "I'm sorry, I didn't mean to say all that."

The only sound the night gave now were the soft sounds of footsteps. Holly walked with her head down and Roland would glance at her, sigh and look away. Holly slowed and lifted her head a little, then said, "Ah live down there."

Roland looked and could barely see the house, sittin down from and off the road, for the darkness. When he looked back at Holly, she turned her face from him and looked down the road.

"Holly," Roland says softly.

"Thanks for walkin me all the way out here," Holly says but keeps starin down the road to where the night is darker. The light from the full-faced moon doesn't shine and the sky over the Back Land stays black.

"Holly, I'll be back and I want to see you."

"Ah don't know . . . Ah don't know," Holly sayin, then sighin.

Roland says, "Well if I just happen to come by, will you shoot me?"

When Holly turns from the road, she has a smile on her face. She looks at Roland and says, "No, Ah ain't goin ta shoot ya, Ah ain't got no gun."

"Then I can come by?"

"Ah ain't said that."

"But you said you wouldn't shoot me."

"Ah said Ah ain't got no gun."

"But you said you wouldn't shoot me, anyway."

Holly's smile gets a little bigger as she says, "Ah might go git one, my daddy got one."

Little sounds of soft laughter wiggle around in the dark, until Roland leans to Holly and kisses her on the cheek, then whispers in her ear, "I'll be back."

Holly lowers her eyes, stares down where there ain't nothin to look at. Roland turns and starts back up the road, stops, spins around, waves and yells, "I'll be back, Holly."

Holly has looked up, she watches Roland seep into the dark of the road, then she turns and starts down the path. She slows, looks off to where the light from the moon does not shine.

12

It was the third week of April, nineteen forty-five, and for a day or so everything and everybody in Supply seemed to stop. Anything that did move, had to move, did so slowly. President Franklin D. Roosevelt had died. Some folks didn't know what to do, didn't know what was goin to happen next. Town folks that had the electric line sat around for days and listened to the radio, some of them kept a handkerchief up to their eyes. Coloreds out in the fields kept turnin that dirt over and pattin on it hard, kept singin sad songs all day too.

Ginger got to listenin to the radio again but still couldn't sit next to it. She still had to have that space between her and it, she'd stay out in the kitchen but she could still hear the radio. In her mind, she could see what the voice on the radio was tellin her about. She could see the horse-drawn caisson bein pulled up a street. Sometimes she could hear, thought she heard the hoofbeats of the horses, the solemn drumbeat had already passed. She would sigh, grab a dish or pan, wash it or put it away. Then she'd hear the scratchy voice again and listen for the sound of Holly's footsteps comin up onto the porch.

April had brought its ways, most things that happened when springtime came happened again. Rains came, pretty-colored flowers were bloomin, warm days cooled at eve. But spring did not bring the changes Ginger was waitin on to come. It did not bring Holly back to herself, bring that life back into her that Billy's death seemed to take away. Ginger listened for Holly's footsteps comin up on the porch and tried not to hear them things in her mind she was wantin to say, sometimes scream. "Where ya been at all day? . . . Ya been down that creek again? . . . Ya got ta come out of it . . . Spendin all that time by ya self ain't good for ya. . . . Ain't no good at all . . ."

Ginger kept herself busy as the supper hour neared. She was at the sink when she heard the footsteps comin up the porch steps. She waited for Holly to come through the hallway, then into the kitchen, but did not turn to her.

"Hi, Mama," Holly's sayin, "ya still listen ta that? That's the longest funeral Ah ever heard of."

Ginger got to stirrin somethin in a pot, she had a big spoon that kept on makin that scrapin sound against the bottom of the pot. She kept stirrin but looked over her shoulder a little and asked, "Were ya down Elsie's, honey?"

"No, Mama," Holly says real fast, then asks, "How long they goin ta keep all that sad music playin?"

"It ought ta be over soon, Ah guess," Ginger says softly, then gently asks, "Where ya been all day?"

Holly gets to peekin in the icebox and sayin over her shoulder, "Ah was just out walkin, Mama, that's all. What we havin?"

"Um fixin that beef stew."

"Oh," Holly says, then closes the icebox.

"Ya hungry?" Ginger asks but only hears the quick sounds of Holly's footsteps leavin the kitchen.

Ginger swirls the big spoon around in the pot, makes it go faster, then slows her stirrin and lets the spoon rest on the edge of the pot. She lowers her head and tries to find some rest for her soul.

Suppertime came and Ginger called Jason, told him to go get his sister and brother. Jason went hollerin for Bobby and Holly to come eat, then he got to the table first. Holly came down from upstairs, she had washed, changed into a light-colored dress and combed her hair. She came into the kitchen with a smile on her face, in a few minutes Bobby came in quietly. He could get a gentleness about his face, smiles had not come yet.

After the silence that followed Ginger's grace, Holly got to talkin to Bobby. He wouldn't say things back, just nod sometimes, but Holly would talk to him anyway. Sometimes she'd say things for him so he wouldn't have to talk if he didn't want to. "Ya want some of Mama's stew?" Holly was askin her brother as she began to fix her plate, then she'd fix his plate, ask him if that was enough. "Ya should have saw what Ah saw," she gets to tellin him now, "Ya know where that big old rock sticks out the creek and all? Ya know where ya caught that big old snappin turtle, ya member? Ah saw the biggest, fattest water snake layin up on it. Ya should have seen that thing, it was just layin there. It wasn't curled up or nothin, it was all stretched out real long. Ya would have tried ta catch that thing, wouldn't ya have? It was lookin like it just ate somethin real big, its belly was all fat and lopsided-lookin. Ya goin down there and do that fishin again? It be nice enough for it now."

Supper would end, days would darken, begin again.

Beyond where the old road came to the Hill's yard path, it became a meandering road. It curved through the shadows of the roadside trees, then sloped and wound down to the old wooden rickety bridge. Beneath the bridge, the Velvet Creek flowed, beyond the bridge the Back Land lay. There wasn't much out there and what was out there hadn't changed much at all, old folks couldn't remember anything changin. Most of the coloreds lived out there on what folks called the Hump, which wasn't nothin more than a withered bare hill with a bunch of slanted shacks and shanties hangin off it. Chickens and bony-ribbed yard dogs scrounged for food, lived up under porches or wherever they could. Brown-faced children, bare-butt on them hot summer days, played in a maze of yard fences and slopin shacks. Some coloreds lived closer to the creek, had them their own plantin land, kept some mules for plowin and haulin.

Back Land coloreds had their own ways about things, didn't need no electric line to find out what was goin on anywhere. They seemed to have a way of knowin, knowin what town folks were doin, knowin which ones they could come around and which ones to stay away from. They could tell who town folks were from where they'd see them at. "Let's see, that's that little white childs live up there past the water. Gots that colored hair the rest of them do, she one of them children belongin ta Miss Ginger."

The Back Land had its own church and courthouse too. Primas Allen did the preachin and the judgin too. Told folks, "Ya better mend your wrong doins. Some of ya ain't fit ta enter your Father's house. Some of ya all ain't even fit ta tend his fields."

Back Land coloreds, even them ones that worked in town for the white folks, could keep to themselves and Back Land ways. All of them knew Sam Fletcher shotgunned that Jimmy Lee Parker for tryin to come around that woman of his, Meta Mae. Sonny Hampton said he saw Sam Fletcher do it, said, "Sam done shot Jimmy Lee. Caught em up there wit Meta when he come home. Ah heard Sam yellin, Ah look, Ah see Jimmy Lee runnin out of there but he ain't run that far fore that shot git em and knock em up in that bush there by Sam's. Then Sam gits him and hauls him off, ain't nobodies goin ta find what Sam dids wit him."

As far as Back Land folks thought, Jimmy Lee Parker got what he went up there askin for. Didn't need that Sheriff LeRoy comin down there for nothin. Town folks wouldn't miss Jimmy Lee Parker anyway, didn't know him from any of them other field-pickin coloreds. If one was missin, they figured he just scooted on up north on one of them late-night freights. Meta Mae was the only one to miss Jimmy Lee.

The Velvet Creek flowed from the north, folks say it came from as far as them mountains in Virginia. When it got to Supply, it cut through the Back Land, then circled east and ran through the fields south of town.

Just before the old rickety bridge, the fat-bellied oak tree sat down near the water's edge. There was a little worn path that went from the road down to the creek. The path would wind down through the high weeds, then dip beneath low-hangin branches until it reached the grassy clearin where the fat-bellied oak sat.

Holly came into the clearin, smiled, took a deep breath. She took a look around, let her eyes wander with the ease of the breeze comin from the creek. She took a quick peek at the dark shade lurkin under the old rickety bridge, then she turned to the fat-bellied oak. She stared for a moment, then turned away.

The waters of the creek ran swiftly, bouncin and splashin over water stones in the midday sun. Its sound was soothin, always soothin. Holly threw her head back, flicked the hair out of her eyes and let her face show a full smile. A moment passed before she took graceful steps to the water's edge, then she walked downstream.

There was a place where the creek widened and seemed to spill over its banks. The water was shallow and flowed gently, almost without ripplin. On the other side of the creek, tall grass sprinkled with pretty-colored flowers covered the face of a small hill. Little trees, still in bloom, scattered themselves amidst the tall grass and flowers.

Holly had her place to sit, a big turtle-like rock that bulged out from the water's edge. She'd take her shoes off, tiptoe through the soft mud until she reached the turtle rock. A couple scoots and she'd be up and sittin on its back. She would sit and watch the water go by, maybe see some water bug buzzin, watch it, stare at it until it wasn't there no more. Sometimes she'd keep starin until nothin was there, until nothin never changed.

Ginger flinched when she heard the footsteps comin up on the porch, then sighed when she heard Elsie callin. She turned and yelled from the kitchen, "Come on in, Elsie."

Elsie came on in callin for Holly and yellin into the kitchen, "Hi, Miss Hill, Holly here, she upstairs?"

Ginger yelled back from the kitchen, "Come on in, Elsie. She ain't here, Ah thought ya were her comin back here now. She ought ta be back here soon, seein it's gettin late. Come on in, sit a while, she ought ta be comin in here soon."

Elsie came into the kitchen askin, "Where she at?"

Ginger sighed and just shook her head.

Elsie sat down at the table and got to sayin, "Ah just come down ta see how she doin and all. She ain't been up since the day fore yestaday. She said she was comin up yestaday."

Ginger was at the pantry gettin supper ready, she turned and went to the stove and asked Elsie, "Ya want some coffee?"

Elsie said she'd take a cup, then told Ginger, "Mama say ta tell ya hello."

"Ya tell ya mama Ah said hello."

"Where she at, Miss Hill? Is she . . ." Elsie let her words end in a sigh, then looked down at the table.

Quickly, Ginger said, "She ought ta be back soon."

Elsie blurts out, "Roland really likes her."

Ginger smiles and says, "He's a real nice boy. When he comes here, he goes on up and sits wit Bobby some. Him bein like a marine and all, bein over there too. Ya can tell Bobby likes him. Ah wish Holly would pay him some mind. He's such a nice boy."

Elsie says, "He likes her a lot. He wants ta take her places, too. Ya know, like the picture show. He even wants ta take her ta one of them nice dinner places and all. He tells me, he always askin her but she always sayin she don't want ta."

Ginger comes over and sits at the table, starts sippin on her coffee tellin Elsie, "This war ain't done nobody any good. Just seem like it ain't never goin ta end. Now, the president done died, God only knows what's goin ta happen now. Them boys still over there fightin, seems like it ain't goin ta end. Um so thankful Bobby back here, Ah just pray them other boys come back home. Miss Bruce say she ain't heard from her Charles in weeks again. She gets so worried, seein how we done lost so many boys just out the ones we got. Ah thank God every day that Bobby come home. Ah hope this boy Roland ain't got ta go back. He seem like he real good for Holly, seem like just what she need. Don't seem ta have that runnin around in him. Poor thing, he just come here as faithful as ya could git. Jason thinks he come here just ta see him, Ah got ta pull him away from that boy every time he come here. Jason would sit right up between him and Holly if Ah didn't make him go on and go somewhere."

It had been the Sunday after Holly met Roland, it was midafternoon that day when Ginger was sittin on the porch and Roland come down the road. She watched him come with his sailor suit on and got to smilin a little as he came down the path. She gave him a nice welcome but still wasn't sure what he was wantin. He stood at the foot of the steps, got a little smile on his face and said, "You must be Holly's mother? My name is Roland Shreck, I've come to see Holly. I was in town and I just figured I'd come out, I hope it's all right, Mrs. Hill? Is she home?"

Ginger had taken a good look into Roland's face, a quick stare into his eyes, then told him, "Why don't ya come on up and have a seat. She's upstairs, ya just have a seat here while Ah go in and tell her ya here."

"Who?" Holly had wanted to know, then wanted to know, "What's he doin here?"

It was quiet in the kitchen now, Ginger was drinkin her coffee and Elsie sat silently not wantin to say things she was thinkin and not wantin to keep sayin things she wasn't thinkin about at all.

"Here she come, Miss Hill," Elsie blurted out when she heard Holly comin up onto the porch. Ginger had put her head down and kept it down when Holly came into the kitchen sayin, "Um home, Mama." Then when she saw Elsie, she said, "Ah was comin up ta see ya. What ya doin down here? Ah was just thinkin about ya, how long ya been sittin here?"

"Ain't been long. Where ya been?"

"Just out, that's all."

"Ah thought ya were comin up yestaday?"

"Ah was, then Ah forgot."

"Ya goin wit us tomorrow?"

"Ah said Ah was," Holly says, pouts and sits down.

Elsie tells her, "Well Ah just wanted ta make sure. Paul says they goin ta be down about seven. He says, they might have a surprise for us."

"Surprise?"

"Yeah, him and Roland got somethin. They sayin it's a surprise and all."

Holly smiled and sat quietly for a moment.

Elsie asked, "What ya wearin?"

"Ah don't know."

Ginger sat with her coffee cup in her hands but not lookin at Holly. Elsie kept talkin for a while, and when she was ready to leave, Holly said, "Ah go up wit ya some."

The sun was way past the Back Land, the old road was darkenin. Elsie was talkin quickly, askin Holly, "Ya think he really likes me? He say he do, he always tellin me things like that. Ah like him, Holly."

Holly walked silently.

Elsie kept talkin about Paul, sayin, "He says when the war is over, he thinkin about just stayin down here. He says it looks like it will be over soon, seein how they already fightin in Germany. He say them Germans ain't got a chance now. What ya gonna say if Roland ask ya, ya know?"

"Askin me what?" Holly wants to know.

"Ya know, askin ta marry ya."

"He ain't askin me that."

"Ah bet he do."

"He better not."

"Why not? Ya know he's goin ta be askin ya."

"Ah don't know him, Elsie. Ah mean, he just come by the house. He comes by and talks ta Bobby, too. That don't mean he goin ta be askin Bobby ta be marryin him."

"He likes ya a lot."

Holly throws her hands up and gets to poutin. "That don't mean nothin, Ah like him and all. He's real nice but why everybody wantin me ta be marryin him for? Ah don't even know him good or nothin. Mama actin like he comes from heaven or someplace. Always askin me when he comin down. Gits on my nerves, Ah mean he nice and all and he nice-lookin, too, but that ain't meanin Um goin ta marry him. That don't be meanin that at all."

Elsie walked quietly for a moment before askin, "Ya still thinkin about Billy?"

Holly's eyes twitched, she turned her head away from Elsie and looked off into the far dark fields. "No!" she shouted, then came to a sudden stop. "Um goin home," she said quickly.

Elsie said, "It just seems like, Ah mean ya still—"

Holly shouted into the sound of Elsie's voice, "Um goin home," then spun around and started down the road.

Elsie yelled out, "Ah just was askin ya, that's all."

Holly kept walkin and did not look back.

Elsie called out, "Ya still comin tomorrow?"

Holly kept walkin.

Elsie yelled, "What's wrong wit ya, huh? What's wrong, Holly?"

"Nothin. . . Nothin. . . Um just goin home, that's all," Holly shouted over her shoulder and kept walkin.

"Holly . . . Holly . . . ," Elsie called out and ran to catch up with Holly.

"Leave me alone. Um goin home, Ah don't want ta talk any-more!" Holly shouted when she heard Elsie's footsteps runnin after her.

Elsie caught up sayin, "Ya been actin so different. Ya just been, ya know since . . . since it happened. Ah mean Roland really likes ya. Ya ought—"

Holly butts in, shoutin, "Just leave me alone. Leave me be. Ah said Ah don't want ta talk no more. Um goin home, that's all. What's wrong wit that, huh? Um just goin home."

Elsie slows her steps and Holly keeps goin.

"Ah see ya tomorrow," Elsie calls out.

Holly keeps goin, she walks quickly, each step finds its way over and around the broken patched road. At her yard path, she slows, stops and takes deep breaths. She thinks of Elsie, can still hear her talkin and askin her stuff. Askin her about Roland, askin her about

Billy. She can hear Billy sayin things, too, she can see his face sayin them. He lookin at her and sayin, "Ya didn't wait on me, Holly, ya promised, ya promised."

She jerks her hands up and puts them over her ears, then she closes her eyes to the night.

13

May came to Supply and brought its bright-eyed way of lookin at things. Them old men that sat out in front of the courthouse said better days were comin, said, "That Hitler can't last much longer."

Folks started takin a likin to Harry S. Truman, sorta liked the way he just said things. Eugene Purvis said, "This Harry makes ya feel like he here talkin ta ya. Ah like him."

Elsie wasn't thinkin about Harry S. Truman, she was just waitin on Paul to give her a ring. She figured it ought to be any day, seein how he was always comin around and had told her he loved her a thousand times. Roland started showin up more often after he surprised Holly with that brand-new car he bought. He told Holly he'd teach her how to drive. Holly said, "Ah ain't drivin that big old thing." Then she asked him, "When?"

Roland would drop Paul off at Elsie's, then come up to Holly's. If she wasn't there, he'd just wait, maybe go up and sit with Bobby a while or talk with Ginger until Holly came home.

It was a Sunday afternoon and Holly was upstairs gettin dressed.

Roland had asked, "Let's go for a ride Sunday afternoon, just us?" Holly had said, "Well, all right."

Ginger called up the steps, "Holly, honey, Roland's here."

When Holly came down the steps and into the kitchen where Ginger sat with Roland, even Ginger smiled. She kept lookin at Holly with that smile, then said, "My, but ya look so pretty."

Holly took a look at Roland to see his expression, he just sat starin before he said, "You really look beautiful, you really do."

Holly had put her white dress on and had let her hair fall over her shoulders. She smiled at Roland and said, "Well we goin, or did ya just come ta see Mama?"

Holly liked Roland's new car and felt comfortable sittin in its big front seat. She would lean back and let her head rest on the back of the seat. Sometimes she'd look out the window, look at things far from the road and just feel the wind comin through a window. She asked, "Where on earth ya takin me?"

Roland had turned north on the highway and headed toward Wilmington, then Holly had seen the signs for Wilmington flash by the window and Roland kept drivin. "I told you, you'll see," he said, then smiled.

Holly giggled a little and asked, "Ya ain't kidnappin me, are ya?"

"Maybe."

"My mama would come and git me."

"Your mama said I could have you."

"No, she ain't said that," Holly says, turns her face to the window, then says over her shoulder, "Where we at, where we goin? Wilmington's way back there. Ya ain't takin me ta no Pennsylvania."

Roland laughs and says, "Hadn't thought about that..That's not a bad idea."

"Ya better not," Holly says, then smiles and giggles.

Roland turned the car off the highway and onto a road that wound through marshy lands. Big gloomy trees stood in the stillness of quiet waters. The air that seemed to hover over the land had its own scent. But it was the silence of the water land that seeped into the car and brought its stillness. Holly was silent and had been starin out the window for a while. Roland was surprised when she turned from the window and asked, "What's all them ribbons for? Ya got some just like Bobby."

Roland was quiet for a moment but had glanced down at his chest enough to get a glimpse of the blur of colors on his white uniform, then he spoke quickly. "They're just what they give you. You get them for where you were and stuff like that."

Softly, Holly asked, "Ya got hurt, didn't ya?"

"How did you know? Did Paul tell you?" Roland asked.

"No, he ain't said nothin."

"Then how did you know? Did Bobby talk about it?"

"No, Bobby don't say nothin about all that. He did one night when he first come home. It was rainin real hard and all, a lot of thunder and lightning come too. It must have scared him or somethin. He went hollerin and runnin outside in all that rain. That's the only time he talked about it. He didn't say nothin then but ya could tell he was thinkin about it. Kept callin for a Sarge or somebody but he ain't said nothin about ya. But ya got one of them Purple Heart ribbons too. That purple one ya got wit a star or somethin on it. Mama said ya had it, she said she saw it the first day ya come by. Said, it was just like Bobby's. She got his in her drawer. She said Bobby didn't even want ta look at it. Ya got hurt too, didn't ya?"

"It wasn't that bad. I got hit a few times but it wasn't that bad. Not as bad as some guys got it."

"Where the bullet hit ya at?" Holly's askin.

"Why?"

"Ah just want ta know, that's all."

"I got hit in the legs, then they got me in the back."

Holly sighed and Roland started to talkin about somethin else, anything else to change the taste of his thoughts to that of a sweeter time. Then he got to glancin over to Holly and when he could, he kept his eyes on her instead of the road. Holly had leaned back in her seat, her blue eyes were soft in the shade of the car.

Roland is sayin, "We're almost there."

Holly leans up in her seat and looks out the front window, sayin, "Where? Ah don't see nothin. Where ya got me at?"

"It's up there."

Holly sees the bright sky and then the white sandy ground, then all the sea came to view. She smiles and says, "That's the ocean. This some kind of beach or somethin. What ya bring me up here for? Ah can't be goin on no beach."

"I thought you would like it."

Holly's still smilin but tryin not to as she's tellin Roland, "Ah done wore these heels. How come ya ain't told me we comin here? Ah know ya ain't thinkin Um goin swimmin in some ocean water."

Roland parked the car, got out and opened Holly's door for her. When she got out, her heels sank into the sand. She stood there lookin at Roland with a half smile and a half-twisted funny face, then says, "How Um goin ta walk in this, huh?"

Roland smiles, says, "Take em off."

"Take what off?"

"Your shoes."

"Ah got stockins on."

"Take them off too."

"What?"

"You can take them off too. Go ahead, do it in the car."

Holly stood beside the car lookin at Roland, then rolled her eyes to the sky. Roland laughed a little, then went to the trunk, got a blanket and picnic basket out. Holly got back in the car and took her shoes off, then pulled her stockins off. When she got out, she saw Roland with the basket and blanket. She stared a little, smiled, then asked, "What's all that for?"

"It's a surprise, everything for a picnic."

Holly stood barefoot and holding her shoes in her hand. The sea brought a breeze to her face and she smiled. Roland took her by the hand and started walkin toward the beach. It was the way he wanted it to be, the bright sky and rollin sea. He stopped and spread the blanket out on the sand and sat down but Holly stood and looked out over the ocean. Waves came in, then went back out again and when they did her thoughts wanted to go too. She flung a quick look over her shoulder, asked, "Were ya way out there?" then just as quick, looked back out across the water.

Roland sighed a little, said, "A couple times."

Holly didn't turn, just asked, "What's it like?"

"Sometimes it's pretty."

Holly stood silent on the sand.

Roland called, "Come on and sit down."

When Holly turned, she had a smile on her face. She came to the blanket, stood lookin down at Roland and just stared for a moment. He was lookin up at her and reached for her hand, she let him take it and ease her to him. Holly sat on the blanket, the smile still on her face, and now the sun was warm. She pulled her dress up a little and let the breeze from the sea cool her legs, it was a soothin feelin.

"You hungry?" Roland was askin.

Holly shook her head no.

A moment passed, then Roland pulled out a bottle of wine from the basket and told Holly, "Let's celebrate."

Holly turned, saw the wine, then asked, "Celebrate what?"

"Oh, I don't know. Let's just celebrate being here, you know, just being here. I have an idea. Let's celebrate you. We'll celebrate you," Roland said as he caught the moment to look in Holly's eyes.

Holly looked away, sayin, "Ah don't want ta be celebrated."

"Okay, well let's celebrate today. It's a good day to celebrate."

Holly turned and looked into Roland's eyes, then quickly looked away again but had asked, "Why ya want ta be celebratin for?"

Roland opened the bottle and poured two glasses of wine and gave Holly one. She just held it for a while, stared through the glass at it. Seen its little sparklin bubbles around the edges of the glass, then looked out to sea and watched the waves hittin the beach. She took a sip, then held the glass again, lookin into it. She asked Roland, "Didn't ya have a girlfriend up there in Pennsylvania? Ya know, fore ya went away and all, didn't ya have a girlfriend?"

Roland was quiet.

Holly turned to him, asked again, "Didn't ya have a girlfriend up there?"

"Yeah, but . . . things just didn't work out after the war started. She's married now. She . . ." Roland let his words drift into a silence.

"Oh," Holly said, then sipped at her wine again and looked out to sea. She was silent for a while, still, even when she felt Roland's hand gently touchin her back. He did not see the smile on her face, but when she got up quickly from the blanket, he asked, "Where you going?"

"Ah want ta see how cold it is," Holly yelled over her shoulder as she started to the water's edge.

Roland stayed on the blanket and watched as Holly neared the water, then crept closer to the incomin waves. He smiled and laughed as he watched her slowly step toward the waves, try and dip her foot into the water, then quickly turn and run away from a rushin wave. The wave came on in again, splashin high, Holly's quick steps backward got her away from it again. Then she pulls the white skirt of her dress up high and eases her way toward the water again.

Roland is laughin, shouts, "Go on in."

Holly turns, gets to shoutin back, "Ah ain't goin in there."

A quick wind rushes through Holly's hair, then a wave splashes her back and gushes through her legs. She spins around and kicks at the wave as it rolls back to sea.

Roland's laughin and yellin. "You might as well go on in now."

Holly turns and comes back to the blanket. Her dress is soakin wet and clingin to her legs, wet sand is stickin to her feet. She sees Roland lookin at her and hears him laughin. She tries not to smile but does, then gets to kickin sand at Roland when she nears him.

Holly sat on the blanket but stared out at the sea, watched its waves rush to shore, then burst into white foamy bubbles. She would take a few sips of the wine, then stare back out to sea.

Roland whispers, "Holly."

Holly keeps her silence.

"Holly," Roland whispers again, sits up next to her. He puts his arm around her and waits, pulls for her to lean to him. "Holly . . . Holly," Roland whispers again.

Holly can feel Roland's breath gettin closer to her neck, then it's his lips on her cheek.

"What's wrong?" Roland is askin as Holly pushes him away.

"Nothin, nothin," Holly's sayin and starin at the sea again.

Roland looks down at the sand pebbles lyin on the blanket. He sits quietly, then asks, "What's wrong, Holly? What did I do, huh? I just want to be with you."

"Ya ain't did nothin, Roland," Holly says, sighs and looks down at the sand, then tells Roland, "It ain't ya. Maybe Ah shouldn't have come up here wit yea. Ah mean, Ah wanted to and all but . . ."

"But what?"

"Ah don't know."

"What am I supposed to do? I really care about you, you know that but you won't let me touch you. What is it?"

Holly sits quietly, looks from the sand to the sea.

"Damn it," Roland mutters but Holly stays in her silence and stare.

Roland sighs, then asks, "Do you want to go? Do you want me to take you home? Is that it, huh?"

"Ah don't know." Holly jumps to her feet and starts walkin down to the sea.

Roland calls, "Where ya goin?"

"Nowhere, just down here, that's all," Holly yells over her shoulder and keeps walkin.

Holly slows and stands still at the water's edge. The waves come in and roll at her feet, the wind blows in her face, tosses her hair across her eyes but she keeps starin out to sea. She can hear Roland callin her name, then she can feel him nearing. She doesn't have to turn, it is his touch pullin at her she feels. She keeps her eyes on the water, its surgin swells and sways. Without turnin to Roland, she asks, "What happens when they put ya in there?"

Roland's eyes widen a little, he stares at Holly, then asks, "Huh?"

"What happens when they put ya in there? How do they do it, they just let ya go ta the bottom? Ah mean, do they know where they put ya? Is there like a special place out there, or they just put ya wherever the boat is?"

"Huh, what do you mean?" Roland asks and looks out to the sea.

"When ya die, what do they do wit ya out there?"

Quietly, Roland sighs and looks down at the incomin waves, he doesn't say anything. Except for the sound of the sea, it is silent until Holly asks, "How come they can't bring ya back? How come they have ta put ya out there where nobody knows where ya at and all? Can't even put a flower or somethin."

Roland stands silently but Holly turns from the sea and walks back up the beach to the blanket, then sits. When Roland gets back, sits, Holly whispers, "Ah think we better go."

"It's Billy, isn't it?" Roland asks.

Holly is quiet.

"It's Billy, isn't it?"

"It's a lot of things," Holly says so softly the breeze from the sea almost carries her words away.

Roland reaches down, grabs a handful of sand, holds it, then watches it fall through his fingers. "How long has it been?" he's askin.

Holly doesn't say.

Roland keeps lookin down at the sand that has fallen from his hand, he is silent for a moment, then says, "I thought it was over with you and Billy. Elsie said you had broken off the engagement. Said you weren't sure you wanted to marry him. What happened?"

Quickly, Holly's sayin, "Ah don't want ta talk about it."

"Did you still love him?"

"Ah don't want ta talk about it, ya hear."

"Elsie said you used to go out a lot but after Billy got it, I mean after he died, you . . ."

Holly throws her hands up, gets to shakin them and shoutin, "Ah don't want ta talk about it, ya hear me? Ah want ta go now, are ya goin ta take me home?"

The ride back to Supply was quiet. Roland didn't say much, he tried to talk about different things. He told Holly about some new guy in his outfit that was from his hometown. Said he knew the guy from high school, they played baseball together. Said he had told the guy all about Holly and said the guy wanted to meet her. Holly sat quietly and just looked out the window.

When the car pulled into Supply, it brought the silence from the road. Supply streets and folks seemed to become a part of the quietness in Holly's eyes. The sun had lost its afternoon glare and was just shinin lazily. The old road seemed to be asleep, just lyin there and not payin the car any mind as it rolled over it. When Roland reached Elsie's house, he slowed the car down, stopped. Elsie and Paul were sittin on the porch, Roland yelled to Paul that he would be back in a bit. Elsie waved from the porch and Holly waved back but didn't yell anything.

At Holly's house, Roland pulled the car off the road by the path, turned the engine off. He sat quietly, rubbed his fingers over the steerin wheel. In the same breath with a sigh, Holly whispers, "Um sorry, Roland."

Roland looked at Holly and asked her what she was sorry about. She put her head down and uttered, "Ya know."

Roland whispered, "Holly . . . Holly, I . . . You know I love you. I haven't said it before. . . . I guess I wanted to wait for the right time. . . . But . . . I guess it's the right time now. . . . I know you're not over Billy . . . but he's . . . He's not comin back, Holly. . . . You have to realize that." Roland stopped whisperin, took a deep breath and looked out the window, then turned and tried to see Holly's eyes. He couldn't see them, her head was hung too low.

"Ah know Billy's dead," Holly starts sayin, "but Ah don't feel it. Ah mean sometimes Ah do but it's not all the time. Sometimes it's like he still here and all. Sometimes it's like Ah ain't here, like there's just some old shell of me or somethin. Ah like ya, Ah think you're real nice but Ah can't feel nothin sometime. Ah want to, like Ah really wanted ya ta kiss me back there. Then it's like Um not there, like Um floatin up in the air or somethin and ya know like

lookin down and seein me. But not bein in me and all. Then sometimes, Ah think Billy might not be dead, ya know, somebody done
made a mistake and all. Like maybe sent his daddy the wrong thing
or somethin. Maybe Um just waitin, Ah mean, Ah know he ain't
comin but maybe Um waitin case he do. But Ah don't know he
ain't comin. Ah know Um goin ta love him, even if he don't come.
But Ah told him Ah was goin ta wait, Ah didn't all the way. But Ah
can still . . . Ah mean, maybe he's still comin. If he don't come, Ah
still want ta git married and have kids and stuff. Ya know what
Ah really want ta do? Ah want ta go far away, be by myself, maybe
up some mountain or somethin, somethin like that. Ah don't want
ta stay forever or anythin like that, Ah just want ta go real far away
for a while. Ah go down the creek, it's quiet there. Me and Billy, we
used ta go down there a lot. There's a big tree down there where
we used ta sit. That's where he asked me ta marry him and all. Ah
don't sit by the tree no more. Ah don't think it's right me sittin
there but Ah go by it some. There's a big rock Ah sit on, it's further
down. Ah think a lot down there, then sometimes Ah ain't got ta
think at all. Ah mean, like there ain't nothin in the world ta be
thinkin about. Nothin, no crazy war and all. It's pretty down there,
it's real pretty. Ah just don't want anythin ta be what it is. Why
can't it be things it used ta be? Why everything happen and all?"

Roland didn't say anything and Holly was quiet for a while, then
she took a deep breath and opened the door of the car.

"Wait a minute," Roland said quickly.

Holly stilled.

"I said, I love you, I meant that."

Holly smiled a little.

"I'll be up next week."

Sunday came again and Holly thought Roland would come by.
Elsie had said Paul said they'd be up. It was late afternoon and Holly
was sittin on the porch. She had put her bright yellow dress on,
combed her hair so that it would hang softly over her shoulders. Roland never came.

14

June had come, then July. Folks that could tried to stay out the heat, keep that sun from burnin down on them. Folks didn't have as much to say to one another, kept that look on their faces that said it's too hot to be bothered. Chucky Bruce's mother didn't have a look on her face at all, it was blank, cold in the heat. Chester Higgens said, "Ah give the telegram to her and she ain't even opened it. Said she been knowin that boy of hers been dead, been knowin it for a while. She just went on back in the house, thanked me though for bringin it out."

Ginger didn't ask about Roland anymore, last time she asked was weeks ago. Holly had just shrugged her shoulders and said, "Ah don't know, Mama, Ah ain't seen him." Holly had started going back up Elsie's and would go down Ben's, sometimes up to Wilmington. Elsie never mentioned Billy and tried not to talk about Christmas either. Holly never talked about Billy at all, just kept his unopened letters and ring in that drawer of hers. Elsie used to talk about Paul, wondered what happened to him. He stopped comin to see her right after Roland stopped comin around, then she stopped talkin about him. The last time Holly had asked her about him, she said that she didn't know why he stopped comin by but wherever he was he could come back and kiss her butt.

It was a late afternoon, one of that kind that has a gentleness to it, even a slow breeze flutterin. Holly was sittin on the porch steps, just sittin and not wantin to think about anything. Ginger had been sittin for a while, hadn't said much either until she sighed a little, then said, "Well Ah guess Ah mise well get supper ready."

Holly stayed on the porch steps, sometimes she'd look down at the old cracks in the steps, then wonder why she was lookin at them. She got up, yelled over her shoulder that she was goin up Elsie's, then started up the path. When she reached the old road, she turned up, then slowed. It had been a while since she had been down the creek. She had got to goin back up Elsie's instead. She'd go up there and sit some like she used to. Sometimes she'd try to say something funny to Elsie, get Elsie to say something funny back so they could laugh.

Holly has stopped on the road and stands starin down at the ground. Slowly she turns and starts walkin back down the road. Where the old road curves, she slows in the shade, stops and thinks about turnin around and goin up to Elsie's. She stands there in the shade, just starin into the shadows. She has on her white polkadot dress. When she starts walkin down through the curve of the road again, the subtle swishin sound it makes with her stride follows her.

In the clearin where the fat-bellied oak sits, it is quiet. She walks softly through the clearing and down to the water's edge. Summer birds sing and dash through the air, land on a bush or limb, still themselves, then sing again. Holly's shoes are danglin from her hands, the soft mud is cool and soothin to her feet. Where the water isn't too deep, she tiptoes through its ripples until she reaches the big turtle rock. She crawls, scoots up on the rock and sits quietly until she flinches. Quickly, her hand comes to her face, brushes the hair from her eyes, but she keeps lookin into the shade beneath the trees on the side of the hill. "What's that nigger doin over there?" she mutters to herself. Her eyes get big and she keeps starin across the creek. She can see a dark figure sittin still beneath the shade of a small tree. She sees it move, then still itself again. Sometimes she'd see old colored men fishing, or children playin. But the dark figure beneath the tree does neither.

Holly keeps lookin, mutters again, "What's he doin?"

She inches up higher on the rock, watches until he looks at her. She sees his eyes, can feel them starin at her. Dark eyes that make her look down, look back into the water. Quickly, she peeks up, looks down again. A moment, then moments will not flow with the water, they still. Holly looks up again, she cannot see his eyes. His face is lowered behind somethin, looks like some kind of board and he got some kind of stick or somethin. She sees his eyes again, lookin right at her. She squinches up her face, stares back and mutters, "What ya lookin at?"

He stares.

Holly lets him stare, stares back, then slides down the rock and splashes through the shallow water, then up the water's edge. She don't look back because she knows he's lookin, can feel it.

Elsie was hanging clothes in the yard when she saw Holly comin down the path. Holly yelled ahead, "What ya doin?"

Elsie had a clothes pin in her mouth but still tried to yell back, "Holly Hill, what the Sam Hill it's lookin like, huh?"

Holly nears and weaves through the hangin clothes sayin, "Ah thought ya said ya were goin ta wait till Saturday."

Elsie makes a face, says, "Mama said Ah ain't get these things washed up and all, she sendin me ta China. Ah got tired of her fussin, she been fussin all day long about this, that and everything else."

"Oh."

"What ya been doin?" Elsie asks.

"Nothin, sittin on the porch, went for a walk and come up here, that's all. Ain't nothin else ta do anyhow."

Elsie didn't ask anything about Holly's walks, didn't ask and didn't want to know. She started talkin about somethin else, she had met this guy named Eddie. He was some kind of truck driver, drove one of them big trucks that would come down the lumberyard and haul off that lumber. He lived up near Norfolk, said he spent most his time on the road. Elsie liked him, met him down Ben's. When she got done hangin up the clothes, she kept talkin about Eddie. She was askin Holly somethin but Holly got to starin off toward the road. Elsie stopped talkin, then said, "Well, ya think Ah should go, huh, huh? Ya hear me?"

Holly turned back to Elsie, sayin, "Yeah."

"Yeah what?"

"Huh?"

Elsie picked up her clothes-washin basket, went on over to the steps. She put the basket down on the top step, then sat down beside it. Holly came over to the steps, said somethin that Elsie didn't hear, then sat down. Elsie muttered, "Huh?" Holly said, "Nothin."

Coloreds started headin down the road and Elsie got to talkin about Eddie again, askin Holly if she should go with him on that truck like he's been askin her to do. Holly kept lookin up to the road, watchin the coloreds go by. "What ya think, huh?" Elsie was askin.

Holly says, "Ah don't know, Elsie. If ya want to, Ah guess."

"He said sometimes he has to go up to Rocky Mount, then just turn around and come back. Said he wants me to go ridin wit him then."

Holly's still watchin the coloreds go by."

"Ya think Ah should go? He said it could be like a picnic and all."

Holly ain't sayin nothin.

Elsie asks, "Ya hearin me?"

Holly jerks her head away from the road, looks down at the ground and says to Elsie, "Yeah."

"Well?"

"Well what?" Holly asks.

"See, ya ain't listenin."

"Ah was thinkin about somethin, that's all."

"What?"

"Nothin."

"Well, what Ah do? Ah like him and Ah don't want ta be sittin around here till the moon fall down or somethin. Ya know, him not bein no sailor or in the army and all, him not bein able ta go, ain't like he goin ta be runnin off and all. He say he like it around here, said Ah might like it up in Norfolk. He said he ride me up if Ah ever want ta go."

Holly says, "Ya just meetin him and all, Ah wouldn't tell him nothin. Ya ain't sure he likes ya. Just cause he actin like he do don't mean he do, member that Paul."

Elsie looks out to the road, sighs a little and says, "Well what Ah do, huh? Ah can't be sittin around here the rest of my life, Ah be crazy fore Um twenty-one and that bein in October."

Holly gits a little smile, says, "Maybe we could git a job or somethin, git us some money and git out of here. Maybe go somewhere, meet some millionaire men. Ya want ta do that?"

Elsie makes a face, says real fast, "Where we goin ta git a job at, huh?"

Holly's still smilin, says, "We can ask Ben. We can ask him ta let us be waitresses. Maybe he let us do that."

"Ya crazy. Ah ain't bein down Ben's and bein no waitress."

"Well, ain't noplace else, less ya want ta git a job down the lumberyard. Ya think they let us work down there? We could cut wood." Holly's smile gets to be a giggle.

"Ah ain't cuttin no damn wood."

"Well, ya could marry Raymond, work at his cleanin shop."

Elsie giggles, says, "Holly Hill, ya can marry my ya know what."

A quiet moment came, Holly looked up toward the empty road, stared beyond its trees that stood on the other side. Elsie got to sayin somethin, talkin about bein tired of goin down Ben's. Holly looked down from where she was starin, sat quietly not seein whatever she was starin at. Elsie said somethin else but Holly butted in sayin, "Ah was down ta the creek taday, just fore Ah come up here. Ah saw this here nigger starin at me."

Real loud, Elsie said, "Huh?"

"He was on the other side. Ya know where that big rock is? Ah was sittin there. Ya know where the creek gits real wide and it ain't deep or nothin, that rock there. Ah saw him, he was on the other side up in them trees like there. He kept on lookin at me and all. He ain't try and say anything or nothin. He kept lookin, then he like look down like he was doin somethin."

Elsie got quiet.

Holly looked back up toward the road, then got to sayin, "He was just lookin, that's all. He ain't said nothin or nothin like that. Look like he had one of them paintin things, ya know them kind ya sit pictures on when ya goin ta draw somethin. Like ya see in the movies or somethin. He was lookin like that's what he was doin, ya know like drawin and all. Ah ain't never seen him down there at all."

Elsie looked up to the road, stared a little and said, "Ah ain't never heard of no paintin nigger before. What he look like?"

"Ah ain't seen him before. He young, maybe in his twenties, somethin like that. He look like, ya know, like he one of them kind that have that different color. Ya know how they can git, lookin like Indian or somethin, wit that real black hair. He ain't said nothin, he'd look and keep doin that fore he look back down. Ah started ta yell over there and ask him what he callin hisself doin and all. Ah could see his eyes when he be lookin. Ah looked back some."

"Ya see him leave?"

"No, he was still there when Ah come on up here."

"Oh," Elsie said.

Holly took a quick deep breath, saw the dark eyes in her mind, stared back again, then started talkin about somethin else, got to tellin Elsie about where they could go and get a job. Elsie was talkin, askin Holly somethin but Holly wasn't sayin anything back. Elsie turned to her, saw her just starin off somewhere.

It rained the next morning and Holly stayed in bed, just lay there enjoyin the cool breeze comin through the window. She had woken, then had slowly twisted and grabbed her pillow, then closed her eyes again. When she did open her eyes, she just held the pillow and stared at the dreary light comin through the window. Everything in the room seemed to be the color gray. Except for the distant barkin of some yard dog, it was a quiet morning. Holly slowly pushed the pillow away, rolled onto her side, then sat up on the side of the bed.

Ginger was sittin on the porch when Holly finally came down the stairs and poked her face out into the day. "Mornin, Mama," she muttered and came out onto the porch.

Ginger just nodded her head and sipped on her coffee. Holly came out on the porch, stood for a while stretchin and yawnin, then went on back in the house and fixed herself some breakfast. When she came back out, Ginger was still sittin and starin up at the road. Holly asked, "What's wrong, Mama?"

Ginger sat silently, then took a deep sigh and said, "Oh nothin, Ah was just thinkin about some things, that's all."

"About what, Mama?"

Ginger smiled and said, "It wasn't nothin. What ya goin ta do today?"

Holly said, "Nothin, Mama," then went and sat on the steps, looked out to the road. She was quiet for a while, then turned to her mother sayin, "Me and Elsie might try ta git a job or somethin. Maybe ask Ben if he let us be a waitress but Elsie say she don't want ta be a waitress there. Ah just want ta git some money, ya know, be able ta have some money. Be able ta go someplace and stuff like that."

Ginger smiled, asked, "Where ya want ta go?" Then she took a long breath and told Holly, "Things ain't the way they used ta be, world done changed. Folks doin things ta folks Ah ain't never heard of. Don't ya and Elsie be gittin no crazy notions in your minds about things ya hear. That grass ain't no greener and sometimes ain't no grass at all. Can fool ya, show ya things ya lookin for but ya ain't seein nothin but what's ya want ta see."

"Ain't nothin ta do around here, Mama."

"Somethin will come along, honey." Ginger's whisper seemed to float in the air, stay there as she got up and went into the house. Holly sat on the steps for a while and thought about places she ain't never seen, but it was only the road she saw.

"Mama, Um goin up Elsie's," Holly yelled over her shoulder, got up from the steps and started up the path. The old road to Elsie's was empty and stayed empty. Holly didn't go that way. The sky over the Back Land had the blue and soft yellow of sunlight again, the gray shadow of rain was passin on. Holly walked slowly, the old road seemed longer. It could seem that way sometimes, it could seem to stretch itself out, be a feelin that lingered beyond its thought.

The secret path was only a space through moments. The clearin beneath the fat-bellied oak, a breath, a sigh and silence. The water's edge was a gushin sound that filled the air. Holly took her shoes off, walked the way the water flowed. When she saw the turtle rock, she slowed and looked across the creek, then up into the tall grass where the trees start growin. He was there again, she could see him and he saw her.

Holly climbed up on the turtle rock, threw her head back to get the hair out of her face, then stared down at the water. It was runnin swift, carrying a breeze that fluttered through Holly's hair. She didn't feel the breeze, only the feelin of his eyes lookin at her. She sat quietly, stared at the water before she looked up and kept lookin at where he sat. She could see his black hair, his copper-colored skin. She wanted to see his eyes again but he lowered them from hers. Holly slid off the rock and walked the water's edge until she could see him clearly, then she shouted across the creek, "What ya doin over there, huh? Just what ya doin lookin at me for, huh?"

She saw him look up, stare for a moment before he lowered his eyes from hers again.

Holly put her hands on her hips and shouted, "Ya hear me? What ya doin, huh? What ya keep lookin at me for?"

She could see sticks holdin up some kind of big drawin board, she waited to see his eyes when he looked up but he kept his head down.

She lowered her voice a little, askin, "Ya paintin? Ya paintin somethin?"

The creek made its little ripplin sounds, some summer birds sang somewhere. Holly got tired of hearin things she wasn't listenin for and got to shoutin again, "Can't ya hear me? What's wrong wit ya, huh?" When she heard his voice, her eyes widened and she shouted, "Don't tell me ta shut up." Now she stills herself, just stares, waits to see his eyes. She sees them as the sound of his voice comes above the waters, he is tellin her, "I did not tell you to shut up, I merely asked you to stop shouting."

Holly's nose got all squiggled up, she pokes her chin out and shouts, "That's the same thing as tellin me ta shut up." Then she keeps lookin at him, he's lookin back but ain't sayin nothin. Holly's waitin on him to say somethin and when he just keeps lookin she shouts, "Ya paintin somethin? Ya a painter, huh? Ah ain't never seen ya before."

Holly waited for him to talk again but the only sound she hears is the rushin of the creek water, the only thing she sees is his eyes lowerin.

"Ya hear me talkin ta ya?"

"I can't hear anything else, except you."

"Then how come ya ain't answerin me?"

"I am trying to paint."

"What ya tryin ta paint, can Ah see?"

"No."

"How come?"

Holly stares, listens but he is silent again.

"Ya ain't no painter," she shouts and is about to spin around when she sees his face again, then his eyes. She stills and watches him look at her, then the sound of his voice comes across the creek. He has said, "All right," but it is only the tone of his voice she hears. She tries to see more of his face, his eyes, but he has lowered his head again.

The water was never deep where the creek widened but it is

flowin fast from the morning rain. Holly lifts her skirt some as she tiptoes into the water. Wherever she can, she steps on a stone, then tries to leap to another. She knows he is watchin, she can feel his eyes.

The water is cold, gives chills as it gushes over Holly's skin. The bed of the creek is soft, squishy, unsettlin to Holly's steps, she is careful. When she slips a little, she steadies herself and quickly glances up, then looks back down into the water. He was watching her, she knows he was. She lets her skirt fall when she reaches the other side of the creek, looks up into the tall grass on the slope of the hill. She cannot see him now but she knows where he is and begins weavin up through the grass.

In the small clearin where he sits, it is quiet, a soft silence seeps from it. She can see him now, she slows her steps but keeps lookin at him. His hair is black but now she can see its dark curls. The side of his face that she can see looks like a new penny, has that copperlike glow. Then it's the shirt she sees, stares at its faded green next, sees it dull next to his shiny skin. She cannot see his eyes, she looks for them but he keeps them lowered and away from her. She comes to his side and sees colors, misty colors, bright colors, colors that were just colors and colors that were the same color of her hair and that old white polkadot dress. She keeps lookin, smiles, shouts, "That's me. Is that me, huh? That's the big rock. Is that me? That don't look like me."

He is not lookin up and is silent.

"Is that me, huh?"

"It's a likeness, that's all," he says, but keeps his eyes down. His hand begins to move slowly, it reaches toward the painting. The brush he holds in his fingers gently dabs a color onto colors.

"That's me."

"It's a likeness."

"Then how come she got my dress on and have hair like mine?"

"I've told you, it's just a likeness."

"Ah don't care, it's still me, ain't it? Where ya from? Ya ain't soundin like ya from around here or nothin. Ya a painter or somethin? Why ya here paintin for?" Holly askin, looks at him, then stares and blurts out, "What happen ta . . . Ya don't have . . ." She catches her words but her thought stays in her eyes that have widened and still stare at the armless dull green shirtsleeve.

He is quiet and keeps paintin. He has felt Holly's stare and knows she has seen his empty dangling sleeve. He feels her sigh and hears her askin, "What's your name? Ya ain't from around here. Ya live out in the Back Land, huh? Ah ain't seen ya before. Ya don't live out there? Ya makin the sky and the creek real pretty and all. Ya a real painter?"

"My name is not important to you, shouldn't be."

"Ah just ask, that's all."

"Elias E. Owens."

"Eee . . . Eee . . . What?"

"Elias E. Owens."

"What's the E for?"

"It's the initial for my second name."

"Ah know that. What's it stand for? How come it's E, like ya first name is? Ah ain't never heard of that before," Holly's sayin, then waitin on him to say somethin back. He doesn't. She watches his hand move in the sky of the painting, watches the brush gently touch a cloud and swish into its whiteness. She smiles, says, "That's pretty. Ya still ain't say what the E for."

"It's Euritides."

"U-what . . . Urithusdies . . . Who name ya somethin like that?"

"My mother."

"How come you sound like some schoolteacher or somebody from the old-time days and all? Ya ain't from around here. Where ya from? Ya a real painter?"

"Why are you so concerned, you shouldn't be."

"Just askin ya."

"That depends on what you consider to be a real painter."

"Ya know, somebody that's a painter and gits lots of money for pictures they paint."

"No, I don't sell my work in galleries if that's what you're asking."

"How come ya can't talk like folks do around here. Ya ain't from here, are ya? What are ya doin down here anyway? Ya ain't said where ya from?"

"Why are you so concerned?"

"Um just askin ya. Ah ain't never seen no, ya know, somebody colored paintin and all, that's all. Ya a good painter, Ah like the picture. It look just like it do over there. Ya can see all the things in it, it's real good 'cept for me. Ah don't think that looks like me."

"It's simply a likeness."

"Ah can see that. But it looks like me but it ain't."

"It's just a likeness."

"What are ya goin ta do wit it when ya done paintin it?"

"I've not decided."

"Ya goin ta sell it?"

His silence has a stillness about it. Distant summer birds are singin, only Holly doesn't hear them, just him sayin, "Why are you concerned?"

"Um just askin. Why ya keep askin me why Um concerned and all?"

There is a silence that Holly hears, stands in when she sees him turnin to her, lookin up into her eyes. "What is your name?" he's askin, then lowerin his eyes from hers.

"Holly R. Hill," she says quickly, then gets to askin, "How come ya want ta know my name for?"

She sees a smile, a gentleness come to the side of his face that she can see until he takes it away. "Where ya from? Ya ain't said that yet," she says, waits for him to look up again. He doesn't but says, "If you must know, Washington, D.C."

"What ya doin down here for?"

"Trying to find a quiet place to paint."

"Ya come all the way down here just ta paint the creek? Ya just picked this old creek ta paint, come all the way down here ta do it? Ya ever see that Harry Truman up there?"

"No."

"Ya colored? Ya don't look like a nig . . . Ah mean ya just don't look colored all the way."

"Are you asking if I am a Negro?"

"Are ya?"

"Am I what?"

"Are you colored?"

"No."

"Oh, what are ya then?"

"Negro."

"That's bein colored."

"It's Negro."

"All right, ya a colored Negro. Ya don't look all colored, don't talk like it either."

"Well, I'm not trying to talk now, I'm trying to paint."

"Ah ain't never met nobody like ya, ya know, a painter and all. And stop tryin ta hush me away."

Elias slows his stroke, the paintbrush hangs loosely from his fingers. His dark eyes look up and Holly knows they are smilin at her, then they lower again.

"What ya look at me like that for?"

"Do you like flowers?"

"What?"

"Do you like flowers? They are pretty, quiet. They don't ask questions."

"What ya tryin ta say, huh?"

"It was just a thought. How old are you?"

"Um twenty. How come ya askin that for? If Ah ask ya somethin, ya say it ain't why Um concerned and all, which ain't nothin but some nice way of sayin it ain't my business. Ya get all talkin down the nose at me, sound like some schoolteacher or somethin. Ah was just askin ya things, that's all. Ah think ya a good painter, Ah like the picture 'cept for me. Then ya say it's just a likeness, Ah know it's me. Ain't nobody ever painted a picture of me. Ah like the picture, Ah just don't like how Ah look in it, that's all. Ah ask ya somethin, ya can't answer witout bein all smart about what ya say back. Ah was just askin things, that's all. Ya don't look all colored, that don't mean ya ain't. Ya know Tessie? She used ta live over here, she live over on the Hump, we used ta play when we were kids and all. We'd play right down there, right where ya paintin the picture of. How old are ya? Ya git hurt in the war? Is that what happen ta ya arm? My brother Bobby, he got shot a bunch of times. He don't talk much at all, he just stay up in his room. Is that what happen ta your arm? Ah was goin ta get . . . His name was Billy . . . He . . . He died and they buried him at sea. Ya goin ta live here now, or ya goin back up ta Washington, D.C., when ya gits done wit the picture?"

A breeze blew that carried a chill; Holly shivered. She lowered her eyes to the ground, then looked back across the creek. She was quiet and kept starin off, then quickly she turned, said, "Ah ought not be talkin ta ya, ya bein colored and all." She waited for him to look up but he just kept his head lowered, kept paintin and said, "Maybe you should go."

"Well, Ah ought be goin."

"I think that would be a good idea."

Holly puffed up her cheeks, put her hands on her hips and said, "Ya just can't be nice can ya? Ah mean, ya ain't mean but ya just can't say somethin nice. Ah ain't done nothin ta ya."

"What does the *R* stand for?"

"Huh?"

Elias looked up, stared and asked again, "What does the *R* stand for? What is your middle name?"

"It's Rachelle . . . Holly Rachelle Hill. How come ya ask that?"

"I just wanted to know."

"Why?"

"It's not important."

"If ya say it, it means somethin, just like when ya askin about flowers. Sayin they pretty and quiet and all."

"I think you better go now, you're on the wrong side of the creek."

Elias didn't look up but Holly kept lookin down, waitin on him to, then she turned when he didn't. The tall grass had his face in it, his face had his eyes, then the grass was just tall and green but the water in the creek had his eyes in it too. Holly was halfway across, carefully steppin, holdin her skirt above her knees and the splashin water when she stopped. She turned, looked back up into the hill, squinted her eyes until she could see him, waited until she knew he was lookin and yelled, "Hey Elias . . . flowers . . . flowers have things they want ta say too. And if they could talk, it wouldn't be some stinkin noise or nothin, they'd say real nice things."

The cold water kept runnin swift, splashin some where Holly was steppin out of it. She let go of her skirt and it swayed with her steps along the water's edge. She kept her chin down, looked at things she didn't care anything about, couldn't think about for the chill that had come again.

It was a couple days after that little rain had come and passed over Supply. Most folks didn't remember the rain at all, didn't do anything to cool things off. Seemed like it got hotter, the old road and anything else dirt would get dusty if somebody just looked at it long.

It was late in the day and them coloreds goin down the road were walkin so slow, seemed not to be movin at all. Dust up on the road just hovered around them, made them look still—silent dark faces in silent dirty dust.

Holly and Elsie were sittin way back on Elsie's porch in the little bit of shade back there. It was too hot to talk but Elsie was sayin somethin just cause she ain't had anything else to do. Holly butted in, askin, "Ah wonder what it be like bein one of them?"

"Huh?" Elsie said and stopped sayin what she was sayin.

"Ya know, bein one of them."

"Bein one of what?"

Holly pointed up to the road.

"Ahh nigger?' Elsie asked, turned and twisted her face up at Holly.
"Yeah."

"What ya askin that for?"

Holly sat quietly and just stared up the road. She had not told
Elsie or anyone about the painter, for she would have had to tell
them she had talked to him. She had not been back down to the
creek. She had gone to the end of her yard path, stood, looked down
the road toward the Back Land, then would look away and go up to
Elsie's.

Elsie's sayin, "Ah wouldn't want ta be one. Why ya askin
that for?"

Slowly, Holly says, "Ah just ask."

Elsie shrugs up her shoulders, shakes her head some and gets to
sayin, "Look at them, all black and all. Some of them nice but they
ain't got nothin. Livin down there in them shack-lookin things. Ah
know Ah wouldn't want ta be one."

"What if ya were one anyway? What would ya do?"

"Probably go git my daddy's shotgun and shoot me in the head.
Why ya keep askin about niggers? Ah damn sure don't want ta be
none. They look like they stink, them ones out in them fields look
like they smell real bad, like a mule or somethin. Them town ones
ain't that bad-lookin or actin, 'cept them ones we see up in Wilmington sometimes. Ah be afraid of them, some of them look like
they do somethin ta ya in a minute."

Elsie is still talkin and Holly asks, "Ya ever see them kind that
don't look like they colored, Ah mean not all the way colored?"

"They still niggers," Elsie gets to sayin and tellin Holly, "My
daddy say, if he had his way he send them all back on the Africa
boat. He say, ya can't trust em. Some of em steal anything ya got. He
say, when Ah was too little ta remember, they had one of them ones
that was out there workin in Mr. Tanner's fields go wild or somethin.
Said, he went ta cuttin up on them other ones that were out there
wit him. My daddy say they had ta shoot that one."

Elsie doesn't hear Holly's sigh, just her askin, "Ya think they
all bad?"

"Why ya askin? Why ya keep on askin about niggers for?"

"Ah don't know, just askin. Ain't nothin else ta ask about. Ah was just seein them goin down the road, that's all," Holly says, shrugs her shoulders and flicks the hair out of her eyes, then looks at Elsie and asks, "Ya still want ta go tonight? Ah git tired of goin down there. Ain't nobody down there no more, 'cept ya know who."

Elsie sighs and says, "Ain't noplace else ta go. Eddie out drivin that truck, Um tired of sittin around here, mise well go down Ben's, listen ta some records or somethin."

Friday night, Saturday night came, went, and on Sunday, Holly told Elsie, "Ah ain't never goin down there, sittin around lookin at the same faces lookin back at me, don't make good sense."

Elsie had said, "Well, maybe next week we can git Raymond ta take us up Wilmington or somethin. Maybe Eddie be back and he take us up on his truck, go someplace wit him," but it was Sunday, with Sunday ways. Holly still had her white dress on, the one she had worn to church. She was sittin on the porch talkin with her mother. Ginger had asked, "What ya thinkin about?" when Holly would seem to forget what she was talkin about and just stare out at the road.

"Nothin, Mama," Holly would answer and start talkin about somethin or anything else. In a while, Ginger got up, mumbled somethin and went on into the house. Holly sat on the porch for a bit, then eased herself up and went and stood leanin against the porch post. Suppertime had passed, the sun was beginnin to cool, it was makin colors in the sky above the Back Land.

Slowly, Holly stepped down the porch steps and started up the yard path. Each step seemed like the one she had just taken, the old road didn't get closer or further away. When it did get close, it was too close. Holly stopped and stood, then slowly looked back over her shoulder. The porch was empty, the yard path lay quiet beneath the silence in the air. Slowly, Holly turned and looked back down the road toward the Back Land.

Where the old road curves, where the shade and shadows are always there, Holly walks slowly. It is dark there, the flow of her white dress flutters through the darkness. Far ahead she can see the top of the fat-bellied oak tree, she lowers her eyes. The secret path is long and lonely. Where it should end, it doesn't. Holly sees the clearin beneath the fat-bellied oak, she has slowed, then stopped on the path. She stares into the clearin, takes a quick breath and eases into its silence. At the water's edge, the breeze from afar slows, chills come through the air. Holly walks quietly along the edges of the creek. The water makes its little ripplin sounds, splashing up against rocks, curlin around old dead brown wood lyin in its way. Summer songbirds perch on branches, peek about, watch Holly walk the water's edge, and sing their summer songs. But where Holly looks, lowers her eyes and looks, peeks real fast, the slopin hill where he sat is empty. She can see where he was, see the spot under the little tree just beyond where the high grass lowers. She can look now, stare, he is not there to look back. Near the turtle rock, Holly has stopped and taken her shoes off. Slowly she steps through the soft mud. When she reaches the turtle rock and goes to ease herself up on it, she stills in the ripplin water. Everything becomes as still as the brightly painted red flower on the back of the turtle rock.

Sunday night came and Holly was in her room sittin on the side of the bed. She had come back from the creek and had sat on the porch with Ginger until evening came. Ginger had asked her, "How come ya so quiet? Did ya and Elsie have a fuss?" Holly had shrugged her shoulders and just said, "Um just tired, Mama."

The room was dark and quiet, Holly sat holdin her pillow on her lap. If there were sounds, bugs hummin, distant dogs barkin, she didn't hear them. Slowly, she edged herself up onto the bed, brought the pillow to her arms. When she closed her eyes, the red of the flower on the rock was still there.

Two days went by before Holly asked Elsie, "Ya ever feel things that ya didn't want to? Ah mean, ya don't want ta feel but ya feel anyway."

It was Tuesday afternoon and Holly was walkin Elsie into town. Elsie slowed her steps some and just looked at Holly before she asked, "What ya askin that for?"

"Ah was just thinkin about somethin. Ya know, how it would be if ya feelin somethin and ya don't want to. Like if ya meet somebody and ya feel somethin but ya don't want to and all. Ya ever feel that?"

Elsie kept lookin at Holly, watched her look down at the road. "Who ya talkin about?" she asked.

"Ah ain't talkin about nobody, just askin."

"Sound like it ta me."

"No Ah ain't."

"Well it sure sound like it ta me."

"Well, ya ever feel like that?"

"Feel like what?"

"Feel like what Ah just said."

"Ya mean like ya like somebody and they don't like ya?"

"No, that ain't what Ah mean. Ya know, just feel somethin ya don't want ta feel, somethin like that."

"Ah feel a lot of things Ah ain't wantin ta feel. Feel me wantin ta go someplace and can't."

"No, that ain't what Ah mean. Say ya see someone, say that. Say that ya don't want ta like them, ya know. Say somethin feels important but ya don't want it ta be important but ya still feel it."

Elsie walked quietly for a few steps, put her head down too, then said, "Ah ain't never felt that way about things like that."

Holly walked quietly for a while and did not answer Elsie when she asked, "Who ya talkin about, huh? Ya meet somebody? When ya meet them?"

Holly kept lookin down at the road and said softly, "Ah ain't met nobody. Why ya keep askin Ah did and all?"

"Sounds like it ta me."

Holly looked at Elsie and said real quick, "Ah ain't though. Ah told ya, Ah ain't met nobody, Elsie Fagen."

Supply's streets were as busy as they could be. The few folks that were walkin on them were mostly women doin their shoppin. Them children that live right in town were makin whatever noise that could be heard at all. Them old men that usually just sit out in front of stores were doin just that. When Holly and Elsie passed the courthouse, Elsie kept on talkin about whatever she was sayin. Holly slowed, as she did all the time when she passed the wall with names on it and the freshly cut flowers beneath them. She looked, stared briefly but kept walkin. She had never read Billy's name on the wall, only knew it was there.

"Wait, Elsie," Holly's sayin.

Elsie keeps talkin, but slows and lets her words drift as she sees Holly lookin back over her shoulder toward the courthouse wall. She starts to ask Holly what she is lookin at but then stands still in the silence that has come.

Holly's whisperin, "Ah want ta see it."

Elsie stands quietly, stares at Holly, watches her lookin back at the wall, then she's whisperin, "Ya really want to?"

Holly shakes her head yes. Elsie has not thought of Billy, has let him rest, but now she stands still as if in reverence, as if he is standin at the wall. Holly stands still until her hand slowly raises and comes to her mouth. Gently she places a finger on her lips, sighs and says, "Ah ain't never seen it. Ah mean got close and all."

Elsie whispers, "If ya want to, go ahead."

Holly starts walkin back toward the courthouse, Elsie follows. The walkway to the courthouse wall is longer than Elsie could remember. Holly's steps are steady until she is within the shadows of the wall. She slows, her steps become hesitant. She stops when she can read the names, she stares when she sees, FELTER WILLIAM J. Elsie hears her whisperin, "How come they put William up there for? Billy hated it when somebody called him that." Elsie ain't sayin anything, she just holdin her breath while she's watchin Holly reach up and touch Billy's name.

When Holly turns and walks away from the wall, Elsie follows and keeps quiet until they are out of the shadows of the wall and back on the sidewalk, then she asks, "Ya ever open up his letters?"

"No," Holly says softly, then asks quickly, "Ya want ta go over Ben's and git a soda or somethin fore we git your mama's stuff? Or ya want ta wait till after and git a soda?"

"Ah don't care," Elsie says, then walks quietly.

Holly didn't say much the rest of the time her and Elsie were in town, even when they stopped and had a soda at Ben's she sat quietly. On the way back home, both Holly and Elsie walked slow with their heads droopin. Holly asked Elsie what was wrong with her but Elsie only answered with, "Nothin, what's wrong wit ya?"

When they got to Elsie's, Elsie asked, "Ya comin down?"

Holly said, "No, Ah feel like goin home."

"Ya comin back up later?" Elsie asked.

"Ah don't know," Holly says, sighs and looks off.

"What's wrong wit ya?" Elsie asks.

Holly looks back at Elsie, twists up her face and says, "Ain't nothin wrong wit me."

"Ya actin like it."

"Actin like what, huh?"

Elsie stands silent, looks at Holly, then looks away.

Holly shouts, "What ya talkin about, huh? Say it."

Elsie turns back, shoutin, "Ya actin funny, folks be talkin some, too. Say ya ain't actin right. Say ya ain't actin like ya used to. Ya down that creek all the time, go down there more than ya go anyplace else. Paul told me what happened and all, he said Roland told him. He said Roland said ya weren't actin right. Said Roland wanted ta marry ya and all, really liked ya but ya actin funny and all. Your mama say it too, she say how ya go down that creek and can git ta bein like ain't nobody in the world but ya. She worried, keep talkin ta me about it. Then sometimes it be like ya makin stuff up, askin stuff about somebody ya ain't met like some fairy-tale land or somethin . . ."

Elsie is still shoutin, Holly screams, *"It ain't none of your damn business. If Ah go down the creek or stand on the moon, it ain't your business or nobody else's. If that damn Roland come by or don't come by it just bein my business. How come that Paul stop comin, huh? Ya actin like he stop comin cause of me or somethin. He want ta see ya and like ya the way ya be thinkin, then he still be comin. He done married ya and all. As far as Um concerned, ya, that Paul and Roland can go ta the devil."*

Holly spins around, starts down the road. Elsie yells, *"Ya know*

*what ya can do, Holly Hill. Ah don't give a damn if Ah see ya again or
not. Ya hear me?"*

Holly stops and jerks around so fast her hair flows like wildfire.
"Look, Elsie Fagen," she's screamin, *"ya and everybody else in this damn
town can go ta hell.* Um fed up wit ya and everybody else. Who ya
think ya are tellin me how Ah ought ta be actin and what Um supposed ta be doin? At least ah had a boyfriend and could have more
if Ah wanted them. Ya just bein jealous, that's all. Ya jealous cause
ya ain't got one and if ya did, ya can't be keepin them anyway. That
Eddie ain't been around either. Don't ya ever be tellin me again how
Ah should be actin. Ya hear me, Elsie Fagen?"

Holly spun back around and stomped down the road with her
cheeks puffed out and blowin the air out of her mouth until she
started cryin. When she got to her yard path she kept on goin down
the road through its shady curve, then bolted off the road and ran
down the secret path. She flicked the hair out of her eyes when she
passed the fat-bellied oak, gave it a quick look, then kept goin to
the water's edge. When she got to the turtle rock, she looked across
the creek, stared into the shade beneath the tree where he had
sat, then turned and looked to the rock. The flower was still there,
she saw its red, saw its thin green stem, its tiny leaves. She splashed
through the soft mud and shallow water, then scooted up on the
rock and sat beside the flower. Slowly she reached down and touched
it, rubbed the tiny cracks and crevices of the rock where the bright
paint colors of the flower had seeped, then looked up and watched
the water in the creek go by. She kept starin at the water goin by until it was just a slow-movin greenish blue blur. She could still hear
Elsie screamin and sayin things. She sighed, closed her eyes and tried
to make Elsie go away. When she opened them, she looked across the
creek and into the shade of the tree, then sighed again but kept
starin across the creek until she felt a chillin feelin come. She lowered her eyes and looked at the creek again, but she could feel herself
touchin the wall where Billy's name was. She could see the letters of
his name stuck neatly on the wall again lookin like some front of a
book. One of them books that didn't have a picture on the front, just

a name without a face. Quickly she lifted and turned her head, looked down the creek as far as she could look. There were just colors there, the greens of the fields and the blue of the sky. But there was an emptiness there where she wanted to go.

Holly stayed on the rock until the sun began to drift beyond the Back Land. Then she slowly started walkin back up along the water's edge. Suddenly, she stopped and stared up at the old rickety bridge. She knew it was him, could see his armless sleeve hangin loosely at his side but it was his eyes she felt. He was standin on the bridge lookin down, then he moved. She watched him cross the bridge, then disappear behind the thick bushes beyond the bridge. She kept still, waited, then she could hear his footsteps comin down the secret path. When she could see him, see all of him, it was still his eyes she watched. He passed the old fat-bellied oak, then slowly came to the water's edge. Holly kept still but kept lookin at him. When he neared, he brought a silence with him. Holly dropped her eyes, looked down at the soft dirt and asked, "Ya put the flower on the rock, didn't ya?"

Holly did not see the quick little smile, only heard him askin, "What flower? There's a lot of flowers down there, which one do you mean?"

She looked up and said quickly, "Ya know what flower Um talkin about. Why ya do that for, huh? Why ya do that?"

She watched his eyes look down and away from hers, then when he looked back up he smiled and said, "I thought you liked flowers."

"That ain't answerin my question. What ya do it for?"

"I don't have a reason, flowers just grow."

"It ain't just grew there, it was painted on there and ya did it."

"I didn't think it would upset you, I'm sorry."

"Ah wasn't upset, it was a pretty flower."

"You're very pretty, too."

"Why ya say that? Ya shouldn't be sayin things like that."

"Why not?"

"Because."

"Are you saying, I shouldn't talk?"

"Ya know why," Holly says, takes a deep breath and looks away, sees the old fat-bellied oak and just stares at it and says, "Ya just ain't supposed ta be sayin things like that. Ah mean, Ah liked the flower, Ah was really surprised and all. Ah didn't think ya do somethin like that, ya know, since Ah bothered ya and all. And ya kept tellin me, nothin was my concern. But ya shouldn't be sayin things like Um pretty and all. Ya shouldn't be talkin like that."

"I should not have done a lot of things in my life."

Slowly, Holly turns from the stillness of the oak tree and asks, "Like what?"

"That's not important."

"How come ya always sayin things, then ya say it ain't important or nobody's concern and all?"

For a moment, nothin made any noise. If summer birds sang, it was a silent song. The creek stilled its ripplin sounds. There was a loneliness, a sadness, deep in the dark of his eyes that Holly could see but knew had been there all the time. There was a gentleness there, too, that she had felt before she saw how dark his eyes were. "Do ya like me?" she asked before she could catch her thought, then she turned away but turned back quickly and waited for his answer.

"Is that important? Or could it ever be important?"

"If ya say it ain't important, Ah guess it ain't. Ya probably goin ta say that anyway or say it ain't my concern or somethin. But Ah ask ya if ya like me and ya ain't answered. Ah just want ta know. Ah just want ta know why ya put that flower down there? Why ya look at me the way ya do? Ya try and say things, try and be all like ya don't care. Sayin things like 'That's not my concern' and 'That's not important.' And Ah know ya colored, Ah mean Negro colored. Ah just want ta know why ya put the flower there. Ah remember your name, it's Elias Urithusdies Owens. Ah just want ta know if ya like me? If it's important enough ta say?"

He wouldn't answer, just looked at Holly. She stared into his eyes, wouldn't turn away. The cold breeze blew but she didn't shiver, she kept starin. He looked down and she said, "Do ya? And don't say it ain't important. Don't say it ain't my concern, don't say that. Ah just want ta know, that's all."

He brought his eyes up, looked at Holly and asked, "Why?"

"Because it's important ta me. Ah just want ta know."

"I don't even know you."

"Then why ya put the flower there? What did it mean? Ya know Ah would come see it. Why ya do that? How come ya did it and ya bein colored and all? Ah mean a Negro, too."

He's silent.

Holly looks away, takes a short quick breath and says, "Ah shouldn't be talkin ta ya. Ah mean like this and all."

"Why are you, then?"

"Ah don't know, Ah think Ah better go."

"Why?"

"Ya know."

Slowly, he steps closer. She can feel him gettin closer, feel herself quiverin until she hears his voice, it's whisperin. When she lifts her eyes, she can only see his face, it is silent and she asks, "What did ya say?"

"I said you're important to me."

"Why?"

He doesn't say anything but Holly looks for the answer in his eyes, quivers and keeps her eyes open until she feels his lips on hers. There was a smell of his breath, the warmth of it, it had come quickly. It was a sweet smell that was warm and kept lingerin until the touch of his lips was there. Slowly his lips were moving over hers and rubbin the sweet smell of his breath beneath her nose. Holly's eyes were closed, she didn't know they were goin to close. In the dark, there was still the glow of his copper-colored face, the look in his eyes that looked back and kept starin into hers. When she parted her lips, feelins poured into the dark. She pushed away from them, opened her eyes, sayin, "What ya do that for? Ya shouldn't have done it, Ah mean ya shouldn't be kissin me. Ya shouldn't have . . . Ah have ta go."

Holly left the breath from a deep sigh trailin behind her as she passed around where he stood. She felt his arm still on hers as she passed. "Ah have ta go," she says quickly and scoots by. Quickly, her hands grab at her skirt, she jerks it above her knees when she begins to run. The silence in the clearin of the fat-bellied oak is shattered by her poundin heartbeats. When she reaches the secret path, she stops and spins around in its shade. She can still see him standin at the water's edge, he has not taken his eyes from her. She yells, "Ah can't like ya, Ah can't."

16

Days went by, but Holly kept thinkin about the kiss. The thought of it was different from the feelin. The feelin lingered, sometimes gently, but the thought of the kiss wouldn't go away. It haunted her mind, stayed in it and wouldn't let her think of anything else. She had let a colored kiss her. She would look in the mirror, go to brush her hair but turn away. The porch was as far as she would go until it was time for the coloreds to pass by, then she would get up, go into the house and up to her room. Ginger had asked, "What's wrong with ya, honey? Did ya and Elsie have a fuss? She ain't been down and ya ain't been out the house since the day fore yesterday."

Holly had just shaken her head no. Then she said, "No, Mama, Ah mean we had a little one. Ah guess Ah ain't wantin ta go up there and all."

Ginger had stood quietly, then asked, "What's got inta ya? Got ya all twisted up, ya ain't even eatin."

Holly had flung her hands in the air, shouted, "Nothin, Mama. Ain't nothin at all wrong wit me. Ah just don't be feelin like seein Elsie Fagen, that's all."

Evenings could be long, take their time passin before the night would come. All them buzzin bugs get to hoverin around things that didn't want to be bothered with them. Holly was sittin on the top step, leanin against the porch post and just lookin out into the dark. Ginger had been sittin for a while but had gone on in and had asked Holly if she were comin in soon. Holly had only shaken her head yes, but stayed on the porch. Night bugs came close, buzzed and nipped at her ears. Sometimes they'd be there nippin or buzzin for a long time before Holly would shake her head a little, swing at them and make them go away, then she'd look out into the dark again. The night seemed to have layers of darkness in it, tops of trees were lightened by star and moonlight, low bushes and dirt were just dark. Sometimes Holly would stare into the darkness around the bushes, then with a sigh she'd close her eyes.

When the next day came, Holly pushed her pillow away and was up, washed, dressed, downstairs and out the door before Ginger could ask where she was goin in such a hurry. When she got to the creek, she went along the water's edge till she reached the turtle rock, looked at the flower, then looked across the water. "Shit," she muttered aloud, took her shoes off, held them in one hand and her skirt up some in the other, then splashed across the creek. She hurried up through the tall grass, through the small trees and bushes till she reached the top of the hill. She could see far from there and stood lookin. The tall grass was there again, it grew down the backside of the hill, grew high and full in a shallow valley before it thinned as it neared the bottom of the other hill. Then the grass seemed to die, lose its greens and yellows, seemed as brown as the bare dirt it was stickin up from. On top of the far hill, Holly could see the outlyin shacks of the Back Land and then it was the high grass she was wadin down through.

Little brown children were playin near some old dark fence, they stopped their play when they saw Holly comin up the hill. They kept starin, brown eyes kept gettin bigger. Holly smiled at them as she neared and asked, "Ya know where Elias is, ya know where he live at?" Holly kept the smile on her face. The children kept smilin back but got to shruggin their shoulders. Holly sighed, smiled and asked again, "Ya knowin where Elias is? Ya know where he live at? He live up there on the Hump? Is he up there?"

"Ah ain't knowin that," the one child answered, then got to lookin down at the dirt some.

Holly looked off, sighed, then looked down at the child with his head down and said, "He paints pictures and things, he just have one arm. Ya seen him?"

The child looked up, his eyes and smile brightened. He got to pointin and sayin, "He be livin up there. That's where he be, he the one-arm man, he live up there."

Holly looked off to where the child was pointin. She could see a shack sittin far away from the others and near the top of the hill. If it was gray or brown like the others, it looked black silhouetted against the morning sky. Holly started up the hill, found paths that weaved around patches of thick bushes, pieces of old haulin wagons that were doin nothin but rustin and rottin. Then near the top of the hill was a piece of fence, didn't have any beginnin, no endin, just a piece comin from nowhere and goin nowhere. When Holly reached the fence, she stopped and stared beyond it, then took a deep breath and held it until she found the path that went around it. Except for the sound of her footsteps there was a silence as she neared the shack. She stood at the porch steps and called out, "Elias . . . Elias . . . Ya in there?"

The door of the shack opened slowly, the squeaky sound it made on its hinges seemed to scratch slowly at the air. Holly stood watchin the door and could only stare in silence as the old woman looked out the door, then crept out onto the porch. She looked at Holly, then kept lookin. Her face was as rusty-colored as some old water bucket that been lyin around for years. Her hair was long and silver-colored but it was her dark, quiet eyes that Holly watched and could not turn from.

"What ya want up in here, child?" the old woman asked.

Holly stood silently.

"What ya doin up in here, huh?"

Holly kept her silence, looked down at the beaten-down dirt of the path.

The old woman spoke again, "Oh, ya that pretty child in that boy's picture he be paintin, ain't ya?"

Holly kept her eyes down, then looked up quickly, sayin, "Um just a likeness."

The old woman kept on talkin as if she didn't hear what Holly had said or if Holly had not spoke at all. "Seems like the only thing make that boy smile is when he paintin on that there picture. He come on in here showin that ta me, say he down there by the creek and ya come on along down there and sit in the middle of what he be paintin. What's ya name child? He tells me but Ah can'ts rightly say Ah can remember."

"My name is Holly . . . Holly R. Hill. Ah live on the other side of the creek. Ah live in the last house on the road fore ya git down ta the creek. Ah used ta play down there when Ah was little. Ah used to play wit Tessie, too," Holly was sayin and findin herself feelin warm in the gentleness of the old woman's eyes.

"Ya come down here ta see him, child?"

"Yes, ma'am . . . Ah just want to ask him somethin."

"He went on out here earlier. Ah fix him some breakfast, then he goes on out of here. He say he goin on up over the hill. That's where he be, right up over the hill, child. He doin that paintin now, that's be all he can do. He say he can'ts plays that piano no more. That war gits his arm . . . takes it off like that. Ya . . . ya git up there, ya just look over some. Ya see him there, he just over the hill there. Ya tells him, Alpha sends ya on over there. Ya go on, child, ya see him there."

The gentleness in the woman's eyes had dimmed. Holly turned away from her, then turned and looked back. She didn't say anything to her, sorta looked at her for a moment, then nodded her head a little before she turned and started walkin around the shack. She found a path goin up through the grass behind the shack, then found herself on it. At the top of the hill, it was silent. Holly stopped and stood on the top of the hill. She could feel a little breeze blowin, her legs quiverin and her heart poundin.

Below the crest of the hill, a cluster of trees clung to the hillside. Slowly Holly started down the hill. As she neared the trees, she stopped and peered into the shade within them and whispered, "Elias . . . Elias . . . ," then slowly and softly she stepped under the low-hangin branches and into the shade beneath them. She could see him, see his faded shirt with its empty danglin sleeve and the back of his curly black hair. She could see his hand stretchin, strokin at the blurry colors before him, but she could not see his face. "Elias," she called again. He jolted, spun around. His eyes were glarin until he saw her, then they calmed.

"Elias," Holly called again and crept through the shade of the trees. When she neared him, he stood but only looked at her lookin at him. Anything that may have made a sound, a flutter of a bird's wings, a crackin of a dried limb beneath their feet, stayed out of their silence. Even the subtle pantin sounds of their breath seemed to still until Elias asked, "Why did you come?" Holly didn't answer, just slowly looked away and sighed.

"Why did you come? What are you doing over here?" Elias asked again.

Holly shrugged her shoulders, then just shook her head. Elias spoke softly and as he did, he placed his hand on Holly's cheek and gently turned her face to his. "Why did you come?" he asked again. Holly kept her eyes down from his but did not turn from his touch, then she whispered, "Is it important why Ah come?"

"Just tell me, why did you come?"

Holly wouldn't look up, just asked again, "Is it important?"

"Yes" Elias whispered.

Slowly, Holly looks up and just stares into Elias's eyes, then says, "Say it again. Say it's important."

Elias whispers, "It's important."

Holly looks away, sighs, says, "Ah just come cause Ah wanted ta ask ya somethin. And Ah didn't see ya . . . ya know . . . Ya weren't down the creek and all . . . and Ah just come, that's all . . . was just goin ta ask ya somethin . . . Can't Ah ask somebody somethin?"

There is a little smile that Holly doesn't see, just feels comin from Elias when he asks, "You come all the way over here just to ask me something?"

"Ya come all the way from some Washington, D.C., ta just paint that old creek. Ya come way down here just ta do that. Didn't ya?"

"What is it? What do you want to ask me?"

Holly stands silently, keeps lookin away. She doesn't see the things she's lookin at, the darkness of the shade, little rays of sunlight sparklin on the edges of low-hanging leaves, but she keeps lookin.

"Holly, what is it you wanted to ask me?"

"What's it like?" Holly begins sayin as she slowly looks up at Elias, then she's sighin and just starin.

"What is what like?"

"What's it like bein ya? What's it like bein ya and colored and all? Ah mean Negro, too? Can ya still like me? Do ya . . . Ah mean can ya really like me? . . . Ah wanted ya ta kiss me . . . then when ya did . . . Ah thought about it a lot. . . . Ah ain't told nobody, Ah ain't did that . . . but Ah was thinkin about why ya kiss me . . . why ya wanted ta, bein colored and all . . . Ah felt like things Ah didn't want ta be feelin like . . . but it ain't made no difference what Ah wanted ta feel cause Ah was still feelin what Ah was anyhow. Ya colored, Ah can't be likin ya . . . Ah feel things anyway. And Ah feel somethin else too, Ah feel when Um near ya, Ah feel it when Ah ain't down at the creek, ya know like when Um home Ah feel it, Ah feel ya like me. Ya ain't said it or nothin but Ah feel that too. Do ya like me and can't? . . . Ah want ta know that"

Even though Elias moved, turned his head and looked off, stared at the rays of sunlight tryin to peep into the shade, there was a stillness about him. Holly said, "Answer me, it's important."

Elias kept lookin at the rays of sunlight but said, "What do you want me to say? Do you know what would happen . . . ?"

Holly was silent, the sound of Elias's voice had drifted. She stood watchin him just look away. She could not see his eyes, just the side of his face. She waited for him to turn and look at her. "Why did ya kiss me?" she asked and kept waitin for him to turn.

"I don't know," Elias said without turning.

"Ya ain't answered my question. Do ya like me? Can ya do that?"

Elias turns, looks in Holly's eyes, stares, then looks off again. "I didn't come down here looking for trouble," Elias is saying, "I don't want any trouble, I don't want to care enough to have any trouble. I don't want to care about you, I don't want to care about that damn town on the other side of the creek or anybody in it."

"Why did ya kiss me? How come ya did that then?"

"Why do you want to know?"

"Why won't ya say it? Ya all hurt and don't want to talk. Ya say things but they just things ta say. Ya say ya ain't carin but kissin is carin. Sayin things ya really feel is carin. Ya ain't sayin things ya feelin but Ah still feelin what ya ain't sayin."

Elias turned, looked.

Holly just stared.

"What do you think would happen if your family, your friends or anybody in that town knew you were over here?"

'That ain't what Um thinkin about now. Ah ask ya somethin and ya ain't answered what Ah ask ya. Ya ask me why Ah come up here and Ah told ya. But ya ain't answerin what Ah ask ya. Ya want me ta go, Ah'll do that. Ah just want ta know why ya kiss me and ya ain't sayin that. Ah ask ya if ya can like me and ya ain't sayin that either."

"I don't know why I kissed you. I didn't come down here to fall in love with you or anybody else, especially a white girl. I just want to be left alone—"

"Did ya fall in love? Did ya, Ah want ta know."

Elias jerked his head, looked away, then just as quick, looked back at Holly and asked, "What difference would it make? Tell me, what difference would it make in this world of yours?"

"It would make a difference ta me."

Elias shouted, "Look at me . . . Look at this world. Look at this place. Nothing can mean anything. Nothing, nothing means any-thing. I wanted to be a pianist, compose my own music. Maybe one day, just maybe, play with the Washington Symphony. That's what I wanted. Look at me, look, there's nothing in this empty sleeve, nothing. And it wasn't my freedom I was fighting for."

Holly lowered her eyes a little and stood silently.

The sound of Elias's voice softened until it was just the sound of words floatin in whispers. "I kissed you, I don't know why, only that I wanted to. I went down to the creek every day after I met you. When you weren't there, I painted you again. I do that, I paint things now, I can paint them the way I want to, I don't need both hands to make things come alive but I can't hear them. I pretend there's music there. You came out of nowhere, I watched you. Every step, I watched you walk along the creek. Then I watched you climb up on the rock. You didn't know it but you had come along and sat in the middle of my picture. You made it a different picture, you added the color of life and what love might look like. I'd never seen you before, I could not have known who you were. I don't know what to tell you now and anything I could say, I don't think would make a difference."

Holly had stared at the darkness of the shade. Elias was lookin at her and she knew it. When she looked up, she stared at him, then said, "Things ya sayin and all, they make a difference ta me. Ah was goin ta git married, was in love, too. And then Ah didn't want to git married, but Ah was still in love. But Ah didn't know that till he died and Ah almost been dead, too. Ah ain't feel things anymore. That's why Ah know how ya feel things that ya ain't sayin, cause Ah feel things Ah don't say. Ah just say things when folks be around but Ah don't feel the things they hearin me say, Ah just say things so they don't git mad at me or think Um crazy or somethin. Ya might not have two arms but Ah don't think about that. Ah think about ya bein colored and all and Ah know Ah can't like ya but that's just thinkin, that ain't what Um feelin. Ya hurt real bad and Ah know that, Ah ain't meanin your arm."

Elias's eyes lowered and Holly watched them, then she whispered,

"Ya still ain't answerin me. Ya still ain't said it. Did ya fall in love anyhow?"

"Don't you understand?" Elias said, took a deep breath and was silent for a moment, then he looked up and said, "You'd be an outcast."

Holly put her head down and whispered, "Um an outcast anyhow . . . Ah feel like one anyhow . . . Ah mean Ah just don't fit no more. Ya want me ta go, too? Just say that then, just say it."

Hours passed in the shade, it was almost dark when Holly got home. Ginger was sittin on the porch, she had watched the road for hours. She could see Holly come through the gray of the early eve, then watched her turn from the old road and come down the yard path. Ginger got up and stood at the top of the steps. As Holly nears Ginger's whisper slices through the air. "Where have ya been?"

Holly shakes her head, gets the hair out of her eyes, glares up at her mother.

"Where have ya been? Ya answer me, ya hear me?"

Holly nears the steps. "Ah ain't been nowhere. What ya standin out here for hollerin? What Ah got ta do, tell everybody where Ah go, tell em everythin Ah do? If Ah want ta go somewhere, that's my business."

Ginger screams, "Don't ya be talkin ta me that way, ya hear me? Ah want ta know where ya been. Ya left out here way fore noon. It's plum near dark, where ya been?"

Holly screams back, "Ah told ya Ah ain't been nowhere. What Ah have ta do, sit around this here house all day? Ah ain't no baby, Ah can do what Ah want."

"Don't ya talk ta me like that. Where have ya been, ya hear me?"

Holly stomps up the steps, whisks past Ginger, then turns and yells back, "Ah ain't been nowhere, Ah told ya. Ah was just down by the creek walkin."

"Don't tell me ya were just out walkin or sittin down by that creek. Ah sent Jason down there lookin for ya. He say he ain't seen hide or tail of ya. Said the only thing he saw was some flower painted on some rock down there. Ah want ta know where ya been all day."

"Where Ah go is my business. Ah went past that old rock down there. Ah went for a walk, that's all, see if Ah could find Tessie's house."

"Tessie?"

"Yeah. Ah wanted ta see what kind of baby she had."

"Ya know ya ain't ta be down there wit them niggers. What done got inta ya? What is wrong wit ya? That ain't noplace for ya ta be and ya know that."

When the night came, Holly held on to her pillow, twisted and turned through the dark hours. The morning slowly came, Holly lay still in its soft light. Her eyes had been open and just starin into the silence of the morning shadows in the room. The pillow was all things warm and close, then it was just the pillow when she pushed it away.

Ginger was in the kitchen and did not turn from the pantry when she heard Holly come through the door. The sounds of Holly's footsteps and some clingin, clangin noise comin from Ginger's stirrin of somethin in a pan were the only sounds. Holly moved around the kitchen slowly, fixed herself something to eat, then ate in the silence.

The morning still had the coolness of a night. Holly had finished eatin, sat at the table for a moment, then quietly put her plate on the sink and went out onto the porch. She stood for a while at the porch post, looked far into the sky, then she looked down at the path. She stared, kept starin until she saw the shade in the trees, Elias's eyes just lookin into hers. She looked up into the sky again, looked where it hung low over the Back Land until she heard the sounds of her mother's footsteps nearin the door. Holly's fingers squeezed into a fist, her teeth bit down on her bottom lip, then she ran down the steps and started up the path.

"Where ya goin out of here this time in the mornin?" Ginger called from the door.

"Um goin up Elsie's. Ah guess Um allowed ta go up there," Holly yelled back over her shoulder.

Elsie's mother was sittin on the porch when Holly came up the road. She gave Holly a big wave and Holly waved back, hurried her stride and turned down the yard path. Elsie's mother got to smilin as Holly neared, shouted ahead to her, "Where ya been, huh? Thought somethin done dragged ya off somewhere."

"Ah ain't been nowhere," Holly answered with a little smile and went up onto the porch askin, "Is Elsie up yet?"

"If she ain't up, ya go on up there and tell her Ah said for ya ta git her butt up," Elsie's mother said, laughed and kept smilin as Holly went into the house.

Elsie had just got up and was sittin on the side of her bed. She heard Holly comin up the steps and yellin, "Elsie . . . Elsie . . . Ya up yet? Ya still mad at me?"

Elsie kept her head down when Holly came into the room. Quiet moments seemed to stick together and get all twisted up before Elsie looked and asked, "What ya doin' up here? What do you want?"

"Nothin, Ah just wanted ta see if ya still bein mad about our fuss, that's all. Are ya?"

Quickly, Elsie says, "Ah thought ya weren't speakin anymore."

Holly says back, "Ah thought ya weren't speakin ta me."

Elsie lowered her head, sat quietly until she said, "Ah was mad, real mad. Ya sayin them things ya were sayin, that stuff about Paul and all. That really made me mad at ya."

"Ya said things too."

"But Ah ain't say stuff like that."

Holly asked real quick, "What ya been doin?"

"Nothin."

Holly went and sat on the side of the bed with Elsie, sat silently for a while, then asked, "Ya still mad at me?"

"Kinda."

"Well, Um kinda mad at ya too."

Elsie asked, "What ya doin up so early?"

"Ah don't know, just felt like gittin up. Ah ain't stayin long, just come up ta see if ya still mad at me."

"What ya been doin?"

"Nothin," Holly says, sighs, looks down at the floor, then says, "Mama all mad at me, she ain't talkin."

"How come?"

"Ah don't know, Ah mean, ya know how she gits."

"Well, what did ya do?"

Holly gets to poutin, sayin, "Ah ain't done nothin. . . . Yestaday . . . yestaday . . . Ah just got tired of sittin around. Ya bein all mad at me and stuff, Ah went for a walk. Ya know, wasn't nothin else ta do. Ah didn't come back for a while. Ah didn't come back till it was almost dark. Mama had a fit."

Elsie sat quietly, Holly took a breath, then told Elsie, "Ah tired of everybody gittin inta my business. Ah ain't did nothin 'cept go for a walk and all."

Elsie got a funny look on her face and asked, "Where ya walkin at that take all that long? Sound like ya walkin out ta California or somethin."

"Ah was just walkin."

"Oh."

"Ah ain't did that, Ah just went down by the creek some. Then Ah just decided ta walk out in them fields some on the other side."

Elsie squinted her eyes up, looked at Holly and said, "Ya walkin around out in the Back Land? Why ya go over there for? How come ya did that, huh?"

Holly gave Elsie a quick glance, then looked down at the floor and slowly said, "Ah was just walkin some. Ah been over there lots of times. Ya member, me and Bobby would go over there. Then Ah used ta play wit Tessie, too. Ah wasn't over there on the Hump or nothin, Ah just went way down the creek some over there."

"Oh," Elsie said. Holly sat quietly again and in a moment, Elsie was saying something about Ben's. Holly butted in sayin, "If Ah . . ." Then she let her words die in a quick sigh.

Elsie stopped talkin about Ben's and asked, "If ya what?"

Holly started starin at the floor real hard.

"If ya what?" Elsie asked again.

Holly kept her head down and sorta whispered, sayin, "If Ah tell ya somethin. But ya can't tell nobody else, Ah mean nobody, would ya?"

"Who Um goin ta tell?"

Holly kept starin real hard at the floor, bit her lip some, then said, "Never mind, it ain't important anyhow. Ah mean it's important but . . ." Holly let her words drift but kept starin at the floor.

"Huh? What ya talkin about?"

"Nothin. What time ya think it is?"

"Ah don't know."

Holly lifted her head and looked out the window and said, "Ah, got ta go, Ah come up later."

Elsie went down the steps with Holly, then out onto the porch. She was goin to stand for a while and talk but Holly started up the path. "What time ya comin back up?" Elsie called. Holly slowed, turned a little and said over her shoulder, "Ah don't know, bout dark maybe. We can go down Ben's, ya want ta do that?"

The sun was gettin high, Holly hurried down the old road until she got near her house, then she slowed and looked back over her shoulder. The road behind her was empty. She waited a moment in the stillness of the road, then slowly vanished into the high bushes along its far side. Beyond the bushes, she weaved through thickets until she was in the dark shade beneath the roadside trees. There she quickened her steps, but walked quietly in the shadows of the trees. She stayed off the road until she was far beyond her house, then she slipped back through the bushes and thickets until she was on the road again.

The waters of the creek seemed to run slow, their ripplin sounds lingered behind their passin. Holly had crossed the creek, stood lookin back across, then climbed the hill. From afar, brown-faced children stopped their play and watched Holly passin. They could see her wadin through the far high grass, see her yellow hair flow in a breeze. They watched, could see her come down through the valley and start up the far hill.

When Holly neared the dark gray shack, she slowed and took

quick peeks at it to see if she could see the old woman, then she quietly went around the shack. She found the little path that led to the
top of the hill. She hurried up the hill, then stopped and took a
quick look back over her shoulder.

A few days passed through Supply, then Sunday came and lingered. Ginger was hummin in the kitchen while she fixed dinner. She still had the peace she had found earlier in church. While others had sung, she had cried, let the tears run free and thanked her God. Bobby Hill had gone to church for the first time since he had come home. Ginger had cried and smiled at the same time.

The smell of chicken cookin filled the kitchen and seeped through the house. A cherry pie was in the pantry, Ginger had chased Jason away from it a few times. It was for Bobby and she wanted him to see it with its crust still coverin all its cherries. But each time she had chased Jason away, she had smiled. She had seen Bobby in Jason, saw a time ago, felt its moments and wanted to keep the feelins.

Holly was upstairs changin her clothes, she had told her mother she didn't want to keep that white dress on she wore to church. When she came back downstairs and into the kitchen, she had on her short red dress with the low neckline and the puffy sleeves. Ginger was at the stove when she heard Holly come into the kitchen.

She kept hummin for a while, then let her hum slow until it became a sigh. Without turnin from the stove, and keepin the smile on her face, she asked Holly to start settin the table. When she turned to Holly, her smile faded and she asked, "Where on earth ya goin in that today? Don't ya think that's a little too much for Sunday?"

Holly kept her eyes away from Ginger's but answered quickly sayin, "No, Mama, Ah ain't goin noplace. Ain't nothin wrong wit this, Ah just felt like puttin it on, that's all. Ah might go up Elsie's some, Ah might do that."

Holly set out the plates and silverware, then helped her mother get the food on the table. Ginger was hummin and would sometimes sing softly. When the table was set, Ginger sighed, wiped her hands on her apron and asked Holly to go tell Bobby and Gus Hill that supper was ready, then she said, "Give Jason a holler, see if he out there and tell him ta come on."

Gus Hill sat at the head of the table and waited for Ginger to sit before he asked, "Where's that boy at? Doesn't he know it's time to eat?"

Ginger kept her smile and said, "He went down June Boy's, he be back in a bit. He knows we havin chicken and he's been eyein Bobby's cherry pie all day." Ginger gave Bobby a quick glance, wanted to see his eyes smile, look back at her. He sat still and silently.

Gus Hill lowered his head and began blessin the table. His words seemed distant, beyond the solemn sound of his voice. His "Ahhmen" seeped beneath the smell of the chicken and seemed to lie on the table, stillin it until the sound of his voice was no longer heard. Ginger had sat in the silence for a moment, she kept her eyes closed and prayed beyond Gus Hill's blessin. When she opened her eyes, she smiled.

Holly picked at the chicken and Bobby flinched when Jason came runnin into the kitchen. Ginger fussed a little and told Jason to go wash his hands and get back to the table. Holly smiled across the table at Bobby and said, "Bobby, ya better hurry up and eat fore Jason gits ta gobblin everythin up."

Bobby looked down at his plate and seemed as if he wanted to smile but Holly only seen him quiver, his hand shakin as he reached for his food. Jason got to the table and got to fillin his plate, then bitin into the fat part of a chicken leg. He was chewin away when he blurted out, "Guess what, Mama? Guess what me and June Boy saw? We were down by the creek and we saw some nigger paintin over there. He was paintin over there. He was paintin and he only had one arm. We seen him, Mama, he just had one arm."

Holly shuddered and when she stopped, her fingers squeezed the fork she held in her hand. She kept her head down, kept starin at the food on her plate and hearin Jason sayin, "He had all kind of paint stuff, Mama, and he just had one arm, too."

Holly could feel her mother's eyes on her, then could hear her sayin to Jason, "Hush now, Jason, go on and eat." Then she heard her mother askin her, "Ya seen him hangin around down there any?"

Holly kept starin down at her plate but quickly answered, "Ah ain't seen no one-arm nigger down there."

Holly tried to still herself, she could feel her stomach quiverin and now her father's eyes glarin at her, she sat quietly. Ginger asked, "Weren't there some kind of flower or somethin painted on some rock down there?"

Slowly, Holly starts pickin at the food on her plate, then throws a quick look up to Ginger, looks back down and tells her mother, "Ah seen some flower, Mama, but Ah ain't seen who did it. Wasn't payin no mind who painted it on there and all. Ah figured somebody felt like paintin a flower and just went on and did it. Why ya askin me about some one-arm nigger Ah ain't seen anyhow? Ain't nobody ever bothered me down there—"

Ginger butted in and told Holly, "Ah think ya need ta be stayin up from down there. Don't need ta be down there all the time. Ain't no tellin about things these days, ya just can't tell what might happen. Ya just stay up here."

Jason got to talkin again, Ginger got to hushin him too, told him to go on and eat before his food got cold. When supper was over, Holly helped her mother clean off the table and wash the dishes. Ginger got to hummin again, the gentle sound floated through the kitchen. Holly didn't say much and when the dishes were done, she told Ginger she was goin up Elsie's for a while, told her, "Me and Elsie might go in town too, Mama."

Holly started up the yard path, then up the road to Elsie's. When she got past the high roadside bushes, she slowed, looked back over her shoulder, then went to the far side of the road and slipped through the high bushes. When she was through the bushes and deep within the shade of the big trees, she stopped and stood in the silence there. The thumpin sound of her heart poundin had followed her and shattered the silence in the shade. Elias was waitin for her at the creek, she had told him, "Ya just wait there, Ah have ta eat and all, then Ah come then."

On the other side of the creek, up there on the hill, Elias stood watchin the far side of the creek. He could see a dab of red comin down through the high greens of the bushes and tall grass. He watched it weave through the green, disappear, but he kept starin until the soft blur of red became Holly, then he watched each step she took. He saw her stop at the water's edge, look back over her shoulder, then quickly take her shoes off and hurry across the creek with the sounds of the splashin water trailin her. Elias watched, then looked beyond Holly, peered into the shadows beneath the trees on the other side of the creek.

"What's wrong?" Elias called as Holly stepped out of the water and started up the hill.

"Nothin," Holly yelled and hurried up the hill.

"What's wrong?" Elias asked again as Holly neared and kept lookin back over her shoulder.

"Nothin," Holly said quickly, then said real fast, "We can't stay here, let's go someplace else. Let's go past your house, ya know, up on the hill."

Elias tried to look into Holly's eyes but she kept lookin back over her shoulder and takin quick peeks across the creek. "What happened, what's wrong?" Elias asked, then looked over Holly's shoulder and stared over the water.

"Nothin is wrong," Holly said quickly, then said, "Git your stuff, git your paintin stuff. Ya go first, Ah wait here, then come."

Elias looked back at Holly, stared into her face, tried to see her eyes again and asked, "What's wrong, what happened? Tell me, what happened."

"Nothin, Ah tell ya when Ah git up on the hill."

When Elias left, Holly stood starin across the creek, she sighed, pulled a leaf from a bush, then looked down at it and stared at its green before she ripped it apart. Its pieces fluttered in the air, then softly fell to the ground. She did not see them fall, her eyes were already lookin back across the creek. She was starin past the gentle ripplin sounds of the flowin water, past the silence beyond the water's edge, past things that had no sound and could never be seen. Billy Felter was there, Mama and days ago were there too.

On the far side of the far hill, Elias was waitin in the shade of a cluster of trees. Holly had climbed the far hill, circled the shack and found the path in the weeds. At the top of the hill she slowed and just stood for a while, lookin down at the grass and weeds at her feet. When she looked up again, she quickly looked back over her shoulder. She stared for moment, looked as far as she could see before she hurried down to the trees.

Elias was in the shade of the trees and Holly saw him lookin at her when she looked for him. He didn't say anything when he saw her, just kept his eyes on her as she neared and came into the trees. She went right to him, sighed in the silence, looked up into his eyes, then lowered her head and leaned it against his chest. Elias put his arm around her, let her lean away from herself, then asked, "What's wrong, did something happen?"

Holly was quiet, she had closed her eyes and was just listenin to the sounds beneath Elias's chest. Soothin, rhythmic poundin sounds, then the soft echoes of heartbeats. She could hear the curlin sounds of his breath makin his words, then she heard him askin again, "What is it, what happened?"

Holly kept silent, kept listenin to the sounds seepin from Elias's chest. She heard a deep breath, then felt him gently pushin her away until he could look down into her face, see her eyes and say, "You have to tell me. What is it, what is wrong?"

Holly whispers, "It's not important," and puts her face back on his chest.

"Yes it is, if it upsets you."

Holly keeps her face pressed against Elias's chest, sighs and whispers, "My little brother saw ya . . . he was down by the creek today, he saw ya paintin. . . . When we were eatin, that's when he said it . . . then Mama was wantin ta know if Ah saw ya. . . . She starts sayin things and askin things . . . she kept on askin if Ah saw ya and sayin ya might be wantin ta bother folks and all . . . sayin stuff like that . . . Ah told her, Ah ain't seen no one-arm nigger like she sayin about . . . Ya a Negro and a real painter and ya ain't down here botherin nobody . . . Ya just don't want folks botherin ya. . . . But Ah couldn't say all that, Ah had ta sit and listen ta it. . . . Jason told Mama about the flower on the rock over there by the creek . . . but he told her that last week . . . When he git ta sayin he seen ya, Mama remember Jason sayin that, then she wantin ta know if ya be the one doin that. . . . Ah just told her Ah figured somebody put it there cause they wanted ta and they could if they wanted ta, Ah said that. . . . They talked like ya all mean and somethin . . . Ah couldn't say things back . . ."

Holly could feel Elias's chest heave and could hear him sigh before he said, "That was your brother, the one with the blond hair, I should have known." Elias's words withered and just became the sounds of slow breaths, then he says, "Maybe we should think about things."

Holly whispers, "Think about what?"

"I told you if they find out about us, you'll be an outcast."

Holly keeps her head pressed against Elias's chest and is silent for a moment, then slowly whispers, "Um already an outcast but when Um wit ya Ah don't feel like that. Ah feel the whole world is a stinkin outcast and Um where Ah belong."

"Listen," Elias is sayin, "I don't have fear for me, death doesn't mean the things it used to. I'm not afraid of dying, I was but not anymore. I was afraid of not living, not being able to do the things I wanted to do. I feared that but that's not important now, don't ask me why, it's just not. What is important is that you are not hurt, and I think you could be if we continue to see one another. Do you understand what I am saying?"

"Ah understand what Ah hear," Holly's whisperin, keepin her head nestled against Elias's chest and tellin him, "Ah hear what ya sayin and all and Ah hear your heart beatin and it don't say go away. And Ah ain't goin anyhow, so ya mise well git that notion out your head now."

Gently, Elias is pushin Holly away, makin her look up into his eyes and tellin her, "It's not that simple. This can never be a place for us. I don't want you to get hurt."

Holly stares into his eyes for a moment, then says, "Um not goin ta git hurt. Ah don't care what they say. They can say what they want about me, Ah don't want them sayin mean things about ya. Ah don't want them ta say that. If Ah thought they wouldn't come down here and bother ya, Ah'd tell em all about ya. Ah tell em how ya can paint real good, make things look just like they look like. An Ah tell em how ya really like music and all and wanted ta play the piano but ya got your arm all hurt in the war. And how ya lived up in Washington, D.C., and how ya try and be mean sometimes but ya ain't."

Holly lowers her face, puts it back on Elias's chest and closes her eyes.

A deep sigh comes from Elias, Holly hears it comin up in his chest and then him sayin, "We can't, we just can't."

Holly lifts her head, waits until she sees Elias's eyes, stares into them and says, "Ya colored and all but Ah still feel things. Ah don't want to, but that don't make no nevermind cause Ah still do. Ah wish Ah could say things like they do in movies or somethin, say all the things Ah feel and all. But Ah don't know what Ah feel, just Ah feel em. Ah don't want to, cause ya colored and all, cause ya different and stuff like that. Ah was in love, was goin ta git married and Ah loved him too. Sometimes Ah didn't think Ah did but Ah did. Ya different, Ah ain't got ta think things, pick that way and wait ta do that. When he died, Ah was real sad and Ah couldn't be happy about things and Ah didn't want ta be happy. Ah was almost dead, too, and Ah wanted ta be, too. Ah ain't felt alive till ya come. Ya different but ya make me feel different. Ah mean ya makes me feel livin can be different, it can be happy. Ya might not have two arms but Ah don't think about that. Ah wish Ah could paint, Ah paint ya, Ah paint ya arm back on, Ah'd do that."

Elias took his arm and brought Holly back to his chest, slid his hand up her back and gently touched her hair. Holly leaned with his touch, closed her eyes again and laid her face against his chest. He sighed, she heard that but did not see him starin off, his eyes searching beyond the shade of the trees.

Holly's days became slow, long hours passin until the moment would come when she could go to the road. Sometimes if Bobby was sittin on the porch, she'd sit with him, talk to him and try to get him to say things back or just sit within his silence. But she would always be waitin for the moment when she could yell over her shoulder, "Mama, Um goin up Elsie's." Then she would go up the yard path, go up the road until she was far past her house. There she would always look around, then go into the bushes until she got to the trees. Sometimes she'd stop there, sigh, listen to the silence before she'd head toward the Back Land.

Elias would wait for her, Holly knew he would be within the cluster of trees on the far hill. He would wait for her there in the shade and the silence of the trees.

The colors dimmed in the shade there, they became soft greens of grass, soft darks of dirt and wood. Elias's eyes were part of the dark, the silence, too. They watched Holly come beneath the low-hangin branches of the trees, then stared into her eyes as she neared and sat next to him.

They had been sittin for a while, just holdin hands, when Elias whispered, "I have something I want to give you."

"What," Holly whispered back, then looked at Elias and smiled.

"Wait here, it's in the house, I have to go get it."

A smile turned into a giggle and Holly asked, "What is it? Tell me first, please."

"No, you wait here, I'll be right back."

When Elias came back, he had a smile on his face. Then as he kneeled to sit again, the smile on his face just became the look that was in his eyes. Holly was tryin to keep her eyes on his and look at the bag he had brought back at the same time. "What ya go and git, huh? What's in the bag, huh? What's that? Say it, Elias," she said before she giggled and tried to keep her mouth in a smile.

"It's a bottle of wine I brought back from Paris."

"Ya ain't said ya were in Paris."

"That's one question you did not ask."

Holly made a little funny face and said, "Ya always sayin Ah talk a lot. Um goin ta stop sayin anything at all. See how ya like that, then what ya goin ta do when Ah don't say things back?"

"I've been saving this for a special occasion," Elias said as he took the bottle out of the bag.

Holly didn't say anything. Elias asked, "Would you like to share it with me?"

Holly pressed her lips together and held them like that real tight.

"Well I had something else for you," Elias whispers. Holly looks up into his eyes, then looks away again and keeps her mouth shut. Elias leans over and kisses her on the cheek, then reaches in his pocket and brings out a little box. Holly's eyes widen and she stares at the box, then looks at Elias and just stares. She keeps her mouth closed until she smiles and blurts out, "What's that? Ah ain't got to be quiet, ya can't stay shut-upped either. What's that, is that for me?"

Elias whispers, "I was going to give this to you, I just didn't know when."

The smile on Holly's face softens.

Elias says, "I don't know whether or not you'll like it but I'd like for you to have it."

Holly whispers, "What is it, huh?"

"Here."

Holly takes the box and slowly opens it, she holds her breath for a moment, then looks at Elias and quietly asks, "Is this mine? It's so pretty, where did ya git it?"

"My mother gave it to me. . . . I used to wear it but when I got overseas, I put it back in the box."

Holly gently lifts the gold cross from the small box, stares at it and asks, "Do ya really want me ta have it, Elias? Is it really for me and all, it bein real special?"

Elias smiles and says, "It's been in the family for a long time. . . . My mother says my great-grandfather made it out of pure gold and gave it to my great-grandmother. . . . My mother gave it to me when I told her I was being shipped overseas. . . . I'm not much on praying but this is the strongest symbol of love I have. . . . I want you to have it."

"Ya sure, Elias, ya sure? This is so special and all."

Elias whispers, "So are you."

For a moment, there was no time in the shade of the trees. It had gone away, left Holly be. She sat for a while and stared at the cross. She sighed, smiled and looked at Elias. He had been watchin her, his eyes had never gone away.

"Did ya have a girlfriend up in that Washington?" Holly asked softly.

Elias smiled, laughed a little, then said, "I had a girlfriend in Washington."

Holly's eyes got big and she asked, "What was her name?"

Elias took a deep breath, then tried to smile but only his lips parted. Holly caught the look on his face and asked, "What happen ta her? Is she still up there?"

"No, she's not there."

"Well, what happen ta her."

"The war . . . the war has done a lot of things to people. . . . She's married . . . I didn't know it . . . I was in the hospital for a long time. . . . They say she married this guy from Cleveland. I knew him, we went to school together . . . Well, anyway, I don't have a girlfriend in Washington."

"How long were you in the hospital? My brother Bobby was in there a long time fore they let him come home. He had ta git some kind of plate in his head and all. He still don't talk a lot, he says some things but not a lot. How long were ya in there fore they let ya come home?"

"Holly, please don't ask about that, I don't want to talk about it."

"It's all right," Holly is sayin as Elias looks away. She hears him sighin and quickly tells him, "Ya don't have ta talk about it if ya don't want ta. It hurts ya ta say stuff about it. It hurts ya just ta think about it, too. Ah can't say things too that hurt real bad. Ah won't ask ya stuff again, but if ya want ta talk about it sometime, Ah mean not now but sometime when ya want to. If ya want ta do that, Ah listen for ya."

Elias was silent, Holly watched him look away. She wanted to see his eyes, maybe in his silence, too. In a moment she whispered, "Elias . . . Elias . . . Would ya plase look back at me? . . . Ah won't say things about that no more."

Elias turned and just looked at Holly and then she smiled, said, "We goin ta drink the French wine, we goin ta do that or just look at it? Will it make ya talk French talk? Say things in French and all? Ah can't have a lot but Ah can have a little bit."

Holly kept lookin at Elias, said some more things about the wine and kept watchin him until he smiled, reached for the bottle. She saw him tryin to get the cap off with his one hand, holding the bottle between his legs and tryin to twist its top. Each twist of his hand, the bottle slips and turns in his legs. He squeezes the bottle in his legs, tries to hold it tight in the grasp of his thighs but it slips and slips and turns again. Holly turns away and will not watch, wants to help but feels a feelin she doesn't know. Quickly it tells her, Don't reach for what he must touch hisself.

There is a quick *piff* in the air as the bottle cap loosens. Holly
turns back to Elias and when she sees him smiling, she smiles too.
Gently, Elias hands her the bottle. Slowly, Holly takes a sip of the
wine, then smiles at Elias. The wine is good red wine. There is a
drop of wine caught in the creases of her lip. She stills as Elias slowly
reaches toward her mouth, then wipes the drop from her lip. His
touch still lingers on Holly's lip for a moment until she smiles and
asks Elias, "How do French people talk? How ya say things in
French, huh?"

Elias smiled. Holly says, "Talk in French, go ahead, say
somethin."

"What do you want me to say?"

"Say somethin."

"What?"

"How ya say . . . how ya say house, huh?"

"*La maison.*"

"La . . . ma . . . what?"

"*La maison.*"

"What's that mean?"

"House."

Holly looked around, smiled, looked back askin, "How ya say
tree?"

"*L'arbre.*"

"How ya ask somebody their name?. . . How ya say that?"

"*Comment vous appelez-vous?*"

"What's that say?"

"What is your name?"

"Say . . . ahh . . . Say wine. . . . Say that."

"*Le vin.*"

"That don't sound like wine. . . . Ya just makin funny sounds . . .
ain't ya?"

"No."

"Yes ya are, Elias."

"No I'm not." Elias says, then laughs.

"Don't ya laugh at me."

"I'm not laughin at you."

"Then what ya laughin at, huh?. . . Ain't nothin else here 'cept me."

Elias laughs again, catches his breath long enough to say, "I'm not laughing at you, I'm laughing at what you said." Then he laughs again.

"That's laughin at me. . . . Ya don't stop Um goin ta beat ya up. . . . Ya can't say French things . . . ya just pretendin . . . ya just makin funny noises and all."

Elias laughs again, Holly scoots closer to him, then straddles his lap and pushes him down to the ground. He's still laughin and she sits gigglin and sayin, "Ya laughin at me, Elias."

"No I'm not . . . I'm not laughing at you . . ."

"Yes ya are," Holly says, scootin higher up on Elias's waist. The hem of her red dress slides way past her knees. She leans over Elias, looks in his eyes, yells at him. Tells him, "Say ya love me. Say that in French words. And ya better say it right. Ya better not say some funny sound."

Elias stills, stares up into Holly's eyes and whispers, *"Je t'aime."*

Holly leans closer, can feel Elias's breath on her lips and tells him, "Say it American now . . . Say it."

Elias can only say, "I love—" before Holly's lips cover his.

"Say it . . . say it . . . ," Holly whispers, waits till Elias's lips part, till she can feel his breath. She waits till the sound of his words tries to come out of his mouth, waits till then, then kisses again. Kisses and says, "Say it." Then kisses when he tries.

"Say it . . . say it . . ."

Holly closes her eyes but she can still find Elias's curly black hair, find a way to put her fingers in it while she wiggles herself closer to him. She can feel his hand slidin up her back and pulling on her shoulder. She sucks in her breath as he pulls her down and slowly slides himself over her. His lips gently nip at her neck. Holly jerks her head back, slowly turns it back and forth. She feels the wet touch of Elias's tongue licking at her neck, it leaves a stream of chills runnin down her skin. She slowly opens her eyes and closes them again. Now she can only feel what she cannot see, feel the touch of lips, then a tongue near her breast. The feelin of the tuggin on her bra comes quickly but the feelin of the air wispin across her naked breast comes slowly. It lasts until she feels the nipple of a breast bein sucked into a warm mouth. She sucks and bites at the air, sighs deeply as her other nipple is sucked into Elias's mouth. She begins turnin and twistin until her red dress is off, thrown aside. Her back arches, her hips wiggle a little until she knows her panties are off and feels the air flowin over her body. She keeps her eyes closed, feels the hair on Elias's chest rub over her naked breast. She gasps for air, keeps gaspin for it and kisses Elias's neck as he enters her, pushes and slides through her inner softness. She is quiverin, her fingernails scratch at Elias's back. Her hips are movin, squirmin, she thrusts herself upward. Her sudden cry leaves her words lingerin in the air until she cries out again, "Ya love me? . . . Say it . . . say it . . . say it . . ."

18

Supply's summer of nineteen and forty-five seemed to be lastin longer, just wouldn't go away. Folks were even lookin the same as the day before, the day before that, too. Days were bitter hot but there was a stillness in the heat. The mid-August days seemed just to stick around like dried sweat on folks. Folks had been sittin around for days sittin still, had that waitin look on their face. Folks that had to move, get up and go someplace, did it slowly, kept lookin at folks they might be passin. Folks still sittin might look back, might say, "Ya hear anythin?" or just let their look on their face say it. Some folks hadn't got out from around them radios, wouldn't walk past where they couldn't hear it. Then the radio told em somethin it took a while for them to say somethin about, had to sit for a moment and just look someplace where nothin was at, shake their head a little bit and wipe at their eyes. The war was over but the heat and stillness lingered.

Reverend Powell was still doin his preachin, told folks, "God been good ta Supply, Supply better be good ta God." Mrs. Bruce was at church when Reverend Powell was talkin about blessins folks ought to be thankful for. She smiled a little, sighed, wiped the tear from her eye. Her boy Charles was the last name to be put up on the courthouse wall, his ship was sunk durin the invasion of Okinawa. Chester Higgens said he was sure glad this here war was over, said, "Ah couldn't take much more of carryin folks that kind of news. . . . It got the best of me . . ." Eugene Purvis said he would keep fresh flowers under them boys' names that didn't come home, he said, "That's the least Ah can do for em."

Days started coolin some when September came, went by. October found Supply settlin back in the shadows of the autumn sun. Folks welcomed the change, with the war gone, most of the boys were home. Except for the empty spaces at supper tables, time started puttin stuff back the way it was. Old men that sat in the shade were tryin to get some sun, tryin to get somethin else to talk about, too. Them coloreds that were workin down the lumberyard had to go on back to them fields. The lumberyard had to cut them long hours back, give them jobs back to them boys comin home, too. Eugene Purvis kept fresh flowers under the names on the courthouse wall but with them cold nights comin, sometimes he'd have to change them flowers in the morning.

Gus Hill was workin daylight hours again, although some days he wouldn't get home until after dark, had started nippin at the bottle again. Bobby Hill had to be put back in the hospital for a while. Ginger didn't know what was wrong with him, he'd start screamin and holdin his head, then start shakin and sweatin all over. The doctors up at the Wilmington Veterans' Clinic gave him some pills, said that ought to stop them fits he was havin. The next day, Ginger had to take him right back up there and leave him for a while.

Ginger seemed not to worry about Holly. Seemed like Holly was just bein herself again, goin down Elsie's all the time, gettin moody if anyone asked her about her business, or where she was goin. Ginger hadn't seen her runnin down that creek, sorta figured she grew past that, got Billy's soul to rest in her mind.

Holly never went down the old road, she always went up toward

Elsie's, then she'd sway to the far side of the road, weave into the bushes until she was deep within the trees. It was there that she'd turn and head toward the Back Land. She kept the cross Elias gave her tucked in the left side of her bra. She had told Elias, "Ah keep it there. . . . Can't nobody else see it . . . but my heart knows just where it's at."

Elias had told Holly everything there was to know about him. He had said that when he got out of the hospital, he thought he needed some time, needed to get away from things for a while. He told Holly, "I thought if I came down here, I could find some things . . . My mother thought it was a good idea, she had been worried about me. . . . My grandmother could use the company . . . She doesn't have anyone since my grandfather died. . . . I was born here, right up in the old house there. . . . My mother took me away when I was just a baby . . . My father sent for us to come to Washington . . . He had left just before I was born . . . He worked his way through school and my mother learned how to play the piano, that's how I learned to play. She wanted me to go to school and get a degree . . . she wanted me to make something out of myself like my father. . . . My father teaches at Howard University, he's a professor of litera- ture. . . . I wanted to play the piano but I went to school, studied art . . . then the war came."

Elias had tried to teach Holly how to paint and had sat still for an hour or so while she painted him. He had to promise her he would not laugh at the picture before she'd let him see it but he couldn't keep his promise.

In a quiet moment, Holly had leaned her head on Elias's shoulder, had closed her eyes and whispered, "When ya goin ta take me away, Elias?"

Elias had whispered back, "Do you really want to go? If you do, you know you'll never be able to come back."

Holly had answered, "Ah want ta be wit ya all the time, that's all. Ah mean Ah love Mama and stuff like that . . . but . . . Well, Ah ain't no little girl no more. . . . Ah want ta be a mama too . . . and Ah want ta be wit ya, Elias . . ."

Elias had taken her under his arm, kissed her on her forehead, then sighed and looked beyond the shade of the trees.

October was nearin its end, gatherin up its time and getting ready to move on, only a few days remained. Holly would remember its passin and one of its lingerin days as "that day." It had rained durin the night and in the morning the sky was still dark and dreary. Holly lay in the bed with her pillow in her arms starin at the gloomy light comin through the window. She pushed the pillow away, sat up on the side of the bed and took a deep breath. When she went to get up, she felt weak and dizzy. When she got dressed and came down into the kitchen, Ginger asked, "Honey, ya feelin all right? Ya look a little pale, ya comin down with somethin?"

"Um all right, Mama," Holly said quickly, then slowly sat down at the table. The dizziness came again and brought a pain that settled in her stomach.

"Honey, ya sure ya feelin all right?"

"Yes, Mama, Um fine. Ah told ya Um feelin all right."

Holly sat at the table for a while and talked with her mother, then went out on the porch to sit on the steps. She sat for a while, stared at the sky before she yelled back over her shoulder, "Mama, Um goin up Elsie's."

Ginger came to the door and called out, "Honey, ain't ya goin ta eat anythin?"

"Ah ain't hungry, Mama, Ah'll eat somethin up Elsie's," Holly yelled back over her shoulder as she started up the path. The walk up Elsie's seemed to last forever, Holly stopped twice along the road when the pain in her stomach made her quiver and weakened her stride. Elsie was sittin at her kitchen table when Holly hollered, "What ya doin? Where ya at, huh?" and comes into the house.

"Um in here," Elsie yells.

Holly goes into the kitchen, sits down, sighs and looks down at the floor. Elsie gets to lookin at Holly, squints up her face a little and says, "Ya ain't lookin right. What's wrong wit ya, ya sick or somethin?"

"Ah don't know, maybe," Holly says, keeps lookin down.

"Ya got cramps?"

"No, it ain't that or nothin. Ah mean it ain't that yet."

Elsie is silent for a moment, then sorta whispers, "Well, what is it?"

Holly keeps her head down, says, "Ah don't know, just sick, Ah guess."

"Ya want some aspirin? That might make it go away. Ya just probably gittin them cramps comin."

Holly shakes her head no, then asks, "Ya mama here?"

"She went inta town. Um glad, she been gittin on my nerves all mornin anyway."

Holly takes a deep breath, lifts her head and looks off toward the window. She stares, the blue of her eyes is stilled by the gray of the gloom comin through the window. In the softness of a quiet breath, Holly's askin, "Would ya go away if ya could?. . . Ya know, go someplace ya ain't never been and all?"

Elsie says, "Yeah, Ah'd leave out of here in a minute."

Holly sits quietly.

Elsie asks, "What's Bobby doin?"

Holly looks away from the window, lowers her eyes to the floor and says, "He ain't doin nothin . . . Ah mean, he ain't had one of them fits or nothin . . . Mama worried and all but she don't talk about it . . ."

Elsie asks, "Ya want ta go inta town? Maybe find somethin ta do?"

Holly shakes her head no.

Elsie says, "Ah wish Ah could go somewhere a ways from here, find some place that got lots of stores and places ta go and all. Find some man that got lots of money and ain't all full of bullshit too."

Holly smiles a little, then asks, "Ya ever want ta go way up ta Washington? Ya ever want ta go way up there or somethin?"

"Ah ain't never thought about goin up there but Ah'd go, long as Ah ain't got ta be sittin around in some house all the time."

Holly asks, "Ya ever goin ta go away? Ya think ya goin ta do that or stay here all the time?"

Elsie is silent for a moment, then slowly says, "Ah git tired of bein around here. . . . Seem like the more ya wait and be hopin ya can be wit somebody, the more that don't come. . . . Mama says it will . . . says, Ah ain't but two time ten . . . Says, enjoy it . . . but ain't nothin ta be enjoyin most of the time. . . . Ah thought that Paul was real nice and all . . . Ah really liked him, Ah keep hopin he'd write or somethin . . . He done probably went and got married and ain't even thinkin about me. . . . That Eddie be thinkin more about that truck he drives than me . . . he out on the road all the time anyway . . ."

Holly asks, "Ya want ta have kids? Would ya have kids wit Paul, ya know if he would have asked ya ta come up there wit him and all?"

Slowly, Elsie answers, "Ah think so. If he would have asked me ta marry him."

Holly says, "Then if ya love somebody, ya go wit them, huh?"

Elsie says back, "Yeah, one thing for sure, Ah wouldn't want ta be married and still livin here wit Mama. Ah'd want my own house, a pretty one, too."

Quickly, Holly says, "Ah didn't mean that. Ah meant, would ya go away wit them, ya know, leave Supply and don't come back? Like go real far and ya couldn't come back. If ya love somebody, would ya do that?"

Elsie stares at Holly for a moment, then says, "Ah might want ta come back, see Mama, see ya if ya still here. Ya know, things like that. Why ya askin stuff like this for?"

Holly dips her head back down and says, "Ah don't know, just askin."

"Oh," Elsie says, then asks, "Ya want ta start goin up Wilmington, start goin up there more like we used ta? Maybe meet somebody up there."

Slowly, Holly looks up at Elsie, then puts her head back down. She was silent for a moment but now she is askin Elsie, "Ya my friend?"

"Huh?"

"Ya my friend?"

"Why ya askin that for?"

Slowly, Holly says, "Ah know we fuss some and stuff like that . . . and ya git mad at me and all . . . Ah git mad at ya, too . . . but Ah always still like ya . . ."

Elsie smiles a little and says, "Well, Holly Hill, if ya thinkin we ain't friends, then ya crazier than what Ah thought."

Holly laughs some, then says, "Ya the one that's crazy, Elsie Fagen." Then she sits quietly again.

Elsie blurts out, "Ah think we should start goin up Wilmington a lot. Maybe we could even git a job up there. Maybe in one of them stores, make us enough money ta git us a place ta stay and all . . ."

Holly looks up at Elsie, sighs and says, "If Ah tell ya somethin, Ah mean somethin real important, ya promise ya won't say nothin ta nobody? Ya promise that fore Ah tell ya?"

Elsie stops talkin, looks at Holly, then just stares at her. Holly looks back down at the floor, tells Elsie, "Never mind."

"Never mind what?"

"Never mind what Ah was goin ta say."

"Why ya say somethin if ya ain't goin ta say somethin?"

Holly whispers, "Ah ain't never told nobody before."

"Told somebody what, huh?"

"Well . . ."

"Well what, huh?"

"Well if Ah tell ya, ya got ta promise ya ain't goin ta say nothin ta nobody. Ah mean ya can't say nothin, Elsie."

Elsie says, "Ah ain't goin ta tell. If it's a secret, Ah won't tell nobody. What is it, huh? Is it somethin about Bobby? Did he do somethin?"

"It ain't him."

"What is it then?"

Holly is quiet, bites down on her lip a little, stares at the floor, now looks up at Elsie and says, "Ya got ta promise ta still be my friend. Ya got ta promise that too. Say it."

Elsie looks at Holly, stares into her eyes and sees them starin right back at hers. Holly keeps starin and tells Elsie, "Say it, Elsie, say ya still be my friend."

Elsie looks away but says, "Yeah, we still be friends. How come ya think Ah wouldn't be friends wit ya? Ya done went out and killed a bunch of people like in some scary movie or somethin? What's wrong wit ya, ya real sick and don't want nobody ta know, huh?"

Holly looks back down at the floor and says, "It ain't that . . . Ah mean it ain't like bein sick . . ."

"Then what is it?"

"Ah might be sick . . . Ah mean not like ya think . . . but that ain't it. . . . It's just a part of what Ah might tell ya and all . . . Ah mean the way Um feelin is important . . . but it's just part of somethin more important . . ."

Elsie takes a big breath, sighs, then stills herself.

Holly is keepin her head down and whisperin somethin that Elsie cannot hear. Quickly, Elsie is twistin up her face and sayin, "Huh?"

Holly whispers again, "Ah can say French words, not a lot, just some."

"Huh?"

"La mayson or somethin means house . . . and . . . la ven, that means wine. . . . Ja tinay, that means when ya love somebody . . ."

Elsie is just lookin at Holly and keeps lookin at her. Holly is still starin down at the floor, she ain't sayin nothin, just starin. Quickly now, Elsie is sayin, "What in the world ya talkin about? What ya sayin French things for, huh?"

Holly whispers, "Somebody loves me . . . Ah mean they just don't say it, they really do . . . they do things that makes ya feel that they really love ya. . . . He's real nice too and Ah love him too . . . Ah mean it's like Ah want ta be wit him always . . . Ah mean, no matter what, Ah want ta be wit him . . ."

Elsie's askin, "Who is it? Who ya talkin about, huh? Ya ain't been seein nobody, what's that French stuff for? Is it somebody that's French or somethin? When ya meet them? Ah ain't seen nobody like that."

"He ain't French, he was in France and all, he was there in the war

. . . he said it was real bad . . . but he don't like ta talk about it much . . . ya know like Bobby . . . Ah mean he talks, he ain't like Bobby but he don't like ta say things about the war. . . . Elsie . . ." Holly lets her words slow, takes a deep breath and looks up at Elsie and tells her, "Elsie, Ah really love him . . . Ah mean Ah loved Billy too and Ah still do . . . but this is different . . . Ah mean, Ah can't say how Ah feel and all . . . Ah just can't stop feelin what Ah feel . . . Ah love him, Elsie . . ."

Slowly, Elsie's askin, "Who is it, huh? Who ya talkin about?"

Holly lowers her head and is bitin her lip again.

"What's his name, huh?"

Holly is keepin silent and just starin at the floor.

"How come ya can't tell me?"

Holly whispers, "Ya don't know him."

"He live around here? Where's he from, huh?"

"He ain't from around here, Elsie . . . Ah mean he was born here and all but his mama took him up ta Washington, D.C., when he was a baby. . . . He lived up there and went ta a university school. . . . He's real smart, too . . ."

"How ya meet him then?"

"It was in the summer."

"Where ya meet him? What does he look like? Ah ain't seen no-body like ya talkin about comin around here. How come Ah ain't seen him? Ya still ain't sayin what his name is."

Holly raises her head, looks past Elsie and stares out the window. Elsie keeps lookin at Holly lookin away and asks, "How come ya can't tell me his name? How come, huh?"

Holly whispers, "It's Elias."

"It's what?"

"Elias."

"Elias what? Where he git that kind of name? Where ya met him? Ah ain't never heard of him."

"Ah told ya, ya don't know him."

"How come?"

"Ah don't know, ya just ain't seen him, Ah guess," Holly is tellin

Elsie and still starin out the window, then she whispers, "Ah seen him down the creek . . . Ah met him down there, Elsie."

"What?"

"Ah said, Ah met him down the creek."

"Down the creek, what he doin down there? That's why ya been goin down there all the time, huh? He ain't no nigger is he?"

Holly's eyes jerk away from the window, stare at Elsie. Elsie is starin back and sayin, "Ain't nothin down there 'cept niggers. He ain't no nigger is he?"

Holly shouts, "He ain't no nigger. Ah mean he ain't all black and all. He got real pretty skin and he got dark curly hair and real pretty eyes. But that ain't why Um lovin him. He makes me feel things, important things, too. He makes me feel alive. Ah ain't all empty inside anymore. Ah love him, Elsie, cause he makes me feel love and bein in it, too. He ain't no nigger either."

Elsie looks away.

Holly shouts, "He's real nice, too."

Quickly, Elsie turns back, shouts, "He's still a nigger. Ya let him kiss ya and stuff?"

"Yeah," Holly shouts and puffs her cheeks out and says, "He ain't no nigger either. He ain't, ya hear me? He's a Negro."

Elsie shouts, "That's a nigger. Ya let him touch ya?"

"It ain't like that, it ain't like that, Elsie," Holly is shoutin back. "It ain't like what ya thinkin. He loves me, Elsie. Ah want ta be wit him, Ah love him, too. It's important, Elsie. It's real important."

"What's so important about bein wit some nigger?"

"It's important ta me. It's important ta me and he ain't no nigger."

"Ya let him touch ya. Didn't ya? Didn't ya?"

Tears are comin from Holly's eyes and rollin down her cheeks. She's tryin to keep her head up but the tears keep on rollin down. She sighs, looks back toward the window where the gray gloom is. "It ain't like ya think and all," she's softly sayin, "It ain't like ya sayin, Elsie. It's important, real important. . . . Important is when ya have somethin . . . have somethin and it's the only thing ya have and it has ya, too . . . And ya want it ta have ya like ya have it . . . It's the only thing Ah have that wants me and Ah want it too . . . It's important . . ."

"Holly," Elsie shouts, now she's lowerin her voice and sayin, "Ya can't be wit some nigger, ya just can't. Folks goin ta have a fit."

Quickly, Holly turns from the window, shoutin, "Ah don't care. It ain't their business, Ah don't care."

Elsie's shoutin, "Ya ain't did it wit him, have ya? Ya let him do it ta ya?"

"Ah did it," Holly shouts, "Ah did it and Ah wanted ta. Ah love him and he loves me."

Elsie sighs, looks away.

It's silent, just sounds of breathin can be heard. Holly puts her head down and starts cryin and whisperin, "Ah ain't sick like ya thinkin, Elsie."

Elsie turns around, says, "What?"

"Ah said, Ah ain't sick like ya thinkin. . . . Ah ain't told him yet . . . Ah was goin ta say it ta ya first . . . Ah was goin ta say it ta ya so ya could be happy, too. . . . Um scared, too . . . Ah mean, Ah ain't never thought things like this would be . . . But it don't make no nevermind now. . . . Ah been wantin ta tell ya . . . been wantin ta tell somebody Um happy . . . ya know, really happy . . . But Um not all the way happy cause Ah can't tell nobody nothin. . . . Ah ain't sick, not like ya think . . . Um gonna have a baby. . . . Ah ain't had my time, it's real, real late . . . it's time for it again and it ain't came either . . . Ah guess that's why Ah be lookin like Um sick and all . . ."

Elsie turns from Holly, puts her head down and sits quietly. Holly puts her head down, too, just stares at the floor again. Any noise would sound as sudden as thunder in Elsie's kitchen until Holly sighs and whispers, "Well, Ah think Ah better go."

Elsie sits quietly.

Slowly, Holly is gettin up from the table. She looks at Elsie and says, "Ah guess Ah see ya later, huh?"

Elsie keeps her head down. Holly stands and keeps lookin at her but Elsie don't say nothin, just keeps her head down. Holly says, "Ah guess we ain't friends no more, huh?"

Elsie doesn't say anything, just sits there with her head down. Holly whispers, "We ain't friends, huh?" as she slowly turns to leave.

Outside the day is still gray. Any greens, blues and browns have weakened into just ghostly shades of what they had been. Holly walks along the old road with her head down. She stares at every pebble and raggedy crack along the way, turns off the road and starts down the yard path. She keeps walkin with her head down. Slowly the hard poundin of her heart begins to make her tremble. Tears stream, then gush from her eyes. She throws her hands in the air, grabs at her hair, spins around and starts runnin up the path. She gets to the road, turns down it and keeps runnin. Where the road curves through the shade she slows, gasps for air. Her legs are wobblin but she runs again. Tears are still fallin from her eyes and when she looks, the top of the fat-bellied oak tree is only a far gray blur. She keeps runnin for the secret path, then down its dips, around its twists, then through the stillness where the old oak tree sits. At the water's edge, she slows, stops and takes her shoes off. The water in the creek is splashin up on her, gettin on her dress, but she keeps runnin through it.

The old woman's rusty-colored face is peerin through the dark screen door. She has heard the shouts turn into cries of, "Elias . . . Elias . . . Ya in there, where ya at?"

The women quietly opens the door and looks. Holly tries to wipe the tears out of her eyes, looks up at the old woman standin in the doorway and asks, "Is he in there?. . . Is Elias in there? Please tell him ta come out, please."

"Come here, child, ya just git on in here," the old woman is sayin, holdin the door open.

Holly stills and just stares.

"Come on in here, baby child. Ya just come on here ta Alpha, come on now."

Holly wipes her eyes, then lowers them as she goes up on the porch. She whispers as she nears the woman, "Is Elias here, is he here?"

"Come on in here, baby child. Ya just come on in here ta Alpha, come on now. Ya bring that hurt on in here, come on, child."

Holly goes on to the woman and through the open door. In the first room of the shack, the walls have a warm blue color. Pictures and a big cross hang quietly on the blue. A couch sits in a far dark corner and a rockin chair sits where the light should come through the window. It is only the faded colors of the woman's tattered dress Holly can see as she keeps her eyes lowered. She raises her hand to wipe at her eyes and in a faint whisper she is askin, "Ya Elias's grandma? Is he here?"

"Ya just sit on down here, baby child, go on now."

Holly looks behind her, eases herself down on the couch. The woman sits down, too, she sits on the edge of the couch, watches Holly lower her head into her hands. She sees Holly quiverin and reaches for her cheek, touches it and says, "Baby child, what's gone and got into ya? Ya just tell Alpha. Ya ain't the first baby child that done tried ta pull this here world behind em. What ya tryin ta pull that done got too heavy for a mule ta be pullin?"

Holly can't stop shakin, she keeps her face down in her hands. She tries not to see Elsie's face, hear her sayin things. But she keeps on hearin things Elsie said.

"Come on ta Alpha, child," the woman whispers and brings Holly to her bosom, then holds her. It is warm in the old woman's arms, Holly cuddles closer. Slowly and gently the woman begins to rock with Holly in her arms. Holly begins to still, only her tears keep movin. Her eyes are open and just stare at the soft blue of a wall.

"What got ya hurtin like this, baby child? Ya got ta tell it now. Say it out, say it out, child."

It is quiet, Holly does not speak. She has tried to say something back, tried to make feelings turn into words. The woman whispers, "Ya can tell Alpha, baby child. Lookin like ya children done went and got feelins, ain't ya? God ain't never got mad at somebody just cause they love somebody." Holly snuggles closer to the woman and closes her eyes.

"Ah done seen it in that boy's face. Been seein ya comin up in here every day. Ah knowed he done had some feelins for ya, knowed it all along. All ya had ta do is look at that boy's face ta see it. He come in here wit that picture he done painted of ya, ya could see it in his face right then. Ya all children just ain't knowin this world, ya just ain't knowin this here old world at all."

The old woman eases Holly from her bosom but keeps her hands on Holly's shoulders. She tries to look into Holly's eyes, but they are lookin down. She asks, "Now, what done got this here pretty face wrinkled up so? Tell it ta Alpha."

Holly keeps her head down but asks, "He ain't went nowhere, has he?"

"Oh no, child, he out there somewhere. He ain't went away on ya."

Holly whispers, "Ya ain't mad at me, are ya?"

The woman smiles and takes Holly into her arms again and rocks her while she's tellin her, "Alpha ain't mad at this child, naw, Alpha ain't mad at ya. Now, who done made ya cry like this? Who made ya come on up here wit all that hurt ya carryin?"

Holly started talkin, just started sayin things, tryin to say the right words about things, then stopped tryin to say the right words and just said what she was feelin. She keeps sayin, "Ah love him. . . . Ah love him. . . . He loves me too. . . . Ah ain't got nobody Ah want ta be wit 'cept him. . . . Ah know it ain't right and all but it don't feel that way. . . . It feels like it's right and everythin else ain't. . . . Ah think Um goin ta have a baby too . . . Ah ain't told him, Ah wanted to, but Ah wasn't sure and all . . . Ah just . . . ."

Holly jolts and turns toward the door. There is a faint sound of footsteps nearin. She watches the door, the sounds come up the porch steps. She keeps starin, the door opens and Elias is there. She hurries from the couch, goes to him and puts her arms around his waist and her face against his chest. Elias puts his arm around her, looks over her head to his grandmother's face, stares and asks her, "What happened, Grandma?"

"She'll tell ya but ya got ta git aways from here. Ya gots ta do what's right and ya gots ta do it now. Ya children gots ta git away from here. Ya don't know them folks and their ways. Ya gots ta do, ya gots ta do, ya hear?" A quick silence comes into the old woman's eyes, then she sighs deeply and quietly leaves the room.

Elias lowers his head and whispers into Holly's ear, "What has happened? You must tell me."

Holly keeps her eyes closed, she can hear Elias's deep sighs and shakes when she feels him tremblin and whisperin again, "Holly, what is it? Did someone find out, what has happened?"

Holly starts whisperin back, tellin Elias about Elsie. Tellin him about things she was still seein in her mind. Elsie wouldn't look back at her and Holly was tellin Elias that. Sayin, "Ah thought she was my friend, Elias. Ah though she'd be happy and Ah wanted ta tell her things that was makin me happy. . . . Maybe she ain't goin ta tell . . . maybe she just look like it or was actin like she ain't my friend no more . . . Sometimes she act like that when we fussin . . . Maybe she was just doin that."

Elias's chest is heavin, Holly is tryin to wait till it stills, make it still by squeezin her arms around him, pressin her head up against it. When she feels it still, can't hear his breath surgin, she whispers, "Ah was goin ta tell ya but Ah wasn't sure . . . but Ah think Um sure now . . . Ah thinks Um goin ta have a baby. . . . Ya still love me?"

A sound of breath comes slow to Holly's ear, it keeps on comin, stays beyond the passin moment. She's shakin, then slowly stillin. Elias's arm is pullin her closer to his chest.

"Ya still love me?"

Dark soft lips find their way to Holly's ear, Elias whispers, "Yes. How come you did not tell me sooner?"

"Ah don't know, Ah wasn't sure, too."

Gently, Elias is easin his arm from around Holly and slowly bringin it up to her face. He touches her cheek, softly nudges at her chin until she looks up at him. Quickly he is sayin, "You must listen and you must know that everything I say is for us. Do you understand?"

Holly begins to lower her head, feels Elias's hand tremblin and looks back up into his eyes. He stares into hers for a moment, then says, "You must listen to me."

Elias's hand keeps tremblin. Holly bites at her lip, puts her head down and looks back up real quick, sayin, "Maybe she ain't goin ta tell. Maybe she was just actin like she was."

"We can't take the chance. We've taken too many already. You must listen to me, it's important."

"Um listenin."

"We must leave here."

"When?"

"You must leave tomorrow."

"Huh?"

"You must go."

"Where we goin? How we goin ta git there?"

"You're going to Washington. I want you to leave in the morning."

Holly's eyes get big, she looks at Elias and says, "Ya ain't sayin we, ya just sayin me, Elias. Ah ain't goin noplace witout ya."

"Damn it, Holly, listen."

"No. Ah ain't listenin ta nothin like that."

Elias takes a deep breath, blows the air out of his mouth, turns and quickly goes to the window. Holly watches him stare out of the window, hears his deep breaths fill the room. He turns back to her, says, "You have to listen to me. You must leave tomorrow, I'll come later. You must leave in the morning to Wilmington. Get the train there."

"No. Um not leavin witout ya."

Elias shouts, "Holly, listen. We don't have a lot of time, listen. I don't have enough money for both of us to go now. I'm going to give you what I have, it will be enough for you to get there. My discharge check will be here any day but it's not here now and you must go now. You must go before anybody says anything."

"No. Ah said Ah go wit ya. Ah said that but Ah ain't gittin on no train or nothin else if ya ain't comin too."

Elias spins around, blows all the air out of his mouth and goes to the window. Again, he looks out, turnin his head back and forth. Holly calls to him but he keeps lookin out the window. She calls again, says his name until he turns around, then she says, "Elias, Ah think ya should go. Ya go git on the train, then when ya git there and ya still love me and ya git that dischargin check, then ya can send for me ta come. Ah'll come, ya know that. Ah want ya ta go, Ah don't want anythin ta happen ta ya ever."

"No. You're carrying our child and I want you and the child around love, not around this. I'm going to give you the money, I have enough to get you there. I'll give you a letter, give it to my mother. When you get off the train, get a taxi, just tell them the address, they'll take you there. I'll come soon, I promise you. But even if I did have enough money, we couldn't leave or be seen together anyway. It's better this way. Alone, no one will say anything to you. Holly, I love you. Please, for me and the child, please go. It's important to me. I have a bad feeling. My God, please go."

Holly lowers her head, whispers, "Ah love ya, Elias. Ah go if ya say go. Ah don't want to but if ya say it's important, Ah go. . . . But ya have ta promise me that ya goin ta be all right and not let anyone be botherin ya . . . Ya got ta promise me that, ya hear . . . and ya got ta promise me that ya comin as soon as ya can. . . . Ah don't ever want anythin ta hurt ya again, ya hear me? . . . Ya have ta promise . . . Ya have ta say that . . ."

Holly looks up.

Elias shakes his head yes.

"No. Ya have ta say it."

"I promise."

"The baby is goin ta be a girl . . . and she's goin ta have pretty eyes like ya . . . and she's goin ta have black curly hair like ya . . . but she's goin ta look like me some, too. . . . we can have a boy, too . . . Ah want one . . . but Ah want a girl first so he'll have a big sister. . . . Ah never had a big sister . . ."

It was quiet in the room for a while, then Elias gave Holly the money he had. He wrote his mother a letter, put her address and phone number on it and gave it to Holly too. She took it and said that she would take the bus in the morning to Wilmington, then she'd get the train. She said, "Ah just tell Mama Um goin inta town. Ah won't take a bunch a stuff. Maybe take some clothes and say Um goin ta put them in the cleaner's or somethin. Ah got a big purse Ah can put stuff in. Ah write Mama from up there, tell her Ah love her and all. Maybe she can come visit me if she wants. Ya know when she's done bein mad and all, she can do that."

Elias watched Holly leave, watched her go down the hills through the valley. When he could not see her anymore, he still stood watchin the valley and the hills. He had told her, whispered into her ear when he was holdin her, when she was cryin and not wantin to go. He had whispered, "Go on, because I love you. You are everything in my life I care for. I'll come too, if I have to I'll get on a freight, or walk if I have to."

Holly's walk home was slow. She took her time crossin the creek, stopped at the turtle rock and touched its red flower. At the old fat-bellied oak, she stood and looked at the old tree, smiled as she saw times of its time. She whispered, "You're goin ta be a little girl, Ah just know ya are. . . . Um goin ta take ya ta Washington and your daddy's comin too."

When Holly got home, Ginger was in the kitchen. Holly yelled, "Um home, Mama." Ginger yelled back, "Tell Bobby supper's ready. Ya feelin better?"

Holly went into the kitchen, Ginger was busy in the pantry and did not turn around. Holly just stood lookin at her mother for a while, then said, "Mama, Um feelin all right and all. Ya can't be worryin about me."

Ginger turned around and looked at Holly, then said, "Um goin ta worry about ya if Ah think you're not feelin well or somethin wrong."

"Ah know that, Mama . . . but . . . well, ya got Bobby, ya don't need me ta be . . . Ah mean, Ah don't want ya worryin about me . . . Um all right . . ."

Ginger kept lookin at Holly, then wiped her hands on her apron and asked, "Honey, are ya all right?"

Holly smiled and said, "Um fine, Mama, Ah was just thinkin. Ah just don't want ya worryin about me."

Holly went on upstairs, tapped on Bobby's door and whispered, "Bobby, Mama says it's suppertime," then she went into her room and closed the door. For a moment, she stood lookin around, then she went and sat on the bed. She put her head down, but looked back up and around the room again. Slowly she got up from the bed and went over to the dresser and sat on the chair and looked at things on the dresser. She saw the chipped knob on the dresser drawer, stared at it before she pulled the drawer open. She eases her hand into the drawer, slides it into the back and gets the little box that has Billy's ring in it. Slowly, she brings the little box out, opens it, and touches the ring with her finger. She closes the box, reaches back in the drawer, sighs, and gets the little stack of letters. She sits quietly for a while, then gently tears the first letter open.

Ginger pokes her head into the room, says, "Honey, ya comin down ta eat? Ah fixed ya a little stew." She sees Holly sittin at the dresser and the letters open, a sudden silence comes over her. She tries to still herself, softens the sounds of her breaths. Holly turns to her and says, "Mama, Um all right, Ah just don't feel like eatin now. But Ah ain't sick or nothin."

Slowly, Ginger walks in her own silence, goes over to Holly and whispers, "Ya all right, honey?"

Holly looks up and says, "Yeah, Mama, Um fine."

Gently, Ginger puts her hand on Holly's shoulder, rubs it a little and asks again, "Ya sure everythin is all right?"

"Um fine, Mama."

Ginger turns to leave the room, Holly watches her walk away. She calls, "Mama."

Ginger turns around, Holly stares up into her eyes, then looks away and says, "Oh nothin, Mama. It wasn't nothin."

"Ya comin down later? Ah think ya should have some of that stew, maybe a little warm tea be good, too."

"Yeah, Mama, Um comin down."

The sounds of Ginger's footsteps are slowly goin away. Holly waits for every sound to still, then looks at the words on the letters again. She can hear Billy sayin things, askin things, she whispers back to him, "Um sorry about doin things Ah did."

Quietly, Holly places the ring on top of the letters and pushes the drawer closed. She's at her closet, gettin her big straw purse out. She starts pickin through her dresses and skirts, gettin some out the closet and foldin them up. Quickly, she's puttin her clothes in the big purse, lookin back into the closet to see if she wants to take anything else. The purse is full, she stills, then slowly reaches into her bra and gets the money and folded-up letter out. She slides the money and letter into the bottom of the purse. A deep sigh fills the room as Holly lies across her bed and closes her eyes. The dark dreary gray outside of the window gets darker, the early night brings a curdlin call.

"Holly, Holly, git down here!" Ginger is screamin up the steps.

Holly's eyes come open, she mumbles, "Huh?" keeps hearin her mother screamin, *"Holly git down here now, ya hear me callin ya, git down here!"*

Holly yells, "What's wrong, Mama?"

"Git down here right now, git down here Holly!"

Holly starts takin deep breaths, her stomach begins squirmin, her hands tremble. She's up from the bed, wipes at her eyes, slows when she nears her door. Her mother's screams fill the hallway when she opens the door.

"Um comin, Mama. What's wrong?" Holly yells.

The steps are dark, Holly is easin down each one, slowin when she hears the voices in the kitchen, creepin when she knows it is Elsie's voice she hears. She nears the kitchen door and she can see Elsie with her mother. Her mother's face is red, drawn up tight and starin at her when she goes into the kitchen.

"*Git in here, Holly!*" Ginger screams.

Holly looks at Elsie but Elsie doesn't look back, Ginger yells. "*What have ya done? My God, what have ya done?*"

Holly keeps starin at Elsie. Ginger throws her hands up in the air and shakes her fist at the ceilin and screams, "*What have ya done? What are ya doin wit a nigger?*"

Elsie looks at Holly and says, "Ah didn't want anythin ta happen ta ya, Ah didn't want that. Ah didn't, Ah didn't."

"*Answer me, ya hear me?*"

Holly turns from Elsie, stares down at the floor. She feels her legs quiverin, something in her stomach is shakin. The floor becomes blurry, dark grays seem to shift and spin. Holly keeps her eyes down, won't look up, won't say nothin.

"*Answer me, ya hear me? Ya answer me. What did he do ta ya?*" Ginger hollers, flings her hands at Holly, grabs her shoulders and starts shakin her. Tears burst out of Holly's eyes, she jerks away from her mother, looks up at her and shouts, "He ain't did nothin. He ain't did nothin ta me."

"*What were ya doin wit him? Trash got better ways. What did he do ta ya? Ya answer me, ya hear me?*"

Holly flings her hands in the air, spins around, keeps her back turned to her mother. Ginger grabs at Holly's shoulder, yanks her around, screams, "*What's his name?*"

Holly shouts, "Leave me alone."

"*What's his name? Is it that nigger that was down there paintin? Is it?*"

Holly stands glarin at her mother. Ginger yells, "*What's his name? Ya hear me, what's his name?*"

"He ain't no nigger, he ain't no nigger."

"*Ah want ta know his name.*"

"Leave me alone, Mama. Um leavin here anyway, leave me alone."

"*Ya ain't goin noplace wit some damn nigger.*"

"He ain't no nigger."

"What's his name?"

"Why ya wantin ta know his name for?"

"Ah want ta know his name! What's his name?"

Holly flicks the hair out of her eyes, throws her shoulders back and just stares at her mother. Ginger turns to Elsie and asks, "What's his name? Did she tell ya that?"

Elsie keeps her eyes away from Holly but utters, "Ah can't remember. She said it was Eleesa or somethin. Ah told her she wasn't actin right, can't be wit some nigger."

Holly jerks her head toward Elsie and shouts, "Ya shut up. Ya hear me? Shut up."

Ginger turns back to Holly and just stares at her, then says with a hissin voice, "Have ya been wit him? Ya been wit that nigger, haven't ya? Haven't ya, answer me."

"It ain't like what ya sayin, Mama."

"Ya carryin that nigger's baby?"

Holly stands starin in her mother's eyes.

Ginger gasps, then utters, "My God."

Holly keeps starin at her mother, then says with her mother's hissin whisper, "God ain't never got mad at nobody just cause they love each other. He loves me and Ah love him too."

"Ya carryin a nigger's baby!"

Tears gush down Holly's cheeks, she shouts back at her mother, "It ain't goin ta be some nigger's baby. It's goin ta be our baby, and Um goin ta be her mother."

"No you're not."

"Um not a little girl anymore, Mama. Um a woman."

"The hell if ya are and you're not havin that nigger's baby!"

Holly stands glarin at her mother, she does not hear the footsteps comin up behind her and shudders when she hears her father shout, "What in the hell is goin on here?"

Quickly, Holly turns and looks up into her father's face, then turns away from it. Elsie looks at the dark outside the kitchen window and whispers, "Ah better be goin now."

Gus Hill shouts again, "What in the hell is goin on in here?"

Holly glares at Elsie as she passes.

Gus Hill looks at Holly, then looks at Ginger and shouts again, "Goddamn it, Ah want ta know what is goin on here, right now."

Holly looks up at her mother, turns to her father, then bolts out of the kitchen, screamin, *"Leave me alone! . . . Leave me alone! . . ."* She runs through the hallway, runs up the steps, gets in her room and slams the door. The room is dark, Holly reaches through it, touches things, feels the bed. She kneels and reaches under. Quickly, Holly's fingers touch the straw purse. She pulls it out from beneath the bed, gets back up on her feet and stares through the dark at the door.

Gus Hill is comin up the steps. Stompin sounds fill the stairway. Ginger is followin, screamin. *"No, Gus, no!"* But he keeps yellin, *"Goddamn you! Goddamn you to hell!"* Spit flies with his words, the sound of his voice splatters against the walls.

Holly hears the screamin and yellin, the thunderous footsteps nearin her door. She keeps starin at the door, tries to brace herself, hold one breath so she won't have to breathe and tremble. The door comes bustin open, Gus Hill barrels into the dark room, shoutin, *"You goddamned little tramp! Ah'll kill you and that goddamn nigger! You goddamned little bitch, you."*

Holly tries to step back, Gus Hill grabs at her, gets her hair and flings her against the dresser, then yanks her against the wall.

Ginger is screamin, *"No, Gus. No, Gus, ya hurt her."*

Holly is screamin, tryin to push her father away. His hand comes smackin across her face. He's yellin, *"You want to be with a nigger, huh, huh? Ah'll kill you first, you goddamn tramp."*

Holly puts her hands over her face.

Gus Hill is swingin wildly.

"Stop it, Gus, no, Gus . . . ," Ginger is screamin.

Tears and blood cover Holly's face.

Ginger is pushed to the side, Gus Hill's arm is jerked from its swing. He is yanked by his neck and thrown across the room. Bobby Hill is shoutin at him, tellin him, *"You leave her alone, Daddy! . . .*

You leave Holly alone! . . . Don't you hit her, Daddy . . . don't you make her cry . . . leave her be . . ."

Holly grabs at the straw purse, gets it in her hand and lunges for the door. Gus Hill yells, *"Ahm goin to kill you, you nigger whore!"* Ginger cries out, *"No, honey, no!"* and grabs Holly's arm. Holly jerks away, shouts back, *"Git off me, Mama. Git off me, Mama, Um goin."*

The sounds of shouts and screams follow Holly as she runs down the steps. Jason is standin at the bottom of the steps, he has tears in his eyes. Holly slows, looks at him, he turns away. She runs to the door, out onto the porch, down the steps and up the yard path.

Ginger runs out onto the porch and screams out into the night, *"Come back here, Holly, come back here. Come back, Holly. Holly, come back."*

"No, Mama . . . No," Holly yells out and doesn't look back. Ginger keeps callin, her screams fill the night. Holly can still hear them as she reaches the road. Distant yard dogs begin to howl. Holly keeps runnin, her heart is poundin with every step. Where the road curves, the darkness thickens. Holly can't see, everything is blurry black through the tears in her eyes. She can't find the secret path, plunges down the dark hillside through the thick weeds and bushes. Thorns rip and scratch at her arms and legs. She moans, cries out Elias's name. She can hear the ripplin sound of water runnin and keeps goin down the dark hillside. She reaches the soft mud along the water's edge, tries to see the turtle rock, see where she always crosses the creek. She can't, stops lookin for the rock and starts across. The water is cold, deeper, flowin faster in the night. The splashin sounds she's makin alarms the night's far stillness. She reaches the other side of the creek, starts up the dark hill. Cold water is drippin from her dress, her legs. She slips as she climbs, grabs onto a branch and calls out Elias's name. In the valley where the brown children play, it is dark and still. Holly wipes at the tears in her eyes, searches for the far hill and screams, "Elias . . . Elias . . . Elias."

A distant light flickers, she runs to its glow. She can see the top of the far hill, the flare of light gleamin down through thick bush

forbidding her way. Elias is callin into the dark, "Holly . . . Holly . . . Where are you?"

Holly runs to the call of her name. Elias puts the lantern down,
lets its flame go out and takes Holly into his arms. Holly is tryin to
say things but her quick gasp for breath silences her words into
moans. Elias holds her in his arms and stares out into the night.

"Boy, what's that child doin out there? Ya all git in here," the old
woman calls from the porch. Elias takes Holly into the shack, she
will not take her face away from his chest. When the light comes, it
comes slow and only to a gentle glow. The old woman brings the
lantern close, Holly closes her eyes to its light. Elias gasps, "Oh my
God, what did they do?" The old woman sees the blood on Holly's
face and asks her God for his mercy, then is sayin, "Ah knowed this
was goin ta happen, Ah knowed it, Lord. Look what they done did
ta this child."

The old woman vanishes back into the shadows. Elias keeps
askin, "Holly, what happened? What happened?"

Holly tries to get her words through the sounds her moans are
makin, she's sayin, "Elsie came . . . she told Mama . . . told Mama
about ya . . . She told Mama about the baby too . . . She ain't had to,
she come anyway . . . Then Daddy come home. . . . Mama told him
too . . . He . . . He . . . Bobby made him stop . . ."

The old woman comes back with a wet towel. Softly, she tells
Elias, "Sit the child down here. Lets me gits this baby child cleaned
up some. She gots ta rest some too."

Holly tries to wipe the tears from her eyes, catch her breath, she's
tellin Elias, "He said he was goin ta do things . . . Bobby made him
stop. . . . Ah told Mama Ah wanted ta be wit ya, Elias. . . . Ah told
Mama Ah was leavin too . . ."

"Hush now, child. Ya just come on and sit down here," the old
woman whispers, gits Holly by the arm and eases her down on the
couch. Elias clenches his fist, breathes quietly and hard, then goes to
the window and looks out. The night has no light. Hills and all the
valleys stand so high and lie so deep in the darkness. Elias keeps
lookin out the window. The old woman calls to him, "Boy, ya gots

ta git out from here. Ya gots trouble comin, ya gots ta go tonight. Ya ain't knowin this here place likes Ah do."

Elias turns from the window, sighs and looks at Holly, then asks, "Do you still have the money?"

Holly mutters, "Ah have it . . . Ah had it in my purse. . . . It's in the bottom."

Quickly, Elias says, "I got to get you out of here."

Holly asks, "Ya comin too, Elias? Ya comin too, now?"

Elias turns back to the window, he is silent.

"Ya comin too, Elias? Ya got ta come too."

Elias jerks away from the window, rushes to the lantern and douses its light. Darkness rushes into the room. Elias hurries back to the window, Holly shakes with his sudden moves. The old woman stares through the dark, she watches Elias at the window, sees his head slowly movin back and forth. She turns and whispers to Holly, "Don't ya be frettin none now, baby child, God's goin ta take care of his children."

In the distance, there is a dog barkin somewhere.

Holly calls to Elias, "Ya have ta come too, Elias. Ya can't stay either."

Elias keeps lookin out the window but quickly whispers over his shoulder, "Be quiet. Grandmama, keep her quiet."

The old woman pulls Holly close to her, whispers, "Hush now, baby child."

Holly closes her eyes, but she can still see her father's twisted face comin at her, see Elsie in the kitchen, Jason turnin away, then she hears the dog howlin and she opens her eyes.

Holly waits for Elias to answer but he does not, he just keeps lookin out the window. The black and dark grays of the night have their ways, a stillness where everything still moves, reaches for you, then stills itself again. Elias won't take his eyes from it. The old woman whispers to him. "Boy, ya gots ta go, ya knows ya have ta go. Ya can't stays here, ya gots ta git ya self out of here."

Holly calls out, "Elias, they ain't goin ta find us. They don't know where ya live, Ah didn't tell Elsie that. Nobody knows that."

Elias hurries a whisper over his shoulder. "I have to get you to Wilmington. You can't wait until morning for the bus. You can't go back down there."

"How we goin ta git there, Elias? How we goin ta do that if we ain't on a bus? Who goin ta ride us there?"

Elias turns from the window. Holly can see him lower his head, his hand come up to his face and rub at his eyes. He sighs and says, "I don't know."

Holly whispers, "Elias, com'ere."

When Elias gets close enough, she reaches and pulls him closer to her. She whispers, "Um sorry . . . Ah ain't meant for all this ta happen . . . Ah just want ta be wit ya, that's all. . . . But Ah don't ever want anything ta ever happen ta ya, Elias . . . Maybe Ah should go back . . . maybe if Ah do that, they won't come. Ya know, come up here and try ta find ya."

"No." Elias shakes his head and goes back to the window. Holly shudders when she sees him flinch at the window.

"What's wrong, Elias?" Holly whispers, gets to her feet and goes to him. She looks out into the night and grabs his hand when she sees the distant lights in the dark.

"Grandmama, there's light way down by the road. I think they're coming."

"Lord have mercy. Now ya children listen ta me likes ya ain't never listened ta nobodies before. Boy, ya take this child on out of here and don't ya ever come back here. Now ya's goes now, ya's goes on out back, goes way around the Back Lands. Ya's goes that way, goes out through them fields, then gits in them woods, then ya starts ta the north. Ya starts there, stay in them woods till ya gits ta the creek, then ya keeps goin till ya gits ta where the tracks be. Ya gits there, ya keeps close ta them tracks. Ya's follow them up ta Wilmington, ya hear me? Ya gits this child on a train, then ya git on one of them long pullin trains. Ya gits on one of them and hides. But don't ya's come back here for nothin."

Elias shakes his head, says, "Grandmama, I'll take her to Wilmington but I have to come back. I can't leave you here by yourself."

"Oh no, boy. My children is the life Ah have. Your grandmama Alpha ain't got no fears. Now ya do as Ah say and ya do it now, ya hear me? Ya's go find someplace where folks is goin ta lets ya be, just lets ya be God's childrens. Ya's go on now."

Elias pulls Holly from the window, quickly whispers, "Wait here." He goes to the back room of the shack and comes back with a big green army jacket and tells Holly, "Here, put this on, it has a hood, put it over your hair." He goes back into the back room and comes back with a dark blanket over his shoulder. He looks out the window again, stares, turns quickly and looks at his grandmother.

"Go on now, boy, ya gots ta go."

Elias rushes to his grandmother and hugs her, Holly follows. The old woman tries to take both of them in her arms, then tells them they got to go. Holly whispers to her, "Ah take care of him, Grandmama Alpha. Ah take care of him too."

"Come on, Holly," Elias whispers and takes her by the hand. He peeks out the window, takes a deep breath and eases the door open. He keeps his eyes on the lights, then slowly steps out onto the porch. Holly follows and stares at the lights she sees. They are far lights, just speckles in the dark, but they shine through and stay in her eyes.

"Come on," Elias whispers, squeezes her hand and starts down the steps. She keeps lookin at the lights, Elias pulls her on. He takes quick steps, soft steps, until he is around and beyond the shack.

The high grass is dark and gray, sometimes black, then it thickens into bush and weeds that jab, scratch at passin arms and bare legs. Holly covers her face with her hand, with her other hand she holds onto Elias's as he weaves through the darkness. Twigs and branches break and snap at their passin.

Elias stops, looks back.

Distant dogs bark and bite at the night.

Shouts comin from afar bring shivers.

Holly whispers, "Elias, ya think they done seen us, huh? Ya think they know where we at?"

Elias pulls Holly on, takes her deeper into the bushes. She follows, slows and pulls on Elias's hand. He stops and she whispers, "Ah think Ah hear em back there."

Lights flash in the bushes. Elias jerks Holly's hand and pulls her on into the thickets. Quickly, he stills, stoops and yanks Holly to the ground, whisperin. "Be quiet, don't move."

Lights flicker and flash.

Holly shudders in the dark.

Silence settles in the night.

Elias stills his breaths, sighs, pulls Holly's hand and whispers, "They're gone, let's go. We have to hurry if we're going to get there before morning."

Quickly, Elias leads Holly out of the thick bushes, through long dark fields. He slows at old fences, climbs them, helps Holly over, then hurries through the night.

Holly pulls on Elias's hand and makes him stop. He turns to her, then leads her to a bare spot beneath a tree where they can sit. She wants to see his face but he sits lookin back through the trees and low-hangin branches. She whispers to him, "They didn't see us, Elias. They won't come this far."

Elias puts his head down, takes a deep breath and says, "We have to keep going, we can't stop long."

Holly got to see his face, she reaches and touches his cheek, makes him turn so she can see his eyes, then she whispers, "Ah love ya Elias . . . Ah just want ya ta really know that. . . . Ah tried ta tell Mama and them it wasn't the way they were thinkin and sayin things like . . . but they . . . Well, it don't matter now. . . . What's important is what Um tellin ya . . . Ah love ya, Elias, and Um where Ah belong and that's wit ya. . . . That's important."

She can see a gentle smile come to his face but he lowers his head again. She reaches for him, brings him close to her, gently brings his head to her breast. She holds him and closes her eyes. He whispers something she does not hear, she just feels the warm flutter of his breath against her breast. Softly, she whispers, "Huh?"

"It wasn't anything."

"It was so, ya don't say anything."

Elias is silent for a moment, his slow deep breaths give rhythm to the passin moments. Holly sighs and holds him tighter when he says, "Sometimes I wish I would have died. I lost more than just my arm over there. I lost what I was and wanted to be. You gave me the feelings again, just the way you are makes me think of tomorrow. I want to see it, I want to live again. When I get to Washington I know people will talk and look at us every place we go. I know they'll say we shouldn't be together, but I don't care what they say. I just want you and my music, that's all. It may be wrong, but I don't care, I love you."

Holly keeps her eyes closed, lets a few moments come and bring their silence, then her lips touch Elias's ear and she whispers, "Ah love ya too, Elias. When Ah say things ta ya, they things Ah feel, things ya make me feel. It ain't like sayin words, it's like sayin feelins back. When Ah think of ya it's way past words and all, it's like one of them pretty songs witout words in em. And when ya listen and say things back, Ah feel different than ever before. Ya say words and all but it's closer than that. Ah mean, like there ain't no space or anybody's old creek between us, like there ain't nothin between us, like we just one thing. If ya would have died in that stinkin war, Ah had been real mad at ya."

Holly and Elias sit for a while, the night that had chased them now lets them rest and hide in its darkness. The late hours are chillin. Elias looks back through the darkness, sighs and whispers, "Come on, we better be going."

Holly follows Elias through the trees, stops when he stops, peeks back when he looks back, then dips her eyes from the night when they move on. When the big trees go away, it is as if they had never been there. Elias stops and looks at the bushes and tall grass ahead, then leads Holly into the dark grays of the fields. The open bushy fields become wooded again, then a slopin weedy hillside. At the bottom of the hill, Elias stops, he can hear the water of the creek running. At the water's edge he searches for steppin stones. Slowly, he leads Holly across the creek. Holly holds on to Elias's hand, lugs the big straw purse over her shoulder. The chill of the cold water lingers. A dark hill slopes into a darker valley. There in the silence of the valley, Elias stops, the train tracks are there. Holly hears him sigh and say, "Thank God, we're at the tracks. I found them, we can follow them into Wilmington."

Holly looks up the tracks, stares out into the darkness and asks, "Is it goin ta be far now, Elias?"

"No, we'll go a little further, then stop and wait for morning."

Holly can walk beside Elias now, he has his arm around her and she leans into his side. Their steps slow, the shiny rails guide their way. Sometimes Holly sees Jason, hears him askin Mama things. Ginger is fixin Holly's hair, makin her stand still while she combs it. Tessie is down the creek, then Billy comes and it's dark. Elsie's at Ben's pointin at Garet Foster. Then Elsie's in the kitchen, Mama's screamin. Daddy's comin up the steps, Bobby comes.

Elias squeezes Holly's hand, whispers, "Look, see the lights, they're coming from Wilmington. It's not far now."

Holly raises her eyes and sees the far glow in the sky. Tiny lights glimmer in the darkness. She lowers her head and walks silently for a while, then whispers, "Elias, ya comin too. Ah want ya ta come, and Ah don't want ta go till ya can come too."

Elias takes his eyes away from the lights of Wilmington, looks at Holly. She is still walkin with her head down, she whispers again, "Ah don't want ta go till ya come, Elias. Ah don't want ya ta be here by ya self."

Elias leads Holly away from the tracks and into some tall grass. He sees a tree and takes her to it. A bare spot is there and he sits and leans against the tree. Holly sits and snuggles up against him, puts her head on his shoulder. She is quiet for a moment before she whispers, "Ah love ya, Elias."

The far, puffin sounds of a comin train come into the night. The sounds come and go until the train begins to near, then the burst of hissin steam and clangin engines fills the darkness. The ground is shakin and Holly quivers in Elias's arm. She keeps her eyes closed to the passin train, but Elias stares and watches it pass. Another train comes and passes. Holly shakes in a restless sleep. Elias does not sleep, sometimes he hears guns in the night, the long whistle of incomin shells, then screams and moans fill the silence in which he sits holdin Holly.

Maybe an hour or so of the night has passed but the darkness is still there. Elias whispers into Holly's ear, "It's time, I think we better get started, it will be morning soon."

Holly opens her eyes, then closes them again and snuggles closer to him. Elias kisses her on her cheek, tells her, "We have to go now, it will be getting light soon."

Elias gets to his feet, takes ahold of Holly's hand. She gets up and looks around, then looks up at Elias and tells him, "Ah love ya." He smiles, and then they go back through the tall grass to where the tracks lay in the stillness of the night. Their footsteps leave one trailin sound. Holly knows the time ain't goin ta be long now, the darkness is beginnin to fade, grasses are showin their color green. Further down the tracks, far buildings of Wilmington can be seen. Elias slows and leads Holly from the tracks again. There is a clearin in the high bushes he sees, he takes her there. When he stops, Holly looks up into his eyes, he looks away. She can hear him takin a long deep breath but she is quiet. Quickly, he turns and says, "Holly, it will be daylight soon and we will have to get off the tracks and up on the road. Give me the jacket and go up on the road, it will take you right into town. I'll follow you from a short distance, don't look back, I'll be there. When you get to the station, check the schedule on the wall, I'll look at it too. Get a ticket for the first train to Washington. When the train comes, just get on it. You'll be all right. I'll wait at the station until you're on the train. We can't be near one another, but I'll be there. I'll wait until you're on the train, then I'll come back here and wait until dark and get a freight. Holly, please do as I say, you have to, I love you and I want you to be my wife."

"Say it again, Elias. Say it and say ya love me too."

Elias sighs, then stills his breath and says, "I love you, Holly, and I want you and I want you to be my wife. Will you?"

"Yes, Elias."

Holly lowers her eyes and Elias can see the tears begin to fall. He takes her in his arm, holds her and whispers that he loves her. "Ah forgot somethin," Holly says softly.

"What?" Elias whispers.

Holly puts her hand down inside of her dress and while she is reachin inside of her bra, she is sayin, "Ah can put my cross on now. Ah put it on in my room sometimes, now Ah can keep it on all the time."

Elias smiles and says, "My mother will like you and my father will too. You'll like them, they're caring people and I love them. I know I have disappointed them. I know they are worried but I needed some time away from everything. I don't think they understood that, but I want to go home now. Tell them I'm coming home. Give them the letter but tell them I'm coming home."

"Elias, do we have ta say good-bye now?"

"Soon."

"Ah don't want ta do that . . . but Ah will cause ya said it was important ta ya. . . . But never again, ya hear me? Ah want ta ask ya somethin too."

Elias smiles and asks, "What is it?"

Holly smiles, looks up in Elias's eyes and says, "Ah was thinkin . . . Ah was thinkin when we were walkin and all . . . And the baby is goin ta be a girl . . . Ah told ya that . . . Can Ah name her if ya like the name too?"

Elias's smile becomes a glow of a gentle feelin. Holly's eyes get real big and she says, "The baby, she's goin ta be half you and half me too . . . but Ah want ta name her Alpha . . . cause . . . well . . . just cause Ah do."

Quickly, Elias turns away.

Holly says real fast, "Ain't that all right?"

She can see him shakin his head yes.

"What's wrong?" Holly is askin when she sees Elias's shoulder shakin. "What's wrong, Elias, huh?" She is askin again as she pulls him around to see his face. He keeps his head down, the tears easily fall from his eyes. Holly grabs him and takes him into her arms.

19

Early light had come but the Wilmington Streets were still gray from the passin night. Road trucks were comin in from the highways, downin their gears makin rattlin turns and squeaky stops. The sidewalks seemed empty, early morning walkers would quickly fade into long lingerin shadows or some doorway.

Holly walks with her head down but tries to listen for Elias's followin footsteps. Sometimes she slows her steps, flicks the hair out of her eyes and looks back over her shoulder. Elias is followin.

Dark gray faceless buildings line Holly's way. A fat man with a straw hat on and a bag under his arm whisks by. Holly sees him comin, lowers her eyes but she can still hear his footsteps nearin and now passin. Her head jerks, her eyes widen, she shakes but keeps walkin. The cat that has quickly meowed scurries away between two buildings. A bent old man folds papers at his newsstand, he glances at Holly but quickly turns back to foldin his papers. Holly looks back over her shoulder, Elias is passin the old man foldin the papers. Trucks pass and leave their rattlin sounds echoin in the stillness they've driven through. Holly can see the train station, she slows her steps, looks back at Elias and takes a deep breath, then walks on.

The black and rusty orange spiked fence in front of the train station is covered with dewdrops. Some gleam and sparkle as they catch a glow of first light. Holly passes silently, she looks beyond the fence, sees the faceless cold walls, then stares at the door as she nears. Slowly she turns and looks back over her shoulder, then slowly turns back and pushes the big door open. Except for the sound of her footsteps, the train station is silent. She quietly walks across its dark wood floors, her head is down but she is takin quick peeks at the long brown benches along the far walls. She can see a few folks sittin and lyin on the benches, she peeks to see if they are watchin her, then she quickly looks back over her shoulder until she sees Elias comin through the doorway. She stares until she knows she has looked too long, quickly she turns and looks for the schedule on the wall. When she sees it, she goes to it, reads it, then reads it again. She sees the big black words sayin, ROCKY MOUNT, RICHMOND, FREDERICKSBURG, WASHINGTON, ALL POINTS NORTH. She looks for WASHINGTON again, looks at the big black numbers beside it. Sees 9:45, sees the words sayin, ARRIVING ON TRACK 1, DEPARTING AT. Then the big black numbers look back at her, saying 10:00. She stares at the numbers, then looks above the schedule to the big clock on the wall, it is six forty. She turns from the clock, looks around, then is lookin for Elias. When she sees him, she waits for his eyes to turn to her, then nods toward the women's rest room. Elias nods his head a little, then quickly looks away.

Holly pushes the rest room door open, looks around, then hurries to a toilet stall. When she comes out, she goes to a mirror, stills, and stares at her face. She sees the bruises on her cheek, the dried blood on her mouth, her father's sneerin face, her mother glarin at her. Elsie's lookin too, Jason's at the bottom of the steps. Bobby's little and so is she, he's tellin her she can't come with him but she knows he's goin to take her anyway. She quickly looks away from the mirror, washes her hands and face, gets lipstick and makeup out of the purse, puts it on and tries to cover her bruises. She combs her hair, hurries and changes into another dress, combs her hair again, puts more makeup on, then stills herself and stares into the mirror again. Slowly and gently, she rubs her finger over the gold cross hangin from her neck, then leaves a soft smile in the mirror as she turns.

The station is still quiet when Holly comes out of the rest room. She looks for Elias, then looks to see if anyone is watching her. When she looks back at Elias, she gives him a quick smile, then quietly walks to the end of the closest bench. She stands by the bench for a while, watches Elias, watches for his eyes to say if she should sit there. He nods to her, then turns and walks away. She watches every step until she sees him go into the colored section and sit on the bench near its edge. She sighs and sits down. From where she sits, she can see the clock on the wall. If she stares, she can see its little black arms pointin to its numbers. It is seven oh-four.

Quietly, the station is beginnin to fill, quiet faces pass Holly in her silence. When they near, she lowers her eyes from them, listens for the sound of their footsteps to go away before she looks up again. Sometimes she keeps her eyes down, looks at the little cracks and grains in the dark wood floor. Sometimes the moments leave her there, let her alone and don't poke at her. Don't show her things she's already seen. Them lights comin in the dark, Mama lookin that way at her. When she looks back up, she looks at Elias, stares. She cannot see his face, she wants to. She keeps lookin, sighs, then looks at the clock on the wall. Quickly, she looks away from it when its moments start pokin at her again.

There is a bright part of the station, its bright lights glare through the dull soft glow of the high-hanging ceiling lights. Holly thinks of Ben's when she sees the waitress behind the bright counter. She watches her for a while, then slowly gets up from the bench.

"What ya havin, honey?" the waitress is askin as she looks up over the counter and glances at Holly. The waitress puts her head back down and busies herself at what she was doing. Holly hurries and reads the scratchy writing on the blackboard menu.

"Ah want two egg sandwiches. And Ah want two cups of coffee."

The waitress looks up again as if she expects to see two faces where she has only seen one. Holly speaks quickly. "Can ya put them in two bags? Ah want ta take one on the train wit me."

"Honey, they feed ya on the train."

"Oh," Holly says quickly, then tells the waitress, "Ah want ta take it anyway, case Ah don't like that train food."

The waitress stops what she's doin and rolls her eyes and asks, "Ya want both them coffees too?"

"Yes, Ah take them too."

The waitress shakes her head, scratches somethin on a piece of paper, turns but says over her shoulder, "It will be a minute, honey."

Holly stands and waits but tries not to look around until she feels the footsteps comin up behind her. She hurries her glance over her shoulder, then quickly turns away when she sees the soldier nearin the counter.

"Here ya go, honey," the waitress is sayin and puttin the two bags on the counter.

Holly hurries and opens her purse while she is askin, "How much for em?"

"Sixty-five cents, honey."

Holly gives the woman a dollar, waits for her change, gets the two bags from the counter, turns and passes the soldier's stare as she hurries away. When she is out of the glare of the bright lights, she slows, looks around until she is sure nobody is comin or lookin at her, then she eases her way as close to the colored section as she can get. Slowly she looks around again, makes sure no one is lookin at her, then she nods to Elias and puts one of the bags down on the far end of an empty bench. Then quickly she walks away and goes back to where she was sittin. She watches Elias, waits for him to get up and go get the bag. When he does, she sighs, sits down and opens her bag.

The soldier comes out of the snack bar, stands lookin around until he sees Holly, then he walks over to her. Holly sees him comin, puts her head down and starts sippin on her coffee. The soldier nears and says, "Hi, I saw you over getting something to eat. Where you headed?"

Holly keeps her head down.

"Are you from Wilmington, or just going through?"

Holly does not answer.

"My name's Gregg Suder. I'm going home, back up to good old Pennsylvania. You going north too?"

Holly sighs and keeps her head down.

"You mind if I sit down?" the soldier asks, then quickly sits next to Holly. "By the way, what's your name?" he's askin.

Holly looks away.

"What's wrong with you? I'm just trying to be friendly."

Holly turns to the soldier, blurts out, "Would ya leave me be? Um gittin married and Ah can't be talkin ta ya."

"When are you getting married? Who's the lucky guy?"

"Just leave me be, will ya?"

"I was just trying to be friendly, that's all."

Holly sees Garet Foster, sees his face comin at her down Ben's. Billy got his sailor suit on smilin, and she was goin to send him a Christmas card. The feelin comes back, she can see the Christmas card, Mama too. The soldier is lookin at her and she's tellin him, "Ah don't need ya bein all friendly. Ya just go on and leave me be, ya hear?"

"All right, all right, I'll leave you alone if that's the way you want it. I was just trying to be friendly," the soldier says, gets up and takes the sneer on his face with him.

Holly watches him walk away, then takes a quick look at Elias before she lowers her head and stares at the floor. Others are passin by her now, when Holly peeks up she sees blurs of passin faces, backs, legs, hands wavin sometimes. Sometimes she hears quick blurts of words. "Ya all come now. Ya hear me, git over here Ah said," a fat colored woman is sayin and gatherin her children. Holly watches her go past Elias and into the colored section. "What time is it?" a wide-eyed hurried woman is askin the stern-faced man that is followin her. "Git over there and sit down," a young woman with a small boy by the hand and a baby in her arm is sayin, pointin toward Holly's bench. The little boy breaks from his mother's hand and runs to the bench. The woman follows with the baby in her arms. Holly looks at the boy, he peeks back, then squirms up onto the bench. The woman sits, gives Holly a quick smile, then begins rockin the baby. The baby gives a little whine and then begins to cry. Holly watches the woman shift the baby from one arm to the other and smiles when she sees the baby's face. She knows it has to be a little girl. The baby keeps cryin and Holly keeps lookin at her. The mother starts rockin the baby again and whisperin to it. Holly wants to whisper too, and she smiles and softly whispers, "You're so pretty, aren't ya." The mother turns to Holly, gives her a big smile and says, "She won't sleep for anythin."

When Holly turns back and looks through the station she still has a gentle smile on her face. She looks to see Elias and keeps the smile, then she looks and stares at the clock on the wall. It is eight twelve or eight thirteen. She has forgotten about the soldier until she catches him starin at her from a far bench. She stares back and mutters to herself. "Why don't ya stop lookin over here?"

The baby is crying and whimperin, then gets to screamin. Holly turns and looks at the child, then the mother. She watches the woman's face, sees it strainin. She looked younger when she came in with the children. Holly wonders how old the woman is and where she's goin. But the woman's face is too strained for questions. Holly turns away and looks toward Elias. Her eyes widen and she sucks her breath in when she sees the policeman walkin through the crowd. She watches him, tries to see his face, wants to see if he is lookin around, searchin, but others pass and leave their blindin blur in her eyes. She leans to the side, stretches her neck and looks again. She sees him again but not his face, then he's gone. Quickly her breath seeps out of her. She looks for Elias, she can see him and stares until she feels the soldier's eyes on hers. She lowers her head and stares at the floor, then jerks her head up and looks at the clock. She sees the policeman again, she shudders when she sees him goin near the colored section. Quickly she looks for Elias but can only see his green jacket. She looks back at the policeman again, he's lookin around. Holly holds her breath until she sees him turn away from the colored section, go someplace where she cannot see him anymore. Quickly she looks back toward Elias, stares at his green jacket until she can see his face.

The mother yells at the little boy, the baby lets out a cry and Holly turns to the woman. "Shish . . . shish . . . ," the mother is whisperin and catches Holly's eye. She smiles at Holly again as the baby hushes.

Holly smiles back and asks, "How old's your baby?"

"She's goin ta be three months next week," the mother says softly.

"Are ya gittin on the train, too?" Holly asks.

"Um gittin the nine fifteen."

"Where's that one goin?"

"Um takin that one ta Charlotte, then Ah got ta git another one up there that goes ta Lexington."

"Ya goin all the way up there? How long that goin ta take ya ta git there?"

"Ah be there tomorrow mornin. Where ya goin?"

"Um goin ta Washington. Um goin up there ta git married and Um goin ta live up there, too."

"Is he from up there? Ya ever been there before?"

"No, and Ah ain't never been on no train either. He was born down here in Supply. That's where Ah live, Ah mean Ah used ta live there. His mama took him up there when he was a baby, too. But he come back after the war. He come back ta stay wit his grandmama. He was goin ta be a big piano player but he got hurt real bad in the war. But he can still paint real good. He's goin ta do that and write songs and stuff since he can't play the piano. He got hurt real bad in the war and all."

Holly talks with the woman, then watches her gather her children and vanish into the crowd. Quickly, Holly looks at the clock on the wall, counts its time until it tells her the train will come in one hour and seven minutes. She looks toward Elias, keeps starin at his green jacket through the blurs of folks passin by. She can't see his face, so she puts her head down and stares at the floor. But the time and the train stay in her mind. She can see it comin on the far tracks of her mind. Bobby's comin home all over again. "Shoeshine time. Gimme ahh dime for a shine," colored boys are callin out through the crowd as they pass. Holly looks up, sees Jason runnin to the train and lookin for Bobby. She's got Mama's hand and lookin for Bobby too. Then it's dark and rainin, and Bobby's out there hollerin in it.

"Come on, Jimmy," some woman calls to her child. Holly turns and looks through the crowd for the child, watches him when she sees him.

A young man is hurryin through the crowd, a young woman has his hand. Holly watches them passin by, then starts when she sees them slow and hears the young man sayin, "We can get the tickets over there."

Quickly, Holly looks at the clock, stares through the crowd at Elias, then watches the young couple weave through the crowd. She can see them going to a dimly lit counter. She looks at Elias again, then lowers her head, sighs and looks at the big straw purse. She jerks her head up again, looks at the clock, looks at Elias, then through the crowd to where she can see the young couple standin at the counter. Slowly, she stands and looks back toward Elias, keeps starin and wantin him to turn around. The soldier is lookin at her, she feels his eyes, then sees him starin at her. Quickly she looks away from Elias, then slowly begins walkin toward the far counter.

There's an old man behind the counter whose face is thin. Thick glasses make his eyes look real big when he looks over the counter at Holly standin there. She doesn't like his eyes, his sudden look, she lowers her head.

"Can Ah help ya here, young lady?"

Holly looks up at the man, sees his eyes starin at her and no smile on his skinny-lookin face. She puts her head back down.

"Can Ah help ya here, miss?"

Holly looks up but does not look at the man's face, she stares at his white shirt. Looks at the top button buttoned, looks at the light brown stains of sweat on the collar, then she puts her head back down and quickly says, "Ah want ta buy a ticket for ta get on the train."

"Where ya want ta go there, miss?"

Holly looks up real fast, says, "Ah want the one that goes up ta Washington, Ah want ta git on that one."

"Ya want a round-tripper?"

"Huh?"

"Miss, ya want a ticket ta take ya on up there and bring ya back?"

Holly lowers her eyes, then looks up again and says, "Ah ain't comin back, Ah mean Ah don't think Um comin back for a long time."

"Oh, well that will be thirty-five dollars and fifty cents. Ya want ta git that northbound *Flyer* comin in here. It will be comin in here on track one. It will be comin in here at nine forty-five, leavin out of here at ten a.m. Ya can git it right out there," the man says, points to a far door, then gets to gettin a ticket from beneath the counter.

Holly hurries and gets her purse up on the counter. She reaches down into the side of it and gets the money out. Quickly she gets two twenty-dollar bills out, takes a peek at what she has left before she puts the two twenty-dollar bills on the counter.

"This here will git ya on up there, young lady. Ya just take it and show it to the man when he ask ta see it. And ya have a nice trip on up there, ya hear?"

Holly gives the man a little nod, waits for her change and the ticket, then turns from the counter. Slow steps take her back through the station to where she sits. A quick look again finds Elias lookin too, she keeps lookin back until he gently nods, turns, and she cannot see his eyes anymore. Passin moments just leave blurs of folks goin by, their loose words still hangin in the air. Sometimes someone passes too close and Holly looks up, watches them, then lowers her head again. Sounds of footsteps go away, lingerin words follow. Mama's face comes, she ain't screamin or nothin, just lookin. Holly looks up and Ginger's faces vanishes in the dark wood of the floor. The clock on the wall stares back, says its time is nine seventeen.

Slowly, the time is goin by, leavin its footprints on the clock on the wall. But it don't go fast enough, and when it moves it goes too quick. Elias is there, Holly can see him but he ain't comin too. Promises made in the dark want to run away in the dim light of the train station. Holly won't stop lookin at Elias. That soldier's watchin her, she can feel his eyes but she won't turn away from Elias. She jolts when she sees him stand, look at her and nod toward the clock. She looks at the clock and looks back at him. He nods toward the door to the platform. Holly looks at the clock again, sees its numbers say nine thirty-five. She looks back at Elias, sees him still lookin at her and noddin toward the platform door. Slowly he leaves the edge of the colored section and starts walkin toward the door. He looks back at Holly as he pushes it open and goes out onto the platform. Holly hurries and gets her purse, gets up from her seat and sees the soldier starin at her. She gives him a quick dirty look and slowly walks toward the platform door.

As Holly nears, the door gets bigger and bigger. She pushes on it and it opens. Morning air and the sunlight rush to her face, she squints but keeps lookin for Elias. He stands on the other side of the doorway. If he had his other arm, he could reach and touch her, but he just looks. Holly stares into his eyes until he turns away and slowly walks toward the end of the platform where the colored section is. Holly takes a few slow steps and stands where Elias has stood, she waits there.

Others are comin out onto the platform, some keepin children by the hand, some carryin suitcases and small boxes under their arms. Sailors pass with their big brown bags heaved up on their shoulders. Some coloreds pass, too, go to the far end of the platform where the last cars of the train will stop.

Above the sounds of chatter, passin footsteps, heavy suitcases bein dragged, there is a silence that hovers over the platform. The cool morning air clings to Holly's face, the sunlight stings at her eyes as she looks down the empty tracks where the far sky hangs so low. It is a soft-lookin sky, its color blue gives peace to a few passing moments. Holly takes a deep breath, lowers her eyes from the sky, and looks down into the shade of her shadow.

The stocky man with the blue cap comes onto the platform, stands and looks down the tracks, then begins pacin back and forth. He stops, reaches inside his vest pocket, glances down at his watch, then looks up and stares down the tracks. Holly was watchin him, now she's lookin as far down the tracks as she can see. Little white puffs of smoke seep into the blue of the far sky, Holly's eyes widen when she sees them. She stares at them, then quickly jerks her head toward Elias. He's standin and leanin against the wall with his head down. He does not see the puffs of white smoke or Holly starin at him or the tears in her eyes.

"Shoeshine time. Gimme ahh dime for a shine," the colored boys pass and call out.

Elias keeps his head down.

Holly keeps starin at him.

The soldier passes, looks at Holly, then turns to see what she is starin at.

Holly is lookin at Elias.

The soldier sees the coloreds and the empty tracks.

A far whistle blows.

"Are you all right?" the soldier asks as he turns back to Holly.

"Huh?" Holly says, turns and looks at the soldier.

"You look like you're crying. Are you all right?"

"Yes, Um all right."

The stocky man shouts, "*Flyer*'s comin in. Keep clear of the tracks."

"Shoeshine time. Gimme ahh dime for a shine."

"Why are you crying?"

"Keep clear of the tracks. *Flyer*'s comin in."

"Um not cryin."

"Why won't you tell me your name?"

"Huh?"

"What's your name? Is this your train coming?"

The far whistle blows, then blows again.

Holly looks down the tracks.

White puffy smoke floats high into the sky.

"What's your name?"

"Shoeshine time. Gimme ahh dime for a shine."

"Please leave me be. Ya hear me?"

"Keep back from the tracks, *Flyer*'s comin in."

"I'm just trying to be friendly."

Holly sucks in her breath.

A huffin sound is nearin.

"Why are you crying?"

Quickly, Holly turns and looks at Elias. He's lookin back, steppin away from the wall but he's still lookin at her. Real big tears slowly roll all the way down her cheeks.

"Why are you crying?" the soldier's askin.

The huffin sounds of the train are fillin the air. The platform begins to quiver. Folks start movin around but Holly keeps lookin at Elias. The soldier keeps lookin at her, askin, "What's wrong? Are you all right?" Holly turns to him, shouts, "Please go, leave me be. . . . Please . . . Please . . . Please go away . . ."

The soldier turns and goes.

Holly turns back to Elias.

The ground trembles and shakes. Puffy white smoke fills the air. Big iron wheels are screechin to a halt. Holly keeps lookin through the smoke, she can see Elias's armless sleeve danglin in the smoky breeze. She keeps lookin until she can see his eyes again.

The train slows to a stop, then settles on the tracks. Dark colored men are lowerin its boarding steps, then they stand silently in the fadin smoke. Others pass like ghosts in a fog, their shouts and whispers float with the smoke. Faces come from the train, look for others that look for them.

The ground has stilled now, but Holly keeps tremblin. Tears won't stop flowin from her eyes, drippin from her face, fallin down to the ground. She hasn't turned from Elias. She can see him across the creek, taste his breath through the smoky air. She wants to touch his face and feel his hair, whisper in his ear, "Ah love ya."

Elias nods to the train, Holly won't move. He puts his head down, then looks up and nods toward the train. Holly won't move, keeps standin still. Elias slowly raises his hand and puts it over his heart, stares at Holly, then nods toward the train. Holly keeps starin at him, then very slowly raises her hand up to her cross and gently touches it. She stands still for all the time the passin moment will give, then so very slowly she turns and steps toward the train. When she reaches the steps, she looks back at Elias. The only hand he has is still on his heart.

20

Far from Supply, North Carolina, was green field, patches of brown land, brightly colored houses and gray old shacks, places that look like any other place the train has passed. Holly keeps lookin out the window, watchin the fields and scattered houses and shacks go by. Sometimes she sees an old truck or some old car goin up some road somewhere. She sees its old dented colors against the field's greens. The old truck or car goes away, tries to take Holly's thoughts with it, but they come back, stay, then go further than them old trucks and cars could ever go.

Except for when a child cries, or someone coughs or talks too loud, the train travels in a silence. The rhythmic thump of its rollin wheels is soothin to Holly's weary soul.

Virginia comes early in the evenin, Holly's blue eyes catch the soft glowin reds and yellow colors of the setting sun. She is tired and has not slept, hungry but does not think of food. The train is slowin, then stoppin. A conductor is callin out, "Petersburg ... Petersburg ..."

Holly sighs, leans back in her seat and lets her head rest against the back of the chair. Lights from the station shine through the window, slowly she turns, looks out onto the loadin platform. Others are rustlin in their seats, some gettin suitcases down from racks. Holly looks at some of the faces she sees on the platform, then wants to lean up in her seat, look back down the platform, look and see if she can see Elias. But she doesn't, she closes her eyes, she knows she can see him there.

The train sits for a while, its empty seats fill again. Soft talk flutters past Holly's ears after the rufflin sounds of suitcases bein pushed into racks go away. The train jolts, Holly turns to the window and watches the lights of the station go by. The evening has gone, beyond the station the night looks into the window, dark shadows begin risin in the train. Holly curls up in her seat, tries to close her eyes and seep into the darkness there. The rhythmic thumpin sounds of the rollin train carry her into soothing, gentle moments. She reaches for her pillow, reaches for it again, then jolts in her sleep.

The train sways in the night, speeds by far flickerin lights Holly doesn't see. Richmond comes, the train slows, stops and settles on its tracks. Lights from the station shine in the window. Holly sits up, wipes her eyes and looks out the window. She watches folks gatherin in the station, sees a young colored soldier hurryin by the window, she watches him until he disappears into the crowd, then she quickly turns from the window and shakes. Chills squirm and wiggle in her blood. She wants to go back, get Elias by his arm. Tell him, "Ya come now."

The train starts movin again. Holly closes her eyes, tries to curl up in her seat. She's still shiverin from the passin chills. She sways with the gentle rockin motion of the train, jerks in her sleep and tries to find her pillow again.

The lights of Washington come out of the dark, big white buildings gleam far off in the night. Holly has woken and has just sat starin out the window. Now, she stares at the far-off lights and buildings in the night. One big building seems to stand alone in a glow of its own. A big white steeple in the night. Holly sits up and keeps lookin out the window at all the lights comin from the city, they get bigger and brighter as the train travels on. It nears, then begins passin over a bridge. The lights from the city have fallen over the water. Dark little waves become bright as they ripple through the fallen light. Holly looks down, sees the big white steeple and the big round buildings glowin in the water all upside down.

"Washington . . . Washington . . . ," a conductor calls out as he nears Holly's seat. She turns from the window, looks up and watches the conductor pass. Others begin stirrin in their seats, Holly looks at some of them, then lowers her head. She tries to find an empty space to stare in, still her thoughts. The bright lights from the city cling to the window, keep ridin with the train, glarin in at Holly, but she won't look up from the empty space she's found. She sits starin down at the floor.

The rhythmic sounds of the train become louder as it begins to slow, takes curves through the city. The lights keep glarin through the window, flashin across Holly's face. They light up the yellow of her hair hangin loosely over her face, the dark red of the settled blood in her bruises, the lighter red of her faded lipstick. The glares of light become gentle with the blue of her eyes.

The train is slowin. When it jolts a little, Holly looks up and out the window. The station lights come, faces are lookin at the passin train. Holly tries to see some of their eyes, see if they're smilin. Everything is as bright as day, dark colored men with bright red caps flash glowin white grins. Other faces stare, quickly turn to others and smile.

The train stops and settles on its tracks. Holly stays in her seat and keeps lookin out the window. Others are gettin up from their seats, yankin at suitcases, gettin children by the hand and movin toward the doors. Holly is still starin out the window, then she slowly turns away and looks back into her empty space. Deep sighs fill long moments before she takes a quick glance out the window, then begins easin out of her seat. She gets her big purse and slowly starts toward the door. When she reaches it and looks down the steps, a dark colored man is lookin up and sayin, "Watch your step, ma'am. Watch your step here."

A slow cool wind is blowin across the station's platform. When it stops, its cold air lingers. Holly shivers from the sudden chill in the air as she steps from the train. She does not go far before she stops, then slowly looks around. Where she can see the far end of the platform, she stares, then turns and looks to the other far ends of what she can see. A loud voice seems to come out of nowhere and hangs in the air. Holly quickly looks up but only sees the high ceilings and the darkness the low-hangin lights keep back. The loudspeaker chants its call again and Holly lets the echoes pass. She looks for a door into the station, sighs when she sees it and others goin through it.

The station is big, light-colored and brighter than the platform. Faces pass quickly in the light, sounds of talk and sometimes laughter follow their stride. Holly's standin still, clutching her purse until she sees the signs for the rest rooms. She hurries through others that are passin by, then she slows and pushes the rest room door open. The sounds of the station do not follow her into the rest room, it is quiet there. An older woman is standin in front of the mirror. She puts the last dab of lipstick on, then gives Holly a little quick smile as she passes to leave. Holly takes a deep breath, takes a few steps and then quietly stands lookin around to see if she is alone. When she sees she is alone, she feels alone. She can feel herself begin to shake, she ain't alone anymore, it ain't quiet either. Mama's screamin, Elsie's sayin, "Nigger, nigger, nigger." Gus Hill is comin up the steps after her and he's screamin, too. Don't nobody like her 'cept for Elias and he ain't here. She don't know where he's at but he better come too. He made her come and he didn't come. He should have come too. She can see Elias, see him there by the wall lookin at her. When she can't see him, she keeps lookin, feels all cold. Tears start fallin from her eyes, she doesn't want to look in the mirror and see them. She hurries into a stall, jams the door closed, gets her dress up and panties down. The toilet seat is cold, she shivers. The quick squirtin sounds of urine splashin in the toilet bowl's water trickle into the silence. Holly listens, she wants to hear somethin else in her mind. She pushes within herself to make the sounds come again.

Pushes within herself to find a different feelin, a warm one. One that has words to say what it is. The urine settles, the flushin sound of the toilet gushes through her mind, leaves it empty. The silence is there again, snarlin. It never left, it stood silently with its quiet, ugly grin. Just waited to show itself again. Slowly, the cold comes back too.

The mirror is quiet, shy, only moves when Holly moves. It watches her with a caringness, is patient with her slow moves. Tenderly, Holly is pattin fresh makeup over her bruises. A deep sigh falls between her and the mirror before she turns, gets her big purse and quietly leaves the rest room.

Faces pass again, the big loud voice seems to tell them where to go. Some hurry, but Holly walks slowly. She sees a clock up on the wall, counts its numbers in her mind until they tell her it is ten thirty-five at night time. Quickly, she turns from the clock, then slowly looks around until she sees a old colored man with a broom cart comin. She waits until he nears, then asks, "Which one of these doors Ah go out ta git one of them taxi cars? Ah ain't never been here before. Ah have ta git a taxi."

The man slows to Holly's voice, turns to her and watches her while she speaks to him, then points to the closest door, sayin, "Ya can git one right out through there. Just ya go on right out through them doors right there. Ya see em right out theres."

Lights are flashin by again, car lights light up the street outside the station. Holly stands on the big wide sidewalk, she can see the long line of taxis parked at the curb. Some are different colors but most are yellow, she stares at them.

"Taxi, missy? Taxi here, missy?" a big shiny brown colored man is callin to her.

She turns to the man, then stares at him as he begins nearin and beckonin to her. He's askin again, "Taxie, missy?"

"One of them yours?"

"Yes, ma'am."

Holly looks at the long line of taxis, then looks back at the man and says, "Ah ain't never been up here before. Ah have ta take a taxi.

Ah have the street name and number and all. If Ah give it ta ya, can ya take me where it's at?"

"Any place ya want ta go, missy."

Holly looks in her purse, gets the letter Elias gave to her and pulls it out. She shows the address on it to the man, then she says, "Ah want ta go here. Seven, two, one, nine Meade Street. It's in a Northwest. Can ya take me there? Is it real far from here?"

"No, missy, it ain't far. Ah have yous up there in no time. Where's your bags? Ah can gets them for ya."

"Ah ain't got no bags."

"Well, just ya come on then. Big John takes yous on up there."

Holly follows the big colored man to a cab. Quickly, he gets the back door of the taxi open. Holly gets in, scoots around a little, then settles herself in the backseat.

The taxi speeds, then slows and stops for traffic lights. Holly looks out the window, sees all the big buildings and says with a sigh, "It's so big." Then she's askin, "Ya live here too?"

The man takes a quick look back at Holly, then says, "Ah come up here in 'twenty-two. Come up here from Mobile. Been here ever since. Where ya from, missy?"

"Supply. It's in North Carolina. It ain't too far from Wilmington."

"What brings ya up here?"

"Um goin ta be married."

"Now that's real nice. Gots ya a good man waitin on ya?"

"He ain't here yet. But he's comin real soon."

"Oh?"

"He's back down in Wilmington. But he's comin real soon. Um goin ta his mama's house ta wait for him there. His name is Elias E. Owens. Ya know him? He used ta live here and all. Then when he come back from the war, that's when he come to Supply. Ah mean, he was born there too. But he come up here when he was just a baby. He come back ta Supply ta be wit his grandmama, her name's Alpha. She's real nice too. Um goin ta name my baby the same name. Ah mean when Ah have one and it's a girl, Um goin ta call her Alpha."

Holly looks back out the window, keeps lookin and asks, "What's that there?"

"Just one of them governments buildins."

"Where folks live at? Ah ain't seen a house at all."

"Folks live all over, some gots nice homes. Some thems ya seein is them big apartment buildins. Some of them big senators and them congressmens gots some of them big apartments up in them."

"Ya ever see that Harry Truman? Ya ever see where he live at and all? Ya ever see him, Ah mean, does he come out and just walk around?"

"Harry Truman ahh good man. Ah done seen hims a few times down the station. He gits the train down there, gots his own car, big ones, too. But Lord, Ah was sure sad ta see Mista Roosevelt pass on. Now that was some kind of president, good man there."

Holly sees a day again, she turns from the window, looks down into the darkness of the cab. Ginger is there too, she's standin in the kitchen but listenin to the radio. Holly can hear the slow drumbeat again, see her mama's back over at the sink. She can hear her washin somethin in the sink and them slow drumbeats come from the radio. She raises her eyes a little and tells the man, "That sure was a long funeral, Ah heard some of it on the radio."

"Just right up here, missy. Should be right up here, what yous say them numbers was."

Holly shudders and looks out the window.

"What's them numbers yous got, missy?"

Quickly, Holly turns from the window and opens her purse. The taxi slows and pulls over to the curb. The man looks over the seat at Holly and flicks a light on. She's tryin to see the numbers on the envelope. When the light comes on, she tells the man, "It says it's seven . . . two, one . . . nine." Now she's lookin out the window and askin, "Which one's that?"

"Lets me see here now. That's ahh seventy-two thirteen. It's be right up there. Lets me pull up some for ya."

Holly's lookin at the houses in the dark. She can see they're dark colors in the night. There are some lights in some of the windows, she keeps lookin back at the ones that have lights on. The cab is slowly easin up alongside of the curb.

"Here it be, missy."

Holly looks at the house, it is dark gray in the night. Darker gray steps go up to its door. There is a soft light in one of the windows, the curtains seem to cuddle it and hold it still. Holly keeps lookin as she takes a deep breath, then asks over her shoulder, "Is that it?"

"This the one, missy."

Holly sits still and keeps starin at the house.

"What's wrong, missy?"

Holly keeps starin at the house.

The taxi man looks at the house, then turns and looks back at Holly and asks, "This is where ya wants ta come, ain't it?"

Holly shakes her head yes.

"Lets me see here, thats will be ninety cents."

"Huh?" Holly says and turns to the taxi man, then quickly says, "Oh, Ah forgot that." She reaches into the purse, grabs around in it and gets the man a dollar, then she reaches back in and gets a dime out for him too.

"Thank ya, missy."

Holly looks at the house again, sits and stares.

"Missy, why don'ts yous go on in? They's probably waitin on yous."

Holly looks away from the house, lowers her head and whispers, "They don't know Um comin. They ain't never met me either."

Holly keeps her eyes down and cannot see the little smile on the big colored man's face. He tells her, "Theys know yous comin one day, theys know that. Now, missy, yous just go on in there, lets them see ya. Go on now, theys can'ts meet ya if you's sittin out here."

Holly eases the door open and gets out of the cab, then stands still on the sidewalk. She reads the numbers of the house again, then sucks in her breath and tries to straighten the wrinkles in her dress before she nears the house.

At the top of the dark gray steps, she sighs, turns when the taxi pulls away and watches it leave. When it turns at the corner, Holly turns back around and looks at the door, its dark brown shows black in the night. Slowly, she raises her hand and gently taps, then stops quickly when the tappin sounds like thunder in the night.

Holly waits in a moment that she will not let move, keeps in the breath she is holdin. Slowly, gently, she taps on the door again. She waits, listens for any sound to come out of the silence. She shudders, steps back when the door opens, then looks up into the face of a tall Indian-colored man. His hair is dark gray, but it is his dark eyes she sees. She stands silently as the man speaks softly. He's sayin, "Yes, dear, may I help you with something?"

Holly stands still but keeps starin at the man.

"Are you lost? Can I help you with something?"

Quickly, Holly's askin, "Are ya Elias's father?"

The man is silent for a moment but keeps lookin at Holly. She's watchin his eyes and can see Elias's, too. A woman's voice calls into the hall, "Who is it, Alex?" The man keeps lookin at Holly and says, "Yes, I'm Elias's father."

"Um Holly."

"Who is it, Alex?" The woman's voice is callin again. The man is askin, "Do you know my son?"

"He sent me . . . He said ta come here."

"Elias told you to come here?"

"Ah come up here on the train."

"On the train?"

"Alex, who is at the door?" the woman's voice is callin as it nears. Elias's father turns and says to the woman, "Elias sent her here." Holly can see the woman now, she is a darker golden color with eyes dark, too, as the night. But they brighten when she hears Elias's name. Quickly she is rushin her words and sayin, "Let her come in, bring her in, Alex."

Holly sees the woman's eyes widen when she looks past her husband and sees Holly. For a moment the woman just stares, then says, "I'm Elias's mother, Marcel Owens. Please come in."

Holly dips her eyes and slowly walks into the hallway, then stands still. She keeps her head down but she can feel the light touch of the woman's hand on her arm. Elias's mother is sayin, "Come and sit down," then leadin her toward the couch. Holly quickly looks around the room, then stills and stares at the piano she sees. Elias's mother is sayin, "Please sit down. May I get you something? Maybe some tea or coffee?"

Holly shakes her head no, then sorta whispers, "No, thank ya." When she sits, she sits on the edge of the couch, keeps her legs together and folds her hands on her lap. Elias's father's eyes have widened, he is askin, "Are you from North Carolina?"

Slowly, Holly looks up and says, "Um from Supply," then quickly she puts her head back down.

"Supply?" Elias's mother says and looks at her husband. Holly looks up and says, "Ah come up here on the train. Elias said ta come here."

Elias's mother asks, "How is he? When did you see him last? Is he all right?"

Holly looks at her and tells her quickly, "He's all right. Ah saw him this mornin. He's comin too."

Quickly, Elias's father asks, "How do you know my son?"

Holly looks up into his eyes, then puts her head down and sits quietly. Elias's mother looks at Holly, then looks at her husband. It is silent for a moment, then Elias's mother is askin again, "Is he all right?"

Holly keeps her head down and speaks softly, her words are fillin up with sighs as she says, "Ah wanted him ta come too. . . . Ah didn't want ta come witout him. . . . Ah wanted him ta come too . . ."

Elias's mother can see the tears comin to Holly's eyes when Holly looks up and tells her, "Ah wanted him ta come too. . . . Ah wanted him ta come and then Ah would come after a while or somethin . . . Ah told him that. . . . He said for me ta come first . . . he said that . . ."

Holly puts her back down into a silent moment. When she sees her purse by her foot, she quickly reaches for it and gets the letter out. She holds it in her hand for a moment, then slowly looks up and tells Elias's mother, "He said for me ta give ya this."

Elias's mother takes the letter, holds it and just stares at it. Slowly she begins to open it. Holly watches her as she begins to read it, then Holly puts her head back down when she hears Elias's mother take a deep breath.

Elias's father nears his wife and tries to read over her shoulder. Holly keeps starin down at the floor and shudders when she hears Elias's mother gasp, "My God."

Holly sees Elsie in the kitchen and Jason steppin away. Elias's mother gives the letter to her husband, then sighs and looks at Holly. She sees her sittin with her head down and can barely see her face for the hair hangin over it but she can see the tears comin down her cheeks. Holly keeps her head down, but utters, "Ah wanted him ta come too. Ah didn't want him ta stay either. He made me promise ta get on the train. He said it was important."

Elias's mother leans toward Holly and softly asks, "Did you read the letter?"

Holly shakes her head no.

Elias's mother asks, "How old are you?"

"Um twenty," Holly answers, then says, "Ah was twenty on Christmas. Ah wanted him ta come too."

Elias's mother gets up and goes and sits beside Holly and whispers to her, "Don't cry, sugar."

Holly whispers back, "Ah don't want ta. Ah mean, Ah want ta be happy and all . . ." Holly lets her words drift, then slowly raises her head and looks into Elias's mother's eyes and says, "Ah wanted him ta come too. It ain't like nobody thinks it is. Ah mean, Ah just wanted ta be wit him. That's real important ta me. Other things are important, too, but Ah just want to be with him. Ah want ya ta like me and all. And Ah don't want to cry either. But Um afraid."

Elias's mother whispers, "There's nothing to be afraid of." Elias's father puts the letter down, lets it hang in his hands and stands lookin at Holly. He takes a deep breath, looks away for a moment, then looks at Elias's mother and says, "I'll leave in the morning." He keeps lookin at Elias's mother, then says, "No, I better leave tonight. I'll call the station and see if I can get a train."

Holly looks up and asks, "Ya goin ta git him?"

Elias's father shakes his head yes, then quickly leaves the room and leaves a silence in it. The quietness lingers until Elias's mother asks Holly if she has eaten on the train. Holly shakes her head no, then sorta whispers, "Um not hungry."

"Well, that's what you say. But come on in the kitchen and let's get you a little something."

Holly follows Elias's mother through the living room. As she passes the piano, her quick peek at it becomes a long stare. In the kitchen, she sits at the table while Elias's mother makes sandwiches and tea. Holly lowers her eyes when Elias's mother sets the sandwiches and tea on the table. She looks away from them and says, "Ah don't mean to be no bother. Ah guess Ah wasn't thinkin. Ah mean, Ah wasn't thinkin about me puttin myself on folks and all."

Elias's mother sits at the table. Holly looks up when she hears the woman softly saying, "Sugar, we have a lot to talk about. This is Elias's home and he has sent you here." Her words slow to a pause. Holly sees Elias's smile on his mama's face. It is a faint smile, a soft smile and when it goes away it leaves a tender look in the woman's eyes. She starts talkin again, tells Holly, "Elias has sent you here. This is his home, you are welcome here. I want you to eat something. You may not be hungry, but that baby is."

Holly's eyes widen and she puts her head down, but asks, "He say that in the letter? Did he put that in the letter too?"

"He didn't have to."

Holly keeps her eyes down. Softly, Elias's mother says, "Go ahead and eat your sandwich."

Holly takes a bite of the sandwich, then asks, "How come ya knew? How could ya tell? Ah mean, Ah was goin ta tell ya all. Ah was goin ta wait till we married and say it then."

"You just go ahead and eat now. I'll be right back, I want to talk to Alex."

Holly sits sippin on her tea and lookin at the sandwich. She can hear the sound of Elias's mother's footsteps going up the stairs, then it is silent in the kitchen. There are pretty flowers on the teacup, Holly begins starin at them.

Footsteps come into the silence, near. Holly looks up as Elias's father comes into the kitchen. She keeps lookin up into his eyes until he asks her, "Does your family know where you are?" Holly looks down, shakes her head no. Slowly she looks up, says, "Ah was goin ta write Mama. Ah mean just somethin short and all, let her know Ah was all right. Ah was goin ta do that when Elias come."

"What's your last name, Holly?"

"It's Hill. My daddy's Gus Hill and my mama's Ginger," Holly's sayin, then turnin to the sounds of Elias's mother comin into the kitchen. She stares at her but for just a quick moment, then lowers her head so that some words can come out easier. They don't want to come, she starts to shakin a little, and they start fallin. "My daddy ain't goin ta be carin where Um at," Holly's utterin and keeps shakin and sayin, "My daddy ain't goin ta ever want ta see me again. Mama ain't goin ta want ta see me either. She got enough ta be worryin about wit my brother Bobby and all. Him gittin all hurt in the war. Ah just wanted Elias ta come too. Ah wanted him ta come but he wouldn't come now."

Elias's father stands quietly as Holly speaks, then lets the sounds of her words settle into his own silence. Elias's mother keeps lookin at Holly, then to her husband. Now, very softly, she's askin Holly, "Did someone hurt you? What happened to your face? Did someone hurt you like that? Who did that to you?"

Holly doesn't say anything, for a moment that seems never to end she can see it all again. Elias's mother places her hand on Holly's shoulder, then gently rubs it. Elias's father turns and quickly leaves the room.

Holly looks up and wipes at her eyes a little, then says, "Um sorry, Ah don't mean at be cryin all."

Elias's mother sits down and asks, "How did you meet Elias?"

Holly wipes at her eyes again and they brighten some. A soft smile comes to her face, the softness stays as she tells Elias's mother all about the creek and how she saw Elias paintin. Then she slowly turns, looks in the other room and asks," Is that the piano in here that he played, is that the one he say he done learn ta play on?"

Elias's mother smiles, glances at the piano in the other room and says, "That's all he wanted to do. I taught him when he was little. Sometimes, he'd sit and play for hours."

Elias's father hurries into the kitchen, sayin, "I've called a cab, it should be here soon. Marcel, first thing in the morning, give Pete a call and see if he'll take my classes. If I can get to the station in time, I can get that twelve ten out. That will get me down there about noon."

Holly's lookin at Elias's father, she can see Elias's eyes in the night, see them lookin back at the lights. Quickly, Elias's father is lookin at her, askin, "Where did you last see Elias?"

Holly answers real fast, "He was at the train station."

"What was he going to do. Does he have any money? How did he say he was going to get here? He's not going back in Supply, is he?"

Holly shakes her head no, then says, "He ain't goin back there. He was goin ta do that but Alpha told him ta come too. She made him go."

"Where do you think he is now?"

"He was ta maybe wait till it got real dark, then he was goin ta get on one of them old freight trains. He was goin ta do that. He was goin back where we were fore it got mornin. He said he was goin back there and wait there."

"Where?"

"Ah don't remember exactly and all, it bein all dark still. But it was just along the tracks, just fore ya git close to Wilmington and all. It was there by the tracks, right next ta them, like in them bushes and all."

Quickly, Elias's father leaves the kitchen. Holly looks, stares into Elias's mother's eyes and asks, "He's goin ta be all right ain't he? Elias is goin ta be all right, ain't he?"

The woman is silent, and just stares off at a near wall. Holly sucks her breath in and looks down at the flowers on the teacup and sits quietly too. They both turn to Elias's father when he rushes back in the kitchen with his coat on sayin, "It's here."

Elias's mother gets up quickly, sighs and says, "I'll go to the door with you." Holly watches Elias's father move like Elias, her eyes follow him. She calls, "Tell him . . ." Her words slow him, he stops and looks back into her eyes. Quickly she's sayin, "Tell him Ah want him ta come right now."

"I'll bring him back."

Holly lowers her head, sits quietly at the table and stares at the little flowers on the cup until Elias's mother comes back. Soft talk goes into the hours of the night. Smiles come about tomorrow, come followin hopes the soft words speak of. Elias's mother says, "He'll be home soon." Holly whispers back, "Ah really love him, Ah mean, Ah love him too."

She is given Elias's room and it is his pillow she takes into her arms and holds through the night. When the morning comes and she opens her eyes, she flinches a little and stares at the wall and its wallpaper, then slowly looks at the light comin through the window. The curtains are soakin with the morning sunlight. Holly closes her eyes again and squeezes the pillow in her arms. Now she jolts, opens her eyes again and stares into the moment until it swells and bursts into the ugly face of time.

She shakes.

Elias is still in the dark.

The lights keep comin.

Dogs barkin.

Mama ain't downstairs and Elsie sayin "Nigger."

Quickly, she closes her eyes again, then opens them and sits up on the side of the bed. She looks at the window, but can only see the light soakin in the curtains. She eases herself up from the bed and goes to the window. Tops of tall buildings stick up in the far sky, smaller ones hide deep in their shadows. Real close, there's backs of big houses that have little yards. When she turns from the window a mirror watches her lookin into her eyes.

"Did you sleep well?" Elias's mother is askin as Holly comes into the kitchen, then she's askin, "Did you find everything you needed?"

"Yes, ma'am."

"Sugar, just call me Marcel. Come on and sit down, I'm fixing some pancakes, do you like pancakes?"

Holly shakes her head yes, then says, "Ah didn't mean ta be sleepin all that time. Ah guess Ah was real tired and all."

"Sugar, you must have been exhausted."

"Ah guess Ah was."

"You want some coffee?"

"Can Ah fix it? Ah don't want ta be a bother."

"Pot's on the stove, cups are right up there. The cream and sugar are on the table. And you are not a bother."

Holly fixes herself a cup of coffee, then asks, "Can Ah help with anythin?"

"No, you just sit down. Do you think you will like Washington?"

"It's real big. It's real bigger than Wilmington."

"You'll get used to it."

Holly sits down at the table and takes a sip of her coffee, then says, "Ah didn't think of Washington till Ah met Elias. He told me about school and things he liked and all. Fore that, the only time Ah think about up here is when somethin be on the radio about the president or somethin."

"Well, when Elias gets here we'll have to take you down to see the White House and some of the monuments."

"Ah thought Ah saw that white house from the train. It looked like it was real big with a round top. And there was somethin that was real pretty, it was real tall and skinny like."

"Oh, that was probably the Washington Monument."

"Oh, it was real pretty. Ya think Elias's daddy done found him yet?"

Marcel Owens was still mixin pancake batter, she stops and just stares down into the mix. She is silent for a moment, then looks up and over her shoulder to the clock on the wall and says, "Alex should be just getting there now. He said he'll call as soon as he finds him." She sighs and says, "I hope it don't take too long."

Holly is watchin Elias's mother's face. It is turned from her a little and she cannot see the woman's eyes. When she does, she lowers her own and looks at the flowers again on the cup, there is a red one on there.

"Do you have any brothers and sisters?"

Holly looks up, sayin, "Ah got two brothers. Bobby, he's twenty-two but he's goin ta be twenty-three come January. He got hurt real bad in the war, too. He used ta be, ya know ..." She slows her words, sighs and says, "He always be talkin and all. He don't say things now, Ah mean he can talk, he just don't, less its real important. He got hurt bad in the head, he was shot there. Jason is my little brother, he ain't but eight. Then there's just me. Ah had a real good friend, her name was Elsie. We were real good friends and all, her livin right up the road and bein the same age as me, too. But . . . well, we ain't friends now."

"I see you have the cross," Elias's mother says softly with a softer smile.

Holly speaks quickly, "Ya can have it back. He give it ta me ta wear. He said ya give it ta him for the war when he was goin. But Ah give it back cause Ah know it's real important."

"Oh, no, sugar. If he gave it to you he wants you to have it. I just noticed that you have it."

Holly dips her eyes toward her breast, gently raises her hand and rubs her fingers over the cross and says, "Ah always wear it. Ah mean, when he give it ta me, Ah couldn't show it ta nobody. Ah couldn't do that, but Ah always had it wit me. Ah kept it real close all the time. Um goin ta always wear it, then when the baby gits big enough, Um goin ta give it ta her. Um going ta do that just like ya gave it ta Elias."

Elias's mother smiles, laughs a little, then asks with a smile, "How do you know it's going to be a girl?"

Holly smiles back and says, "Ah don't know, Ah guess Ah just feel it and all. Ah mean, if it's a little boy, Ah be real happy too. But it's goin ta be a girl."

Slowly, Holly's smile fades, she lowers her eyes, looks at the flower again and without lookin up, she's askin, "Does Elias's daddy know too? Ah mean does he know about the baby too?"

A silence brings its stillness, Elias's mother stands quietly in the middle of it. Holly can hear the suddenness of a breath gatherin the woman's words, then the softness of her voice sayin, "Yes, I told him last night, he had to know. I told him not to mention the baby, that you and Elias would want to tell him. But I thought he should know before he left to go down there."

"Was he bein mad at me? Ah mean, thinkin Ah was a . . . Ah mean, thinkin Ah ought not . . ." Holly doesn't finish what she was sayin, just lets the sounds of her words go away.

Quickly, Elias's mother tells Holly, "No one is angry with you, sugar."

Holly looks up and stares, then keeps lookin at the tear she sees comin out of Elias's mother's eyes. Other soft words the woman is sayin are comin too. "He . . . he . . . he was always so gentle," Elias's mother's tellin Holly. "He cared so much about things, he was always like that. He loved flowers, always loved to draw. When he was still just a little boy, he would get so quiet after I read him a poem. Oh, did he like poetry, flowers and the gentle things in life. He was like that, he was special. And when he played his music it was like it was the music of the world." Elias's mother looks off to the other room, stares at the piano. Holly turns and looks too, then she turns back and lowers her eyes, keeps them down and sometimes closes them tight when Elias's mama gets to sayin, "I didn't know him when he came back. He was different, mean, you couldn't get near him. He wouldn't let me touch him. God only knows what happened over there. Elias would never talk about it. I didn't know what to do except pray. I just didn't know what to do. He started drinking, fighting inside himself. You could see it every day. You couldn't talk to him, his daddy couldn't even say anything to him. He wouldn't even touch the piano and went running out of the house if I played. And the nights, I'll never forget. He'd scream all night sometimes, scream in his sleep until he woke himself up, then he'd just lie there and shake. We got him in a hospital but he wouldn't stay. He kept fighting with people . . ."

Holly keeps her eyes down but sometimes reaches up and gently catches a tear before it falls. The soft words come again, Elias's mother is sayin, "We hadn't heard from him in months. We knew he was down there. We wrote and wrote, but he never wrote back. . . . In the letter he sent with you, I could hear that gentleness again, he sounds himself again. He says when he comes home, he's going to try and play again. He thinks he may be able to play enough to be able to compose. The letter is an answer to a lot of prayers. He's going to play his music again and he's coming home."

Holly doesn't see Elias's mother lower her head and the gentle smile that comes to her face. A silence comes with the smile, then Elias's mother whispers to Holly, "He says in his letter that he loves you very much."

Holly raises her head a little bit and whispers back, "Ah love him too."

Elias's mother keeps her head down and is silent for a moment. Holly lowers her eyes from the woman as she hears her sayin, "Sugar, I don't think you and Elias were thinking. He's my son and I love him very much, but I don't think you two saw beyond yourselves. I don't think you realized what you were doing." Holly hears the woman sigh before she hears her sayin, "But I guess the most important thing is he's coming home." Holly slowly looks up and sees a smile on the woman's face. Holly's eyes brighten when she hears Elias's mother sayin, "Come on, I'll show you some pictures of Elias when he was a little boy."

Gently, coffee cups are set on a coffee table. The little rattle of china goes away, but the brightness in Holly's eyes stays. A dark-haired baby with a smile and big dark eyes is lookin up at her. His mama is sayin, "He was about three in this one."

"Here's one of him at the piano. I think he was about six in this one. Have you ever played?"

Holly looks up from the pictures and stares at the piano, then she says, "Ah ain't never played one of them. We had one in the school and there's one in the church, too, but Ah ain't never played them."

"Do you want to play?"

Holly smiles, giggles and says, "Ah can't play. Ya think Ah can? Elias tried ta show me how ta paint and all. Ah painted a picture of him, and Ah made him promise not ta laugh fore Ah showed it ta him. He laughed, too. Ah can't play that."

Elias's mother smiles, says, "Come on, I'll teach you a song and you can play it for him when he gets home."

"He'll laugh at me."

"No, he won't, he'll be surprised. Come on, I'll teach you something to play."

Holly is gigglin as she sits on the piano stool next to Elias's mother. Slowly a smile comes to her face and the morning becomes music. Long dark golden fingers touch soft white and gentle dark keys. Moments fill with melodies and slowly go on by.

"Come on now, you try it."

Holly's fingers touch the piano keys, her eyes widen as the sound of music seeps into the moments again. She giggles and says, "Did Ah do it right?"

"Almost, try it again."

Holly stares down at the keys, then pushes the ones down that made the tune come before. Softly, Elias's mother whispers, "That's good, you're doing good. Now try it again now."

A bell rings and Holly stops playin and looks up at Elias's mother. She sees a quick smile come to the woman's face, it stills itself there. The bell rings again and Elias's mother quickly gets up from the stool, sayin, "That's the phone. I'll be right back."

Holly watches Elias's mother leave the room and go into the hallway, then turns and looks back down at the piano keys. Very softly she touches a key, then listens for the little sound of music to seep into the room. She smiles and touches the key again until she hears

Elias's mother scream. Now Holly is tremblin, turnin and lookin toward the hallway. She can hear Elias's mother cryin. It is a distant sound now, like that sound from the piano that can still be heard after it's played.

The music is gone away, only its sound is lingerin.

21

The same sun that had risen over Washington and lit the tall buildings that Holly had seen had quietly risen over Supply. It was past
the noon hour and Supply folks weren't talkin yet, just whisperin.
Everybody knew about Holly Hill and that one-arm nigger. Chester
Higgens sorta passed the word with the mail. Some folks said, "It
was a cryin shame, that nigger doin what he done." Said, "If he ain't
hang the way he did, they should have hung him anyway." Chester
Higgens told folks, "Ah saw him when Sheriff LeRoy bringin him
on back from up there in Wilmington." Told folks, "They catch him
up there by the train station. It was lookin like they gits him up
there just in time fore he could git one of them trains. They gits him
up there and the sheriff bring him on back here and put the nigger
in his cell." Chester Higgens told folks, "Gus was over there wit the
sheriff. Him wantin ta see the nigger, bein his daughter and all. The
sheriff tell me, he and Gus went on over there ta the courthouse ta
see Eugene and git all them official papers filled out. He said he
knew it was rape and might be murder, too, seein how they can't
find that poor girl. Said, that nigger wouldn't tell em nothin. Said,

when he done over the courthouse and goes back over the jail, said, he went ta feed the nigger. That's when he found him hangin. Sheriff said, he just let him hang, seein though that's what the nigger wanted ta do."

Chester Higgens told folks that were askin, "Them Hills ain't fit ta be tied, they done had their troubles. Ya know that boy of theirs still ain't right."

Reverend Powell did his walkin and talkin too, told folks he saw, "Lord put his vengeance on that boy. That colored had devil ways. Ya still have ta pray, ya know, things like this show ya. This here kind of evil can come at ya anytime. Ya gots ta pray."

Elsie told Garet Foster and Lucy Belmar, "Ah told Holly, ya can't be trustin and thinkin about likin some damn nigger. She ain't been actin right at all."

Gus Hill told Eugene Purvis, told him right over there by the courthouse, "I went lookin for that nigger. I went and got LeRoy last night. We looked for that nigger all up in them Back Lands. If I'd found him then, he'd still be hangin up in there, 'cept I'd taken his other damn arm off."

Ginger had just sat all night, then into the morning, too.

Bobby Hill looked out the window of his room with a tear in his eye.

Jason went to school but June Boy wouldn't walk with him.

Dewey Evans, that old colored man that used to work for Ryan Witek in his undertakin shop, told them Back Land coloreds, "Sheriff LeRoy call me over there ta the jail. Ah had ta cut that boy down. Ah went over there and seen him hangin, just hangin like Ah finds Mr. Witek hangin. If Ah ain't had the Lord's strength wit me . . . That boy lookin like . . . Ah ain't never seen nothin likes it, less it be some coon the dogs done got ats. Ah tries ta clean him up some fore Ah takes him on up ta Alpha . . . tries ta gits that blood and beatin off his face . . . tries ta make him look like . . . So folks, Ah did the best Ah know how . . . Gits a box for him . . . gits the wagon and carries him on up ta Alpha . . . Ah ain't knowin what else ta do. . . . Ah was goin ta do him right . . . find him some quiet place, puts him in there fore Alpha . . . Ah was goin ta do that. . . . His daddy done come for him, gonna takes that boy back on up home wit him. . . . Lord gots ta have some mercy . . ."

Alpha told her God, "Looks what they done ta this child," then she held her hand up to the sky and put her tear-filled eyes to the ground. She told Elias's father, "Ya take him on back up there. Ya puts him in that dirt up there. Don't lets this boy lay down here forever. Ya takes him on home wit ya, son."

Holly had not eaten for two days and nights. Two nights had no stars, moons. Holly would not let sleep take her away, she kept holdin on to Elias's pillow and starin into the darkness. The days that had passed took the color from her face. Sometimes, it was only the movement of her tears that showed any signs of a livin soul.

A soft tap comes to Holly's door, she turns to its sound. It comes again, then the door opens slowly.

"I brought you up a little something. Thought you might like a little cup of soup and some tea," a woman is sayin as she comes into the dark of the room. Holly can barely see her, she tries to see the woman's eyes in the dark. Softly, the woman is speakin again, "Why don't you try and sit up and get something in you? It might make you feel a little better, honey."

Holly sits up on the side of the bed, turns the light on, rubs her eyes and looks at the woman, then lowers her head. The woman speaks again. "You have to eat something, honey."

Holly keeps her head down.

The woman sets the tea and soup down on the little table where the lamp sits, then she stands lookin down at Holly. She is a tall stout woman with soft wrinkles in her brown glowin skin. Slowly, Holly looks up and utters, "Ah thank ya, but Ah ain't hungry. Ah don't feel hungry."

The woman sits down beside Holly, sighs and takes her by the hand sayin, "Honey, why don't you try a little something?"

Holly just shakes her head no.

"You want to talk a little bit?"

Holly just stares at the floor.

"I'm Elizabeth Lewis, Pastor Lewis's wife. He's downstairs with Marcel. She asked me to come up and see if you wanted to come down. Would you like that?"

Holly keeps starin at the floor.

The woman sits quietly for a moment, then whispers, "That's a pretty cross."

Holly whispers back, "Elias gave it ta me."

"That was one fine boy. I watched him grow into a fine young man. Seems like only yesterday he was sitting on Marcel's lap and trying to play as much piano as she was. He was the sweetest child you ever wanted to see."

Holly keeps her head down.

"Marcel tells me you were very special to Elias," the woman says softly, then leans in a way so she can see Holly's face.

Holly sees the train comin, can see the gray smoke fillin up the station.

The woman sighs and says, "You have to trust in Jesus, honey."

Holly can see Elias noddin toward the train.

"Why don't you try a little soup?"

Holly sees Elias's hand on his heart, she gets on the train.

"Come on now, let's try and take a little bit of soup."

Holly utters, "Ah wanted him ta come too."

"I know, I know." The woman's words fall heavy from her mouth.

"Ah didn't want ta come less he come too. Ah didn't want nothin ta happen ta him that didn't happen ta me either."

The woman jerks her chin up in the air and quickly says, "Jesus knows, honey. Jesus knows, and nothing is ever going to change that. Jesus knows what's in your heart. He put it there."

"Ah ain't got no heart no more."

"Yes you do, honey. You talking about too much love not to have a heart. Jesus knows what you feeling."

Slowly, Holly takes a sip of tea, then a spoonful of soup. Elizabeth Lewis is a gentle woman, she is gentle with Holly. If Holly lowers her head, begins to shake at all, quick, soft words rush to her, tell her the Son of God ain't too far and he'll come to her if she calls. Holly gets up and washes her face, combs her hair a little and slowly straightens herself up some. Elizabeth Lewis stays with her. Sometimes she talks to Holly, says and asks little things. Sometimes Holly says something back, sometimes she cannot hear the woman talkin. The train is comin into the station and it is makin too much noise for Holly to hear anything else in her life.

The livin room is full with colored faces that have come in the night. Holly can feel their eyes but she reaches for Elias's mother's hand that is reachin out for hers. Another older woman who sits beside Elias's mother hurries up out of her seat so Holly can sit.

Murmurs and soft talk fill the room.

Holly lowers her head and leans toward Elias's mother.

Someone whispers, "I just can't believe it. I can't believe he's gone. Oh Lord."

A fat yellow-faced woman keeps lookin down and shakin her head.

Elias's mother has Holly's hand in hers.

Pastor Lewis talks about how dark a road can be at midnight.

It is dark, but Holly can see the top of the old fat-bellied oak.

The house is silent now, the faces have gone back into the night. Holly is sittin with Elias's mother, she sits and stares at the piano. The hours after midnight come, the silence stays. Another train is on the way, it will be here in the morning. In one of its back cars, where it carries big trunks and suitcases, Elias sometimes sways with the motions of the train. The coffin he rides in is too heavy to sway. His mother and Holly wait for the train, they will not sleep or close their eyes.

At the end of the night the train slows, and begins crossin the bridge above the river. The lights of Washington have gone out, the big tall and round buildings do not glow as the train begins curvin into the city. The station lights have gone out too, the platform is covered with the early gray first light.

Elias's father has come with the train and now stands at the far end of the station's platform. He waits until Elias's coffin is unloaded, then he waits by its side until the long black hearse comes.

A church is fillin up with different-colored solemn faces. The early morning sunlight has come but is too weak to brighten the pretty pictures in the stained-glass windows. In one of the windows, the glass face of the Son of God meekly looks into the church. Holly does not see Him, she sits starin at the closed-up coffin covered with flowers. Elias's mother is sittin next to Holly and also starin at the flowers. Elias's father is sittin next to his wife, he has lowered his eyes away from the flowers and closes them when he thinks of the battered face beneath the pretty-colored wreaths.

A piano is playin softly, its music seems to hover over the flower-covered coffin. A dark-faced woman begins to sing, long words bellow from her mouth. Her eyes are closed and she sings of a place she sees. She sings of the Garden of Eden and the dewdrops that she sees, that are still on the roses.

The music begins to fade when Pastor Lewis rises from his seat behind the pulpit and softly asks for silent prayers. In the silences of the passin moments, Holly keeps starin at the flowers, some of them are red.

Pastor Lewis begins to speak.

Holly keeps starin at the flowers. The tears in her eyes are gentle with her, they stay cuddled up in the corners of her eyes, and only drip down her cheeks. Pastor Lewis's words come slow, but fill the church with his voice. He is sayin, "The almighty God has spoken. . . . The Lord hath spoken and called the earth from the rising sun unto the going down thereof. . . . Our God shall come and not keep silent. . . . A fire shall devour before Him . . ."

Holly shudders with his words but keeps starin at the flowers. Pastor Lewis is saying, "Elias's father, Dr. Alex Owens, will give the eulogy."

Holly watches Elias's father rise and go past the flowers, she watches him go up behind the pulpit, then looks back down to the flowers as he begins to speak. She feels Elias's mother quiverin beside her as Elias's father says, "It is with my son's strength that I speak, not mine. It is with his artistry that I try and bring meaning to this day, not my intellect. We all knew Elias, I knew him as a father knows a son, his mother and I had no greater joy . . . could ask for nothing more . . . Blessed we were. . . . When he went off to war, we agonized. . . . When he came home we were grateful for his life, but he had lost an arm and to him that was his life, it was his music. . . . His soul had been silenced . . ."

Elias's father's words begin to slow and when his voice begins to waver, Holly looks up and sees the tears in his eyes. "When he came home, he had bitterness in his heart. It was deep in his heart, it was there where he kept his love for music. He exiled himself . . ."

Holly sees Elias across the creek.

"It was months, an endless time for his mother and me, then in the night a letter was brought to us."

Holly's eyes widen and tears start gushin out.

"The letter simply said, he was coming home, he had found his music. He said he was going to play again, play with the hand God left him. And if he could not do that, he was going to compose the music for others to play. There's a young woman here sitting beside my wife . . ."

Holly lowers her eyes and trembles.

"I think my son would want me to say of her . . . no, I know and feel Elias would want me to say of her . . . that he dearly loved her. . . . I think he would want me to say that. . . . She sits beside my wife now . . ."

Holly cannot see the flowers now, she cannot see through her tears.

Others get up and speak.

An old woman is sayin, "Ah can still hear that boy play, they can't take that away."

A young man says, "I'll never have a better friend."

A dark-faced man cries when he says, "They should never have done that boy that way . . ."

Pastor Lewis stands again and the music begins to play softly. Elias's mother utters his name, "Elias." Then her cries curl into the sound of the music.

Pastor Lewis sighs and looks out over the faces. The music begins to soften, slow, then stops.

"Ah want ta say somethin. . . . Can Ah say somethin too?"

Pastor Lewis looks down at Holly and says, "Please come forward."

Colored faces watch, then still in the silence that has come. Slowly, Holly gets to her feet and takes the steps she has to take, then she stands by the flowers. She begins to quiver as she is saying, "Um goin ta say somethin . . . Um goin ta cry because it hurts real bad . . . but Um goin ta say it till Um through. . . . He's all closed up . . . and he's dead, too . . . but he ain't either. . . . Ah mean, he give me somethin that ain't all closed up. . . . Ah can say things . . . Ah can say Ah love him . . . cause Ah feel it . . . and it ain't all closed up. . . . And if somebody want ta say bad things . . . say things that try and make it ugly and all . . . say things mean ta ya just cause ya love somebody . . . and they love ya too . . . if somebody ever holler and say that ta ya too . . . ya just tell em God don't git mad at ya cause ya love somebody and they love ya too. . . . Elias is in that box and all . . . and they done killed him real bad . . . but they ain't killed him all the way . . . cause Um still alive . . . and Ah ain't nothin but him, too. . . . Ah loved him . . . Ah loved him . . . Ah love ya, Elias."